TO REMEMBER

"I'm going to be honest with you, Cassandra. I didn't come here to renew a romantic interest in you, but now that I'm here, now that I've seen you again, I find that's exactly what I want to do. In fact, I'm going to kiss you right now."

Dustin bent his head and pressed his lips to hers in a gentle yet powerful kiss. A breathless fluttering filled her stomach. His mouth and tongue ravaged hers in a slow, savoring kiss meant to seduce and be victorious. Pleasure curled inside her. Cassandra melted against Dustin.

He slid his arms around her waist and pulled her close to his chest. "I've wanted to do that since the night Landon kissed you. I didn't want you going to sleep with the taste of him on your lips."

Remembering she wasn't supposed to enjoy Dustin's kiss, Cassandra pushed out of his embrace and raked the back of her hand across her mouth.

"Landon kisses much better than you."

"You're lying, but that's all right. It gives me the opportunity to prove you wrong."

> *"CASSANDRA* is a page-turning adventure with characters you'll take to your heart. Great characters, great setting, great romance."
> —Patricia Potter, author of
> *The Scotsman Wore Spurs*

RANSOM

"A tale full of passion, humor, and adventure that readers will treasure. This finely crafted story shows Ms. Skinner's writing at its best. Superb!"

—*Rendezvous*

"The authentic western dialect and spicy love scenes tickled the senses."

—*Rawhide & Lace*

"Excellent historical. Ms. Skinner proves once again that she can write and write well. Four bells!"
—Donita Lawrence, Bell, Book & Candle

"A rootin'-tootin', old-time romance that made me believe Cupid uses six-shooters too!"
—Melinda Matuch, The Book Rack

"Strong characters, great story line make *Ransom* a book you can't put down until you've read the last word. Great!"
—Margaret Stilsen, Paperback Exchange

"*Ransom* is a touching western romance that will capture the reader's heart and hold it for ransom."
—Sharon Walters, Paperback Place

"Marvelous characters that stayed in my head long after finishing the book. This author never disappoints."
—Lucy Morris, Lucy's Book Exchange Inc.

"Emotionally charged, a powerful story of the Montana frontier, with a love story that leaves one breathless even until the last page."

—Donna Harsell, Voyager Books

Books by Gloria Dale Skinner

Ransom
Juliana
Cassandra

Published by POCKET BOOKS

GLORIA DALE SKINNER

CASSANDRA

POCKET STAR BOOKS
New York   London   Toronto   Sydney   Tokyo   Singapore

This book is a work of fiction. Names, characters, places and
incidents are products of the author's imagination or are used
fictitiously. Any resemblance to actual events or locales or persons,
living or dead, is entirely coincidental.

An *Original* Publication of POCKET BOOKS

A Pocket Star Book published by
POCKET BOOKS, a division of Simon & Schuster Inc.
1230 Avenue of the Americas, New York, NY 10020

ISBN: 0-671-01138-3

First Pocket Books printing January 1998

10 9 8 7 6 5 4 3 2 1

POCKET STAR BOOKS and colophon are registered
trademarks of Simon & Schuster Inc.

Cover art by Lina Levy

Printed in the U.S.A.

For my parents,
Lester and Margaret Bass.
Thank you
for all you taught me.

CASSANDRA

· *Prologue* ·

Kansas City
September 1889

A lover's moon shone against the midnight sky. Excitement danced through Cassandra's senses making her feel a bit naughty about meeting Dustin in the wee hours of morning.

The faint chirp of crickets and distant calls of night birds wafted past her as she stole quietly through the back garden of the house her grandfather had rented for the summer.

Dustin had finally asked her to meet him in secret. Tomorrow was their wedding day, but like her, he couldn't wait any longer for them to spend time alone together. Since their courtship had started three months ago their embraces had become increasingly passionate.

The air was crisp with late night breezes. She shivered and wrapped her beltless robe tighter about her. She caught a whiff of the pungent scent of wildflowers as she took the path that led her away from the house and into the shadows of the trees.

Ahead she saw Dustin standing in the middle of the flower-covered arbor. Soft moonlight showered him.

He'd taken off his jacket, cravat, and waistcoat and was dressed only in his collarless white shirt and black trousers. His dark blond hair had been ruffled by the wind, but he'd never looked more handsome.

Cassandra picked up the skirt of her robe and gown and rushed into his waiting arms.

"Dustin." She wound her arms around his neck and pressed her body against his. His arms circled and tightened around her.

"Cassandra," he whispered softly into the warmth of her neck. "Mmm, you feel so good." He paused, an inquisitive expression on his face. "Why aren't you dressed?"

"I wanted to meet you like this." She pulled away from him and opened her robe and twirled. The thin sleeveless gown accented her young womanly body. Her soft, youthful laughter tingled on the air. "I love you, Dustin. I don't want to wait any longer to be with you."

His eyebrows drew together. "Cass, this isn't why I asked you to meet me."

Cassandra denied the concern she saw in his face. She dismissed the edge she heard in his voice. They were going to be married tomorrow. There was no need for him to worry about her innocence. She walked up to him and arched her body against his. She felt his hardness and moved against it. "Tell me what I want to hear. Tell me you love me and you can't wait one more night to make me yours."

"Don't do this to me, Cass. You know I want you." His voice was husky, pleading.

She placed a hand on each side of his face and smiled. "Then let's make love, Dustin. I don't want to wait."

His mouth came down hard on hers as his arms scooped her up against his chest. Cassandra melted against him. She opened her mouth. His tongue darted inside with quick, deep strokes that made her hot and breathless.

Dustin's lips left hers. He kissed his way over her chin,

2

down her neck, giving her gentle love bites. He buried his face in the warmth there and whispered again, "No, Cass. I came here to talk to you. Not to do this."

How could he say no to such dizzying sensations that made her feverish with desire? She loved him all the more for wanting to wait for their wedding night but she wanted their first time together to be outside, under the full moon and twinkling stars.

"Dustin," she answered softly. "We'll talk later. This is what we've been waiting for. Kiss me. Touch me." She looked into his eyes with all the love she was feeling.

Dustin moaned his approval. His lips moved hungrily over hers. His hands sailed up and down her back, under her arms and up to cup her breasts. The palms of his hands massaged the taut nipples, sending shivers of wicked desire shooting through her.

A shudder rumbled through his body. "You're so damn tempting," he said.

Cassandra gasped with delight. She felt free to have Dustin touch her so intimately.

With nimble, confident fingers she pulled at the buttons of his shirt and unfastened them. With haste she tugged the tail of his shirt from his trousers. His skin was warm, firm, muscular. He trembled, leaving her no doubt this was what they both wanted.

"Oh, God, Cass, I have to taste you." He grabbed his jacket off the railing and laid it on the wooden floor of the arbor. He helped her sink onto the silkiness of his satin-lined coat and lie down. He pillowed her head with his waistcoat before he stretched out beside her.

"I swear to God this isn't what I intended when I asked you to meet me tonight. But right now all I can think of is how much I want to be inside you."

"I love you, Dustin. I want to be yours."

He pushed her robe off her shoulders and shoved her gown up past her breasts. Holding and caressing first one breast and then the other, he kissed and suckled them as he pressed his hard loins against Cassandra's cushioned womanhood.

Soft, feminine murmurs of pleasure escaped past her lips. She gloried in the feel of his mouth on her heated skin. She thrilled to the sensation of the cool air pebbling her flesh when his tongue left a trail of moisture on her breasts, on her stomach. She was eager and responsive to his every movement. A storm of rich fulfilling emotions drenched her. She was aware of nothing but Dustin.

Dustin's movements were jerky and frantic as he tore open the buttons on his trousers and shoved them past his knees. He spread her legs with confident hands and lowered his body between her thighs. He pressed hard and urgent against her softness until he joined his body with hers.

Cassandra moaned quietly. She flattened her palms against his chest and pushed against him.

"Stay with me, Cass," he murmured, breathing quietly into her ear as he insistently pushed his erection deeper, fitting himself completely inside her. "The discomfort will pass."

She hid her face against the smooth, firm skin of his chest and waited for the thrilling sensations to return.

He rocked back and forth inside her, kissing and caressing her. The throbbing pleasure returned. His movements became easier until she felt as if she were exploding with the most exquisite pleasure she'd ever experienced. Dustin responded to her and moments later his rigid body relaxed.

He raised his head and stared down into her eyes. "That was over too quickly. Was I too rough? Did I hurt you?"

She shook her head, smiling. "No, I loved every second of it. I didn't want it to end."

"Cassandra, I didn't want this for you. I shouldn't have—"

"No," she whispered with a finger pressed to his lips. "I'm glad we made love out here under the stars. It reminds me of being at the ranch in Wyoming. Dustin, we have so little time before dawn, let's don't waste it talking."

Cassandra paced. The petticoats underneath the full skirt of her wedding dress rustled. The heels of her satin slippers clicked on the wooden floor. The flowers in her hair wilted.

"Where is Dustin?" Thomas Rakefield barked again as he stared out the window of a small room in the back of the church.

"Be patient, Thomas," Gordon Bennett answered, keeping watch by the door. "I admit it's unusual for my son to be late, but I'm sure he'll have a good explanation when he gets here. I've sent a man to check his house. We should know something soon."

Cassandra wouldn't allow herself to worry. Dustin loved her. Last night he'd shown her how much he cared for her. She'd felt it in every kiss, every touch, every time they'd joined their bodies. Dustin had loved her so thoroughly they hadn't left the garden until the sun broke on the horizon.

Suddenly a chill of dread shook her. Had Dustin actually told her he loved her? Quickly her mind searched for a day, a time that he'd said, "I love you," but all she could remember was him telling her how pretty she was, how good they would be together, and how much he wanted to make her his wife.

No, he loves me. She had to believe that. He was going to be her husband. She couldn't doubt him.

"I can't imagine what's kept him," Cassandra offered in Dustin's defense. "But it must have been important."

"It damn well better be," Thomas exclaimed. "More than an hour late for his wedding is no way to start a marriage. He better be sick, hurt, or damn near death when they find him or I'm going to make him wish he was."

Cassandra's stomach cramped as the minutes ticked

by. She remembered that Dustin had acted hesitant when they first met last night, but it was only because he loved her. He had told her that last night, hadn't he?

No, he only admitted he wanted you.

A knock sounded. Relief so heady surged within Cassandra she thought she was going to faint. A smile jumped across her face.

Gordon jerked the door open. Cassandra recognized the man Gordon had sent looking for Dustin.

"What did you find out?" Gordon asked.

"No sign of him at the house, but there was a young boy standing in front of the church. He said he'd been paid a dollar to deliver this envelope to a Miss Rakefield. It's from Mr. Bennett."

A whimpered cry of denial slipped past Cassandra's lips. She backed away from the three men who stood rigid, staring at her.

"I know my son. He wouldn't do this. Give me that." Gordon jerked the envelope from the man and ripped it open.

Frozen by disbelief, afraid to even breathe, Cassandra watched in stunned silence as Dustin's father's read the page. He looked up at her, a furious expression on his face. "He's not coming. He's decided he can't go through with the wedding."

"What the hell do you mean? You better be lying." Thomas growled and took a step toward Gordon.

"I—I don't believe you," Cassandra managed to say. "Let me see the letter."

Gordon shook his head and stuffed the paper into his jacket pocket. "No, dear. It will only upset you more to see it in print."

"But it's my letter. I want to see it." Tremors shook her. Tears blurred her eyes. Her body felt as if it were made of water. She didn't know what was holding her up.

"It won't change what it says for you to see it. He's not coming. Tell her, Thomas."

6

"This can't be true. Dustin wouldn't do this to me. He loves me."

"This is unforgivable. I'll kill the bastard," Thomas roared, his face reddening with fury. "Where is he?"

"If I knew that I'd go after him myself," Gordon exclaimed. "Dustin knew how much I wanted this union to take place. I can't believe he'd do this to me."

"You! What about Cass?" Thomas thundered.

"Of course, I meant Cass. I'm—I don't know what to make of this. I'll try to find him and talk some sense into him."

"We have over one hundred guests sitting in the pews. If he thinks he can get away with jilting my granddaughter I'll see him burn in hell."

Cassandra heard their outrage, felt their wrath, but she couldn't move. Why would Dustin do this? She didn't understand. She had freely given herself to him last night because she loved him, because they were to be married today. If he didn't love her why didn't he stop her from making a fool of herself last night? Why didn't he tell her? A sharp pain pierced her heart. She remembered Dustin saying last night that he wanted to talk. He came last night to tell her he didn't love her, then didn't have the guts to do it.

A cry of agony tore from Cassandra's throat. She hurled her wedding bouquet across the room. The flowers smacked against the window pane and scattered across the floor.

Dustin had jilted her! "Grandpapa," she cried between sobs as she fell into his arms.

Thomas wrapped her in a bear hug and supported her weight. She heard her grandfather and Dustin's father shouting angrily but she was too distraught to make out what they said. The only thing she could think was that she wanted Dustin to appear and tell her everything was going to be fine.

But that didn't happen. As her sobs died to heaving gasps she fought between loving and hating Dustin.

"The guests have to be told there'll be no wedding today or any day as far as we're concerned," Thomas remarked coldly to Gordon.

"Be reasonable. Let me announce that it's just a postponement."

"Never," Cassandra said bitterly, pushing away from her grandfather. She had to put an end to this nightmare. In a voice that trembled with pain she said, "Grandpapa, make the announcement there'll be no wedding. Tell them Dustin didn't have the guts to show up."

"Now see here. There's no cause for that kind of drama," Gordon shot back quickly. "I'll announce that something urgent came up at the last minute that took Dustin out of town."

Thomas threw up his hand to silence Gordon. "Your son had the last word for your family. I'll have the last word for mine."

Chapter

· 1 ·

Wyoming
May 1894

Cleaning stalls wasn't Cassandra's favorite job but someone had to do it. She'd much rather be riding the range searching for strays or mending fences with Jojo and Red Sky than filling the water trough and throwing hay down for the horses.

The dry, musty scent of hay mixed with the scent of horse and cold earth helped fill her mind with all the things she was going to do when she got her money. The first thing she had to do was re-hire all her ranch hands and add to her herd. She could think about new cow ponies and equipment later.

Her mind flooded with memories of her beloved grandfather and his last words to her before he died. "The Triple R is yours now, Cass. Don't let anyone take the land away from you. It will always be your home."

Why did her grandfather have to die right after he'd finished this enormous house, and leave her with a big mortgage? How many times had she told him they didn't need a larger place? Why hadn't he understood that it was his love, the ranch, the sky, and the river that ran

9

behind the small ranch house that were important to her? All she needed was a place to feel safe, a place to belong and for him to love her.

A shadow fell between Cassandra and the doorway but she didn't immediately turn around. Thinking of her grandfather always made her sad and she needed a moment to wipe the sorrow from her face.

She finished spreading the pile of hay she was working on, then jabbed the pitchfork deep into the bale. She raked a gloved hand across her forehead and turned to see who had walked into the barn behind her.

Her breath caught in her throat, choking her. A chill of denial bolted through her. Her hands clenched into tight fists by her sides. "Get the hell off my ranch," Cassandra demanded.

Dustin Bennett took off his broad-brimmed felt hat and smoothed his dusty blond hair with an open palm. "It's good to see you, too."

His cool blue eyes scanned her face with a feather light caress. Cassandra's heart pounded with amazing force against her chest. She was so shocked by his sudden appearance she couldn't think straight.

"What are you doing here?"

"The woman at the house told me you were in the barn. I came to talk to you."

"You bastard," she blurted out in a breathy voice. Cassandra dropped her hand to her holster and drew her Colt. She leveled the pistol at Dustin's chest. "You're five years too late. Now get out."

Dustin's eyes flashed surprise. He eased his hands up in the air in front of him and took a step backward. "I know it's been a long time."

Cassandra didn't flinch. "Not long enough. Forever would have been too soon for me."

"I always knew we'd meet again, Cass."

His voice softened as if he were trying to soothe her. She wasn't going to fall for it. "The name is Miss Rakefield to you." She pulled back the hammer and slid her finger around the trigger. "That is, if you were going to be here long enough to call me anything, which you're not."

"Stop fooling around and put that gun down."

"You're not in the big city of Kansas, Dustin. This is Wyoming. We don't aim a gun around here unless we intend to use it."

A frown of irritation creased his brow. "I'm serious. Put that thing away before somebody gets hurt."

"Somebody?" A rueful smile lifted one corner of her lips. "Now who do you think that somebody is going to be, considering I'm the one with the gun pointed at your black heart?"

"You know you're not going to shoot me."

He was too damn confident. Always had been. "Do I? Do you? I promised myself that I'd shoot you right between the legs if I ever saw you again." She lowered her aim to just below Dustin's belt.

"Now, wait a minute, Cassandra." He backed up again. "You might accidentally pull the trigger."

"Grandpapa Rakefield taught me how to use this when I was twelve years old. I've never *accidentally* shot anything in my life."

"You're loving this, aren't you?"

A satisfied smile fell across her face. "You're damn right. You don't know how many nights I've dreamed of doing this. You seduced me, then jilted me. I'd say I have good reason to blow your head *and* your butt off."

"I admit I wanted you but you were the aggressive one that night and don't pretend otherwise. We both know. We both remember."

"You bastard," she muttered again. "You asked me to meet you in the garden an hour after midnight. What was I supposed to think?"

"I explained everything to you in the letter I wrote you the day of the wedding," he said.

Cassandra bristled. Her throat burned from holding back all the pain she wanted to fling at him. "How like

11

you to think a letter of rejection could explain anything, let alone everything."

"I told the truth. I thought you'd appreciate that."

The truth. Her mind flashed back to that day five years before. What had Dustin's letter said? I'm sorry, Cass. I can't go through with the wedding.

Pain from the past rose up within Cassandra with such fury she groaned from its sharpness. She dropped her aim to the open space between Dustin's feet. She pulled the trigger and rapidly fired the gun three times, hitting the ground between Dustin's boots.

Dustin jumped. "Dammit, you little hellcat!"

He rushed her and grabbed her wrist, shoving her arm into the air with one hand and yanking the pistol away from her with the other. Cassandra caught him in the stomach with a hard fist, and she heard the sharp intake of his breath. The .22 fell to the ground with a thump.

Cassandra swung to sock him again but he caught her hand mid-air and bent her arm behind her back. She winced from the pain and kicked his shins with the toe of her boot.

"Let go of me, you double-crossing snake!"

He danced out of her reach and tightened his hold on her wrist. Dustin jerked her up to his solid chest. He twisted her other arm behind her back.

"It would serve you right if I turned you over my knee for that fool stunt, but I think I'll kiss you instead."

Cassandra gasped. "You wouldn't dare."

"In a heartbeat." He slowly lowered his head toward her face. "And yours is beating wildly right now. I feel it pumping against my chest."

"What's going on in here? Who's shooting at who?"

They both turned at the sound of Olive's voice. The plump, gray-haired housekeeper marched into the barn with a shotgun under her arm, pointed straight at Dustin.

"Turn her loose or I'll make mincemeat out of your hide and feed it to the chickens."

Cassandra took a deep breath and jerked away from Dustin. "It's all right, Olive. Nothing's wrong."

"I'm not blind and my hearing's not bad."

"Dustin's—an acquaintance. I shot the pistol by accident."

"Three times? You expect me to believe that?" the woman asked.

"It doesn't matter what you believe. I said everything's fine."

Cassandra brushed her hair away from her face and willed her legs to stop trembling and her pulse to stop racing. For a moment she'd really wanted to shoot Dustin. That startling realization calmed her and forced her to take control of her actions. She took a deep breath. The scent of hay, horse, and earth filled her head again.

"Does every woman around here carry a gun?" Dustin remarked and reached down to pick up Cassandra's pistol.

"I wouldn't do that unless you want buckshot for dinner," Olive said.

He straightened and backed away from the Colt. "I was going to hand it to you for safekeeping," he told Olive, then glowered at Cassandra. "I don't want any more accidents while I'm here."

"I'll get it myself." Olive motioned with the shotgun. "Move away."

Dustin moved further inside the barn.

"Oh, for heaven's sake," Cassandra said in an exasperated tone. "I'm not going to shoot him." She scooped up the pistol and slid it back in her holster.

"Those shots are bound to bring Jojo and Red Sky running if they were close enough to hear. You want me to send them down here?"

"No, of course not. I'm fine. Dustin and I were just talking about old times. Get back to your work."

Olive gave Dustin the once over before she turned and walked away.

As soon as she'd cleared the doorway Dustin strode

13

over to Cassandra. "You're crazy. You damn near killed me."

"What a pleasant thought," she answered tartly, folding her arms across her chest. "However, I was only trying to make you a steer, not a steak."

A twitch of a smile relaxed Dustin's features. His eyes swept down her nose, across her cheeks, and over her lips, then glided along the front of her plain white shirt, fawn-colored trousers, and dusty boots before resettling on her face again.

"When did you start wearing a gun strapped to your hip?"

"When I got old enough to shoot trespassers like you."

"You've grown up, Cass."

"Don't." She choked on the word, tension knotting in her throat. From somewhere deep inside she summoned the courage not to crumble into an emotional heap before him. "Don't call me by that name. Only people who love me are allowed to call me Cass."

"I see you still like to give orders."

She lifted her chin and her shoulders. "That's right and I want you off my land. How many times do I have to say it?"

She didn't want to look into his eyes or stare at the lips that once promised she'd carry his name. She didn't want to think about that time with him. It was over. Forgotten. But unbidden, memories of the way he'd held her so closely and kissed her so passionately came too easily to her mind. The forbidden touches and caresses they'd shared that night in the garden stirred her like nothing ever had before or since. No, God help her, she had never forgotten Dustin Bennett.

"I've always liked the way your beautiful brown eyes sparkle when you're angry."

Her stomach knotted. Her hands trembled. "I'm more than angry, Dustin. I'm furious you'd have the gall to set foot on my property after what you did to me."

"You always were the prettiest girl in the West. That hasn't changed."

Cassandra brushed at her hair with the back of her hand. "Your flattery no longer impresses me, Dustin."

"It was never that, only the truth." He searched her face. "Look. I'm not here to upset you."

"You could have fooled me. You have some nerve coming here at all."

"Can we forget what just happened and start this conversation over?"

Cassandra felt that familiar tightening in the bottom of her stomach as his seductive voice turned low. She flinched from the betrayal. Even though five years had passed since she'd seen him, her body reacted to this ruggedly handsome man. His easygoing, laid-back demeanor turned her legs to mush.

How could she still be drawn to this man?

Damn him!

She had gotten over the heartache, her bitter feelings toward him, and now he shows up at her door, bringing those buried emotions rushing back to overwhelm her. Somehow she had to remain in control of her anger, her shock, and not draw her pistol again.

"I didn't realize you would be so angry, since so much time has passed."

Dustin remained as calm as if it were only yesterday since they'd last spoken. She felt as if a lightning storm was exploding around her.

"Did you think I would welcome you with open arms after you jilted me on our wedding day and left my grandfather to explain to over a hundred guests that the groom hadn't bothered to show up? Pardon me, Dustin, if I'm not forgiving."

"I'm not asking you to be."

"Damn you, Dustin Bennett. How can you show your face to me?" Her voice shook and tears stung the back of her eyes. She clamped her mouth shut and held her

15

breath. She refused to do something stupid like cry in front of him.

He picked up his black Stetson from the ground where he'd dropped it when she fired the gun. His face was etched with concern. "I didn't think you'd want to see me after I'd explained everything in the letter I wrote you that day."

Cassandra laughed harshly. "How can jilting me be explained? It can't. Just go away, Dustin."

His self-assured attitude faded and he struck a more relaxed stance. A glimmer of tenderness flashed across his face.

He shifted his weight and Cassandra's attention was drawn to slim hips and long muscular thighs, hidden beneath fresh-pressed trousers the color of a newborn palomino. His expensive leather boots showed no signs of trail dust, even though the ranch was over a two-hour ride from Cheyenne.

Cassandra swallowed hard. No one ever wore a white shirt and black string tie with more ease and sophistication than Dustin Bennett. Oh how she hated admitting that he was the most handsome man she'd ever seen, the only man to ever make her want to smile just from the sight of him.

The only man she ever loved.

Dustin's expression became gentler. "I'm sorry about Thomas," Dustin said. "You know I respected your grandfather. He was a fine man."

Cassandra's heart constricted at the mention of her beloved grandpapa. Sorrow mixed with her anger. Dustin had always been skillful at knowing when to change the subject and what to say to calm her. Not wanting him to see any sign of weakness, she dropped her lashes over her eyes and managed a softly spoken, "Yes, he was."

"Gordon told me about the new ranch house Thomas built." He glanced through the open doorway to the large stately house in the distance. "I can't see much of it from here."

Thomas Rakefield was always trying to make up to her for the fact that her parents were dead, that her governess had left her to get married, and that Dustin had jilted her. Her grandfather's love and attention had helped ease her sorrow, but nothing could ever take Dustin's place in her heart and her life.

"I'm not inviting you to look around because I don't care what you think about the ranch, the new house, or the weather for that matter. How many times and how many different ways do I have to say it? You aren't welcome here, Dustin. I want you to leave."

He brushed dust from his hat with its stylishly braided hatband, then pushed aside his black jacket and settled his hands on his narrow hips. "I can't do that."

A chill of apprehension scurried up her back and settled in her neck. "What do you mean? The last I heard, my grandfather left everything he owned to me. That makes *me* the one in charge around here."

"I don't doubt that for a minute."

"Good." Cassandra walked past him with long easy strides. Her dusty work boots crunched on the dry earth beneath her feet. She walked to the open doorway, then made an ushering sweep with her arm. "With that taken care of you can go. I'd like to say it was nice to see you again, Dustin, but it wasn't. I have to finish strowing the hay, then round up the horses and bring them in for the night. You're wasting my time."

"Too bad, because I'm not leaving. And, just to put your mind at ease, I'm not here to take up where we left off."

"Thank God," she answered quickly. "I'd rather be burned on my backside with a branding iron than hear that you have designs on me again."

A flicker of irritation flashed across Dustin's face and Cassandra could see he was growing impatient. She was sure he thought her attitude toward him irrational, but where Dustin was concerned her emotions had always been strong. It bothered her that he could rile her like no other. He could make her feel more anger, more passion, more happiness than anyone she'd ever known.

"You're not fifteen anymore, Cass. You're—"

"Don't call me Cass," she interrupted.

He shifted his stance again. "All right, Cassandra, but it's time you stopped letting what happened between us influence you. Put your feelings aside and trust me. I'm here to help you."

She laughed. "Help me? Trust you? I beg your pardon?"

He cleared his throat. "Listen, I didn't come all the way to Wyoming to rehash what happened between us."

How was she supposed to react to the man who'd broken her heart? Did he think she should let bygones be bygones and give him a smile of friendship?

Why had Dustin shown up just as she was beginning to get on with her life? Just when Landon Webster had talked her into thinking about marrying him. One look at Dustin told her that Landon would never set her soul and body on fire the way Dustin had, and judging from the way her stomach was jumping and from the speed her heart was racing, the way Dustin always would.

Cassandra gave herself an internal shake to clear her thoughts. She was letting her emotions control her. Dustin should be the last person to know how deeply his jilting had affected her.

"The past has nothing to do with why I'm here now," Dustin continued. "That was personal. This is business."

She fought to tamp down her raging emotions. She wanted to hate him. She had reason to hate him, but all she could think was that looking at him made her heart beat a little faster.

"What business could I possibly have with you?"

"My father sent me to find out exactly what made you

ask for such a large sum of money from your inheritance."

Gordon Bennett? What must Dustin's father be thinking to send his son to her? Cassandra lifted her chin a notch more, swallowing past the growing lump in her dry throat.

She bristled. "Why? In my letter to him I asked that he send money. *Not you.* I need cash to buy horses and cattle. I have to pay my ranch hands so they can come back to work." Cassandra paused and rubbed the back of her neck. "Don't do this to me, Dustin. I'm fighting to save the ranch. I didn't know I was going to have to fight to get my inheritance, too."

"I'm not here to fight you."

"Then why does it feel that way? Look, Dustin, let's get this straight right now. Your father manages my trust, not the Triple R. He has no say here whatsoever. So go on back to Kansas City. I don't need you."

"You might be in charge of this ranch. But—"

"I *own* this ranch," she cut in, a defensive crispness edging her voice.

"Gordon is in charge of your money. I have to stay for a few days and evaluate the status of the Triple R to see if I think you need the amount of money you're asking for."

"If I need it?" A chill of trepidation shook her. "I don't understand this. My grandfather told me the firm manages the money for me."

"That means they are allowed to control who is paid from your accounts, and that includes you."

"They can't do this to me," she said, outraged by his words. She was furious that he remained so calm, so unruffled.

"They can. But I'm here to help you, Cassandra. Gordon let me read your letter to him. I know you're frightened."

Her eyes widened in shock. "Frightened? I didn't say anything about being frightened."

19

"You didn't have to. I read between the lines."

She was stunned that he'd been so perceptive, but she was not about to admit it. She needed that money to save her ranch.

"There was nothing between the lines," she fibbed without conscience.

His features softened. "You have several thousand acres of rangeland and, according to Gordon, at least fifteen hundred steers, yet the bunkhouse is empty. What's going on?"

"Red Sky and Jojo are the only men I have left. My hands are gone because there is no money to pay them and no work for them to do. There wasn't much of a roundup this year. Every rancher in the Northwest lost sixty to ninety percent of their herds because of the severe storms. The Triple R was hit hard. We had less than two hundred steers make it through the winter."

"Damn. I didn't know it was that bad. I thought the newspapers were exaggerating the numbers just for the headlines."

"No. Red Sky and Jojo can help me keep an eye on what few cattle we have left. I didn't want to, but I had to let the others go."

Dustin gave her a thoughtful look. "Why didn't you buy more calves and keep the hands?"

She didn't want to tell him anything about her life, but it looked as if she had little choice. Anyone around the area could tell him about her troubles. She had been to every bank in Cheyenne asking for a loan, hoping to avoid asking for money from her inheritance. If spilling the whole story to him would get her the money she needed to save the ranch and pay her cowboys their wages, she'd do it.

"We had some good years. Cattle business was booming because of the completion of the railroads and the slaughterhouses. We were a cattleman's paradise. Grandpapa thought every year was going to be better than the last so he tore down our small house and used all the cash we had plus a loan from the bank to build this one. He put everything we had into it. But with no herd to sell this year there is no extra money for more cattle, the mortgage, or the hands."

"Then the trouble with rustling, poaching, renegade Indians, everything I read was true?"

"Yes. Everyone is hurting. There aren't enough steers left for the Army to buy for the Indian allotments so the Indians are stealing from the ranchers, and out of work cowboys are rustling. Vigilante groups are hunting down poachers and rustlers and hanging them on the spot. So you see there's no reason for you to stay."

"I have to do the evaluation and report back to the firm what I think your needs are and the approximate costs."

Cassandra's hands made fists. "It's my money. Why can't he just give it to me?"

"From what I've been told, the rules of the trust were set up by your mother's will, which was first controlled by your stepfather, then your grandfather."

Cassandra couldn't take her eyes off the tall, broad-shouldered man as he talked. How could he walk so calmly into her life, her ranch, after what he'd done to her and act as if they'd never shared a moment of passion? How could she be physically drawn to the man who'd broken her heart?

God, why does he affect me this way?

Why was she allowing herself to become caught up in a past she thought she'd forgotten? She'd already wasted too many years doing that. Cassandra mentally shook herself. She hadn't felt sorry for herself in a long time, and she refused to let this man bring back those unwanted feelings to torture her and leave her vulnerable to him again.

"Is there anything else about my trust I don't know?"

"It states that your guardian can withdraw money for your care. That's what your stepfather did before his death. He lived quite a lavish lifestyle for a few months and spent heavily from your funds. After his death, your grandfather became your guardian. He chose the other extreme and never touched the money."

Another chill shook her, and she looked away from him for a moment. "I never wanted to touch it either." Cassandra had always thought it tainted, nothing more than blood money. Because of that money her stepfather had murdered her parents, and he had tried to kill her when she was six years old.

But I can't lose the ranch. It's all I have left. I must use that money.

Cassandra rubbed her arms to ward off the spring chill. She took a deep breath, looked directly into Dustin's eyes, and without flinching said, "I have no guardian now, so the money should be mine to do with as I please."

"The law firm is your guardian until you're twenty-five. At that time the money is all yours without any stipulations."

A groan of protest escaped her lips. Cassandra fought hard to keep tears of frustration from prickling her eyes. "Three more years?" The news couldn't have been worse if he'd said forever. "You know I can't wait that long. I will have lost the Triple R long before then."

Cassandra's strength impressed Dustin. It always had. He remembered back to when he first met her. At Dustin's father's invitation Cassandra's grandfather had agreed to bring her to Kansas City to see what life was like where she'd been born and to experience the life her parents had lived.

She was pretty, friendly, and as comfortable as a well worn saddle in her new environment. She'd had her pick of all the eligible young men in the city that summer, but she'd chosen Dustin right from the start. That had made it easy for him to carry out what he and his father had planned.

Cassandra couldn't have been any plainer about how

she felt about him now than when she fired her gun at his feet. He'd heard that things were different in Wyoming and Cassandra had just made him believe it.

It was odd, but he hadn't realized until now that he'd missed Cassandra. He thought he'd told her the truth when he said he hadn't come back to pick up where they left off, but now that he'd spent a few minutes with her, he wasn't so sure.

He still loved looking at her. That hadn't changed, although she had. If possible, she was more beautiful than he remembered. Her shimmering dark brown eyes looked wiser, more mature than when he'd last seen her.

He watched the rapid rise and fall of her breasts beneath the crisp white shirt she wore. The wide leather gun belt accented her small waist and lightly flaring hips.

Oh, yes. You've grown up, Cassandra Rakefield.

Her hair was a dark shade of shining brown that danced down her back when she moved. He liked the way she pulled it up on the sides and left the rest of it to tumble in soft waves.

When he'd walked into the barn, his first thought was that he must have been a fool not to have married her when he had the chance, no matter the reason. He couldn't believe some wealthy rancher hadn't taken her to wed and given her a handful of children to care for.

He hadn't minded one bit the anger she'd spit his way a few moments before. It proved that she was still accustomed to getting her way. If she wanted it, her grandfather saw to it that she got it. Dustin had always appreciated the challenge she presented. She'd never tried to be coy or bashful around him, preferring to be his equal. There was a strength about her that he recognized from their first meeting when she'd asked him if he was courting anyone.

"Listen, Dustin, I don't care who controls the money. Just tell me what I have to do to get what I need," Cassandra said, breaking into his thoughts.

"I'll spend a few days here at the ranch and assess the

damage from the winter, then go back to Gordon with my recommendation."

"You can do that in an hour. It won't take days."

"What I'll do won't be as easy as I made it sound."

"Why? I assume you are the successful lawyer your father always wanted you to be."

Dustin shrugged. A familiar tightness attacked his stomach. He was a damn good lawyer, but recently he'd become restless with his work and his social life. After years of fighting Gordon, Dustin had jumped at the opportunity to come to Wyoming to see Cassandra.

"After I file a report with the firm, the executive committee has to meet and approve the expenditure before the money can be wired to you."

"That could take weeks. Isn't there enough money to give me twenty-five thousand?"

"You're worth several million dollars."

Cassandra's eyes widened in disbelief. "You're joking."

He shook his head. It surprised him that she didn't know the value of her inheritance. "Gordon told me your grandfather wasn't interested in your money, but surely he was kept informed about your funds."

"Not that I'm aware of. I haven't seen any paper-work."

"Thomas should have kept a check on the firm."

"We didn't need the money. I guess he trusted your father to do the right thing. If there's so much money, why do I have to prove I need it?"

Fighting twinges of guilt he admitted, "The firm is paid a yearly retainer for managing the trust. One half a percent from the bottom line at the end of each year. That's a substantial amount. Your trust is the largest source of income the firm has. The more you are worth at the end of each year, the more money they make."

"They, Dustin? Don't you mean you? You are at the firm, aren't you?"

"You're not going to give me an inch, are you?" He

didn't blame her and it didn't bother him. Her sharp tongue and quick wit had always excited him.

Cassandra walked over and pulled the pitchfork out of the bale and started strowing the hay into a stall with quick, sure movements.

Gordon had often asked Dustin to come to Wyoming and see Cassandra, make amends, but he had always resisted, until Gordon had shown him the letter she'd written asking for the money. Deep inside, he knew he'd always wanted to see her again. He'd never forgotten her, and now he knew why. He was very much attracted to Cassandra Rakefield. Even more than before, he thought, if that were possible.

He'd been a bastard about the whole affair. What a fool he'd been to court Cassandra and win her hand just so the firm would remain guardians of her money. The hell of it was, he hadn't married her and the firm had continued to control her trust.

"I don't care how much your father makes," Cassandra said as she threw a forkful of hay into the air. "I hate that money. I've never wanted it. I wouldn't touch it now if I had any other choice. Tell your father that."

She spoke with such honesty it touched his heart. He knew he should do as she asked and go back to Kansas City and insist his father wire her the money. The amount she wanted wouldn't make a dent in her accounts anyway. Because of their past, he owed it to her to do it the easy way.

The trouble was, he didn't want to leave. Not yet. He wanted to stay and spend more time with Cassandra.

"I'll make sure he knows when I return."

Cassandra shot back around to face Dustin. "Is there any way I can get control of that money before I'm twenty-five?"

Unbidden, memories of their night together in the garden stole over him. A cool breeze had stirred the leaves on the trees and shrubs. The scent of wildflowers hung in the air. She had run into his arms and embraced him with youthful eagerness and passion. Her mouth tasted so sweet he'd been lost to everything but Cassandra and his need to possess her. But his most vivid memory was of the love shining in her sparkling eyes.

If he held her close now, would she feel the same way she had five years ago? Would her womanly scent be the same if he breathed in deeply and let his lips nip the soft skin of her shoulders? If he put his fingertip on the pulse point in her neck would her heart race with excitement the way it used to when they were alone? Would she taste of the same sweetness if he parted her lips and slipped his tongue inside her mouth and sipped her passion?

A hot shiver of anticipation rose up inside Dustin. "Well, there is one other thing you can do."

Hope shone in her eyes. "What?"

"If you marry, your husband will become your guardian and thereby control the trust. And, it just so happens I'm available."

Chapter

· 2 ·

Why in the hell did I say that?

Dustin's heart thudded crazily. He couldn't believe those words had come out of his mouth. Judging from the incredulous expression on Cassandra's face she couldn't either.

She threw the pitchfork down and glared at him with eyes so dark he felt as if he were looking into a smoky abyss.

"Your joke is in poor taste, Dustin."

Her voice trembled and that bothered him. "I wasn't trying to be funny. You asked me if there was another way to gain control of your inheritance, and I told you about the only other alternative."

Cassandra folded her arms firmly across her chest, remaining rigid in her stance. "I wouldn't marry you if you were the last man on earth."

Dustin wasn't sure which he felt more, disappointment or relief that she had rejected his spontaneous proposal. "I wonder why that doesn't surprise me," he said in a light tone, trying to inject humor into his words. But something inside him knew how tempting it would be for him to take her words as a challenge rather than an insult.

From the corner of his eye Dustin caught a movement. The woman named Olive had returned. This time without the shotgun at her side.

"Olive, what do you need?"

"I didn't mean to interrupt, Cass, but it's time to start dinner. I was just wondering if anyone would be joining you and Mr. Webster tonight?"

Dustin stiffened at the mention of another man's name and that surprised him.

"Yes. There will be three of us. Unfortunately, Mr. Bennett will be a guest for a day or two.

"Olive takes care of the house and the cooking," she said to Dustin. "She has a room on the first floor. Should you need anything while you are here, see her and she'll take care of it for you."

"I'll be sure to do that," he said to the housekeeper, but knew if he needed anything he was going straight to Cassandra, not the short, apron-clad woman with the plump waistline.

Without further comment, Olive turned and walked out of the barn.

Cassandra turned her attention back to Dustin. "I've no doubt you came prepared to stay awhile. You can put your things in the first room on the left at the top of the stairs."

Another surprise. "So you're going to allow me to stay in the house. I thought for certain you'd make me sleep in the bunkhouse."

"I would if I thought you were tough enough to handle it. Your father would never give me the money I need if I let anything happen to you while you're here. The way I see it, I'm forced to take care of you."

Her verbal swipe at his manhood stung, and he chuckled to cover the bite. "I guess I'm going to have to prove to you I can ride a horse as well as any of your hands."

"Just stay out of the way."

Damn, she was tough on him. He stared at the soft set to her lips and realized she was still smarting from his sudden appearance. Her straight back and stiff shoulders let him know she had grudgingly accepted what he came to do, and she was holding herself in check.

Dustin's gaze swept across Cassandra's face. Her silken skin looked as if it had been brushed with a hint of gold dust. Its softness invited him to touch. None of the beautiful, elegantly clad women he'd courted in Kansas City could compare with Cassandra's wholesome beauty. She'd grown from the prettiest girl he'd ever seen to an exciting and capable young woman. One quick appraisal of her told him that the rigors of ranch life had kept her body in perfect condition.

He had no doubt that Cassandra Rakefield had the power to make him want her, but he knew she wouldn't be eager to give him the opportunity to get close to her again. He could understand her feelings. What he didn't know was if he was going to accept them or try to change her mind.

What in the hell was he thinking? He came here on business. Cassandra had made it clear she was no longer interested in him, and he wasn't supposed to be interested in her.

"I know you don't believe me, Cass—sandra, but I'll try to make this assessment of your ranch as painless as possible for you."

"Just do what you have to do to get that money released." She looked him up and down in a quick, perusal. "If you stop talking and make short work of changing your clothes, you can get on with whatever it is you plan to do here. It's two hours until dinner."

Dustin easily forgave her caustic comments, and an amused smile lifted the corners of his lips. "So I don't get to rest after my long journey to the Triple R?"

"I assume you got enough rest on the train ride from Kansas City to Cheyenne. You know the rules of ranching. A man works from sunup to sundown. No exceptions. Dinner's served an hour after sunset. Don't be late."

"Do you dress for dinner?"

"This isn't Kansas City. All we expect are clean clothes, clean hands, and no hats."

"And your other guest this evening—Mr. Webster. Shouldn't I know something about him before he arrives?"

"If you want to know anything about him you can ask him tonight. Right now, you're burning daylight." She grabbed the pitchfork and started throwing hay into a stall.

The enticing sway of her bottom was slight but Dustin saw it. He couldn't help noticing again her small waist and the gentle flare of her hips. Watching her now he wondered why he'd resisted coming to see her.

He settled his hat on his head and walked out of the barn. He'd left his hired horse tethered to the hitching post in front of the house so he headed that way.

Cassandra was such a strong, self-assured woman, yet she didn't know how much money she had or how her trust fund worked. Why? The only indication she'd given was that she'd never wanted to touch the money, but why not? It was her inheritance. And why hadn't Cassandra's grandfather taken more of an interest in her affairs, if for no other reason than to make sure no one embezzled from her funds?

Dustin would have those questions answered before he left the Triple R.

He reached his horse and patted the gelding's warm neck. The animal shuddered and snorted disagreeably. The livery in Cheyenne didn't have a lot of stock to choose from. Dustin couldn't ever remember riding such an ornery mount.

He looked over the animal's back to the craggy mountain peaks rising up toward a glistening blue sky that was spotted with white clouds. The green hillsides rolled and sloped in every direction. A vast number of ponderosa pines and Douglas firs dotted land peppered with sagebrush, juniper, and grass brown from the late winter.

There was something wild about being so far away from civilization, yet the buttes in the distance seemed to stand guard in a protective way. The terrain around Kansas City couldn't match the beauty of the land surrounding the ranch.

The only sound Dustin heard was the cry of a black crow and an occasional snort from his horse. It felt good to be away from the law firm and the city. He liked the stillness, the quietness of the land. It was never this peaceful in Kansas City. From the early hours of morning to the last minute of darkness, the clanking of wagon wheels, the clopping of horses' hooves on the hard road, and the lively tinkling of piano music could be heard.

Dustin liked the way the sun warmed his face while a cool vagrant breeze nipped at his nose and cheeks. He liked how the air smelled on the Wyoming rangeland. It helped wash from his mind the scents of stale tobacco, whiskey, and food that escaped from the open doors of businesses that lined the streets of Kansas City.

As Dustin removed his leather satchel from the horn of his saddle, angry shouts rent the air, startling him. The horse snorted and jerked and pulled against his tether, sidestepping nervously.

Dustin patted the animal's neck and felt him tremble. "Easy, boy. Easy," he soothed.

Loud talking and swearing drifted to Dustin from the rear of the house. He set his bag on the porch and automatically felt for his Remington two-shot. He strode toward the commotion.

Cassandra rushed out of the barn and Olive hurried down the steps at the back door at the same time Dustin rounded the corner. Cassandra glared at two cowboys who were trying to subdue a young man about seventeen or eighteen.

Dustin assumed the older men were the cowpunchers

Cassandra mentioned earlier, Jojo and Red Sky. Kicking and punching, the young man struggled to free himself. He alternated between cussing and yelling as if the hounds of hell were after him.

"Good gracious!" Olive gasped.

"What in heaven's name is going on here, Jojo?" Cassandra asked in a voice that strained to be heard over the youngster's noise. "Turn him loose."

"Can't. He'll run away."

"No, he won't. There's nowhere for him to go. Now turn him loose."

The two men let go of their captive. He immediately swung his arm around and planted a bony fist into Red Sky's stomach, then nipped Jojo's chin with the tips of his knuckles before Cassandra called out, "That's enough. If you don't settle down right now I'll have them tie you up."

The dirty-faced lad glowered at her. Sweat or tears, Dustin wasn't sure which, had streaked the dirt on his face. His blue eyes were red and swollen. His ripped shirt hung off his shoulder and his trousers were caked with blood and mud.

Dustin stepped up beside Cassandra. He knew she didn't want him butting in to her business, but he wasn't going to stand by and let the belligerent young man take a swing at Cassandra, too.

"Need some help?" Dustin asked.

"No. Stay out of my way."

"Who's he?" Jojo asked, nodding toward Dustin.

"Never mind him. What are you two doing with this kid? Where did he come from?"

Jojo, a short, rotund cowhand with a red mustache that curved upward on the ends, lowered his head so Cassandra couldn't see his face. "I don't want to tell you because you won't like it."

Making an exasperated noise, she turned to the Blackfoot Indian with a leathery face and a coarse black braid hanging down his back. He remained silent.

"Spit it out, Red Sky," she ordered.

"We were out scouting for strays when we caught this one"—he pointed to the young man—"and his father up on the north hill. They were skinning a steer with our brand on it."

An ominous feeling stole over Dustin but he remained quiet. Cassandra flinched slightly, letting him know she was worried, too.

"Where's his father?" she finally asked.

"Dead!" the young man cried out in pain. "They killed my pa. They shot him down like he was a wild animal."

Dustin tensed.

Cassandra gasped. "No." Her alarmed gaze darted from the young man to Dustin to Red Sky. "Tell me it's not true."

"It is," the Indian said.

Cassandra felt as if a hand had clasped her around her throat and started squeezing. She couldn't breathe. Her chest tightened. Pressure bore down on her. She quickly took three deep breaths. For as long as she could remember she'd fought the affliction of feeling that something was smothering her whenever she was frightened. She couldn't let that happen.

She tried to remain unruffled by Red Sky's comment but couldn't silence her groan of disbelief. She hadn't felt so alone since the day her grandfather died.

Seeing her shock, the young man continued angrily, "They shot him down like he was no more than a mad dog."

"May God have mercy on his soul," Olive whispered.

The young boy pointed at the cowhands. "And I'm going to kill those bastards the same way."

"Sounds to me like there's been one too many killings already," Cassandra said.

It was well known all over the territory that because of

the scarcity of cattle, rustlers and poachers were being shot on the spot, but she'd never expected it to happen on her ranch.

She turned to Jojo and said, "Tell me everything that happened."

"We saw smoke up on the north pasture so we rode that way to check it out. From a ridge, we saw him and another man carving up a side of beef." Jojo paused for a moment and fiddled with the bandana tied around his neck. "We left our horses and eased down on foot. I held my gun on them while Red Sky looked at the markings. It was the Triple R brand, all right. Looked like it wasn't the first steer they'd carved, either. Several hides were laying around they hadn't bothered to burn. Other brands, too. We told him we'd have to take him in to the sheriff."

"Did not!" the young man yelled. "He just pulled the trigger and shot my pa in cold blood."

Cassandra heard pain in his voice and that bothered her. Having lost so much when she was young, and having so recently lost her grandfather, she knew what he was feeling.

"You'll get your chance to tell your side of the story," Dustin said.

"Stay out of this," Cassandra told Dustin without bothering to look at him. "Tell me the rest of it, Red Sky." She knew she could depend on the Indian to tell the truth even if it was unfavorable to him.

"It wasn't cold blood. The man went for his gun. Jojo had no choice. He had to shoot him."

Cassandra wanted to swear to the heavens, but with Dustin standing beside her she didn't even dare flinch. She'd told him she would handle this and she would, but *what* was she going to do? Was she now responsible for this young man?

"How old are you?" she asked.

"Old enough. I've had my first whore."

Olive gasped.

Dustin took a step forward. "Watch what you say or you'll be answering to me instead of the lady."

Cassandra glared at Dustin and elbowed him out of the way. "I said I'd take care of this."

"Do I have to listen to this woman? Whose ranch is this?" the poacher asked Dustin. "Yours or hers?"

"It's mine, and I'm tired of wasting time on you," Cassandra said firmly. "Now what's your name, how old are you, and where can we get in touch with the rest of your family?"

The belligerent expression seemed frozen on his dirty face, but finally he said, "My name is Rodney. Don't know my age. Pa never told me. Don't have no family neither. It's been just me and Pa for as long as I can remember."

Again, Cassandra's heart went out to him. She swallowed hard, not wanting to be affected by his story but unable to remain unmoved.

"Surely you have an uncle, an aunt, grandfather, or—someone we can contact."

"Not everybody has kin. I don't. Pa was all I had and now he's dead!"

A pang of sadness hit Cassandra. She didn't have any relatives either, now that her grandfather was gone. The closest person she had to family was the woman who'd been responsible for bringing her to Wyoming when she was six years old. But Juliana Banks and her husband Rill had been in Texas all spring because Rill's father was ill.

Cassandra forced those lonely feelings away as her grandfather's words came rushing back to her: "Remember, if a man sees a softening in you he'll take advantage of you quicker than a horse's tail can swat a fly."

"It's part of life to lose those you love," she said, straining to make her voice hard and unyielding. She hated that her words wouldn't offer him any comfort.

"You put things like this behind you and deal with it, that's all." Cassandra turned to Jojo and asked, "Did you bury his father?"

"Felt it was the right thing to do. I didn't mean to kill him. I said a word or two before the boy started running away and we had to hightail it after him."

"I ain't no boy. I'm a man."

"What was your father's name?" Dustin asked Rodney.

He glanced up at Dustin. Rage showed in his red eyes and his bottom lip trembled. "Charlie Mixon, not that it makes a difference now he's dead."

"The grave should be marked, Jojo," Cassandra said.

"I'll take care of it," the cowboy answered.

"Did you check the man's pockets to see if he had any papers on him?" Dustin asked.

"He was clean. Not even a coin or tobacco."

Cassandra took a deep breath. Dustin was determined to have his say. "All right, Olive," Cassandra said, "get back inside and tend to your cooking." The housekeeper immediately turned away and headed toward the house.

"Red Sky, ride into town and tell the sheriff what happened to Rodney's father. If he has any questions about it tell him to come see me. Jojo, take Rodney to the bunkhouse and feed—"

"Wait a minute. I want to discuss this with you," Dustin said firmly. "Keep an eye on him, Jojo."

Dustin grabbed hold of Cassandra's upper arm and started ushering her away from the others.

"What do you think you're doing?" Cassandra struggled to tear away from his grasp and keep pace with his long strides at the same time.

"Keeping you from making a big mistake."

She tried to pull free but his hand held her like an iron band. "Who do you think you're manhandling?"

"You, and it looks like you need it. I want to talk to you alone. We're in trouble here."

Cassandra jerked free of his hand. She couldn't believe what she'd just heard. *"We?"* she asked incredulously. "Since when are you a part of what goes on at this ranch? And what do you mean by ordering me around?"

"I'm trying to get through to you that you need me and I'm here to help you."

"You must have been into the locoweed. I don't need you. Not with the ranch, not with anything." She kept her voice low and gritty.

"You can't let Rodney stay here."

"My men killed his father. That makes me responsible for him until he's old enough to be on his own."

"Like hell it does. He's angry and he's dangerous. He's already promised to kill your men."

"That was nonsense talk because he's hurting and he's frightened. He can't be more than sixteen."

"He's at least eighteen if he's a day and probably much older."

"I'm not throwing him out on his own. You heard him. He doesn't have anywhere to go. He doesn't have anyone to count on for help."

"That's the way he's used to living. He'll survive. I know you're thinking about your own life—"

"No," she interrupted him. She couldn't bear the thought of him knowing what she was feeling right now. "You don't know anything about me, Dustin. Now I'm tired of fighting you and tired of telling you to stay out of my business." Her words sounded far too hollow. She turned and walked away.

"Red Sky, if the general store is still open get Rodney a new shirt and put it on my account. You've got a long ride ahead of you, best get going. Jojo, give Rodney a bed in the bunkhouse."

The cowpuncher slung all his weight to one leg and jutted out his hip. He looked at Cassandra as if she'd lost her mind. "You're not going to bunk him with us, are you?"

"It's the best I can do for now."

"I'm not going with him," Rodney said in a grumbling tone. "He killed my pa and you want me to bed down with him?"

It seemed no one liked her plan. But there was no reason she couldn't give the young man a chance to do a decent day's work. If he continued to poach he'd end up dead like his father.

She stood motionless. "Both my men say your pa went for his gun."

"What if he did?"

"That means it was self-defense and Jojo's not at fault."

"That weasel bastard could've shot him in the leg. He didn't have to kill him."

Cassandra's heart constricted for Rodney, but she had to let him know she was the boss. "First, we don't allow name calling around here. Second, what's done can't be undone. And third, if I thought you were over eighteen I'd send you packing off to the jailhouse and let the sheriff deal with you. Since you're not, I'm willing to let you live here until you're old enough to be on your own."

"I'm already old enough to take care of myself," he argued.

"No one takes kindly to poachers and rustlers in Wyoming. Next time it will be you who's shot. At least here you can have a bed instead of the ground to sleep on. You won't have to steal your food, but you will have to work for it. Jojo and Red Sky will tell you what to do."

"I ain't learning nothing from an Indian. I want to go to the sheriff and tell him that bastard-coward killed my pa." He jabbed a finger toward Jojo.

"That's an excellent idea," Dustin said, stepping into the conversation again. "I'll be happy to ride along with you to make sure nothing happens before you get to town."

"Fine," Cassandra said evenly. "Go if you want to,

Rodney, but I won't stop the sheriff if he tries to throw you in jail—or worse. Last I heard, poaching was a hanging offense. From what my men told me the Triple R wasn't the only brand they found in your camp."

Rodney looked, wild eyed, from Dustin to Cassandra. "All right, I'll stay—for a while."

Cassandra nodded. "We don't allow slackers. I'll expect you to work hard and do whatever Jojo or Red Sky tells you. If I hear of you causing trouble, I'll take you to the sheriff myself." She turned to Jojo. "Show him where to bunk."

Shaking his head, Jojo turned and walked toward the bunkhouse. Rodney followed silently.

Cassandra's throat ached, her stomach roiled, and her head pounded. She looked at the western sky. A shield of blue was etched in a blaze of orange, mauve, and mulberry colors as the sun melted toward the horizon. Not more than an hour or so until sunset. She glanced over at Dustin. Her eyes raked up and down him.

"I see you haven't changed clothes yet."

"I see you still expect people to do whatever you tell them."

"I am the boss around here."

He studied her face for so long before he answered she became uncomfortable.

"That you've made clear more than once." He paused again. "You were always demanding, but I don't remember you being so downright rigid. You know, it won't break you to bend and accept a little help."

Cassandra flinched. His words stung. A long time ago she'd learned how to cope with fear, disappointment, and loss.

"I can't afford to. There's too much at stake. I know that no one is happy with my decision, but it was *my* decision to make."

Dustin nodded. "Come on, I'll help you round up the horses and get them in the barn."

"With those fancy clothes on?"

"They'll wash. Wouldn't want you to think I'm a slacker." He turned and headed for the corral.

A brief smile touched Cassandra's lips, making her feel a little better. Why not let Dustin stay for a couple of days and see for himself that she'd gotten on with her life? Without him.

Chapter

· 3 ·

After the horses had been caught and stabled, Cassandra left Dustin to take care of his own mount and went into the house to wash and change for dinner. Dustin walked his gelding to the barn and unsaddled him, then fed and watered him. With that finished, he picked up his satchel from the porch and headed inside.

He briefly glanced around the darkly paneled foyer and down the wide center hallway dotted with large arched doorways on either side. It was evident Cassandra's grandfather had used only the best materials to construct the house. He found the room Cassandra had told him to use without any trouble.

His thigh muscles felt strained and tight as he climbed the stairs. He didn't get to do much riding. He'd forgotten what a day in the saddle could do to a man. The two-hour ride from Cheyenne was telling on him.

The large bedroom was sparsely filled with only a bed, night stand, short chest, and slipper chair. The draperies and the bedcover were a pink rose print more suited to a woman's taste than a man's. He assumed Cassandra had put him in the room on purpose, hoping to make him uncomfortable. He chuckled to himself and placed his satchel on the flower-printed coverlet. Nothing feminine could bother him.

Even though he had only been in Wyoming a few hours, he knew he'd made the right decision in coming to see Cassandra. She might never admit it but he knew she needed him.

After placing his shaving gear on the chest, Dustin washed his face and hands and changed into a dark blue chambray shirt with two rows of silver-colored buttons forming a V on the front. He put away the rest of his clothing in the chest, then walked down the stairs and made his way down the long quiet hallway, sticking his head in each doorway until he found the one from which the delicious scent of fresh-baked bread emanated.

Olive stood at the stove, humming to herself. Steam rose from all three pots in front of her. Before her a wall of curtainless windows showed a wide expanse of dark blue sky, and the bold outline of craggy buttes in the distance. A pleasant, homey feeling washed over him. He wondered what it was about this ranch that made him feel so comfortable, as if he belonged here.

Dustin was often invited into the best homes in Kansas City for dinner and parties. He'd felt at ease in all of them but hadn't felt at home in any of them.

"Looking for a cup of coffee?" Olive asked, her back still to him. "Or something stronger?"

Dustin hadn't been aware that she'd noticed him standing in the doorway. He stepped further into the room. The kitchen was spacious, with a rectangular table flanked by two benches on either side sitting in the middle of the room. The shotgun she'd pointed at him stood in the corner by the door.

"Something stronger. I was hoping you had some liniment."

A knowing smile appeared on the older woman's round face as she turned toward him. "Been a while since you've been in the saddle, has it?"

Dustin rubbed his clean-shaven chin, realizing by the twinkle in her eyes that she teased him. Maybe she'd decided it wasn't any of her business why Cassandra had shot at him. "I didn't think it had been that long, but I guess it has."

"Time passes faster for some than it does for others."

Her words reminded Dustin how long a day at his office could seem when the weather was warm and inviting him to get on a horse and ride the countryside. "How long have you been here at the Triple R, Olive?"

"Long enough so that I've figured out who you are. I came to help Cass take care of this new house. It was so much bigger than the one they moved from she couldn't take care of it and help Mr. Rakefield run the ranch, too. His health was already failing but Cass doesn't like to admit that."

Olive placed a lid on the pot she'd been stirring and walked over to a handsome wooden cabinet that stood on the far side of the room. "This doesn't smell like wildflowers," she said, handing him a small jar filled with a milky white substance, "but it will help take the soreness out."

He unscrewed the lid and was hit in the face by a strong rancid smell. Coughing, he recapped it quickly. He shook his head at the offensive odor. "Whew! Are you sure this is all you have?"

She nodded. "It's the best. You won't have to use it more than once or twice," she assured him. "If you're here long enough to get used to riding again."

Dustin smiled to himself. Obviously, Olive had overheard his conversation with Cassandra. "I'll try this tonight." Then wash it off first thing in the morning, he thought. If he didn't, Cassandra would be sure to notice and make a comment.

Olive walked back over to the stove. With a big fork she turned over large slices of ham sizzling in a skillet. "There's a creek not more than half a mile from the back of the house. Water's cold this time of year. You can probably stand the smell better than the water. If you decide to wash, you better get up early if you don't want Cass to catch you. She's never been one to slouch in the mornings."

For a moment Dustin thought Olive could read his mind.

"Her grandfather's death," Dustin asked Olive in a somber tone, "was it hard on her?"

A sadness crept into the woman's features. "Good gracious, yes. It just about killed her when the doctor told her he didn't think Mr. Rakefield was going to make it through the winter. Poor thing, she never left his side during the last days. She had Red Sky ride into Cheyenne and bring out some new doctor she heard was coming to town, but there was nothing that could be done for Mr. Rakefield. His lungs were too far gone. Most folks think Cass has a heart of iron but truth is it's softer than kitten fur."

Olive's words struck a chord in Dustin. Again he was hit with the thought of just riding out of Cassandra's life and telling his father to send her the money. She'd been through too much for him to add to her worries. The trouble was he didn't want to leave. He knew he could help her. All he had to do was convince Cassandra of that.

A loud knock at the front door interrupted Dustin's thoughts. He looked over at Olive.

"Oh, that will be Mr. Webster come for dinner."

"Mr. Webster." Dustin said the name out loud.

Mischief shone in the old woman's eyes. "He's Cass's beau."

"He's courting her?"

"Yes. A real handsome man. He's been coming to see her since before winter broke." Olive put down the large fork and started untying the strings of her white apron. "He works for one of them big banks in Cheyenne."

"Is that where she met him?"

"No. He just showed up here one day shortly after Mr.

Rakefield died. Said he was new in town and had heard about her loss and wanted to offer condolences. Cass approved of that."

"Sounds odd that he just showed up here."

"Not really. Folks came from everywhere to pay their respects. Next time he came he asked her if he could come courting. It took Cass a while to warm up to his attentions, but she lets him come to dinner every Saturday night now."

If Gordon knew about Landon Webster, he'd failed to mention him to Dustin. Now that he thought about it, Dustin wondered just how well his father had kept up with what went on in Cassandra's life.

"I'll let Webster in for you, Olive," Dustin said. "And one other thing before I forget. A word of warning. Be careful as long as Rodney is around. I don't trust him."

"I was thinking the same thing myself."

Cass is courting? Dustin thought as he walked down the hallway and into the foyer. He knew that shouldn't bother him, but it did.

Dustin opened the heavy front door to a handsome man of average height, not much past twenty years. His wide smile quickly faded. His eyes and his expression questioned Dustin, though Webster said nothing at first. He wore a fashionable plaid suit that told Dustin the man came from money. Bunched in one hand was a cluster of flowers that were very close to wilting and under his arm he held an expensive felt hat.

"Good afternoon," the man said, quickly recovering from the shock of seeing Dustin. "I'm Landon Webster, here to see Cass."

Cass? Apparently Dustin was the only one not allowed to call her Cass anymore. That bothered him. Five years ago she wouldn't let anyone call her Cassandra. It wasn't hard to figure out where that left him as far as she was concerned.

"Yes, I believe we're expecting you for dinner. I'm Dustin Bennett, an—old friend of the family."

Dustin stuck out his hand and Webster shook it. The man's grip was firm, his shake steady, and his palm dry. Dustin didn't like what that said about Webster—a confident man. Truth was, Dustin would have felt better if he'd been a little nervous.

"Pleased to meet you, Mr. Bennett."

Dustin opened the door wider and stepped aside. There might be several years' difference in their ages but Dustin didn't want to be called Mister. "Call me Dustin, Webster. Come in and hang your hat."

As he stepped into the foyer Dustin heard Cass coming down the stairs. He turned and looked at her. That familiar tightness attacked his stomach again. She was beautiful, but the strain of the afternoon showed on her face. She had changed from her trousers and gun belt into a wine-colored skirt and blouse. A wide strip of white piping edged the high neckline and banded her small waist. Her hair was piled on top of her head in a ringlet of curls. He couldn't help thinking she looked very kissable.

He glanced over at Webster. It wasn't difficult to see that the banker was lovestruck, and Dustin knew exactly what the other man was feeling.

Dustin noticed that Cassandra deliberately let her gaze skip over him and linger on Webster. He walked over and met her at the bottom of the stairs, holding out the wildflowers to her. She took them from him and he grasped hold of her other hand, squeezing gently for a moment before letting her go. Dustin stiffened. He didn't want the dandy touching her.

She smiled sweetly at Webster. "The flowers are lovely, and sweet of you, Landon. Thank you." She turned to Dustin, almost looking through him and removing the smile from her tempting lips. "I see you've met Dustin. He arrived just this afternoon and will be visiting us for a day or two. Isn't that right, Dusty?"

Dusty? The pet name crawled up his back like a slithering snake and Dustin knew that was exactly what she wanted. Dustin held her gaze. "It's true that Cassandra and I have known each other for a long time."

"Cassandra?" Landon looked at Cass. "I didn't think anyone called you by that name."

"Well, I—"

"I'm the only one allowed to call her that," Dustin said with a satisfied smile on his face. "She told me so just this afternoon. Isn't that right, Cassandra?"

Her mouth tightened. "Yes, I did say that."

Dustin winked at her, thinking that the more he called her Cassandra the more he found it suited her far better than Cass anyway.

"Let's not stand here in the foyer talking. We'll go into the parlor and sit down." She reached for Landon's arm before he offered it. "I'm sure Olive will be calling us in to dinner soon. In the meantime, I'll pour you both a drink."

"I hope you've had a good day," Landon said.

"Not exactly. It's been hectic, but let's don't talk about that right now. I'd rather hear about your week."

Dustin waited and watched them disappear through the doorway. He didn't like the way Landon looked at Cassandra or the way he touched her. But worse, he didn't like the way she looked at him. Webster was no sap. And he didn't appear the least bit intimidated by Dustin's presence.

"Not yet, anyway," he whispered to himself and followed them into the parlor.

Cassandra had never sat through a longer, more tedious dinner hour. If she hadn't known better she would have thought Olive was deliberately making the meal take longer than necessary. Cassandra had been tempted to have Olive skip serving the raisin pudding altogether because the strain of sitting at the table with Dustin and Landon was almost more than she could bear.

Polite conversation was the last thing she had on her mind. She had to force herself to be good company when all she wanted was to walk down to the bunkhouse and see how Jojo was getting along with Rodney.

Despite her outward show of confidence earlier in the afternoon, she wasn't sure she'd done the right thing in allowing Rodney to stay on at the ranch.

It would be impossible to talk to Landon about what happened to Rodney and his father. Landon would use it as leverage in his quest to convince her to give up the ranch, move into town, and marry him.

She had done her best to ignore Dustin, but he would have none of that, finding ways to break into her conversations with Landon. Dustin had not been such a talker five years ago. At times it seemed as if he was drilling Landon with questions on his banking business and his family. She was tempted several times to tell Dustin he wasn't her grandfather and to stop acting as if he were.

Finally the two men finished their second cup of coffee. She rose from the table, eager to get away from Dustin. She turned to him, again avoiding looking directly into his eyes, and said, "If you'll excuse us, Dustin, I'd like to spend a few minutes alone with Landon before he rides back into town. We don't get to see each other often."

Dustin hesitated for a moment, then said, "Of course. I understand. We'll catch up on old times later. Goodbye, Webster."

"Enjoy your visit and have a safe trip back to Kansas City," Landon said as Cassandra slipped her arm through his once again.

She tried to relax her tense muscles as they walked out onto the front porch. Dusk had given way to night and the black velvet sky shone with twinkling stars. She drew her woolen shawl tighter about her shoulders. The cold air was still and night sounds seemed far away. They sat down on the deacon's bench in front of the window and Landon took her hand.

"Thank you for getting us away from your guest. I

wanted to spend some time alone with you, and I'm
pleased you wanted me all to yourself."

She smiled at Landon. It was his hand that held hers,
but it was Dustin on her mind. Why did he have to show
up and upset her life? She was just beginning to get
comfortable with Landon as a suitor.

"Cass, I don't like the idea of Dustin staying in the
house with you."

"Don't be ridiculous," she said, dismissing Landon's
objection. If he'd ever been told the name of the man she
was once engaged to he'd obviously forgotten it. She
wasn't going to remind him. "He—he's a family friend.
I've known him for years. I'm perfectly safe with him, I
assure you," she hedged, seeing no reason to tell him
about her past relationship with Dustin. "Besides,
Olive's room is directly under mine and Red Sky and
Jojo are always nearby to come to my aid should I need
them."

Landon smiled, a boyish expression that she found
engaging. "You'll have to forgive me if I appear jealous.
I'm the one who has the long ride back into town tonight
and he gets to stay here with you."

"Just believe me when I tell you Dustin and I have
absolutely no interest in each other."

"I'm sure I worry for nothing. I guess you feel about
him like you would a brother."

"Something like that," she said, knowing she wasn't
telling the truth. The darkness enveloped her, yet she felt
exposed and vulnerable.

Landon placed his hand on her shoulder. "I don't
want to discuss him anyway," he said, moving closer
beside her. "What I want to do is remind you that I
asked you to marry me and you haven't given me an
answer yet."

"I know."

"Marry me, Cass. Leave the problems of this ranch to
someone else." He slipped his arms around her waist
and pulled her close. His eyes narrowed and he lowered

his lashes. "I promise I will make you so happy you'll never miss this place. Say yes, Cass," he whispered, then placed his lips against hers.

Cassandra didn't know if it was the shock of all that had happened during the afternoon or the need to erase Dustin from her thoughts but she allowed Landon to kiss her. She couldn't feel his lips at first, there was so little pressure from him, but when she didn't protest he held her tighter and kissed her with more passion.

Her mind tried to focus on what Landon had said rather than on what he was doing.

I want to marry him.

Do you?

Yes. He can take care of me, the ranch.

He doesn't want the ranch. He wants you to leave it.

Not forever. Just for a little while.

You're lying to yourself.

No.

You're still carrying a flame for Dustin. Admit it.

It's a flame of anger, resentment, bitterness.

Not anymore.

Cassandra wrapped her arms around Landon's neck and pressed him close to her. When he parted her lips she allowed his tongue inside her mouth. She wanted him to erase the passion of Dustin from her heart, from her life. She desperately needed to be in love with Landon so she could forget Dustin.

Landon's hand inched down her back and around her rib cage to cup her breast. A small sound of protest came from the back of her throat and she pushed at Landon. She slid away from him as she caught her breath.

"I'm going too fast, aren't I?"

She rose from the bench and went to stand by the porch railing. "Yes," she whispered, unhappy with herself that she'd allowed thoughts of Dustin to infringe on her time with Landon. "It's getting late. Maybe you should go. As I said earlier, it's been a hectic day, and I have some things I need to check on."

"All right." He reached inside the front door and plucked his hat off the hat tree in the corner and placed it on his head. "I told you I wouldn't press you for an answer to my proposal and I won't, but I'm not going to give up until you are mine."

Cassandra remained quiet.

Landon pulled her to him and gave her a soft kiss on the lips. "Good night, my darling. I'll see you next Saturday afternoon."

She merely nodded and watched him mount and ride away.

She needed to be alone. She had never pushed away from any of Dustin's kisses. No, never.

This whole problem with Landon was Dustin's fault, she concluded. She would have been able to enjoy Landon's kisses if Dustin hadn't come back, if he wasn't in her house and on her mind.

Landon was a good man with a good job. She would have already said yes if he had agreed they could live at the ranch. Why couldn't he understand that she couldn't give it up? Through years of following her grandfather around the ranch checking the rangeland, the timber, the water, she had come to love every inch of the Triple R. She wouldn't give it up.

Cassandra stood in the chilling darkness and watched Landon ride away until she no longer heard the horse's hooves on the dry packed dirt. It was so quiet she thought she could hear the rushing water of the creek that flowed behind the back of the barn.

She closed her eyes, but instead of remembering Landon, her thoughts went back five years to Dustin's lovemaking and the way she had clung to him, not wanting to let him go.

The front door opened. Cassandra turned around and looked at Dustin.

Already she had forgotten the touch, the taste of Landon's lips.

Chapter

·*4*·

"I heard Webster's horse leave but you didn't come inside." Dustin stepped out onto the porch.

"I'm surprised you're not in bed. I thought you were tired after your long journey out here." She shifted her gaze away from his, looking past him.

"I wanted to make sure everything was all right."

Cassandra took a deep breath and sucked the chilling air into her lungs. The scent of burned wood lingered in the crisp spring night. The welcoming glow from lamps inside her house reminded her of the night she and Dustin made love under the stars.

She didn't know why after all these years she remembered everything about Dustin. She didn't want to remember anything about him. Especially the taste of his lips on hers.

Tossing aside those unwanted memories she said, "I don't need anyone looking after me."

Dustin eased up beside her and leaned against the porch post. He said, "I didn't know exactly what to expect from you after all these years."

"Really? I always thought I'd behave badly if I ever saw you again and hopefully I have."

Dustin chuckled attractively. "I'm glad you haven't lost any of your wit or charm."

"Nor have you, but I'm too tired to banter with you any more this evening."

"Seeing you again has reminded me of why we were once so attracted to each other."

"Yes, well that is about as clear as a muddy creek to me. I'd say you did me a favor by not marrying me." She turned toward him. "I need to walk down to the bunkhouse and see how Jojo and Rodney are getting along."

Dustin reached and closed the door behind him, shutting out the little light the open doorway had afforded. "I'll go with you. I wouldn't mind knowing the answer to that."

"Suit yourself."

They stepped off the porch and headed toward the back of the house. There was just enough light from the moon and stars to light their way. Cassandra noticed that Dustin was walking stiff-legged and smiled.

"A long time since you been in a saddle, has it?" she remarked innocently.

"Not too long."

"Guess it was the train ride that made your legs sore."

"I'm glad you looked me over so carefully you noticed."

"I didn't. I'd have to be blind not to see your legs bow with every step."

"You don't have to deny your interest in me, Cassandra. I like the idea of you looking me over from head to toe."

She didn't have to look at him to know he was smiling, but what surprised her was that it didn't bother her. She wanted to be furious with him but already she was relaxing around him.

"There's some liniment in the kitchen if you're interested."

"Your concern is noted."

They walked in silence for a few moments before Dustin said, "I noticed you didn't tell Webster about what happened with Rodney this afternoon. Any particular reason why?"

Yes. Landon is looking for a reason for me to give up the ranch. "No," she fibbed. "I just didn't want to talk about it and possibly spoil our evening together."

"If what happened to you had happened to the woman I was courting I'd want to know about it."

Cassandra stiffened but kept walking. Dustin's tone let her know he didn't think much of Landon. "I'm sure Landon would have liked to know, too. He's very protective of me."

"But you didn't want to spoil his evening," Dustin mocked.

She bristled again. *"Our* evening," she corrected, throwing him a sidelong glance he couldn't possibly see in the dark.

They walked on in silence for a few moments, their footsteps crunching and shuffling on the dry earth. Cassandra curled her fingers into the soft yarn of her shawl and wrapped it tighter about her neck and shoulders to keep the cool night wind from penetrating her blouse.

"Does the bank where Webster works hold the mortgage on the ranch?"

"No," she answered. "Why?"

"Just wondering. Did you ever think of going to him for a loan to pay off the mortgage?"

She glanced over at him again and wished she could see him more clearly in the shaded moonlight. "I tried to get a loan from every bank in town. I told you I never wanted to touch the money my mother left me. I finally decided I had no other choice if I was going to rebuild the ranch. How was I to know it would be so difficult to get?"

"Have you talked with the bank about an extension?"

"That was the first thing I did."

"They wouldn't give you one?"

"No." Her voice suddenly sounded dry and brittle. "There was no loyalty to the Triple R even though my grandfather had done business with them for years. The problem is that everyone had a bad winter and everyone wants an extension. The banks aren't giving them to anyone."

"That doesn't sound like a good way to keep customers happy."

"The bankers don't care. There are too many Easterners wanting to buy our land and cattle. We have groups of them coming from England and other countries, bidding on property and paying double its value. The bankers have made it clear to everyone. If your payment isn't made by the end of the day it's due, your land will be put up for auction the next morning. No exceptions."

"And when is your mortgage due?"

"The first day of July."

"Two months?"

"Yes. I should have the money I need from the law firm long before then, right?" It bothered her that the night was too dark to clearly see his face.

"I see no reason why not. I can have the money wired as soon as I get back to Kansas City. Tell me, does Webster know you're an heiress?"

An heiress? That statement almost made her laugh out loud. She didn't feel like an heiress. Gordon Bennett and the rules of her trust had her feeling like a beggar.

"Why are you asking me all these questions that are none of your business?"

"Webster seems anxious to marry you."

Cassandra didn't like what that statement implied. "What is that supposed to mean?"

"That he seemed to be pressuring you for an answer to his marriage proposal."

Cassandra stopped walking and stared at Dustin. "How would you know that?"

Dustin paused too. "Ah—I accidentally overheard some of your conversation with him."

"Overheard? Accidentally?" She stepped closer to him. "You eavesdropped on me?" Dark gray clouds sailed past the moon and the light brightened his face.

Dustin stood his ground. "Not exactly."

"How dare you."

"Look, you and Webster were sitting in front of the window that is by the chair I happened to be sitting in. I didn't want to interrupt to tell you that your conversation could be heard through the closed window."

She let go of her shawl and jerked her hands to her hips. Her face burned hot even though the wind was cold. "I'm sure you chose that seat on purpose so you could sit in there and listen to what we said to each other. That's a despicable thing for you to do."

"Now, wait a minute. I'm sure I didn't hear everything you said."

She was furious he'd heard anything.

"Or see everything you did."

"You deliberately spied on me. I don't believe this. You—you—you're incredible."

"Thank you," he said dryly.

"That wasn't a compliment." She started walking again, faster this time, stomping through the ankle-high grass. Light from the bunkhouse came into view. "My relationship with Landon is none of your business so keep your nose *and* your eyes out of it."

"We can argue the finer points of that later, Cassandra. What happens to the Triple R if you marry Webster?"

"What you mean is what happens to my inheritance, right?"

"No, that's not what I mean. It's clear that Webster has no intention of working or living on the ranch and you're damn eager to save it."

Cassandra felt a sinking in her stomach. She didn't want to think about that right now. She'd worry about

Landon and what he wanted later—if she decided to marry him.

"I'll never give up this ranch," she finally said.

"Does Webster know that?"

"He knows." Her voice softened. "He just isn't ready to believe me."

"You were going to give it up five years ago and live with me in Kansas City."

Why did he have to remind her of that? She had been so happy, so in love back then. "I wasn't really giving up anything. My grandfather was still here. The ranch wasn't in any danger of being auctioned. And I knew I could always come back here to visit."

"But you don't have that assurance if you marry Webster, right?"

It hurt to admit that she no longer had that security. She wished Juliana was home so that she could ride over to her ranch and talk to her. Juliana was the only one who could understand what losing her grandfather had meant. He'd been a hard man, but she'd always felt loved. When she was ten he stopped treating her like a girl and started treating her like the person who would one day take over running the ranch.

Thomas Rakefield forced her to grow up and learn how to shoot, ride, and rope as well as any of his cowpunchers. By the time she was thirteen she could help tie off a calf's hind legs and brand him.

"You know, I could loan you the money you need until the law firm comes through with your request."

"And be indebted to you? I'd rather be yoked with a rabid wolf."

Dustin laughed.

The front door of the bunkhouse opened and Jojo stepped out. "Is that you, Miss Cass?"

Light from the room behind Jojo fell on Cassandra's face. "Yes," she said, lifting the hem of her skirt and walking closer to the wide plank porch.

Jojo warily eyed Dustin, then glanced at Cassandra. "Is everything all right with you?"

"I'm fine."

"Well, if you don't mind me asking, who's this feller to be hanging around you all the time?"

"I guess there wasn't time to introduce him this afternoon. It's no wonder with all that was going on. Jojo, this is Dustin Bennett. We were once—we met the summer I spent in Kansas City."

"He going to be here awhile?"

While Dustin and Jojo shook hands she answered, "It appears so. Remember I told you I had some money in Kansas City coming to me? This is the man who's going to help me get it. He'll be here looking over the ranch for a couple of days."

"Let me know if there's anything I can do to help," Jojo said to Dustin. "We could sure use some money around here."

"I'll do that," Dustin told him.

Cassandra knew the thing Jojo needed most was his wages and it bothered her that she hadn't been able to pay any of the hands who'd stayed on with her most of the winter. She'd let some of them take their horses as partial payment. She hated losing her work animals but it was better than sending the men away empty handed.

"I wanted to see how it was going with Rodney," Cassandra said, trying to keep concern out of her voice.

Jojo hitched up his brown trousers and said, "I gave him some beans and bacon and cut him some of the bread Olive sent down to us. He might have missed a meal or two but he wasn't starving. After he ate I showed him which bunk to take, then he fell on the bed and he's been snoring ever since."

"Good," she said, pretending she wasn't concerned. "I'm glad he hasn't given you any trouble."

"Didn't say a word to me. But I'm not ready to turn my back on him."

"That's a smart idea," Dustin said.

"Jojo, give him some time," Cassandra said.

"I did the right thing. It was his pa or me."

"I know." She gave the ranch hand a reassuring smile. "Everything's going to be all right."

"Just the same, I'll feel a whole lot better when Red Sky gets back. He should be riding up any time now."

"Let me know if he's not back in an hour or two."

"Let us know if *anything* changes," Dustin added to Cassandra's comment. "There's no harm in being careful."

"I aim to be."

"I'll talk with you in the morning," Cassandra said. "Good night."

She and Dustin turned and headed back toward the house. Cassandra's nose was cold and her fingers had stiffened from the crisp air. She shivered when a gust of night wind whipped across her face.

"That little scrap of wool you're wearing isn't enough to keep you warm tonight. You need something heavier." Dustin took off his jacket.

"I don't need your coat. I'll be fine. It's only a couple of minutes back to the house."

"You're not fine. You're chilled. Now put your arms in the sleeves." He picked up her arm and started stuffing her hand inside. He pulled the coat up over her shoulders. "Now, wear the shawl inside as a scarf. Like this."

Cassandra couldn't have been more shocked if Dustin had put his arms around her. She remembered the familiar way he'd touched her with loving hands. A shiver spread through her even though the heat from Dustin's coat warmed her immediately. A vision from the past flashed before her. She remembered the evening they made love under the full moon. Dustin had given her his coat to keep her warm as she walked back to the house.

Suddenly Cassandra spun away from him as if he'd

59

touched her with a hot branding iron. She hadn't meant to react to his touch, but Dustin made her aware of far too many things she'd hoped she'd forgotten. Silence fell between them and all she heard was the lonesome sound of the wind whipping past her ears.

"Hey, it's all right. I'm just helping you with the coat. I'm not going to do anything like kiss you. Even though I don't like the idea of you going to sleep with the taste of that banker's kiss on your lips. He doesn't suit you, Cassandra."

"You lowdown spy. I can't believe you'd do that, then have the nerve to tell me you didn't."

"I wasn't spying."

"What would you call it?"

"Being in the right place at the right time."

"You're impossible." She started walking again. "I can't believe I have to put up with you for two days."

"You're enjoying my being here and you know it."

"About as much as I'd enjoy having a rattlesnake in my bed."

Dustin laughed, an attractive, softly seductive sound that for a moment had her wishing things were different between them, and that angered her all the more.

"Tell me, are you warmer now?"

"I'm fine," she answered tightly.

Cassandra thought they were going to make it back to the house without another word spoken between them, but as they neared the back porch Dustin stopped her and said, "Before we go inside I want to get something straight between us. No one made me come here. I could have said no when Gordon asked me to check on you and the ranch. I have no ulterior motive for being here. I only want to help you save your ranch. How long are you going to hold it against me for making love to you and not marrying you?"

"I don't know," she admitted honestly as the hurt and bitterness welled up within her once again. "I was seventeen and in love. It's been easy to hate you all these years. I've never had a reason to stop."

"Until now," Dustin said.

No.

Maybe.

"No!" She swung her tight fist upward and caught Dustin under the chin, snapping his head back.

Dustin grunted. His eyes widened in surprise as she connected with another blow that glanced off his cheek.

"You little hellion," Dustin muttered and grabbed her arms in his hands. "Beating me up won't change the past."

"No, dammit, but it will make me feel better," she said, jerking away from him. Cassandra sobbed with anger, with cold, with frustration. "I loved you! I gave myself to you and you left me, you bastard."

His expression softened as he rubbed his chin, but he didn't try to touch her again. "I'm sorry. I deserved that."

"Sorry isn't near good enough. I would have done *anything* for you. You have no right to come here and—upset my life again." She sniffed and pulled his coat tighter about her, trying to stop the shaking.

"I know. I only meant to help. I didn't mean to make you cry."

She wiped her eyes and her cheeks with the back of her hand, hating herself for showing him tears. "I'm *not* crying," she snapped. "I wouldn't shed another tear for you to save your life."

"Then I guess that's frost running down your cheeks."

"Yes—I mean, I don't know what it was but it *wasn't* tears."

The back of her hand hurt where her knuckles had made contact with Dustin's jaw. She sniffed again, her fury ebbing at his quiet tone, his remorseful attitude. But Cassandra wasn't sure she wanted to let go of the hurt and anger that had filled her. It had been a part of her for so long. She'd always thought if she forgave him she would have to forget and she didn't want to forget about Dustin Bennett.

"I have every right in the world to hate you, you know."

He nodded. "For the past yes. But will you at least admit that I have nothing to gain by being here now?"

Her heart skipped a beat. She couldn't concentrate on the present until they'd settled the past. "Why, Dustin?" she asked earnestly. "Why did you make love to me then leave me at the church to face my grandfather, your father, our guests?"

His brows drew together in a frown. "Didn't you read the letter I wrote you?"

"Yes, damn you!" she swore, but the piercing way Dustin looked at her made her thoughts fly back in time to that fateful day. She shuddered. "No, I didn't actually read it. Your father read it to me. He said you weren't coming. You couldn't go through with the wedding."

"I suspected as much when I mentioned it today. I didn't know my father had even seen the letter. He's never mentioned it." Dustin rubbed his chin again. "Cassandra, I told you the truth. You were set up before you ever set foot in Kansas City."

She blinked rapidly. The chilling wind chapped her wet cheeks. "I don't understand. What do you mean I was set up?"

A frustrated sigh passed his lips. He ran a hand through his dusty blond hair and said, "I don't know where to begin." He shook his head. "Money and prestige were always extremely important to my father. That's what motivated him and me. We had to live, look, and talk as if our firm was the best in town and we did. And we are."

She eyed him warily. "What had that to do with me?"

"Everything. You were the key to our success. I had just finished my education and joined the firm when

Gordon came into my office and told me about your trust. He said you were coming of age and would soon be looking to marry. Gordon suggested he invite you and your grandfather to Kansas City, and that I should court you and offer marriage. Gordon told me I needed to make a big contribution to the firm. Arranged marriages weren't all that uncommon. I was willing. By becoming your husband I would be keeping your trust under the direction of the firm."

It was so cold and calculating Cassandra found it hard to believe. "Which would mean keeping the large income you told me about?"

"Yes. Handling the Rakefield fortune gave us a lot of clout in the firm. Using it as a reference brought in other wealthy clients from cattle barons to prospectors who'd struck it rich in the gold mines."

"You and your father decided this *before you even met me?*"

"Yes. I set out to win your hand right from the beginning."

She drew in her breath with a sharp gasp. Her hands balled into fists. "That was an unthinkable, abhorrent thing to do. You used me, you bastard!"

Dustin held up his hands to calm her. "Don't take another swing at me. You're right. I'm not proud of the way I treated you. That's why at the last moment I couldn't go through with the wedding."

Cassandra shuddered with fury. "So jilting me was the only thing you could think to do."

He flinched. "I was a bastard. I admit it. I was exactly what my father had taught me to be. No excuses. At the time I didn't know any different. Money, prestige, standing in the community were the things that were important to me because that's what Gordon had taught me. I was young and eager to make my mark at the firm and establish myself as a lawyer to be respected. And of course when I met you—" He paused and his eyes softened. "It was easy to court you and want to marry you. Not only did you have money, you were beautiful, self-assured and—"

"You lowdown son of a bitch!" Pain tore from her throat. "You never loved me, did you?"

Denial flashed across his face. "Sometimes the line between loving and desiring is extremely fine for a young man. I hadn't planned to make love to you that night in the garden. I swear that's true, Cassandra. I didn't want to do that to you, but you came expecting that was what I wanted. I couldn't deny I wanted to make love to you. I'd wanted you from the moment I saw you. I was desperate to possess you. I know now I didn't really try to stop it from happening."

"But you didn't love me."

He sighed again. "Cassandra, I don't know that I loved you the way you're talking about, the way that makes a man forsake all others, but I do know I wanted you more than I'd ever wanted any woman."

She tamped down the hurt that rose within her. She appreciated his honesty. "Why didn't you tell me this after—we made love?"

"After I'd taken your virginity I decided I had to marry you. It was the right thing to do. I went home with that idea in mind, but the closer it came to the wedding time I felt like such a bastard marrying you for your money. I knew you deserved someone better than me. You should have the chance to fall in love with someone who loved you for yourself, not because of your money, so I wrote you the letter explaining all this."

"Because you didn't have the balls to come tell me to my face. I should have shot you when I had the chance."

She heard the uneven leap of his breath and felt some satisfaction that her words had wounded him.

"No," he answered emphatically. "I knew if I saw you dressed in your wedding gown I would have married you because I wanted you. I hated like hell giving you up,

Cassandra. I know it's no consolation, but to this day my only regret in life is that I didn't marry you."

"It's no comfort at all."

"But it is the truth. I know it doesn't mean anything to you now, but I'm not the same person I was then."

With soft light from the moon, Cassandra searched Dustin's face. She believed he was being honest with her and he wasn't trying to blame anyone else for what he did.

Trying to hang on to her fading anger, she said, "So what happened to you? You're still with your father, two bastards working together."

"Something like that. We work in the same firm but seldom see each other. We're more like business partners than family. That's why I call him Gordon. He's happy with that and so am I. I occasionally accept a social invitation from him, but the rift that happened between us when I didn't marry you is still there. Gordon has never forgiven me either."

"Don't expect me to feel sorry for you."

"I wouldn't like that, any more than you would want someone to feel sorry for you. When Gordon showed me your letter I knew I had to come. I saw this as my chance to make amends. I didn't treat you right then, although I didn't realize that at the time."

"You're damn right."

"I was young and cocky and insensitive to your feelings. I thought only of myself, what I wanted and what was best for me."

"That's a fair assessment."

Cassandra desperately wanted to hate him, but her thoughts betrayed her. She looked into Dustin's eyes longer than she should have. She wasn't fighting mad with him anymore. She had every right to be. She wanted to be but she wasn't. Now that she was getting over the shock and hurt of seeing him again she could listen to his explanation, but she wasn't sure she was ready to forgive him.

Gently, with his fingertips, he lifted her chin until her

eyes were staring up into his. He lowered his head until his face was only inches from hers. Her breath quickened. Her stomach fluttered.

"I want you to believe me, Cassandra. Right now, I'm thinking only of what you want and what you need. I want to make amends for the way I treated you. Let's make peace and start over, working together to save your ranch."

Start over. Why did that sound so tempting? She fell victim to his gentleness, to his sincerity. Was she so vulnerable to his charm she was willing to forget the past to gain his help in saving her ranch?

"All right." She swallowed hard and turned her head away from his touch and stepped back. She took a deep breath and squared her shoulders. "The past can't be changed. I'm willing to put it behind us. As you said this afternoon, the only thing between us now is business."

Dustin nodded.

The next morning Cassandra walked into the warm kitchen filled with familiar smells of coffee, fried bacon, and fresh-baked biscuits.

"Good morning, Olive."

"Morning, Cass. It's a little late in the day for you to be coming downstairs, isn't it? Sun's already on the rise."

"I didn't sleep well the first part of the night," she admitted honestly.

"Too much happen yesterday?"

"You could say that." She walked over to the big window that overlooked the eastern hills. That was the one thing she liked better about the new house. She and her grandfather had made sure that every room had a large window that looked out over the rolling hillsides or sloping rangeland.

"Have you seen any sign of Dustin?"

"Mr. Bennett left about an hour ago, saying he was going to wash off the—I mean wash up in the creek."

"Guess he decided to use the liniment."

"He told you about that?"

"He didn't have to. It showed that he hadn't been in the saddle in a long time."

"It took me a while to figure out who he was. But I said to myself, I don't know of but one man Cass would want to shoot."

Cassandra had all night to think about her conversation with Dustin. Sometimes fate knew when to take control. Maybe it was best that Dustin had written her that note. She was so young and so in love with him she would have probably begged him to marry her and she would have hated herself for that.

There was Dustin's father to think about, too, and the fact that he'd lied to her about what Dustin's letter had said. She should have never let Gordon Bennett read the letter. She should have demanded he give it to her but she had been too devastated by what Dustin had done. But there was nothing to be gained by going over what should have been. She had to put all that behind her and concentrate on saving the ranch.

"I would have had a good night's sleep if you'd sent him packing instead of to the barn to find me," Cassandra said on a wistful note.

Olive poured steaming coffee into a china cup and handed it to Cassandra. "I couldn't have kept him from finding you any more than you could have made him leave yesterday when you kept telling him to go."

Cassandra wrinkled her brow at Olive. "I'm beginning to think the walls around here have suddenly grown ears. Seems I can't say or do anything anymore without someone hearing it or seeing it."

"I accidentally—"

"No need to say it, Olive." Cassandra held up her hand to stop the woman. "I've heard that story before. I'll remember to be more careful from now on."

"Do you want to wait for Mr. Bennett or are you ready to eat your breakfast?"

"No reason to wait for him. I need to ride up to the north pasture and see for myself what the area looks like where Rodney and his father made their camp. Jojo and Red Sky might have missed something that might tell me more about Rodney."

Alarmed shouts sounded in the distance. The two women looked at each other.

"What was that?" Olive asked.

"I'm not sure." Cassandra thumped down her coffee cup. "It sounded like someone yelled fire." She ran to the back door and yanked it open, then rushed out onto the porch. She scanned the area around the barn and the trees beyond. There was no smoke.

"Fire!" Another shout of alarm sounded from the south.

Cassandra jerked toward the bunkhouse. Smoke poured out of the open front door. Jojo emerged from the burning building dragging Red Sky by his arms.

A breath of panic rose up inside Cassandra, choking her.

"Fire!" Jojo shouted again.

"Grab a bucket and come help," Cassandra yelled over her shoulder to Olive, then fled toward the bunkhouse.

She was breathless with fear when she reached Jojo but kept panic at bay. She took hold of one of Red Sky's arms and helped the cowboy drag the Indian farther away from the bunkhouse.

"What happened? Where's Rodney?"

"Gone. He got the jump on us, set the fire, and ran. I saw him hightailing outta here over the east ridge on one of your horses and my pistol's gone. He must have stolen it too."

She looked down at Red Sky and quickly forgot about the horse and gun. Blood trickled from a gash in his forehead and slithered down past his eye. There was no movement in his pale face.

Alarm triggered a tightening in her chest. "He isn't dead, is he?"

"No, but he's out cold. That son of a bitch hit both of us with a skillet. I have a goose egg on the back of my head, too. The no-good horse thief tried to kill us!" Jojo spit the words with so much anger his mustache quivered.

A nervous twitching attacked Cassandra's stomach. "Where's Dustin?"

"Haven't seen him," Jojo said as they lowered the Indian to the ground well away from the bunkhouse.

Cassandra dropped to her knees and put her ear over Red Sky's heart. Thank God it was still beating. Jojo hustled back to the porch, grabbed a pail off the wall, and filled it from the horse trough.

Cassandra looked more closely at the cut on Red Sky's head. The skin was broken and there was a large purple swell above his eye.

Olive ran up beside her. "Good gracious, heavens above!" She gasped and dropped the bucket she held to the ground. "What happened?"

"I'll tell you later," Cassandra said. "Wash his face and see if you can bring him around. We have to put the fire out."

Cassandra rose to her feet, picked up the tin bucket Olive had dropped, and rushed to join Jojo. She dipped her bucket in the water, then headed up the steps. Heat from the fire hit her at the bottom step, almost taking her breath away. When she reached the porch a hand grabbed her arm, halting her.

"You're not going in there."

Her heart jumped to her throat at the sight of Dustin. His hair was wet and his shirt was only half buttoned. She knew he must have been in the creek when he heard the shouts of fire.

Frantically, she tried to push away from him. "I've got to help."

"Not by going inside, you don't."

Jojo came running out of the doorway coughing.

Dustin said, "Wet your bandana and tie it over your mouth and nose before you go back inside." Dustin dipped his kerchief in the pail of water Cassandra held as he told Jojo what to do. "You do it too," he told Cassandra.

"The fire's spread across the front room to the beds. I don't know if we can put it out in time to save the building," Jojo offered.

"We have to." Her muscles jerked.

Dustin took the heavy pail from her and gave it to Jojo and picked up the empty one. He turned to Cassandra. "You fill the buckets and hand them to us at the door. Don't go inside under any circumstances."

Her heart drummed wildly. She started to protest his taking over but realized they didn't have time to argue. Her grandfather was right when he said men like to take charge and sometimes you have to let them.

"All right. Just hurry," she said, her throat already clogging from the dark gray smoke that billowed out of the bunkhouse.

They worked as a team, like a piece of well-oiled machinery, for what seemed hours. A film of moisture caused by the excitement and the heat of the flames ran down her face and collected under her chin, but she didn't dare stop to rest. Her arms trembled from carrying the buckets laden with water. The palms of her hands were raw and hurting from working the wire handles. Even with the bandana tied across her nose and mouth, her lungs and throat burned from the smoke. Somehow, she managed to meet each man at the door with a filled bucket.

She tried to block from her mind the smell, the sounds, the heat of the fire, of burning, crackling wood as she worked at a feverish speed.

After a few minutes of running in and out of the house, Dustin leaned against the porch railing. Gasping for breath in between spasms of coughing, he managed to say, "It's n—no use." He stepped in front of the doorway blocking Jojo's reentry. "These small buckets—are no match for the—flames."

"We can't stop now!" Cassandra exclaimed desperately, coming up the steps behind Jojo. "You must go back in."

"It's too late," Dustin said, pushing Cassandra and Jojo back down the steps and away from the house.

Cassandra felt the wild beat of her heart, the trembling in her body, and she couldn't control either one. Her eyes teared from the sting of the smoke. "You don't understand. I can't lose the bunkhouse." She'd lost too much already.

Dustin yanked his bandana down from his face. "It's gone, Cassandra."

"That's right, Miss Cass," Jojo said, lowering his bandana. "That wood caught fire as fast as summer pine. We have to give it up now."

"No! I'll go in myself!" She tried to rush past him but Dustin grabbed her arm and halted her mid-stride. He stripped the full bucket from her hands and water sloshed down her legs and over her feet.

"Let me go!" She struggled to get away from him.

"Don't be stupid, Cassandra. You'll be killed."

"Who would give a damn if I was?"

"I would." He swung his arm around her waist and caught her up against his chest. "I'd go back inside for you if it would do any good. It won't. We can't save it." His voice was low and firm.

His gaze finally penetrated hers and she understood. Inside Cassandra moaned her despair, but outwardly she pushed away from Dustin and yanked her kerchief from her face. She looked over at Olive and Red Sky, then back to the hissing, crackling sounds of the burning building.

A loud crash sounded and Cassandra jumped as part of the roof caved in. She watched in horror as huge flames licked toward the clear blue sky. Her chest tightened, cutting off her breath.

She shivered from the fear of what would have happened had the men been trapped inside when the roof fell. What was wrong with her? She should have been pulling them out of the house, not begging them to go back inside and risk their lives again. What was she thinking? The bunkhouse could be rebuilt.

She had to think fast. She had to act quickly.

"Jojo, check on Red Sky. If you can't get him to come around, get the wagon and take him into town to see Doc Smithers. Dustin, go to the barn and get a shovel and start digging a trench around the bunkhouse to keep the fire from spreading. Olive, you pump more water into the trough, then start wetting the ground where Dustin's digging."

Without waiting for anyone to answer her, Cassandra turned and strode toward the barn at a fast walk.

"Hey," Dustin called to her. "Where are you going? What are you going to do?"

She threw him a glance over her shoulder. "I'm going after Rodney."

Chapter

· 5 ·

"The hell you are." Dustin reached out and snagged her arm, spinning her around to face him.

"Let go of me." Cassandra wrestled away from his grasp only to be quickly caught again.

"Going after Rodney is the sheriff's job."

"No, it's mine. Rodney burned down *my* bunkhouse, almost killed *my* ranch hand, and stole *my* horse. I can't let him get away with that."

"He won't."

"That's right, because I'm going after him." She tore away from him again.

Dustin reached for her but she sidestepped and eluded him. "Listen to me, Cassandra, we'll find him. I'll help you once we're finished here."

Cassandra's head was pounding and her throat felt as dry and brittle as the tumbleweeds that blew across the flatlands during a sand storm. The pain of losing the bunkhouse and anxiety over Red Sky's injury mixed with fatigue and suddenly threatened to overwhelm her. She thought she might faint from lack of air but sheer willpower forced her to remain on her feet.

Slowly she shook her head and breath returned to her lungs. A breeze cooled her heated skin. "This is all my fault," she said. "Why couldn't I see what Rodney had in mind?"

"You couldn't have known he would do something like this. You were trying to be nice to someone who didn't deserve it."

Her gaze zeroed in on Dustin. His face was red as an apple and he had a deep scratch just below his jawline. His hair fell shaggily across his forehead. The edges were singed where he'd come too close to the flames. He'd never taken the time to button his shirt. It hung sloppily on his shoulders, showing his smooth, firm chest and abdomen.

"Why don't you say what you're really thinking, Dustin?"

"What do you mean?"

"Go ahead and say, I told you not to let him stay. That's what you're thinking."

"Cassandra."

"It's true." Her voice trembled and that made her angry. "You tried to warn me and I wouldn't listen to you."

"It was your decision. It could have turned out differently."

Cassandra brushed loose strands of hair away from her face with a shaky hand. From the corner of her eye she saw the popping, blazing fire. She felt its consuming heat.

"Yes, but it didn't." Her words sounded bitter and that bothered her.

Her fingers were raw and hurting. The stench of burned wood filled her mouth, her nose, her lungs. From behind her she heard the crackling and hissing sound of the bunkhouse burning to the ground.

All of a sudden the task seemed too great. She felt like walking away from it all. Why try to save any of it?

Maybe she should just give up and let Rodney win, let the fire win, let the bank win.

As if sensing her dramatic mood change, Dustin said, "Don't worry about the loss. You can build it back."

"With what?" Pain edged her voice this time. Her head pounded.

"I'll see you get your money, Cassandra. Trust me," he said earnestly.

Trust Dustin? How could she? Emotions warred inside her. She watched as flames leaped out of the fallen roof. The past rose up to remind her this man couldn't be trusted. Yet, as she looked at him another voice told her to give him another chance, to take the comfort and strength he offered and lean on him.

"Remember last night?" he said. "You agreed that I was on your side. Now start acting like you believe that I'm going to help you."

"How can I? I can't believe any of this." She squeezed her hands into fists, trying to stop the flow of pain building in them but only making it worse. "Up until yesterday when you came walking through my door, I thought things would finally get back to normal. Now look what's happened. I'm losing everything."

As if sensing she was on the edge, Dustin took hold of her upper arms and forced her to look into his eyes. This time she didn't move away from him. His hands felt as hot as the fire behind her.

"Thomas Rakefield wouldn't have given up and neither can you," Dustin said. "I'll help you find Rodney."

She tried to take a deep breath but her lungs hurt too badly. "Yes," she agreed. She didn't have time to feel sorry for herself. Her grandfather would have fought to the end and so would she. Dustin was going to see that the law firm gave her the money she needed to save the ranch. Now it was her responsibility to see that she didn't lose any more of her home to the fire.

"But first things first," she said, taking charge once

again. "I need to make sure the fire is out before I go chasing him. We have to dig a trench and clear as much brush as possible to make sure the house and barn are safe from the fire."

She shook away from Dustin and hurried over to where Jojo hovered around Red Sky and Olive. "How is he?" she asked.

"Still out cold," Jojo reported. "That son of a bitch must have whacked him a lot harder than he hit me. I was only stunned for a minute or two."

"He hasn't even fluttered an eyelash once, Cass," Olive said. "I'm worried about him."

Dustin knelt down beside Red Sky and looked over his injury. "Could be that most of the swelling is inside his head. That's dangerous." He looked up at Cassandra.

"Better get him to a doctor. Get the wagon, Jojo, and get him into town as fast as you can," she said.

"You reckon Doc Smithers will tend to an Indian?"

"He'll do it if he knows he'll get paid. After you take care of Red Sky go tell the sheriff what happened."

Jojo rose and took off running toward the barn.

"Olive, go to the house and get some blankets. I want you to ride in the wagon with Red Sky and cushion his head. Get the medicine chest in case he wakes up and is in a lot of pain."

"I'll do that," Olive said as Cassandra and Dustin carefully lifted Red Sky's head from her lap.

The older woman rose from the ground with the agility of a much younger person and hurried toward the house. Cassandra then turned to Dustin.

He silenced her by lifting his hand before she said a word. "I know what to do. I'm going to the barn after a shovel and ax. If the wind picks up and the brush around the bunkhouse catches fire, we could be in for big trouble. You stay here with Red Sky until Jojo or Olive gets back."

Cassandra merely nodded her approval, then looked

down into Red Sky's pale face. She heard the crunching of Dustin's boots on the dry ground as he strode away.

A crashing of timber sounded behind her again, but Cassandra didn't even flinch. She kept her gaze on Red Sky. He'd been a faithful ranch hand at the Triple R for close to ten years.

It was a two-and-a-half-hour wagon ride to town. She whispered a silent prayer that Red Sky would make it.

After Dustin helped Jojo lift Red Sky onto the bed of the wagon, he and Cassandra worked throughout the day. Her grandfather had been smart to build all the buildings so far away from each other. Dustin was convinced that was what saved the barn and house.

Once they had cleared away as much of the vegetation as possible, the two started digging a six-inch trench and wetting the ground around the fire. Shortly after midday, the leaping flames had died down enough for them to get close. They started throwing buckets of water on the remaining heap of burning wood, hoping to extinguish the last of the fire.

The day had remained sunny and crisp with only a hint of a breeze. Dustin was sure he'd never worked so hard in all his life. His arms, back, and legs ached from digging, chopping, bending, and lifting. His eyes and throat felt seared by the smoke. His lungs burned with each breath he drew, but there had been no time to stop and rest.

By late afternoon, the sweat and smoky tears, along with a little help from mother nature, had paid off. They were going to save the house and the barn. It looked as if the fire was going to completely burn itself out without spreading.

The large clump of burned wood that was once the bunkhouse merely smoldered and popped like a dying campfire in the wee hours of morning.

Now satisfied that the flames were under control,

Dustin stopped and leaned against his shovel. His eyes searched for and found Cassandra. She stood pumping more water into the trough. She had to be as tired as he, if not more so, yet he hadn't seen her slow down once.

Her clothes were wet and muddy, her face smudged with dirt. Her chestnut colored hair hung around her face and neck like strands of matted horsetail.

Dustin smiled. She was a mess, but to him she'd never looked more beautiful in her life. He'd always believed that her inner strength was one of the main things that attracted him to her. After today he had no doubt that was still true. She was a woman of rare strength. He'd been a fool not to marry her when he had the chance. At the time, leaving her had seemed like the right thing to do.

He remembered how he felt when he saw Webster kiss her the night before. A possessive hunger had welled up inside him. It surprised him how strongly he reacted to seeing her in Webster's arms. He'd wanted to rush out and tell the banker to get his hands off Cassandra. She didn't belong to him and he had no right to touch her that way. But Dustin had managed to remind himself that he didn't have any rights either.

Yet. With any luck their talk last night had started the healing for Cassandra.

He laid the shovel down and walked over to Cassandra on legs so weak he had to force them to move. "Let's call it quits," he said in a voice so scratchy and gravelly from smoke it didn't sound like his own.

She kept pumping as if she hadn't heard him. He took hold of the handle and stopped her movement.

Through eyes red and swollen, she looked up at him. The blank expression on her face told him she was so tired she was working strictly from willpower.

He gently took hold of her wrists and eased her hands off the pump. "We can stop now. The fire's out. We've done all we can do." Denying the pain in his raw throat and lungs he said, "The scrub grass is gone and the ground is plenty wet. Let's go get something to eat and rest."

She moved slowly away from him and looked at the rubble. "It's still smoldering."

He stared at the soft set to her lips and knew she didn't want to give up the fight as long as there was any chance the fire might re-ignite "Yeah, but I don't think there's enough wind to worry about sparks at this point. I think we're safe to leave the rest of it. Let's go to the house and wash up."

Cassandra's gaze slowly fanned across Dustin's face and down his body. He suddenly felt hotter than he had when the raging flames had been mere inches from his face. Her appraisal wasn't sexual but it might as well have been for all that it did to his insides.

She rested her hands on her slim hips, cocked her head to one side, and said, "You don't really think I'm going to let you inside my house looking like that, do you?"

A good feeling drenched Dustin. As tired as he knew her to be, she was teasing him. He peered down at the dirt and mud caked on his trousers and boots.

He lifted his head and grinned, hoping to stem the sudden rise in his lower body. "Well, I was going to take off my boots first."

Cassandra shook her head. "We're going down to the creek and wash."

Dustin's stomach clenched. He held his breath and envisioned stepping nude into the chilling water with Cassandra warm beside him. "We're going to wash up—in the creek?" He repeated her words as a rush of desire skittered along his heated skin.

She nodded.

"Together?"

"That's right. Clothes and all."

He blinked. "Oh, you meant with our clothes on."

Cassandra laughed softly, lightly. "Surely you didn't think I meant any other way."

"Surely not," he lied. "But take my word for it, that

water is colder than a January night in the north country."

She brushed a strand of hair away from her face and smeared a dirty streak across her cheek. Dustin had a strong urge to wipe the dirt from her cheek.

"I believe you, but we can't go inside the house looking like this. Olive would have a few things to say to both of us if we did."

She pointed to her riding skirt that was caked with mud, but Dustin didn't bother to look. Instead his gaze lingered on her features, lightly brushed across her cheeks and lips, down her breasts, and over her small waist to the slight flare of her shapely hips before returning to her face.

Cassandra quickly lowered her dark lashes, hiding her eyes from him. For a moment he thought maybe she had reacted to him looking at her the same way he had a few moments ago when she had given him the once-over. That thought made his loins even tighter.

There was no longer any doubt in his mind that the passion that had burned between them years before smoldered as hotly as the remnants of the bunkhouse fire. But would Cassandra ever admit that?

"You aren't too tired to walk down to the creek with me, are you?" Cassandra asked.

The cold water was sounding better and better. He needed to cool off and quick. "I might be more tired than I've ever been in my life, but I can keep up with you," he said in a voice raspy from the smoke.

He touched the small of her back to usher her in the direction of the creek, and to his surprise, she didn't move away from him.

"I wish there was word about Red Sky," she said as they trudged away from the simmering heap.

"We should be hearing something soon. Jojo and Olive have had just about enough time to make the round trip to town and back."

"I'll never forgive myself if Red Sky doesn't make it."

He heard the pain choked in her voice but didn't know what he could say to alleviate her fears. They both knew when Red Sky didn't wake up within a few minutes of being struck that it wasn't a good sign.

"Don't go borrowing worry," he said, trying to soothe her. "Let's just wait until Jojo gets back and we find out what the doctor says."

They fell silent and Dustin was thankful. It gave him time to think. He was getting used to the idea that he was so attracted to a woman he thought he'd forgotten about. There was no use denying anymore that he wanted her even more than he had before. He couldn't help wondering if they had a chance now that the past was in the open and they were on equal ground. She was no longer an impressionable seventeen-year-old and he wasn't interested in her money anymore.

There had been a certain exhilaration in working by Cassandra's side to put out the fire. She'd worked harder than most men he knew would have. She hadn't rested or complained.

Suddenly Cassandra picked up her pace. Dustin's tired body resisted when he tried to keep up. "Hey, what's the hurry?"

"Sundown is a couple of hours away. If I hurry, maybe I can find Rodney's trail."

Dustin grimaced and raked a dirty hand through his hair. Starting his law practice hadn't been easy, but dealing with the many criminals he'd defended over the past four years gave him amazing insight into how the human mind worked in different people. Rodney obviously had no fear for his own life and because Cassandra had been nice to him he had no fear of her. He knew better than anyone that some people couldn't be redeemed and that most people cheated and lied to varying degrees.

"You can't go looking for Rodney until you've rested and had something to eat. You're about to drop from exhaustion as it is."

"No. I can't wait that long. Every minute he's getting farther away and on my horse."

He took longer strides and managed to stay beside her. "Forget the horse. You can buy a thousand horses with all the money you have."

"Obviously not until I turn twenty-five, which is not going to happen anytime soon. My grandfather didn't spend years building up a prosperous ranch only to lose it because of one bad winter and a poacher with meanness on his mind."

He had no comeback for her comment. What she said was true. Dustin could blame a lot of things on himself and his father, but not this. How the will and trust were set up had been determined by Cassandra's mother and Ward Cabot.

They reached the creek and both sat down with groans. Dustin shucked his boots first and rose. He held out his arm to Cassandra, offering to help her up. She just stared up at his hand for a moment.

"Come on. I've been helping you all day. Why stop now?"

She laid her hand in his. A sizzling tingle shimmied up his arm. He felt something else, too. He gently pulled her to her feet, then turned her hand over and looked at her palm. The skin was red, broken, and split as if it had been plowed with a blade. He dropped that hand and picked up and examined her other. It was the same. A surge of anger shot through him. He was furious at himself for not recognizing she needed gloves on her hands to carry those buckets and pump the water.

But as he looked into her palms he thought back to the time when those same beautiful hands had lovingly touched and caressed him. He remembered Cassandra's soft lips and the sweet passion inside her mouth. He recalled pressing her firm young breasts against his chest and—

"Damn," he swore softly, forcing his thoughts from

the past and back to the future. "Look at this. Your hands must be killing you."

She slid her fingers through his. "I'll live."

"Cassandra, you should have taken the time to get your gloves."

"You know there was no time. Don't worry, they'll heal. Besides, yours are probably as bad as mine."

"Why are you always so hard on yourself?"

"I'm not. I just don't like to complain." She didn't want to tell him of the many times her grandfather had told her, "If you whine like a girl you'll be treated like a girl."

Dustin couldn't help wondering if that was because she never had a mother to wipe away her little-girl tears. She'd been raised by her grandfather most of her life. Maybe he'd taught her to be tough like a man. She was, on the outside, but Dustin was beginning to see a far different woman on the inside, a woman he was drawn to and wanted to know more about.

Leaving him standing on the bank, Cassandra turned and walked slowly into the water. Dustin followed. Even though he'd been hot as hell all day, the frigid water made him gasp when he first set a bare foot in the icy creek. His whole body shrank from the cold. He couldn't bear walking in a little at a time, so as soon as the water was waist high, he held his breath and dove under.

He was gasping when he came up for air.

"You're crazy," Cassandra called to him as she continued to ease into the water.

"After that inferno we've been in all day this feels great," he said, knowing his lips must be turning blue as he spoke. "You should try it."

Dustin dove under the water again and scrubbed at his face and hair and the legs of his trousers to loosen the caked mud. When he came up again, he didn't see Cassandra. He waited for a moment searching all around him. Suddenly she popped up out of the water like a bobbin, gasping, coughing, and shivering.

"You lied," she called to him. "This water is colder than a frozen lake."

A chuckle rumbled from his chest. "I didn't say it wasn't cold. I said it felt good." He swam over to her and stood up, the water hitting him just below the waist.

"Is my face clean?" she asked in between the chattering of her teeth.

Just looking at her made his blood thicken. Her face was perfect. Rivulets of water ran down her cheeks and dripped off her chin and the tip of her nose. Her hair hung slick, black, and shining on her shoulders. Her white blouse became translucent. It clung and molded to her. He liked that she didn't try to hide her perfectly outlined body or her firm puckering breasts from him.

Dustin wanted to pull her to him and kiss every drop of water from her lips and cheeks. He was dead tired. The icy water had him feeling frozen, yet his lower body came to life at the sight of Cassandra.

"No, there's a smudge here." He stepped closer and dragged his thumb over the soft skin of her cheek. Suddenly the water seemed July hot. With the tips of his fingers he tilted her face up toward his. He knew she wasn't ready for a romantic kiss from him but maybe she'd accept a kiss from him that said, I'm sorry for all the pain I caused you.

Dustin bent his head and softly brushed her lips with his. They were cold, wet, inviting him to deepen the kiss. His body trembled. All he could think was that she had once belonged to him.

As if remembering she wasn't supposed to enjoy his kiss Cassandra pushed against his chest. Dustin lost his footing and splashed back into the water.

She glared down at him. "You shouldn't have done that."

"I know, but I had to wash Webster's kiss from your lips."

Cassandra raked the back of her hand across her mouth. "Landon kisses much better than you."

He smiled. "You're lying, but that's all right. It just gives me the opportunity to prove you wrong."

"Over my dead body. Stay the hell away from me."

He watched as she sloshed out of the water. Her riding skirt hugged her bottom in all the right places. Yes, he'd been right. Ranch life had kept her body in temptingly good shape.

Dustin joined her on the bank and they shoved their feet back into their boots. After stomping in the shallow water to clean the mud off the soles, they started toward the house at a fast walk.

The sun floated low in the western sky and wasn't nearly hot enough to warm them quickly. If they were lucky, their clothes would no longer be dripping by the time they made it to the house.

"As soon as I've changed, I'm going to ride out and pick up Rodney's trail," Cassandra said. "If I can establish the direction he's heading, I can start after him at first light."

"We," Dustin said. "We can start looking for him and that sounds like a good plan to me with one exception."

"What's that?"

"Neither of us has eaten all day. You find us something to eat while I ride out and find Rodney's trail."

A smile that lit the sky like a summer sunrise spread across Cassandra's face. She chuckled lightly under her breath and shook her head. It made him feel warmer just knowing what he'd said pleased her so.

"You've got to be joking, Dustin. You don't know anything about tracking a man. You don't even know this area. You'll get lost, then I'll have to spend precious time trying to find you. You can think of more ways to waste my time than a saddle-sore horse."

Dustin flashed her a grin. "You don't think very much of my skills, do you?"

"So far, I have no reason to think you have any tracking skills, however I'm quite confident that no one could best you in a courtroom."

"I do all right," he admitted, knowing he was much better than all right, but since he'd realized he didn't want to be the kind of man his father was he wasn't sure he'd ever been happy being a lawyer.

"That's my point. You stick to your work and I'll handle mine. I've been trying to tell you ever since you came that I don't need your help around here."

"I know more about tracking than you think I do," he said, remembering all that he'd learned from a Pinkerton agent he'd defended two years before. During the man's trial Dustin had picked up more details than he wanted to know about ferreting out a person in hiding.

"Yes, well, think that if you want, but I'm not letting you go alone to prove me wrong."

"Cassandra, it's the only thing that makes sense. Jojo said he saw Rodney heading out over the east ridge. I can certainly find that and the horse's tracks, too. You can have dinner on the table and a pot of coffee ready by the time I get back."

"What gives you the right to order me around on my ranch?"

Dustin stopped and took hold of both her upper arms in a gentle grasp and peered down into her eyes. "I'm not ordering you to do anything, Cassandra. I'm telling you what I think is the best thing for us to do."

He felt her relax. Her expression changed to one of acceptance. He supposed it was only natural for her to think he was bossing her when she was so used to telling others what to do and having them obey her without question.

"All right," she said. "Get into some dry clothes and ride."

Chapter

·*6*·

Sunrise had barely kissed the land with the first rays of light when Cassandra and Dustin walked their horses out of the barn the next morning. Cassandra wore her sheepskin-lined jacket and brown wool riding skirt. Her Colt was strapped to her hip. Dustin had donned a short-caped overcoat.

The air was crisp as midwinter but clear skies promised a sunny day to help keep them warm. Spring had officially come to Wyoming but someone had forgotten to tell mother nature. The unusually harsh winter had left its telling mark on the late days of spring too.

Jojo and Olive had made it back to the ranch last night before Cassandra and Dustin had finished their meal. The doctor had confirmed their suspicion that Red Sky's condition was grave. Only time would tell if the swelling inside his head would go down in time to save his life. The sheriff and one of his deputies were out looking for a band of rustlers, but Jojo had left word with the officer in charge about Rodney burning down the bunkhouse, nearly killing Red Sky, then running away.

The ranch hand wanted to join them on their search at

first light, but Cassandra insisted he stick close by in case Rodney should return with the idea of burning down the house and the barn, too.

Dustin and Cassandra rode to the place where Dustin had found the half-moon tracks leading away from the ranch, then started their manhunt.

Daybreak shed its brown and orange colors and gave way to a blue sky filled with wispy streaks of feathery white clouds. Rain had been scarce for weeks and the ground was hard, leaving few places a hoof could make its mark.

Cassandra couldn't help noticing that Dustin rode taller, straighter, better than any of her ranch hands. That surprised her because she knew living in Kansas City he had little time to spend on a horse.

Mid-morning they stopped to let the horses graze. Cassandra was used to hard work but today she felt as if every muscle in her body had been stretched out of shape and she struggled to do the simplest task. Her palms ached but she didn't dare take her gloves off for fear she wouldn't be able to get them back on.

She sipped from her water container. Over the top of her canteen she watched Dustin drink. The slender column of his neck was clean shaven and masculine. She liked the fact that he'd taken time to shave before they left. One thing she knew from living on a ranch was that most cowboys shaved once or twice a week. Many grew beards so they'd never have to shave.

Dustin's lips pressed solidly against the opening of the canteen and as clearly as if it had been yesterday, she remembered the last time Dustin's lips had fit passionately over hers.

The sweet memories rushed back with clarity. Cassandra remembered the way his kisses had made her feverish with wanting. She remembered the way he'd lovingly touched her cheeks with the tips of his masculine fingers after they had made love.

"Is something wrong?"

Dustin's question jerked Cassandra back to the present. She blinked and cleared her throat. "No, why?"

"You were staring at me the way a hungry mountain lion stares at an unsuspecting jackrabbit. I thought you were going to pounce on me."

His perceptive remark caused her cheeks to flame. She turned away as she capped her canteen. "Don't be ridiculous."

"I'm only stating what I saw in your face."

"Well you know what they say about only seeing what you want to see."

"No. What do *they* say about that?"

She heard the amusement in his voice. How like him to have fun at her expense. She threw the straps of her canteen over the saddle horn. "That you're blind as a bat in one eye and you can't see out of the other."

Dustin chuckled but remained quiet. Thank goodness he knew when she'd had enough of his teasing.

Cassandra looked at the buttes to the north, the rangeland to the south, and the jagged hills to the west. "It's getting harder to follow the tracks because of the rocky ground. He could have gone in any direction when he left but he chose the hardest. He knows what he's doing."

"Looks to me like he's headed for those hills. You ever been up there?" Dustin pointed to the scattered clump of bleached white boulders and short hills which were about an hour's ride away.

"Not for a long time, but I'm headed there now."

"It looks dangerous."

"That's no reason not to go." She spurred her horse and took off, not waiting to see if Dustin followed.

The hill was steep and covered with loose stones, gravel, and low-growing prickly bushes. Shortly after she started up the incline she heard Dustin swearing at his horse. She smiled. Hired horses were known for being ill tempered and stubborn. She should have offered him one of her cow ponies.

A few minutes later Cassandra no longer heard Dustin's swearing or the horse's snorting. She stopped and looked behind her. Dustin was about thirty yards down, struggling to get his horse up the hill. He'd pulled the reins short for better control but the gelding was fighting him. Cassandra saw trouble.

"He doesn't want to climb," she called to Dustin. "He's frightened. You're going to have to go back down."

"I'm not leaving you," Dustin answered. "Wait up."

"I don't have time to coddle you. Get back down the hill."

As soon as the words left Cassandra's mouth Dustin's mount went down on his front knees. Dustin flipped into the air over the gelding's head. Cassandra's heart jumped to her throat. Dustin landed with a hard thump, then rolled down the side of the hill and over a ledge.

"Dustin!" Cassandra screamed.

Frantically, she turned her horse around and let the mare pick her way back down to where Dustin had disappeared. His horse had recovered and seemed to be unharmed.

Cassandra jumped off her mount and ran to the edge and looked over. Dustin lay face down about twelve feet below. "Dustin!" she called again. He didn't move.

She ran back to her horse and tied the reins to the center stalk of a large shrub. She whipped her lariat off the saddle and tied one end around the horn, then yanked on it to make sure it was secure. Without thinking for her own safety she walked to the edge of the cliff and peered over. Cassandra froze.

Fear gripped her. She felt that familiar pressure building in her chest but refused to let it take over. She squeezed her eyes shut only for a moment but her breathing slowed. The trembling didn't stop, but she knew what she had to do. She stretched the rope tight and started her climb down the rocky embankment.

The rope burned her hands beneath her gloves but she held tight and continued her descent. She didn't allow herself to think, only to move. Loose stones and dry earth shifted beneath her feet, making it difficult to keep her footing stable. She felt the tug on her arm muscles and strained to keep the rope tight.

Her mare snorted and the rope went slack. Cassandra slammed into the side of the hill, knocking her knees and elbows. Her weight fell to her hands and arms. She cried out with pain and bounced against the embankment again, scraping her face against a jutting rock. She clawed the side of the hill with her feet looking for a hold as she dangled in the air, less than halfway down.

The pain in her limbs became unbearable and she struggled to regain her footing. Her horse moved again and she swung from side to side. She thought about taking her chances and dropping to the ground but knew she would be of no help to Dustin with a broken ankle or stove-up leg.

"Hell no, I won't give up," she muttered to herself, then braced the pads of her feet firmly to the hillside and pushed out. The rope caught, tightened. She trembled. Quickly she let the rope slide through her hands and lowered herself the rest of the way down.

Panting for breath, Cassandra dropped the rope and ran over to Dustin. She fell on her knees beside him and helped him roll over.

He looked at her with glazed eyes. "Damn, what happened?"

"You went over the cliff."

"How did you get down here?" He tried to rise.

"Don't try to move. Something might be broken."

"No, I think I'm all right. The fall knocked the breath out of me." He groaned again as she helped him to sit up.

"Are you sure you didn't break anything?"

"If you're just dying to feel of my legs to see if anything is broken, go ahead. I might enjoy it."

"Be serious, Dustin. That was a bad fall and there's blood on your forehead." With aching hands she quickly untied her kerchief and dabbed at the cut.

"If you say or do anything more for me I'll think you're actually concerned about me."

"I told you I feel responsible for you."

He took the bandana from her. "I don't like to be coddled any more than you do. Besides, you look like you fell off the side of the cliff, too. Your cheek's scratched. What happened?"

"Nothing. I'm all right."

"So am I. Why don't I stand up and show you I can walk." Slowly, he rose and stretched out his arms. "See, I'm fine."

Suddenly Dustin pounced on Cassandra and knocked her to the ground. Dustin fell on top of her and rolled. Bullets plowed up the ground around their feet and legs. Something stung Cassandra's foot. Fear bolted inside her.

Someone was trying to kill them!

Cassandra pushed Dustin away from her with one hand and reached for her pistol with the other. The holster was empty.

Dustin rose up over her. Cassandra saw Rodney smiling down on her with evil in his eyes. His gun was pointed at her face.

A bullet splattered the dirt beside her head and she jumped. Two red stains appeared on Rodney's shirt directly over his heart. His eyes widened. His gun dropped harmlessly to the ground. Rodney's knees buckled and he fell face down.

Cassandra thought her heart would beat out of her chest. Tremors of shock and relief shook her. Dustin remained with his gun pointed up the embankment. "Do—do you think you killed him?" she asked, even though she knew.

He turned to her and lowered her pistol. "I had to. It wouldn't have done any good to wound him. His gun was pointed at you. His next shot might not have missed."

She nodded, trembling. She'd seen the wild look on

Rodney's face. He meant to kill her. The sun beat on her back and shoulders. She was suddenly so hot she felt sick to her stomach. She turned away from Dustin.

"Cassandra."

"Don't, I'll be all right."

"Let me help you."

"No. Just leave me alone for a minute."

She heard his exasperated sigh. "I'll climb up, then throw the rope back down to you when you're ready."

Cassandra couldn't move. She tried to take a deep breath but her stomach was too shaky. The sick feeling hadn't passed. She was mad as hell that Rodney had injured Red Sky and burned the bunkhouse, but she didn't want him dead.

From above her she heard Dustin dragging something and finally digging in the hard ground. She knew what he was doing and she needed to help him.

She rose to unsteady feet and settled her hat on her head, then called to Dustin. The climb up was easier knowing she had Dustin to help her. She was grateful he'd taken his bedroll and placed it over Rodney.

Dustin pulled her gun from beneath his waistband and handed it to her. "I had to grab yours when I jumped you. I didn't have time to get my derringer from under my coat."

She stared at the pistol for a moment. No one had ever been killed with her gun before. Don't ever be afraid to use this on man or animal, her grandfather had told her. It will save your life one day.

"You're looking green. Why don't you sit down over there until I finish this."

She took the gun and dropped it into her holster. "If I look green it's because you've had too much sun in your eyes."

Dustin grunted. "Rodney didn't have a gun when he came to the Triple R so I guess this one belongs to Jojo or Red Sky."

It was still hard to believe Rodney wanted to kill them.

He was so young. She shook those feelings aside and said, "It's Jojo's."

"I'll see he gets it." Dustin looked down to where he had been digging. "It'll be a shallow grave but there's plenty of rocks to stack on top."

Cassandra nodded and started gathering the largest stones she could carry.

"Why are you limping?" Dustin asked. "Let me take a look at your foot."

"My foot's fine. A bullet shattered the heel of my boot and ricocheted off my ankle, but it's only bruised, not bleeding."

"That bullet was too close. I could have never gotten my derringer out in time. I'm glad you were wearing your gun."

"Yeah, I reached for it but you were faster."

"Because you were in danger."

His words brought her up short. She stared down at Dustin. He stopped digging and gave her a gentle smile. Sometimes, like now, she wanted to believe he cared about her.

"You gave Rodney the chance for a better life and he didn't take it. Don't blame yourself for what happened to him."

"I don't," she said, keeping her chin stiff. "I tried. That's what's important." She had learned a long time ago that death was part of life. There was no choice but to accept it and keep going.

"Why don't you let me finish this?" Dustin offered as she dropped an armful of stones beside him.

"Burying Rodney's my job. I'm just letting you help. Keep digging."

She glimpsed Dustin's grin of approval as she hobbled away.

The sun floated high in a bright blue sky when Dustin and Cassandra stood over the grave, hats held in their hands.

"Lord, Rodney's in your hands now. Good luck."

Cassandra put her hat on and started limping over to her horse.

"Is that all you're going to say?" Dustin asked, following her.

"No time for more. I've got time to ride by and check the herd on the north pasture before sundown. If there are any breaks on the fence I'll have to get Jojo on it first thing in the morning."

"You look like you're about ready to drop."

"Work doesn't stop just because something bad happens and rustlers don't stop for anything. Now that Red Sky is hurt, I'll pick up the slack. The herd has to be checked every day and we have to move it every three or four days to stay ahead of the rustlers."

Her bravery and courage astounded him, impressed him. "All right," he said. "I wanted to have a look at the herd anyway so let's ride."

They mounted their horses and headed back toward the ranch. Wind rustled the leaves of the aspens and cottonwoods that dotted the base of the hills. The sun lay warm on their backs while a cool breeze nipped at their noses and cheeks.

Dustin settled deeper into the saddle with a groan.

"Something wrong?" she asked.

"Yeah, there's not a place on me that doesn't hurt like a son of a bi—son."

"Bison?"

Cassandra laughed. That made Dustin know she was leaving Rodney behind where he belonged.

"I've been acquainted with the word *bitch* for a long time, Dustin. You keep forgetting you're not in a Kansas City parlor anymore. The language out here can be as rough and wild as the land. You're just not used to hard work, admit it."

"No one can be used to the kind of work we've done the past two days. Not even you. Anyway, it was probably the tumble down the mountainside that has me aching."

"I'm all right and you'll get over your soreness in a day or two."

"I guess I'm not going to get any sympathy from you."

"I don't think you really want any."

Dustin watched the wind whip at the strands of shiny hair that had escaped the confines of Cassandra's braid. He liked that golden tint to her face from just enough exposure to the sun. It made her look wholesome, healthy, kissable.

"You've changed so much from the young lady I used to know that I hardly recognize you," he said when they'd ridden in silence for a while.

"No doubt you're thinking for the worse."

"For the better. You were always self-confident in so many ways. You were never intimidated by the parties we attended or the people you met, even though it was your first time being exposed to the lavish lifestyles of wealthy cattle barons and railroad stockholders. I remember I couldn't believe that your grandfather had kept you from the lifestyle you were born into."

"You make it sound like I never left the ranch, Dustin. We had dances and parties in Cheyenne. Maybe not as elaborate or formal as Kansas City but I knew how to dance and socialize. I had been kissed once or twice before we met."

"And all this time I thought I taught you how."

"I'm glad you believed I was a complete innocent."

He smiled. "You fit very nicely into my world. You seemed eager and ready to accept the way I lived. I think because of that I saw you as someone I could manipulate. I couldn't do that now."

"I never saw myself as someone you could control. I was simply willing to give up my life on the ranch and accept your way of life as mine because I loved you from the moment you first took my hand and smiled at me."

96

Her voice had softened, so she cleared her throat and continued. "I've always been strong, aggressive, able to take care of myself. My grandfather wouldn't allow me to behave any other way."

"Just because you acted that way doesn't mean that's how you felt inside or how you appeared to me. Now that I've seen how you work the ranch, take care of your men, I believe you are that woman."

"Are you trying to compliment me, Dustin?"

"Yeah, so accept it gracefully."

She threw him a cocky smile. "Thank you."

He loved the way she kept him on his toes, never giving an inch. And now he couldn't help wondering if Cassandra had ever let another man make love to her.

She was twenty-two years old. There was always the possibility that some smooth-talking cowboy had kissed his way into her bed. But, God, he hoped not. It was strange, but now that he'd seen her again, talked to her, spent time with her, he knew she belonged to him. Dustin didn't want anyone touching her but him.

Over the years he'd made love to his share of women, but not a one of them had he ever considered marrying. Right now he couldn't bring any of them to mind. Cassandra was the only woman he wanted to remember, and he remembered everything from the curve of her waist and roundness of her shoulders to the taste of her sweet lips and satiny feel of her skin. He even remembered the astonished noises of pleasure she made when they'd made love in the garden.

The horses snorted, rousing Dustin from his reverie. What was he doing wondering about Cassandra's love life? It wasn't going to do him one bit of good. She had made it clear she was only tolerating him in order to get the money she needed from her inheritance. She might be attracted to him, but he'd broken her heart once. She wouldn't give him the opportunity to do it again.

A couple of hours later Dustin and Cassandra stood on

a rise and peered down on the steers below. A quick assessment told him there were no more than a hundred and seventy-five head grazing the hillside.

An unfamiliar feeling stole over Dustin. His saddle creaked as he turned and looked at the peaceful scene around him. He felt free. Suddenly he knew what it was. He loved being out on the land. Now he understood why Cassandra didn't want to give up the ranch.

He faced Cassandra. *She belongs out here and so do I.*

Dustin's own thoughts startled him. Yes, he liked it here but did he really think he belonged here? He recalled what they'd been talking about just an hour or two ago. Once, Cassandra had been willing to give up her life for him. She admitted she'd loved him that much. Would he be willing to give up his life in Kansas City for her? His gut instinct was yes.

"Looks like we made it through another night without losing any," she said.

"Maybe the sheriff caught the rustlers," he answered, still thinking about his own feelings about Cassandra and her ranch. "Jojo said he was out hunting them."

"I doubt if there is only one band of rustlers working these parts. But since there are so many vigilante groups around now maybe the rustlers are heading south." She faced him. "I guess you've run into a lot more than you bargained for when you came out here," Cassandra said when she looked up and caught him watching her.

Dustin's throat tightened. He knew she was referring to Rodney. A man did what he had to do. Cassandra knew that. "I was thinking I came at just the right time."

She nodded and he knew she understood that he was all right with what had happened.

The wind whipped a loose strand of hair in her face and she brushed it away with her gloved hand. A steer bellowed in the distance.

"I take it you're not married," she said. "You haven't mentioned a wife."

He sensed that the atmosphere between them had

changed. "Being engaged to you is as close as I've ever come to getting married."

Her lashes flew up and her gaze locked with his. He could tell that his honesty surprised her. Dustin hadn't realized just how powerful, how truthful that statement was until it was said.

"Kansas City, has it grown in the last five years?"

"Like a weed in clover. The railroads, the stockyards, the opera houses, the people. Everything changes quickly and often."

"I remember I enjoyed the city the summer I was there. It was so different from what I was used to. My grandfather hated it. He only stayed because of me."

"I remember he complained a lot about needing to get back to the ranch. Now I know why. It seems like you're busy every minute of the day."

"If it's daylight, there's something to do."

"I've found that out. I like this land of yours. You have freedom, space. You've obviously done a good job taking care of the ranch since your grandfather died," he said.

"It hasn't been that long. And—you've successfully changed the subject back to me again."

He winked at her and smiled. "There are some things a lawyer is naturally good at and changing subjects quickly is one of them."

"So I've noticed. We should head back. Tomorrow I'll ride into town and check on Red Sky and see if the sheriff is back. I need to tell him that he doesn't need to worry about looking for Rodney."

Cassandra started for her horse, but Dustin stopped her. Their eyes met. She didn't pull away from him. He liked the way touching her made him feel so he left his hand on her arm.

"I can pay the doctor for you," Dustin said. "I can also pay your mortgage and the men you owe wages."

Shaking her head, Cassandra said, "The only thing that will do is change who I'm beholden to from them to you."

"That's true, but you're forgetting one thing. I'm not in need. I can afford to wait months for you to return my money. Your ranch hands need their wages."

She looked away for a moment. "I don't like the thought of turning any part of my life over to you, but my men deserve their pay. I'll tell Jojo to put out the word, but I'll only borrow enough to cover wages and the doctor. I still have time to make the mortgage payment."

He appreciated her honesty and admired her courage. Tenderness for her welled up inside him. He understood what it cost her to agree to accept help from him.

She asked, "Why are you looking at me like that?"

Dustin knew he was staring at her, but he couldn't help it. "I enjoy looking at you. I always said you were the prettiest girl in the West and I always meant it. You are the only woman I know who can look beautiful with trail dust settled across her nose."

She turned away from him. "Don't say things like that."

"Why? Because you don't like to hear it, or is it that you don't believe me?"

"Both will work. You are here on business and don't forget it," she started to move again.

Dustin held her arm and her gaze darted back to his face. "I'm going to be truthful with you, Cassandra. I didn't come here to renew a romantic interest in you, but now that I'm here, now that I've seen you again, I find that's exactly what I want to do." In a rush of pent-up awareness he said, "In fact I'm going to kiss you right now."

Dustin bent his head and softly pressed his lips to hers in a gentle, almost protective, yet powerful kiss. A warmth of pleasure, a keen satisfaction curled inside him, reminding him of a time long ago when youthful eagerness ruled his head and his heart.

It pleased him that Cassandra didn't flinch or pull away, even though she wasn't as responsive as he would have liked her to be. He pulled back, giving her time to let the kiss settle on her lips. He didn't want to anger or frighten her so he kept the kiss brief and lifted his head to look into her eyes again. Her breath, like his, was short, shallow.

While he had the upper hand, he slid his arms around her waist and gathered her up close to his chest. Her soft breasts cushioned against his heart and reminded him of years past when he'd first held Cassandra and wanted to make her his. She felt good, right, at home in his arms. He tightened his hold. He wanted desperately to lower her to the ground and press his body against her and reveal the desire he felt for her, but he was reluctant to push his luck.

When she remained silent, he bowed his head and softly brushed his lips against hers again. His body trembled. It was torture holding himself back. She had once belonged to him and he wanted nothing more right now than to reclaim what had once been his. He wanted Cassandra.

He stared down into her dark brown eyes and asked, "Are you afraid of me, Cassandra?"

"Where you're concerned I'm afraid of both of us." She shoved out of his arms and headed for her horse. "Do whatever it is you came to do here at the Triple R, and then leave."

One fairly innocent kiss had Dustin's blood pumping with so much excitement he was eager to kiss her again. He was desperate to know if there was anything he could do that would lead him back to Cassandra's heart.

Chapter

· 7 ·

The sun hung low in the western sky when Cassandra and Dustin made it back to the Triple R. Cassandra's hands continued to hurt. Handling the reins and the rope had only made her wounds worse. The late afternoon cold seemed to seep right through her worn gloves and stiffen her fingers so that she could hardly hold on to her reins.

They rode past the burned-out bunkhouse that was no more than a cold heap of charred wood and twisted metal framing from the bunks that had lined the walls. The chimney and the cast iron stove also remained as testament to the building that once stood there. The stench of fire and smoke clung to the air.

Their mounts started trotting as they came up from behind the barn, knowing that water and feed were close by. From the corner of her eye Cassandra caught sight of three horses tied to the hitching rail in front of the house.

"Looks like you have company," Dustin said.

"I see. That's Landon's sorrel, but I don't recognize the other two mares."

"One of your guests is that outstanding kisser Landon

Webster?" Dustin mocked her. "How fortunate for you."

Cassandra wanted to ignore Dustin's attempt at humor, but found herself shooting back, "You are so right, Dustin. It's always a pleasure to see him and kiss him."

"I'm up for a repeat challenge if you are."

It bothered her that Dustin hadn't for a moment believed her fib about Landon being the better kisser of the two. She wasn't about to give Dustin further reason to pester her about Landon again.

"I wonder what he's doing here," she said more to herself than to Dustin.

"Maybe Webster doesn't know his days of the week?" Dustin offered. "He wasn't due to come back until Saturday."

With the backs of her fingers Cassandra pushed her gray hat off her head and let it hang down her back against her shoulders. She frowned at him. "I suppose you just happened to overhear that bit of information the other night, too. And to think I believed you when you told me you didn't hear everything."

Dustin shrugged and smiled affectionately. A brisk gust of wind tugged at the ends of his kerchief. His face showed signs of light stubble that added a ruggedness to his good looks and reminded her how much she'd always enjoyed his kisses. Nothing about Dustin would suggest to anyone that he was a successful Kansas City lawyer. Right now he looked and behaved every bit like a cocky Wyoming cowboy trying to impress a woman.

Always their kisses had been impatient, passionate, youthful. Every kiss had been like a new discovery they couldn't wait to explore. That hadn't changed either. Dustin's kiss earlier had been tentative, as if he wasn't sure of himself or her reaction. Never before had he shown that side of him. Even from their very first kiss Dustin had been masterful.

Cassandra appreciated the fact that Dustin hadn't assumed he would be welcomed or even accepted. He'd walked so boldly back into her life it surprised her that he should be in the least mindful of her.

"I'm sure I didn't hear everything." He winked at her. "Sometimes you spoke so low I couldn't understand what you were saying."

Determined not to let Dustin rile her again she said, "No doubt Landon is here because he heard about the fire and what happened to Red Sky. I'm certain he just wants to make sure I'm all right."

"If he'd been worried about you, he wouldn't have taken time to bring company." They stopped their horses in front of the barn and Dustin said, "You know what I'm thinking?"

"No, and I don't want to know," she said, trying to convince herself that was true. "You can keep your opinions to yourself."

"I'll make a little bet with you."

"I don't gamble. You have to go into Cheyenne if you want to do that. In fact that's a good suggestion now that I think about it," she said, and swung her leg over the saddle and hopped down. "Why don't you ride on into town and catch the first train back to Kansas City."

"Can't go yet. Got too much to do here at the Triple R." He glanced in the direction of the horses again. "I'm thinking Webster is with some men who want to buy the Triple R."

"What?"

Dustin dismounted and stood beside her. "It fits. He wants you to sell the ranch, doesn't he? And now he shows up here with two people you don't know."

"You're full of horse manure. I wish you'd mind your own business and stay out of mine."

"If this was just a social call he would have come alone."

There was no point in denying the obvious but Cassandra couldn't help herself. "I don't know any such thing and neither do you. For all you know that's the sheriff's horse. Stop trying to figure out every little thing."

"Can't. I was trained to question everyone's motives."

Thankfully Jojo came shuffling out of the barn and took Cassandra's horse's reins. She refused to look at Dustin. It hadn't entered her mind, but now that Dustin mentioned it she was afraid what he said about Landon might be true.

"How'd it go?" Jojo asked expectantly, his eyes darting from Cassandra to Dustin. "I hope you found that no-good sidewinder and shot him dead."

Cassandra's stomach lurched. She didn't want to remember. "He's dead," was all she managed to say.

"He was shooting at us," Dustin said, giving Jojo the pistol Rodney had stolen from him. "I had to kill him."

The cowpuncher wrinkled his nose and his handlebar mustache twitched. "Much obliged," he said to Dustin, and took his gun and reins.

Dustin took his gloves off and stuffed them in the pocket of his coat. Cassandra wanted to take her gloves off too, but was afraid to until she was alone. She had a feeling they would have to be peeled away from her skin. Her fingers had swelled and her palms had a continuous dull ache. She knew it was going to hurt like hell when she finally took the leather off and washed and bandaged her hands.

Cassandra glanced over at the house and nodded in that direction. "Who's with Landon?"

"Two men in fancy suits with collars starched so stiff they can't move their necks. Sounds like they're some of those English folk by the way they talk. Been here for a while. They rode around the ranch an hour or two, then asked me a few questions about rustlers, the weather, and such. They've been waiting inside the house for you ever since."

Cassandra cringed. That wasn't what she wanted to hear. With achy fingers she took the reins of Dustin's horse away from Jojo and threw them back to Dustin. He caught them against his chest. "Take care of your own horse."

"There's no reason to get mad."

"Nobody said I was mad. Jojo's too busy to be catering to you."

Cassandra turned away from the men and headed for the house. It bothered her that she liked the sound of Dustin's chuckle as she walked away. It irritated her that she actually enjoyed being with him.

A brassy sun hovered just above the horizon, outlining the large white house that sat atop a grassy, sloping hill. It didn't matter if she'd been riding the range or picking up supplies in Cheyenne, it always felt good to come home.

Landon and two short, rotund men as handsomely dressed as Jojo had indicated walked out on the front porch and met her as she started up the steps.

"Cass, my love, you're limping. What's wrong?"

"I'm fine. It's only a broken heel."

"Good. At last you're here. I thought I heard you ride up. We've been enjoying Olive's hospitality while we were waiting for you to return," Landon said. He reached down and took hold of her hand.

Cassandra hid her gasp of pain and quickly pulled her hand out of his grasp. "Hello, Landon," she said in a voice that was still husky from yesterday's smoke. Her eyes searched his face and she wished for the same wonderful feeling that she had every time she looked at Dustin. But with Landon, it wasn't there. No man had ever made her feel the way Dustin had.

"I didn't expect to see you today."

"I know. What luck that I could get away. I want you to meet two distinguished brothers from London who are visiting our fair city of Cheyenne. Cassandra Rakefield, meet Mr. Rory and Mr. Baker Quattlebum."

Cassandra politely greeted the men with a hello but didn't extend her hand.

"They're here in Wyoming looking for land and property to buy. And of course I told them they had to see your place. Your land is absolutely the best in this section of Wyoming. It's close to town, plenty of water and pasture." Landon kept the confident smile on his face as he looked hopefully from the brothers to Cassandra.

"After riding over some of your ranch land, I must say we wholeheartedly agree with Landon, Miss Rakefield," Baker said.

"Oh my, yes." Rory picked up the conversation. "It's far superior to some of the available properties we've considered. Your land is especially appealing because, if a man so desired, he could make it to town and back in a day's ride."

Cassandra's temper boiled, but she managed another fake smile at the eager brothers. It wasn't their fault that Landon had misled them. She couldn't take her anger out on them.

In a low voice she said to Landon, "I guess you didn't hear about the trouble I had with the poachers yesterday and the fact that one of them burned down my bunkhouse and injured Red Sky."

Landon's eyes widened as if realizing he'd made a big mistake. "Yes. Yes, I heard this morning. I was lucky to be able to get away to come see about you. It was a dreadful thing to have happened. Just horrible. I'm glad you're all right." He touched her arm and looked over at Rory and Baker. "Don't let us keep you standing out here. Please go back inside and finish your tea. No reason for it to get cold. Cass and I will be in shortly."

"Certainly. We'll see you inside," Baker said.

As soon as the door shut behind the brothers, Landon settled a concerned expression on his face and said, "Of course I heard about the fire and your ranch hand who was injured. I arranged my schedule so I could come check on you. I wanted to see you."

"Then why are the brothers with you?"

"Ah—I knew these two fine gentlemen were in town

looking over various properties so I asked them if they'd like to ride out with me and have a look around since I was coming here anyway."

Landon wasn't any better at lying than he was at kissing.

"Why would they want to look over my ranch? You know I'm not interested in selling."

"Now, I don't want you making any hasty decisions. The trouble you had yesterday proves what I've been saying all along. It's too dangerous for you to live out here now that your grandfather is gone. I simply can't allow you to continue to stay by yourself any longer."

Cassandra's back stiffened. "What do you mean you can't *allow* me to stay here by myself?"

"Be sensible, Cass. You're a beautiful young woman. You could have been the one almost killed yesterday instead of one of your men. When we marry I can't work at the bank and live out here with you. And I'd never agree to you staying out here alone. Don't you see that selling the ranch is the only sensible thing for us to do?"

"Us? This is my decision to—" Cassandra stopped. She was too tired and her hands hurt too much for this conversation. She really didn't want to have it at all, but she was afraid Landon's persistence would only get worse if she put it off any longer. "Landon, I don't know why you thought you could come here and start taking over my life. I haven't agreed to marry you."

"That's not a problem. I've agreed to give you more time to make up your mind. Your property won't go into foreclosure for—what is it? Six or eight weeks?"

A raw tension stiffened Cassandra. "Eight," she said tightly.

"Exactly. Barely two months. You won't get as good a price for the land once it goes into foreclosure. I'm only trying to help you get the best price for it to make you feel better. You don't want to watch it be sold on the auction block for a fraction of what it's worth."

Disbelief filled her. "What makes you think the bank will foreclose on my ranch?"

Landon grunted in frustration. "I know you have no money. I've talked to the other banks in town. I know that you couldn't get a loan."

In spite of herself her hands jerked to her hips defiantly. "The other bankers told you about my business? I'm beginning to wonder if there's such a thing as privacy anymore."

"Well—er, it's not that I was actually told anything. I'm afraid I—might have assumed some things. Every rancher I know in Wyoming has asked for either loans, extensions, or both."

Cassandra knew he was lying. He'd been discussing her affairs with others and that angered her all the more.

"And you did ask me to speak to the loan officer where I work about helping you, but I had been there such a short time there was nothing I could do."

And I'm sorry I asked for your help. She took her hat off and shook her braid loose from her collar. "Well, I won't lose my ranch, because it just so happens that I have the funds available to pay my mortgage and buy cattle, horses, and feed to keep the ranch going."

Landon's lips drooped and his eyebrows drew together. "You don't plan to borrow money from that man I met the other night, do you? I don't think you should trust him even if he was once a family friend."

And he doesn't trust you. "No, I don't have to borrow from anyone," she answered confidently. "The money I'm referring to is mine. I've never needed it before now." She didn't want to tell him that she had never wanted to spend one nickel of that money. Her grandfather had told her it was there if she ever decided she wanted to use it, but she never had. Until now. If there was any other way to save her ranch, other than marrying someone like Landon or Dustin, she'd do it.

A doubtful expression eased across his face. "Don't

fool yourself, Cass. Take the Quattlebums' offer and marry me. Leave all the worry of this place to someone else. These men are eager to buy American soil. Listen, I have these men talked into a price that is twice what you could normally get for this land."

"Landon, I've been trying to do everything in my power to keep the Triple R. I'm not about to sell it, and I'm not going to lose it to the bank. Now if that's the only reason you are here, then you can ride back into town as fast as you rode out here."

"No, no, of course not." His tone lowered to a soothing level. "Don't get so upset."

"It's hard not to when you're trying to sell my home," she said with a flash of anger in her voice.

"Cass, dear, I don't know what I was thinking to mention all that to you right now. I came to see you, you know that. We don't have to talk about your ranch at all. I can't help it if I worry about you being here alone, can I?"

She couldn't help thinking that the pain in her hands was one of the reasons she felt so snappy. She took a deep breath to calm herself. She shouldn't let Landon get to her, but she was worried about losing the ranch and she didn't need him reminding her.

"I'm not alone. I have Olive and Jojo. I'm quite safe here."

"That's debatable. But tell me more about this money you say you have available. Where did it come from? What bank is it in?"

She was too tired to get into that but said, "It's money left to me by my mother. It's in Kansas City where I lived before I came to live with my grandfather."

"Yes, that's right. I remember now that you moved here when you were quite young."

Cassandra wouldn't have called her wild journey across the state of Kansas in the Conestoga with Rill, Juliana, and Cropper a move. She and Juliana had been on the run for their lives from Ward Cabot, Cassandra's stepfather.

"Didn't you tell me that Bennett was from Kansas City?"

"Yes," she answered in a guarded tone.

Landon straightened his tie. "And you say there is enough money to pay the mortgage?"

"More than enough, I'm told."

"Hmm. Who has this money? Where exactly did you say this money was kept?"

"She didn't."

Cassandra and Landon swung around to see Dustin striding up behind them. He touched his hat with two fingers when he looked at the banker with an unfriendly smile.

Landon gave him a curt nod, rolled his shoulders, and pulled on the tail of his coat. "I didn't realize you were still here."

Dustin met his uncomfortable gaze. "I didn't realize it was Saturday."

Chapter

· 8 ·

It was dark. Cassandra couldn't breathe. She struggled but didn't know who or what she was fighting. She only knew she couldn't get air. She twisted. She turned. She kicked. She cried out.

Cassandra's eyes popped open with a gasp. She bolted upright in bed. Quickly, she scanned the moonlit room and satisfied herself that she was alone. It was only the same dream that had plagued her for years. Forgetting about her injuries, she squeezed her hands into fists in frustration and then cried out from the throbbing pain in her palms.

Since she had been a young girl she'd wake in the middle of the night fearful, breathless, her chest feeling heavy with a pressing weight. Her grandfather had told her they were childish nightmares and nothing to worry about. He said she would outgrow them, but she hadn't. Cassandra stopped telling her grandfather about the dreams, but she never stopped having them.

The room was cold but she didn't bother to put a robe on over her white flannel gown as she rose and lit the lamp on her bedside stand.

Cassandra held her hands up to the light. They had bled again and the white cloth she had wrapped around her palms had stuck to the wounds. She poured water into the basin and took it to her bed and sat down. She dipped her hands into the frigid water. The coldness made them hurt more at first but slowly the cloth loosened and settled to the bottom of the bowl.

A knock on the door startled her. Knowing it had to be Olive or Dustin, she yanked her hands out of the water and hurried to the door. "Who is it?"

"Dustin. Open up."

Something must be wrong. Why else would he come to her door in the middle of the night? With the pads of her fingers she grasped the handle and opened the door.

Dustin stood in front of her wearing only a pair of black trousers that snugly fit his slim hips and muscular legs. Moonlight from the window at the end of the hallway glinted off his broad naked chest.

"What's wrong?" she asked on a breathy note, forcing her gaze back up to his face.

"I thought I heard something so I got up and walked around downstairs, but I didn't see anything out of place. When I came back up I saw a light on. I wanted to make sure you were all right."

"A dream woke me, but I'm fine now."

"Are you sure?" he said, pushing on the door, forcing her to back up and allow him entrance into the room. "You didn't come down to dinner. I've been worried about you. It wasn't an easy day for you with everything that happened."

His words touched her. It felt good to know there was someone in the world who cared about how she felt. When Dustin had joined her and Landon that afternoon, Landon said he had to go, stating that he had to get the Quattlebums back to town for dinner. Cassandra had known Landon expected her to invite them to stay and dine with her. It was the polite thing to do, but she felt too bad to deal with the looks she would get from Dustin, and Landon had already worn out his welcome.

After Landon left she hadn't waited around to banter with Dustin. She'd washed, tended to her hands, and gone straight to bed.

"Really, I'm all right," she said, breathing a little easier now that she knew he'd checked the house and nothing was wrong.

She watched his gaze scan the room and too late remembered the basin sitting on her bed. He must have caught sight of it too, from the confused expression on his face. He strode over to the bed and picked up the basin filled with bloody water.

"What's this?"

"Ah—Nothing." Her hands automatically slipped behind her back.

"What are you hiding?" He plopped the basin down on the dresser and took hold of her arms, pulling them around so he could see them. "Open your hand."

He wasn't asking. He was demanding. Cassandra knew she had been caught, and for the life of her she couldn't figure out why that didn't upset her. Slowly, she uncurled her fingers.

He looked down at the infected flesh of her palms. "Dammit," he swore. "Cassandra, why didn't you tell me your hands were getting worse? You could get blood poisoning from these cuts."

"I've put medicine on them, they'll be all right," she said defiantly. "This isn't the first time I've been hurt and it won't be the last."

A silvery fire shone in his eyes. "You worked those damn reins and that rope to help me and never once complained."

"I told you before, I'll live. This is a working ranch, Dustin. I can't let pain stop me from doing my work. I'll be fine in a day or two."

"Is that what Thomas told you? That you have to keep working even when you're hurt?"

"He told me the ranch comes first. *Always*. Now leave my grandfather out of this." She was the one not wanting her grandfather treating her like a little girl. Cassandra had always wanted to be grown up.

"From now on I'm taking care of your hands. Come over here and sit down." He ushered her to the bed by her upper arm.

"I'm not an invalid. You don't have to help me."

Dustin looked down into her eyes and said, "Cassandra, let me do this for you. I want to take care of you."

A tiny moan of protest died in her throat as she saw the concern etched in his features. His presence had always stirred her senses. But she didn't want him to know that she was vulnerable to his attentions.

No, she couldn't submit to his tenderness, but she didn't know how to stop all the wonderful feelings that bubbled up inside her when he teased her, when he smiled at her, when he offered help.

Cassandra opened her eyes and stared up at him, savoring his strong, handsome features, enjoying the feel of his touch on her skin.

She relaxed. She shouldn't want him to be nice to her or take care of her, but she did. Yes, she'd stop fighting him and let him take care of her tonight.

Tomorrow she'd have to go back to being the hard-nosed, demanding mistress of the Triple R. She couldn't afford to let him know how vulnerable she was to him.

"All right," she whispered.

"What are you doing to treat this?"

"I have salve on the dresser. I've soaked my hands in cold water a couple of times tonight."

"I'm going downstairs to get some salt to go in the water. That should help draw the infection out of the wounds."

He picked up her feet and swung them up on the bed, then pulled the covers up around her waist. He pointed a finger at her and said, "Stay put." He picked up the basin and left the room.

Stunned, Cassandra leaned back against her pillows. When Dustin took over he didn't give her time to argue with him. She loved being in charge. She enjoyed telling other people what to do and how to do it, so why had she followed Dustin's orders so easily?

The answer was simple. She respected Dustin's judgment. She wanted to please him. She wanted to love—No, she couldn't admit that even to herself. If she let herself love him again she would lose him again, and she wasn't strong enough to endure that heartache a second time.

Cassandra squeezed her eyes shut for a moment and shook her head. She was a fool for even thinking about falling in love with Dustin again. He would be leaving in a day or two and she'd never see him again.

She prayed he would leave the ranch before he suspected the truth, that she was dangerously close to being caught up and consumed by all the things that had first drawn her to Dustin. His handsomeness had always pleased her but it was the way he'd smiled at her, talked with her, teased her that had enchanted her and made her feel she was the most important person in the world to him. And he was doing it again. But now she knew, and she had to remember it had all been an act to win her hand in marriage so Dustin and his father could control her inheritance.

It seemed Dustin was hardly gone two minutes before he was back in her room with the salted water and another piece of white cloth. He picked up the salve from the dresser and knelt down beside the bed.

He settled the basin on the mattress beside her. "I want you to soak your hands. It will probably burn but you have to keep them in the water for a few minutes."

"I can do it," she said bravely.

She dipped her hands into the salty water. It stung her open wounds. To take her mind off the pain she looked at Dustin. His skin was a natural shade of golden brown. His muscles were firm, rippling every time he moved.

Her gaze slipped down his smooth, hairless chest. She had a great desire to reach over and touch him.

He looked up and caught her gaze with his. She shivered, but not from cold. She shook from wanting to be held against his muscular chest. It was crazy. He had loved her before and left her. She had to remember that and deny the romantic desires boiling inside her.

"You're going to catch cold. You should put something on," she said, realizing it was difficult for her not to look at him and admire his masculine beauty.

"I'm all right. I'm worried about you right now."

His words warmed her more than the covers she was under. He was worried about her. Could he look inside her and know how safe those words made her feel?

"You don't have to stay in here with me. I can do this myself."

His eyes held fast to hers. "I know what a capable woman you are, Cassandra. I *want* to do this for you."

Her bitter feelings toward Dustin were dissolving because of his kindness. She wanted to believe he wanted nothing more than to help her save her ranch.

She watched as he slowly looked around her bedroom. It was spacious but contained only a bed, a chair, and two chests. His gaze lit on the doll sitting in the rocker on the other side of her bed. Miss Watkins had been with her since before her mother died.

Cassandra's throat thickened as she remembered her dear friend Cropper and how the doll had pulled him through when he'd been shot fifteen years before. If only the cantankerous old man were alive she wouldn't feel so alone. He'd survived the gunshot to his side and lived another five years with Rill, Juliana, and their little girl, Cassie.

"What was your dream about?" he asked when he turned his attention back to Cassandra.

"I don't recall," she said, knowing that was only a half truth.

"Do you have them often?"

She lightly shrugged her shoulders. "What's with you? You're suddenly acting like you're my mother."

He shook his head. "The feelings I have for you are not motherly. I know you were young when she was killed. Tell me, do you remember her at all?"

She drew a deep breath. "Not really. Sometimes when I'm alone, I like to think I do. Why do you ask?"

"Just wondering. I don't remember my mother at all. She died when I was born."

"I remember you telling me that once. I'm sorry."

"If you want to talk about your parents, I'll listen."

A sadness filled her. She was touched that Dustin wanted to listen but the shame of it was that she didn't remember enough to talk about them. Her father had been killed when she was three years old. Her mother when she was six.

"Sometimes I can't help but wonder what my life would be like if they'd lived, but I try not to think about it too often. My experience with thinking about the past is that it causes pain and I don't want that. I love this ranch and right now I can't imagine living anywhere else."

"When you thought about your inheritance, what did you plan to do with it?"

"I never thought about it. I didn't have to. I had all I wanted or needed right here until this past winter. Somehow it just never seemed right that I should get money from my parents' deaths."

"But they wanted you to have that money no matter the circumstances of their deaths."

She nodded, and for the first time she found herself wishing she knew more about them. "Maybe when I get the ranch back on solid ground I'll come to Kansas City and see if I can find anyone who knew my parents and talk to them." Cassandra didn't know what in the world had made her say that. It was the first time that idea had popped into her mind and she blurted it out without thinking.

She had to be careful. Dustin had her thinking things she shouldn't be thinking and saying things she shouldn't say.

"You could start with my father. He knew them both."

"I'm not sure I could believe anything your father said."

"Maybe you're right."

Wanting to change the subject she said, "Dustin, if you insist on staying at least get off the floor and sit here on the bed with me." She moved her legs over, giving him room.

He chuckled lightly as he rose and joined her.

"What's funny?"

"You inviting me to sit on your bed. Did you ever think you'd do that?"

She smiled, too. "No, guess not. Up until three days ago I never thought I'd see you again."

"I always knew we'd meet again."

Cassandra remembered that he'd said that the first day he arrived at the Triple R. "Because your father controls my money."

"That and more. Tell me, why don't you go ahead and let Webster know you're not going to sell the ranch and you're not going to marry him?"

"I don't know that I'm not."

"Liar."

His one word didn't condemn her. With it he challenged her to speak the truth they both knew, but Cassandra remained silent.

"You wouldn't be working so hard to save the ranch if you were thinking of selling it and you wouldn't let me sit here on your bed half dressed, thinking the kind of thoughts we're both thinking, if you were seriously considering marrying that banker."

She wished she didn't feel so many different things

when he was around. She enjoyed his lighthearted humor, his easy take on life, yet she feared the man who'd once destroyed her life. She feared what loving him again would do to her if she lost him.

"I might have to marry him just to get the money I need," she said. "I haven't forgotten your advice that if I marry, my husband gains control of my inheritance. That idea has some merit."

"Only if you marry the right man. I've told you not to worry about not getting your advance. Besides, something tells me you'd have better luck getting money for this ranch out of my father than from Landon Webster."

"Well I certainly didn't get anywhere when I wrote your father. He sent you, not money."

"True, but can you see Landon letting you spend one penny on this ranch? If he controlled your money, he'd sell the Triple R before the sun set."

"I've thought about that, but there are ways to get around him getting complete control of everything. I could have him sign papers before we marry that he will never sell the Triple R."

He lifted her hands out of the water and placed the basin on the floor. He then took the towel and gently dried her hands. "Webster is no fool. Believe me, he'd find a way around any papers you might have him sign."

Dustin applied the ointment over her palms. His touch was soothing, tender. He was caressing her hands as if they were made of the finest silk and he didn't want to damage it in any way.

"How does that feel?"

"Better."

And it did. She couldn't remember being so well cared for. Her grandfather had loved her but when she'd gotten older he hadn't known how to kiss her hurts and make her feel better. He'd tell her not to cry and that she'd be all right no matter how badly she was hurt.

"You don't even know Landon, yet you don't like him very much. Why?"

"Lawyer's instinct, and because he wants to marry you and I know he's not right for you."

"How do you know that?"

Dustin looked directly into her eyes. "Because I'm the only man who's right for you."

Her pulse quickened. She was suddenly conscious of how close they were. With the basin no longer between them, Dustin was so near she could smell the woodsy soap scent on his skin. No, she couldn't even think about what his words might mean.

Cassandra looked down at her hands. In the pale light she saw that some of the redness and swelling had abated and the cuts had been washed clean. Dustin tore a length of cheesecloth in two strips and loosely wrapped the palms of both hands, leaving her fingers free.

"I'm not going to let you ride into town tomorrow."

"You can't stop me," she protested. "I need to check on Red Sky and—"

Dustin held up his hand to quiet her. "I didn't say you weren't going. I intend to drive you in the wagon. Your hands need a few days to heal. They won't as long as you wear gloves and handle reins. We'll go check on Red Sky first, then we'll have a visit with the sheriff, get something to eat at the hotel, and pick up any supplies you might need before we head back. How does that sound?"

Like you are fitting too nicely into my heart and my life.

"Like you are doing much more than you bargained for when you agreed to come to Wyoming."

"I don't mind."

"You've been here two days already and you haven't even begun your assessment of the Triple R."

He smiled. "You're a hard taskmaster. Don't worry, I'll get that work done and in plenty of time for you to get your money. I've learned a lot just talking to you and listening to Webster talk about the economy of the area. But first I'm going to see that you take proper care of yourself." He turned serious. "When we go into town tomorrow I want the doctor to take a look at your hands. He might have something stronger to clear up that infection before it gets worse."

"All right." She looked down at her palms again before lifting her lashes to gaze into his deep blue eyes. He was mere inches from her. Her heart filled with appreciation. She was so tempted to reach out and touch him just once.

The first day he arrived at her ranch she would have sworn on a stack of Bibles that she couldn't be tempted by him again. Now she knew she was only lying to herself to cover the hurt of years past.

"Thank you. For everything. I don't think I properly thanked you for helping me put out the fire or for saving my life. I know Rodney would have shot me."

He nodded. "I didn't expect or want any thanks."

She suddenly felt breathless again. She gave herself an internal shake but the hunger to touch him didn't leave her. "I don't know how to repay you for all you've already done to help me."

His eyes glistened in the yellow glow of lamplight. He reached out and cupped her cheek with his open palm. "How about like this?"

Dustin reached over and kissed her with exquisite tenderness.

Chapter

· 9 ·

Cassandra surrendered to him with a surprised gasp. His lips moved sensuously against hers. Her head fell back, lifting her face to his. His mouth moved powerfully over hers, drenching her in shock waves of desire. Her body reeled from his unexpected assault on her senses.

Instantly she knew this kiss was far different from the sweet ones they'd shared up to now. He no longer questioned his right to kiss her. He was demanding her surrender. He was taking charge and she was letting him.

She knew she should push him away but with his lips so warm, so moist, so soft upon hers, she had no will power to use against him. Her body was too attuned to his touch. She was too ready for Dustin. Cassandra feared she'd been waiting for this moment since she opened her bedroom door and saw Dustin standing there so invitingly.

Common sense, the hurt of the past, faded from her thoughts. Her feelings of bitterness dissolved into the darkness. Determination not to give in to her loving feelings for Dustin deserted her.

Heedless of the dangerous position they were in, Cassandra thought only of long past kisses, and thrust out her tongue, wanting, needing to taste the flavor of Dustin. Quickly he captured her tongue and gently sucked it into his warm mouth. Cassandra's stomach did a somersault. Dustin made a low moan deep in his throat as she plundered his mouth. He yielded to her demanding search, allowing her to forge deeper.

She wanted him to wrap his arms around her and pull her against his massive chest and cover her with his hard, powerful body. Her arms slid around the smooth, taut skin of his back. She cupped him to her. Not allowing her hands to be still, her fingers played over the smooth contours of his shoulder, back, and waist. He was firm, lean, muscular. She pulled him closer, held him tighter.

Dustin lifted his hand to her cheek and with his fingertips he traced the bone under her eye, trailed down the soft skin beside her ear before gliding over the straight set of her jaw to the curve of her chin. He skimmed his fingers down the slender column of her throat to the neckline of her collarless nightgown. With gentle tugs he pulled on the ribbon and untied the bow that held the front panels together.

He fondled the hollow of her throat with the pads of his fingers. Her pulse pumped with longing. Oh, how she'd missed his touch. She couldn't count the nights she'd lain awake and dreamed of lying like this with Dustin.

With strong arms, he gathered her closer to him as if trying to fit her body beneath his. He moved his feet onto the bed and gave her another devastating kiss as he leaned her back against the pillows and stretched his long, lean body on top of hers. She felt the rigid evidence of his desire for her press between her thighs. Shock waves of heat consumed her.

His lips moved from hers to her cheeks, along her hairline. He touched the lobe of her ear with his tongue, then slowly moved up to kiss her eyelids, her nose, and back to her lips once again. He kissed her the same way he had years before: as if he treasured her. Cassandra savored his lovemaking and melted against him.

Tenderness for him welled up inside her. She'd hated him for so long there should be no way she'd accept him in her life like this, but she did.

She wanted him to touch her hair and her face and her hands again. She felt as if she'd been waiting for this, for Dustin, all her life.

With a gentle hand he cupped the fullness of her breast through the cloth of her nightgown and kneaded the firmness with his large hand. He found the puckered nipple and rubbed it between his thumb and finger.

"I must be dreaming. If I am, don't wake me up."

She pressed her chest into his hand. "You're not dreaming."

"I have to be. Lying here touching you like this is a dream come true."

She threw her arms around his neck. "I've had dreams like this, too."

He kissed her hard, with long thrusting jabs of his tongue. Cassandra met his fervor. She felt a throbbing between her legs and rose up to meet the bulge snuggled against her.

A sweet unfurling seemed to be taking place in her body. Cassandra sucked in her breath and she murmured a softly spoken, "Yes."

Yes to his touch, yes to his words, yes to the past, yes to the future.

He reached down and grabbed the hem of her nightgown and pulled it up past her breasts and over her head and dropped it on the sheet. He straddled her thighs and looked down at her. She hooded her eyes with her lashes and followed his gaze down her uncovered body. Lamplight shone on her breasts. They felt full, tight, and deliciously achy. The wide band of her knee-length drawers fit snugly around her small waist, hiding her legs and that secret part of her no one but Dustin had ever touched.

With an open palm he raked over first one breast and then the other, teasing her. "Your skin's soft and silky. You feel so damn good to me."

Her shallow breaths made her chest rise and fall rapidly. He lowered his head and took one erect tip between his lips and closed his mouth around the dusty-brown peak. He sucked gently, drawing on her nipple with possessiveness while his hands kneaded both breasts.

His hand strummed down her ribs to her abdomen, then lower. His hand slid beneath her drawers to the downy thatch of hair between her legs to caress her. Her body arched against his touch.

Cassandra gasped, shocked by the feeling of hunger, an emptiness that needed to be filled by Dustin. Desire, hot and sweet, rose up inside her. She felt she might go mad from the sheer pleasure his fingers were creating.

"You're wonderful, Cassandra." He breathed softly against her ear. "God, it excites me to touch you like this."

"I like to touch you, too," she answered, then kissed the base of his neck. Her hands roved over and up and down his shoulders and back. When she reached the waistband of his trousers he didn't stop her. Her hand slid down his slim hip and over the curve of his firm buttocks. He trembled. A feeling of exhilaration washed over her. She liked the fact that she could make him weak with desire for her.

A passionate, masculine sound drifted past Dustin's lips before he murmured, "Cassandra, at times I thought I'd forgotten you, but now I know I never did."

"I never forgot you, either."

"In all these years, I was searching for someone and I now know that it was you I always wanted."

A smile played on her lips. His words pleased her.

Somehow it made her feel better to know that he'd never forgotten her.

Dustin picked up one of her hands. The loosely bound cheesecloth was falling off. He kissed the tips of her fingers, then lifted his head a little and gazed down into her eyes. "I always thought you were the prettiest young lady in the West."

"You told me many times."

"Now you've grown into the most beautiful woman I've ever seen." His voice was husky, tender, and filled with honesty.

"And you are the most handsome man I've ever known."

He smiled at her. It was sweet, appreciative, and full of surprise for her unexpected praise.

"I'm not sure I should admit this, but I've been waiting to touch you like this since I first saw you again," she said.

"It's okay to admit it. I've felt the same way about you," he whispered again into the curve of her neck as he gently rocked against her lower body. "I never forgot how it was between us, Cassandra."

She matched his movement, unable to resist him. "I shouldn't be doing this," she murmured softly as his kisses and caresses continued to take her to new heights of desire. "But my body isn't listening to my mind."

"Thank God."

With the tips of his fingers he touched her chin and lifted her face to his. Their eyes met. Held. Blue and brown melding into one.

"We were meant to be together, Cassandra. Sometimes late at night I would think about you, dream about holding you in my arms again and making you mine. I often wondered if I ever truly loved you the way a man loves a woman he wants to spend the rest of his life with and now I know I did because I've never stopped loving you. And I don't think you stopped loving me."

His eyes were clear as a summer lake. His expression

was soft and serious. He loved her? Cassandra trembled. No. Her heart beat erratically. She couldn't trust him to love her. She didn't want him to love. He'd had his chance and he'd walked away.

She could admit to herself that she had never stopped wanting Dustin, but loving him?

Cassandra went still.

No, she couldn't accept that possibility either. If she did, she'd have to accept that he might leave her again and she couldn't bear that. A poignant sense of loss shot through her. How could she have let a few kisses and his tender caring for her wounds get so out of hand?

She must have been crazy to let herself fall victim to his charm again. With their first kiss she'd lost all reason. She was so caught up in loving him that she'd begun to trust him. For a few minutes she'd forgotten their past and denied the pain he'd caused her.

What was the matter with her? How could she have let him touch her, kiss her, stroke her with such shameless abandon? Why had she been so eager to explore all those wonderful feelings he created inside her? How could she have responded so wantonly to a man she was supposed to hate? But she knew the answer. He stirred her as no man ever had or ever would.

She had to deny those newly reawakened feelings for Dustin because he'd be gone in a few days, and God help her, she couldn't let him take her heart with him.

"We shouldn't be doing this," she said abruptly, and pushed against his chest. She struggled to move out from under him. She grabbed her nightgown and jerked it over her head, then shoved it down her body.

She thought her heart would hammer out of her chest. He wanted her. She wanted him. It had always been that way between them and now she was convinced it always would. Letting him make love to her would be easy. The hard part would be letting him go.

Dustin held her impatiently. "Why? Neither of us are committed to anyone else."

"No." She pushed again, harder. She saw the confusion in his eyes. She needed someone in her life whom she could trust not to leave her alone. "I don't want this. I don't want you!" she fibbed again.

Dustin rolled away from her to the other side of the bed. He was crazy with need for Cassandra. He felt as hot and hard as newly forged iron. His arousal filled his trousers and ached to be released from the pent-up desire pumping furiously through his body. He'd been with more women than he could remember but he'd never wanted one more. Tonight he had thought Cassandra would be his again.

His breathing was labored. He leaned against the bedstead. The cold wood was a shock to his heated skin and he hoped it would help cool him off. Exhaling heavily he turned to look at her. She was adjusting her nightgown with trembling fingers. He wanted to help her but was afraid to touch her again.

"Cassandra, I have to admit I don't know what the hell is going on. I thought we both wanted to do what we were doing. What happened?"

She kept her head bowed and didn't look at him while she tied the ribbon at the neckline of her nightgown. "I just decided I didn't want to—do what we were doing."

"Why?" He didn't like the way her rebuff made him feel. He needed to understand why she suddenly shied away from him. "You were as eager for me as I was for you when we started kissing. Something happened. What?"

"I came to my senses, all right?"

"About what? Did I say something wrong? Was I going too fast for you? Tell me."

"No, none of those things, and yes, all of them." She jerked her head up. "Dustin, I'll admit that you have proved to me that you and I are strongly attracted to each other. I won't deny any longer that something powerful exists between us. It probably always will." Her voice softened. Her eyes glistened. "We can make each other see stars, but it's not love."

A pain caught Dustin in the stomach and floored him. It felt as if she had sucker-punched him. He moistened his lips. "If it's not love, what the hell do you think it is?"

She looked away from him and shrugged her shoulders. "I—I don't know. Desire. Sex."

"I've finally figured out that those things are a part of love."

"And that's the only part we have. I wish I could find a way to turn off or destroy the way you make me feel."

Pain tore at his gut again. "Why do you want to do that? Call it love. Call it attraction or call it sex. It won't change the way we feel, Cassandra, by giving it a different name."

Her eyes searched his face and for a moment he thought he was getting through to her. "It doesn't matter. I just can't—go any farther. What we had is over and we can't go back."

She sounded so final, without any sign of hope. Her words hit him hard and for a moment he was too stunned to reply. "I'm not trying to go back to what we had. I'm going forward. You aren't the same person. I'm not either. Oh, there are some things about us that are the same, but we've grown up in the years we've been apart, Cassandra, and we feel the same things we did back then. That tells me we belong together."

"No."

She was emphatic. She always had been. There was no middle of the road for Cassandra. But Dustin wasn't about to give in to her so easily. "Why?"

"I don't trust you not to hurt me again."

There were pain and bewilderment in her voice. Tears beaded the top of her lashes but didn't spill onto her cheeks. Her pain was visible and that bothered him more than when she pushed him away. He stared at her and for the first time he saw a frightened little girl who needed to be hugged and soothed and told that she wasn't alone.

"You haven't forgiven me, have you?"

"I guess not. What you did hurt me very badly," she whispered earnestly. "I won't take a chance on you again."

Dustin's breathing slowed. Her honesty touched him, wounded him, enlightened him. For the first time he saw that her hurt went far beyond the anger she flung at him when she shot at him in the barn or when they'd talked last night.

He rubbed his eyes with his thumb and forefinger. "No, I won't accept that." He rose and walked around to her side of the bed and looked down at her. "I know without a doubt that I love you—the woman you are today. I know that as surely as I know my name."

"You're too late, Dustin. It took you too damn long to figure that out."

"Maybe it did take me a long time, but you know what they say. Better late than never. Now that I've found you, now that I know I love you, I'm not going to let you go without a fight. You can count on that, Cassandra."

Dustin blew out the lamp and turned and walked out her door as boldly as he'd walked in.

Chapter

·10·

The two-and-a-half-hour ride to town was harder on Cassandra than she had thought it would be. She was constantly rubbing elbows or brushing knees with Dustin. Far from assuaging and satisfying her hunger for him, last night's passionate encounter had only heightened her awareness of him.

Even when she wasn't touching him she felt the warmth of his body, the sweetness of his smile, and the sheer pleasure of being with him. She was acutely aware of his every breath and movement.

Gray skies covered them all the way to the city of Cheyenne. A brisk wind kept her chilled and produced a light scattering of snow flurries that blew in their faces, chilling and dampening their skin.

Cassandra was glad she'd worn her woolen drawers and stockings and her heavy velvet traveling dress and jacket. She'd bound her palms with clean cloths and kept her hands snug and warm under her wool cape. Dustin had insisted they bring along a blanket to help buffer the wind. It lay covering both their feet and legs.

The timbered mountain slopes that shot up to the sky

in the distance were barely visible in the gloomy morning. The rutted road to town lay dotted occasionally with a barren juniper or ponderosa pine. Gusts of wind sent tumbleweed and sagebrush skipping along the flatland on either side of the wagon. Cold temperatures at night and early-morning frosts kept the hop sage, prickly pear, and most of the other ground grasses dormant.

When they first started their journey that morning they were careful what they said to each other. Neither mentioned their midnight interlude or the money she was desperate to receive from his father. They talked about the gloomy weather, the cattle trade in Kansas City, and how stuffed they were from Olive's big breakfast of flapjacks, homemade sugar syrup, and thick slices of smoked bacon. But after the first half hour of the trip they settled down to the quietness of their own thoughts.

Cassandra couldn't help wondering if Dustin, as she was, was replaying every touch, every kiss, every caress, and every word that passed between them when he was in her room.

As they entered the town, Cheyenne was bustling with activity. People milled about the streets and boardwalks. Some horses trotted along the dirt road and others stood tied to hitching rails. Several wagons and a few fancy carriages stood vacant in front of the stores.

The town was getting ready for summer. Shop owners were repairing damage from the winter storms, putting fresh coats of paint on their doors and signs, and washing a year's worth of dirt and grime from their windows.

Cassandra didn't make it into town more than every three or four months, but over the years she'd watched the small Western town evolve into a dignified city. More women were seen in the shops when she came into town now. Strangers were accepted a little better than they once had been and shootings in the streets were less common.

Her grandfather would complain about the growing

town every time he rode into Cheyenne. He'd settled far out of town because he liked the isolation, the freedom, and the vast amount of land between him and his neighbors. Prosperity and progress brought rules, laws, and people he didn't care to be involved with. He wouldn't even join the local cattlemen's association.

She'd always thought she agreed with Thomas Rakefield about Cheyenne. Now she wasn't so sure. As they passed the women walking in the streets in their fancy hats and stylish clothes and the gentlemen in their plaid suits and top hats she wondered why she hadn't been to town in months.

With directions from Cassandra, Dustin stopped the wagon in front of Doc Smithers's office, which was located on the opposite side of town. Dustin jumped down and reached up to help her. She hesitated for only a moment, then placed her hands on his shoulders. A shiver of excitement sizzled through her at his touch and for a fleeting second she didn't want her feet to touch the ground.

They stepped up onto the boardwalk. Dustin opened the door for her and they went inside. Cassandra was immediately hit with warmth from the flames leaping in the fireplace. She had never liked coming into Doc Smithers's office when she was in town. The room always had a chemical smell to it that she found so offensive she could hardly keep from wrinkling her nose. Today that scent was mixed with the smell of burned wood and beeswax.

A portly woman rose from the small desk that stood in the far corner of the room.

"Cass, dear, how are you?" she asked, but kept her eyes on Dustin. It was easy to see the older woman had no problem appreciating Dustin's good looks, though she didn't offer to speak to him.

"I'm fine, Mrs. Smithers," Cassandra said and reached up to untie her bonnet.

"Doesn't look like it to me. What have you done to yourself? What happened to your hands?"

"Oh," Cassandra said, having forgotten about her palms. The soaking in the salted water and the brown salve she'd used had her hands feeling so much better it was easy to forget how much they'd hurt just yesterday. "This is nothing to worry about." Too late, she realized a doctor's office was not the place to come with bandages showing. She held up her hands. "I failed to wear gloves when I was carrying buckets of water to put out a fire. I'm going to be fine."

"But we'd like the doctor to have a look at them since we're here," Dustin said. "He might have something stronger or better than what Cassandra is using."

Mrs. Smithers looked Dustin up one side and down the other, appreciation and curiosity showing in her features. "Cassandra, is it? Well, that's a new one. Folks around here call her Cass. Always have. Who might you be?"

Most everyone in town knew that Cassandra and her grandfather had gone to Kansas City and that she'd been engaged for three months that summer, but if anyone ever knew her fiancé's name it was never mentioned to her after she returned.

Cassandra spoke up and said, "This is Dustin Bennett, Mrs. Smithers. He's visiting here from Kansas City." Not wanting further questions about Dustin, she hurried on to say, "I really came to see about Red Sky and to let you know that I will pay you for his care."

Mrs. Smithers's expression changed to one of distaste. "Oh, the Indian."

Concern struck Cassandra. "He is here, isn't he?"

"Oh, yes. Harvey took him in just like you asked. He doesn't like to, you know. It's not good for his other patients to know he treats Indians, too."

Cassandra's back stiffened, even though she knew Mrs. Smithers was only telling the truth. Many people

135

refused to associate with an Indian or half-breed. "How is Red Sky?" she asked.

"I can't rightly say how he is. The doctor's been looking after him just like you asked. Harvey's in the back room with him right now. Let me go get him. He'll talk to you about the Indian." She started to walk off, then turned back. "And we knew you'd pay for his care. Wouldn't have taken him in otherwise, you understand."

"Why don't we go ahead and take care of that bill right now, Mrs. Smithers," Dustin spoke up as he reached into the pocket of his jacket and pulled out a small bundle of paper money. Mrs. Smithers's eyes lit up like a candle when she saw how much he had. He extended several bills to the woman.

She looked at Cassandra for approval and for a moment he didn't think she would give it. Her eyes locked on his as if they had a battle of wills going and she was determined to win. Finally she gave one nod of her head.

"It's perfectly all right to take the money, Mrs. Smithers," Dustin said. "Cassandra will repay me when we get back to the ranch. This should be enough for his care through several more days."

She took the money and counted it before looking up and saying, "Well, that depends on how long he'll have to stay, you understand."

"Of course. And how much more you receive will depend on how well he says he was treated when he returns home," Dustin said with a pleasing smile. "You understand?"

The old woman grunted and folded the bills into her hand. She cut her eyes around to Cassandra. "I'll go tell Harvey you're here." She turned and waddled down the hallway and into another room and closed the door.

Cassandra turned to Dustin, ready to give him a piece of her mind, but he held up a finger to silence her.

"It's clear she doesn't like taking care of an Indian. Believe me, he'll get much better care from her now. And

I meant it when I said you could pay me back." He paused. "Whenever you want. In whatever way you choose."

Her heartbeat quickened at his words. She knew what he meant and her body responded to his overt insinuation. She'd wished a thousand times it wasn't so, but it was.

Dustin's cheeks were ruddy from the cold wind and his hair was creased from his hat. There were so many things about him that appealed to her. He had done the right thing for Red Sky.

"I'll repay you with money," she finally said.

"It's your choice."

Cassandra paced for a few moments in front of the fireplace. The warmth penetrated her clothing and took the chill off her skin. "I don't think it's good news," she said, shaking her head.

"There you go borrowing trouble again."

"You saw the expression on Mrs. Smithers's face."

"That could have been for several different reasons, including the fact that she didn't know for sure they would get paid for taking care of Red Sky. I think you like to worry about things you can't do anything about. Seems to me you do a lot of it."

"And you act like you don't worry at all." She paused and looked into his eyes. "Do you ever worry?"

"Sometimes." He fiddled with his fancy braided hatband. "But I learned a long time ago that worry doesn't change anything."

A door opened and Cassandra looked down the corridor. A tall, lanky bearded man came striding her way. "Cass Rakefield, good to see you. How are you?"

She smiled at Doc Smithers. She appreciated how hard he'd tried to save her grandfather. "I'm fine."

"I know it's been hard on you since Thomas's passing." He looked over at Dustin. "And who's this?" He stuck out his hand.

"Dustin Bennett," he said, giving the doctor a good,

strong handshake. "My family has known the Rakefield family for years."

He eyed Dustin from over the rims of his small round spectacles. "Is that so? Not from around here, are you?"

"No. I'm from Kansas."

"First time you ever been here?"

"Yes, but I don't think it will be the last."

Cassandra snapped her head around to glare at him. Dustin smiled and winked at her.

"And what's this with your hands all bound? Let me take a look at them."

Doc Smithers turned back to Cassandra without pursuing Dustin's comment, for which she was grateful. "No, really, they're much better." She looked at Dustin. "I soaked them in salted water last night and this morning and it's already helped. What I really want is to hear about Red Sky, and I'd like to see him if possible."

"Of course you can. He woke up about four o'clock this morning."

She took a step forward. "That's wonderful! Oh, I'm so relieved."

"Well, that might not be as good as it sounds. He's not out of the woods yet. Naturally he's in a lot of pain. It will be a slow recovery until all the swelling goes down inside his head. I can't tell if he's disoriented or if he just doesn't want to talk to me. You know how Indians are. They don't talk to white folks much."

"But his chances are better for a full recovery now that he's awake, aren't they?"

The doctor shrugged.

"I mean, if he's not getting worse, he must be getting better, right?"

Doc Smithers nodded and watched her from over the rims of his glasses again. "In most cases that's true."

"Do you think he'll recognize me?"

"He might. Come on, I'll take you to him."

Cassandra turned to Dustin. "Do you want to go with me?"

"No, I think I'll go get those supplies you wanted while you spend a few minutes with Red Sky. Why don't we meet at the sheriff's office in half an hour? That should give us both plenty of time."

"It won't take you half an hour to pick up what I have on that list."

"I might stop in a saloon and have a drink before I meet you."

Cassandra's stomach knotted at the thought of him standing at a bar with a scantily clad woman hanging on his arm, purring at him. "Oh, well, I—I—

"Not jealous, are you?"

"Of course not," she snapped. "Have two drinks for all I care. I don't need you with me to talk to the sheriff."

"I'm not going to let you talk to him alone. I'll be there."

Cassandra spun on her heel and stomped after the doctor. She huffed. How dare Dustin suggest she might be jealous of him having a drink in the saloon? It didn't matter that it was true and he didn't have to know.

She followed the doctor into a cold, small room. Red Sky lay on the white bed, unmoving. She walked over and looked down at him. He looked so peaceful, so unlike her grandfather, who had coughed, fretted, and labored for each breath until the fight became so overwhelming he had to give up.

"I gave him some laudanum for the pain just before you came so he might sleep for a while."

The bruise on his forehead was better. She reached down and touched his skin. He wasn't fevered, which was a good sign, but she didn't like the chilly feel of his skin.

"It's so cold in here." She looked up at the doctor. "Can't you move him to a room that has a wood heater or a fireplace?"

"Don't have one available right now. He has enough quilts on top of him to keep him warm."

Cassandra remembered her grandfather's illness started with a chill. She was certain the reason Red Sky had been given the small dark room at the end of the hall with no heat was because of his heritage, not from lack of rooms.

She took a moment to think about what she wanted to say, then lifted her shoulders and chin a little higher. She fixed the doctor with a hard expression. "Mrs. Smithers has already received more than enough payment for the care you've already given Red Sky. There will be more forthcoming and that amount will depend on the quality of the care this man gets." She gave him a tight smile. "I suggest you find a warmer room for him to stay in even if you have to give him your own."

"I don't believe your grandfather would approve of you talking to me in that tone of voice."

"And I don't think he would want you to endanger the life of a man be he white or red skinned. I assume you take your oath seriously, as well."

He cleared his throat. "I believe we do have a patient that will be leaving sometime this afternoon. I'll see what I can do about having him moved into that room."

"Thank you," she said, knowing she felt no real appreciation after having to shame the man into doing what was right.

The doctor walked out of the room without another comment. Cassandra took a deep, settling breath. She felt better for having stood up to him. She turned her attention back to Red Sky. He slept so peacefully she didn't want to disturb him but she desperately wanted to talk to him. She wanted to tell him what had happened with Rodney. She wanted to tell him that she wished she didn't always feel that she had to be in control.

If she admitted she had been wrong, maybe God would forgive her and let Red Sky live.

Chapter

·11·

Fine flakes of wet snow continued to fall, but hadn't started sticking to the ground when Dustin drove the wagon from the saloon to the other side of town. Women strolled the boardwalk with their parasols open and men lifted the collars of their coats against the blowing flakes.

Dustin had walked into a saloon not far from the doctor's office hoping to have a shot or two of whiskey to help get him through the long ride back to the Triple R. It had been hell having Cassandra so close and not being able to reach over and pull her to him.

As soon as his snow-covered boots hit the plank floor of the saloon a barmaid sidled up next to him and asked him to buy her a drink. He obliged her and had one drink himself before buying a bottle of good brandy from the barkeep and leaving. He'd take the bottle to bed with him tonight instead of a woman.

He knew what the problem was. Cassandra had spoiled him for other women. She was seductive to the point that he thought about her constantly. She was the only one he wanted.

Hell, he wished he could change the past, but he

141

couldn't. What he'd done was a shitty thing to do. He was a cocky bastard who was more interested in making a name for himself at the law firm than protecting the love Cassandra had for him.

It was a lot to ask, he knew, but he wanted her to forget who he had been and see only the man he was today. He loved her and he was committed to helping her save her ranch. Once he'd done that maybe she would see he was no longer the bastard who had jilted her. He was a man who loved her and would do everything in his power to make her happy.

Dustin set the brake on the wagon in front of the general store, which was located on the main street of Cheyenne, and jumped down from the driver's seat. He took the blanket and spread it over the seat to keep the snow off. Dustin then stepped up on the boardwalk right in front of Landon Webster.

"Well, well, look who we have here," Webster said in a sneering voice. "On your way to the train depot, I trust."

"You aren't that lucky today, Webster," Dustin said and walked right past him.

A bell on the door of the general store dinged sharply when Dustin opened it. He saw Webster's reflection in the window pane and knew the banker was coming up behind him, but Dustin stepped inside and closed the door behind him anyway. He didn't have anything else to say to Webster.

Dustin knocked the snow from his boots and his hat on the rug provided for that purpose and looked around.

The store was spacious, with wide aisles separating counters that held everything from bolts of cloth and ready-made clothes to kitchen utensils and gardening tools. An older man stood behind the counter wearing a gray striped apron and sporting the long handlebar mustaches that seemed to be so fashionable. Shelves lined the walls behind the man and were filled with an array of canned and boxed foods, dry goods, and spices.

"Good day," he called to Dustin. "What can I help you with?"

Dustin tipped his hat and walked up to the man. He pulled the quickly scribbled note from his coat pocket and read. "Three large sacks of flour, two bags of potatoes and three of sugar and two of coffee beans." Dustin heard the door open behind him and knew that Webster had followed him. He knew the banker was itching for him to get out of town and away from Cassandra.

"Sounds like some little lady is going to be baking with all that sugar. Anything else?" the man asked.

"Where can I buy a bottle of perfume or cologne?"

"I have plenty of that. You'll find the sweet-smelling things ladies like right over there." The man pointed behind Dustin. "You look around and I'll get these other things loaded for you right away. Good day, Mr. Webster. What can I do for you?"

"Nothing, right now, Mr. Pippin. I just came in to talk to this man."

The owner nodded and walked to the back room while Dustin strode over to the ladies' counter. He picked up a beautiful crystal bottle that had been fashioned in the shape of a heart. A blue tassel hung from the delicate stopper. Uncapping the bottle, he held it under his nose and sniffed. It had a wonderful spicy scent to it that reminded him of Cassandra.

Webster sauntered up behind Dustin and cleared his throat loudly. "I want you to know that I found out why you are here."

Dustin didn't bother to turn around but answered, "All right."

"I don't intend to let you get away with what you plan to do."

Dustin picked up another bottle. "All right," Dustin repeated.

"I'm going to tell Cass exactly what you're up to."

"Go ahead, but I don't think she'll have any doubt about what I'm up to once she sees this bottle."

Webster grunted. "You won't be so sure of yourself once she learns why you came to town."

"You think so?" Dustin turned around and faced the banker. He gave Webster's brand-new three-piece suit a quick glance. Dustin couldn't help wondering if he, like Webster, looked like a smug ass when he was dressed that way. No wonder Dustin always felt more comfortable in banded collar shirts and leather waistcoats.

Dustin put the bottle down and picked up another and sniffed. The scent was loud and sweet smelling. It reminded him of too many women he'd paid for. He replaced the bottle and looked around.

On a table not far away he saw ladies' knitted shawls and walked over to look at them. A black one caught his eye. It was almost the color of Cassandra's hair and it had a row of beads on the end of the fringe. It was thicker, wider, and longer than the one she had worn down to the bunkhouse that first night he arrived.

"Yes," Webster was saying. "Early this morning I sent a telegram to a friend of mine in Kansas City asking a lot of questions about Cassandra Rakefield and you. I just received a reply. Quite a lengthy one, I might add."

Hell. That meant Webster had found out that Cassandra didn't just have a little money in the bank but that she was a wealthy heiress. He'd be sure to keep the pressure on for her to marry him now. Dustin wished Cassandra hadn't told the banker about her inheritance. That changed everything. Dustin wouldn't have time to court and woo her the way he wanted to. The way she deserved.

Ignoring Webster, Dustin took the shawl and strode back over to the perfume table. He looked over the bottles again but was still drawn to the heart-shaped one with the fancy stopper. He picked it up and took the perfume and the shawl up to the counter with him.

"Cass is not the kind of woman who can have her head turned with gifts."

"Already tried it, have you?"

"I—ah—well, that's none of your concern."

Dustin turned to Webster and asked, "Is there a particular reason you're following me?"

"Yes." Voices and the shuffling of feet sounded from the back. "I'll wait outside for you," Webster said and hurried out of the store as Mr. Pippin walked back into the room. A young man with a fifty-pound bag of flour thrown over his shoulder followed him.

"Need some help with that?" Dustin asked.

"Naw, I do this all the time. Is that your wagon out front?"

"Yes, the one with the gray mare hitched to it."

"I'll have this loaded by the time you pay for it," the young man said.

Mr. Pippin said something to his young worker, then walked behind the counter. "Now, what else can I get for you today?"

"Wrap these two together for me." Dustin pushed the shawl and the bottle toward the man, then he pointed to a large jar that was filled with homemade tea cakes. "I'll take a dozen of those."

"A dozen?"

"That's right." Dustin didn't feel right about taking gifts back to Cassandra without having something for Olive, too, and she looked like the kind of lady who enjoyed having a little something sweet to nibble on that she didn't have to bake.

"Why, sure. The missus made them just this morning."

True to his word, Webster waited for Dustin outside the door but Dustin didn't stop for the chat the banker wanted. Dustin strode over to the wagon where Mr. Pippin's helper was loading the last sack. He carefully arranged his wrapped gifts in the corner under the driver's seat so they wouldn't be stepped on, then walked to the back.

"You want me to help you get the canvas tied over these supplies?"

"I appreciate the offer of help, but I can do it."

The young man waved and strolled back inside the general store. Dustin climbed onto the wagon bed and stretched the canvas over the bulging sacks.

"I have to tell you I don't want you giving Cass those items you purchased," Webster said, stepping down into the muddy street beside the wagon. "It's not appropriate."

An itch started at the back of Dustin's neck. He'd had about all of Webster he could take for one day. Dustin threw a glance at him. "You still trying to pester me, Webster?"

The banker moved closer and placed his hands on the side of the wagon. "You know damn well I am and I intend to until you leave Cass alone. Stop by one of the saloons on your way out of town. Any of those whores will be happy to accept what you just bought and they'll give you what you want in return."

Snowflakes blew in Dustin's face and cooled him. He looked down at Webster. "You'd do well to handle your own affairs and let me handle mine," he warned in a low voice.

"I'm Cass's fiancé. I have a right to—"

"You have a right to nothing," Dustin interrupted. "She hasn't said yes, yet. You know it and I know it so don't try to convince me otherwise."

Webster straightened his shoulders and stood rigid as the flurries fluttered around him. "She hasn't said yes only because I'm being a gentleman and giving her time to make her decision. When she does I'm confident she will agree to marry me."

"I'm not and frankly I wouldn't care if she had. I'll give her anything I damn well please. Now stay out of my business and out of my face before I decide to rearrange your nose for you."

"It doesn't surprise me that you'd resort to fisticuffs

now that you know I'm on to you. And I intend to stay on you now that I know about you. I know you were once engaged and that you jilted her."

"She knows that, too."

Dustin jumped down and tightened the rope that stretched the canvas across the wagon bed, then tied it to a nail that had been hammered in the side panel. He couldn't afford to let Webster think he had an edge.

"But I intend to remind her of it often. God only knows what kind of lies you've fed her trying to work your way back into her life. Thank God she can see through your schemes."

Dustin strode around to the other side of the wagon and stretched the canvas and rope tight.

Landon didn't know when he was ahead. Dustin was itching to put his fist through the man's face. He hadn't felt like doing that since he was a rowdy youth.

"No doubt you've decided you'd like to have her fortune after all and that's why you're here." Webster chuckled. "I'm sure you didn't count on having me around to spoil your little plan."

"I didn't know you'd be around. That's for sure," Dustin admitted, as Webster joined him on the other side of the wagon. "You know, Webster, you're getting under my skin about as bad as any man ever has and I'm tired of it."

"I'm not afraid of you, Bennett."

Dustin pierced Webster with his eyes. "Right now you don't have reason to be, but you're working hard to change that."

"I'm going to be the one Cass marries and takes to her bed and don't you—"

In a flash, Dustin snapped around and shoved his face so close to Webster's their noses almost touched. Startled, Landon drew back so quickly he stumbled over his feet and fell down into the muddy street on his rump.

Dustin merely brushed his hands together and chuckled. It would have felt good planting his fist on Webster's face but not as good as seeing the dandy fall in the mud by tripping over his own feet.

"I'll get you for this, Bennett!" Webster yelled. "You'll pay for this. Stay away from Cass, you hear me? She's mine. You stay away from her."

"We'll see about that."

Lifting his collar against the snow, Dustin climbed up on the driver's seat and headed for the sheriff's office to meet Cassandra. He didn't bother to look back at Webster. He didn't want the man to know that he considered Cassandra marrying Webster even a possibility.

He squeezed the reins as he remembered the way she responded to him with such passion and fervor when he had been in her room. But Cassandra had a mind of her own. Always had. He wouldn't put it past her to marry Webster if she got it into her head that marriage to the banker was the best thing to do for the Triple R.

That left it up to Dustin to prove to her that marrying Webster was the last thing she wanted to do.

By the time they finished answering all the sheriff's questions, snow covered the canvas on the wagon, making it look like a pristine white sheet. Dustin had wanted to take Cassandra into one of the hotels for a hot meal before they started the long trip home, but seeing that the snow was sticking to the ground he decided not to take the time. If the snow continued at the rate it was falling, they needed to get home before dark.

An hour or so into the trip Dustin was beginning to think they should have stayed in town for the night and waited out the snow. The temperature had fallen rapidly and the snow was getting deeper and heavier the farther they traveled away from town.

The wet snow turned to larger flakes and it fell quickly. It became more difficult to see and the ruts of the road had been completely covered over.

"It's a little late in the spring for it to be snowing this

hard, isn't it?" Dustin asked Cassandra when the wind picked up and started blowing wet heavy snow in their faces.

"No. It's not unusual at all. Grandpapa used to tell me that up here in this part of the country it could snow on a sunny day in July."

Dustin chuckled. "Kansas City can get downright frigid at times, but I can't ever remember having a storm this late in May."

He looked over at Cassandra. She smiled at him. Her bonnet partly shielded her face from the snow, but downy flakes had collected on her lashes and in the small amount of hair that framed her face. She was beautiful with her pink cheeks and red nose.

"I am surprised that the snow seems to be getting worse instead of better, the way most snows do this time of year," she offered in answer.

"It's all right if you come closer and lean against my arm. You'll stay warmer that way and so will I. It'll help keep the snow off your face, too, if you look at me and not straight ahead."

"What about your face?" she asked.

"One of us has to watch where we're going, but believe me I'd rather look at you. If the blowing gets worse, I'll pull up my kerchief. Now move closer to me. I promise you I'm not going to stop the wagon to kiss you. If I wanted to do that I could reach over like this and do it." He bent toward her and planted a cold kiss on the top of her nose.

"Dustin." She brought her hand out from under the blanket that wrapped around their legs and wiped her nose with the back of her palm. "I wasn't afraid you were going to kiss me until you did."

"It was only your nose and doesn't count as a kiss. Now come get me warm."

Cassandra scooted over closer to him. He felt her warmth immediately as her thigh, her leg, her side brushed against him. He put the reins in one hand and pulled her close to him with the other. "Mmm. I like the way you snuggle. I'm warmer already."

"Don't get too used to it. As soon as we see the lights from the house I'm moving back to my side of the seat."

"Tell me, what did the doctor say about your hands?"

"Oh—Ah—I—"

"You didn't let him look at them, did you?"

"No. I forgot about them. When I said they were much better today it was the truth. They are. When we get home I'll show you."

When we get home. Her words sounded beautiful in his head and struck a chord of longing within him. That's the way he'd felt these past few days helping Cassandra with the fire, Rodney, and the doctor. She wasn't ready to admit it but she needed him and he needed her, too. He knew now that whenever he was with Cassandra he was home.

His throat tightened at the thought of Webster kissing her again. Dustin wished he had more time to court Cassandra.

"You know, I've been thinking. The way you responded to my kisses last night is just another reason you shouldn't consider marrying Webster."

Cassandra stiffened, then moved so she could look at his face. "Where did that come from?"

She wasn't happy with his comment, but he hadn't been able to stop himself from saying it. Webster's little visit was too raw and Dustin knew how determined Cassandra could be once she made up her mind.

"I was just thinking about you and me—and him."

"Well, don't."

"He wants your money, Cassandra."

"Thank you, Dustin." She pushed away from him. "I'm thrilled to know I have no personal attributes that might attract him."

"Dammit, Cassandra, I didn't mean what I said that way and you know it. All you have to do is look in the mirror to know how beautiful and desirable you are and

I can't count the times you've proven how capable you are."

"You know that he only found out yesterday afternoon that I have money available to me. He asked me to marry him more than a month ago. I think you're jealous."

"Hell yes, I am."

"I'm not ready to turn my life, my ranch, or my inheritance over to any man."

This was coming out all wrong. He was sounding like a weak-kneed ninny. If he wasn't careful he'd chase her right into the banker's arms. "I just saw Webster in town today and he told me he'd telegraphed a friend in Kansas City and asked questions about you."

"You didn't tell me you saw Landon today."

"He seems to always be around."

Cassandra laughed lightly. "I think he said the same thing about you."

A gust of wind blew so fiercely it shook the wagon. Dustin had to brace himself with one hand and hold on to his hat with the other. He realized the ride had become bumpy and they were no longer following the ruts in the road.

He looked ahead of them. Snow flew furiously all around them. The wind fiercely tugged at their clothing.

"I think we're in the midst of a ground blizzard," Cassandra said, trying to hold on to her bonnet and the blanket flapping around her legs. "We have to stop."

He'd heard of the wind blowing so fiercely it whipped the snow off the ground and made it impossible to see, but he'd never experienced a ground blizzard.

"We need to keep going. I don't want you out in this weather all night."

"This time of year the storm shouldn't last more than a few hours, but the way my luck has been running lately this storm could last a week."

"Damn," Dustin whispered to himself. He wished he'd followed his first inclination and stayed in town. Now it looked as if he was putting Cassandra's life in danger. He could see the concern on her face and knew he was responsible for putting it there.

"How far do you think we are from the ranch?" he asked.

"It's hard to say." The wind caught her words and carried them away. "How long have we been traveling?"

Dustin had to shout to be heard over the howl of the wind. "An hour and a half maybe, but we haven't been making as good time as we made going into—" Suddenly the wagon started shaking and the ride became very bumpy.

Dustin put both hands on the reins and started pulling the horse to a stop. The right wheel made a screeching noise before it stopped.

Cassandra gasped and struggled to keep from falling off the seat as the wagon tilted. The supplies tumbled and shifted to the low side of the bed.

"Damn!" Dustin swore again.

"What's happening to the wagon?"

"I don't know. We must have hit a hole. We might have broken something. Hold on to the seat. I'm going to have to check it out."

The wind almost flattened Dustin against the side of the wagon as he jumped down. He tightened the strings of his hat tight under his chin to keep it from blowing off his head. The horse whinnied and stomped from fear.

Dustin struggled to get to the wheel but once he knelt in front of it, it was impossible to see the problem with the blowing snow swirling around him like a whirlpool. The icy wind blew down his back. He felt as if the cold was going to break off his ears.

He was angry with himself for getting Cassandra into this situation. He held on to the wagon and walked back up to the front where she was seated.

"I'm going to unharness the horse and we'll ride him on to the house. Do you think you can find the way?"

"I'll try."

He reached up and helped her down. "Bring the

blanket with you so it won't blow away. Hold on to me. Don't let go."

The horse snorted and stomped as Dustin worked with cold fingers to unhitch the animal. As soon as the last hitch was unfastened from the shaft, the horse shot away from them, pulling the harness behind him.

"Whoa!" Dustin yelled. He ran a few steps, hoping to catch the horse, but the animal bolted away and Dustin found nothing but white air in front of him.

The fierceness of the wind intensified, swirling the snow so fast and furiously that suddenly Dustin couldn't see a foot in front of him. Snow blanketed his face and eyes like stinging pellets of fine hot rock. He turned back toward the wagon and Cassandra. His heart jumped up to his throat. He couldn't see a damn thing. All he saw was white. The ground, the sky, the air were white.

"Cassandra," he called. "Cassandra!" He yelled her name again. The wind caught his words and returned only a mouthful of white ice.

Chapter

· 12 ·

Dustin disappeared into the white mist.

Cassandra's heart lurched. "Dustin, no!" she screamed. "Don't leave, you'll get lost in the snow!"

She started to rush after him, but common sense stopped her. If she left the wagon, they'd both be lost in the snow with no hope of finding the shelter the vehicle could provide or each other. It was better she stay put and continue to call his name in hopes that he would hear her and find his way back to the wagon.

Fear for Dustin's safety cloaked her with weakness. She took a deep breath and strove to force the debilitating emotion away. She couldn't help him if she fell apart.

Gripping the rim of the wheel to steady herself against the gusting wind, Cassandra called Dustin's name again. She trembled as she searched the sea of white for any sign of Dustin's dark coat. The driving snow beat against her face and eyes. The wind whipped furiously at her bonnet, nearly ripping it off her head. She braced herself and shouted into the air.

When she realized she was clutching the blanket that had covered their legs in the wagon she knelt down with

154

her back pressed solidly against the wheel. Quickly she found the flapping ends of the blanket and tied it securely around her shoulders like a cape, then rose again.

"Dustin!" she called over and over until her throat felt dry and ached. Her eyes watered from the wind and snow, but frantically she kept searching the white landscape in front of her, praying Dustin would appear as quickly as he had disappeared.

The minutes ticked by. Cassandra knew she had to do something fast. Dustin could be wandering farther away in the wrong direction. Fear of losing him a second time overwhelmed her. She couldn't let anything happen to him.

She covered her face with her hands to block out the snow, the panic crawling around inside her. She had to think fast. Suddenly, she remembered a story her grandfather had told her when he was once trapped in a snow storm.

She couldn't see anything but she turned toward the wagon and felt along the top of the sideboard until she found the end of the rope near the front of the wagon that held the canvas over the supplies. If she could manage to free enough of the rope, she could tie one end around her waist and walk away from the wagon and search for Dustin without losing her way back to the shelter it afforded.

She shivered violently. Her clothes were not nearly warm enough for the spring blizzard but she forced herself not to think about the cold. Her injured hands were stiff and achy, not wanting to move, but she worked her fingers until she managed to untie the simple square knot Dustin had used.

When the rope was freed the loose end of the canvas started flapping, making a horrible sound in the wind. She pulled on the rope and several more feet of it tumbled out of the wagon bed and onto the snow. There was plenty for what she needed. She hurriedly tied the excess rope around her waist.

Trembling from cold and fear, she felt her way back to the wheel so that she could walk in the direction in which Dustin had disappeared minutes ago. A wave of panic sliced through her again. Her chest tightened. She felt the familiar pressing weight on her chest. No, she had to keep control. She had to. Dustin needed her.

Cassandra inhaled deeply. The cold wind stung her lungs. Fear twisted down her throat, strangling her, but she had to step out into the white depth and find Dustin. She tugged on the rope. It was secure.

Without further thought she took her first step out into the white swirling mist. The fierce wind and collected ground snow made walking difficult but she trudged on.

After several tentative steps she stopped and looked behind her. There was no sign of the wagon. It had already been swallowed up in the sea of snow.

Alarm shot through her again, and for a moment she wanted to rush back to the safety of the wagon. She turned around again and closed her hands into tight fists, clutching the blanket tightly against her chest, and started walking. She tried to call out, but her teeth chattered so badly she couldn't get her mouth working properly.

Suddenly, through the white swirling mist of snow ahead of her she thought she saw a dark outline. She stopped and rubbed the snow from her eyes. The figure appeared to be coming closer to her. Hope surged within her. She recognized Dustin's black greatcoat only a few feet away from her.

"Dustin!" she called.

"Cassandra!"

Her heart leaped with relief. She'd found Dustin!

"Stay where you are. I'm coming after you!" she shouted into the wind.

"No! Lost! You stay."

All she could see was a dark shape but she heard enough of what Dustin said to know he thought they'd both be lost in the snow. With the length of rope secured around her waist, she continued toward him, until she was close enough to reach out and touch his arm.

Dustin's hand closed around her wrist and she started pulling him forward. "Follow me!" she shouted to him, and with her other hand she held tightly onto the rope. Using it as a guide, Cassandra led them safely back to the wagon, where the loose canvas continued to flap wildly in the wind.

As soon as she felt the wood with her hand, she turned toward Dustin. He gathered her up in his arms. She didn't think she'd ever been held so tightly, felt so warm, or been so relieved. Now that they were together she knew they would be safe until the storm lifted.

"Cassandra," he whispered with his lips pressed very close to her ear. "I was so damn scared that you were lost in the snow."

"I was worried about you," she answered into the warmth of his neck. "You shouldn't have run off like that."

"I know. It was a gut reaction to try to catch the horse. I ran before I realized the danger of not being able to find my way."

"I was so frightened for you." She held him closer. She liked the strength she felt from being in his arms and having hers around him. "I kept calling your name."

"I called for you, too. You must have heard me."

"No, I didn't. I was frantic."

"How did you find me? How did you find your way back here to the wagon? I couldn't see a damn thing out there."

"Your black coat. I saw your shape in the distance."

He lifted his head and looked down into her eyes. "You shouldn't have risked getting lost coming after me, Cassandra. You should have stayed where you were safe."

His face was so close to hers that even in the blowing snow she saw the concern, the appreciation, the admiration in his features for what she'd accomplished. "I wasn't in any danger of getting lost. I took the rope from the wagon and tied it around my waist. See?" She took hold of his hand and led it down to her waistline.

He chuckled softly, briefly, and hugged her tightly to his chest again. "You're one smart lady, Cassandra Rakefield. And I'm a hell of a lucky man you were with me today."

She smiled, appreciating his words more than he would ever know. She took the opportunity to snuggle deeper into his embrace. The scratchy wool of his coat scraped her chapped lips and cheeks but she didn't care. Dustin's breath was warm on her cheek as he held her. His body shielded her from the cold wind. Her shivering stopped. She felt safe, secure. In that moment Cassandra knew she was where she wanted to be, where she'd wanted to be for a long time. She was in Dustin's arms with his warm breath falling softly upon her.

"Let's get in the wagon and under the canvas with the supplies until the storm blows over," Dustin said. "That will give us some protection."

Cassandra knew she had all the protection she needed in Dustin's arms. She also knew the danger in feeling that way, but suddenly that fear was no longer real. The only danger she'd felt was in the thought of losing Dustin again.

"Do you think it's safe? What if the wind gets stronger?" she asked. "It could blow the wagon over on its side."

"That's a chance we have to take. We need shelter. If it doesn't get much worse than it is right now, the wagon will remain standing. Let's take the rope from around your waist so you can climb in. I'll crawl in behind you, then tie down the canvas to the sideboard again."

She nodded and Dustin untied the knot around her waist. His hands were sure and fast against her waist as he helped her climb into the wagon.

Cassandra wiggled under the canvas and smack on top

of a lumpy sack of potatoes. She grunted and scampered over that bag and fell upon a softer sack of flour. While Dustin worked to control the wildly flying canvas and tie it down to the wagon side again, she shivered as she took the blanket from around her shoulders and made a pallet on the center of the wagon bed.

It wasn't as dark as she expected it to be under their makeshift shelter. She could actually see better now that the snow wasn't pelting her eyes. She took a deep breath and caught the scent of damp, dank earth that clung to the potato sacks.

A few moments later, Dustin threw his hat underneath the shelter and scrambled up beside her. "Let's shove these sacks up against the corners to help keep the blowing snow out," he said. "That will get them out of our way and give us more room to stretch out."

With the canvas stretched tight, they only had about two and a half feet of working space from top to bottom. They crawled on their stomachs and pushed all the sacks into the corners and along the perimeter of the wagon.

Cassandra heard Dustin knock his knee or elbow on the plank floor. He swore softly under his breath as the wind continued to howl outside.

"You all right?" she asked.

"Yeah. There's not much room to move around in here, is there?"

"No, but it feels much better in here than out there," she said as she made her way back to the center of the wagon and the wool blanket. "I don't think I've ever seen a spring storm come up so fiercely and so quickly. I hope Jojo got the horses in the barn."

"I'm sure he did. Don't worry about the ranch right now." Dustin moved back to the center with her. "Here, I know a way to make us warmer."

"How?" she asked and then realized he was unbuttoning his coat. "Are you crazy? You can't take off your coat. You'll freeze to death."

"Not if I have you to keep me warm. We're going to

use the coat as a blanket. We'll use our body heat to keep us warm." Remaining on his back Dustin continued to twist and turn until he shrugged free of his caped coat.

A funny feeling fluttered deeply within Cassandra. "We—we have to be close together—touching—to generate body heat."

"I know," he said, straining to take his boots off in his awkward, half-sitting position.

After his boots were thrust to the end of the wagon, Dustin reached up toward the top and felt around. Cassandra had no idea what he was doing until he dragged another sack toward them.

"The flour might not be as comfortable as a soft pillow but I think it will feel better than the wood against our heads."

Dustin then stretched out his body and settled down on his side, facing her, and threw his coat over them like a blanket.

He immediately reached over and wrapped his arms around her waist and pulled her close, letting his hand come to rest at the small of her back. "Come over here and let me keep you warm."

Cassandra's temperature shot up immediately. She didn't know if he meant to make his voice sound seductive or if these funny little feelings crawling around inside her were of her own doing. She was certain she could feel the steady thump of his heart against her breasts.

She knew all the reasons she shouldn't allow Dustin to take her in his arms and hold her so close, but right now not a one of them mattered. All she knew was that his powerful body was hard and warm against hers. She had begun to forget the pain of the past. She scooted closer to him. He slipped one arm under her neck and tightened the other around her waist. He pressed her close. His hold on her was firm, confident.

It surprised her that she didn't feel awkward or stiff.

Instead, she felt as comfortable and at ease as she had when Dustin had lain on the bed with her the night before. She turned her face toward him. She didn't have to see him clearly to know he was smiling. That was Dustin. He didn't take anything too seriously. Not even such a dangerous situation as getting lost in a snow storm.

"You're shaking. How are your hands and feet? Cold?" he asked.

"Not too bad now that we are out of the wind. How about you? You're breath is frosty."

"I'm fine now that I'm in here with you."

"Good. I'm glad you're safe."

"So am I. You saved my life, you know."

She shrugged and moved her hands up between them to rest on his chest. "It was nothing."

He touched her chin and tipped her face closer to his. "It was something. You didn't have to risk your own life to help me, but you did. Both of us could have been lost in that and frozen to death. Thank you."

He bent down and kissed her tenderly, briefly, as if he were shy. His lips were warm, soft. Cassandra's breath came in little gasps. She knew their feelings were running high because of the danger from the storm. A part of her reminded her she needed to stay in control of the situation they were in and another side of her wanted to let go of every little past hurt and just enjoy being with this man who had dominated her mind, her thoughts, her dreams for all these years.

Nothing had changed, yet everything had. She wanted to hate Dustin because of the past, but she couldn't. She'd tried ignoring him but that didn't work either. All those unwanted feelings of the past had begun to dissolve and she saw only the Dustin she had loved.

"I would have done the same thing for anyone."

"I believe you, but that doesn't make what you did for me any less important."

His lips touched hers again, the same as before, brief, non-threatening. She didn't know how or why such an innocent kiss should send a thrill of desire spiraling throughout her body but it did. He might as well have been kissing her in the heat of passion, with the intensity of desire his chaste kisses created inside her. She was falling victim to his words, to his touch.

Her heartbeat sped up, warning her he was getting too close, but she was reluctant to break away from his soothing warmth.

When he'd been in her room it had become clear to her that in an intimate situation with Dustin, Cassandra lost all self-control. She wondered if he thought about her as much as she thought about him. She wondered if, like her, he had an ache of longing, of denial centered in his midsection that wouldn't go away.

"Here," he said. "Let me take off your gloves and warm your hands."

"No, they're all right. I'm getting warm. Really."

"I won't hurt your palms. It gives me something to do. Besides, I like touching you—your hands."

He slipped the gloves off and gently took both her hands in his and warmed them in his own. He rubbed the outside of her palms and tenderly caressed each fingertip, careful not to disturb the area of her wounds. He carried her hands up to his lips and blew his breath on them. It warmed her all the way down her body. He gently pressed the pads of her fingers to his lips, then to his cheeks.

"Does that feel better?" he asked.

"Much," she said breathlessly, not only feeling warm, but positively glowing. And no wonder. She was disturbingly aware of every masculine contour of his body. They were alone in the storm and she was pressed close enough she could feel the rise and fall of his chest with each breath he took.

"Hey, I can't have you getting sleepy on me. That won't do."

"I'm not sleepy," she admitted honestly. "Just resting." And enjoying the feel of you so close.

"I bet your nose is cold, too, isn't it?"

"My nose?"

"Yes. Let me see if I can warm that for you." He reached over and kissed the tip of her nose.

Cassandra couldn't keep a small smile from forming on her lips. Filling with tenderness toward him, she reached up and softly caressed his cheek.

"And your eyes?" he asked. "Are they cold too?"

As if with a will of their own, her lashes lowered. She felt Dustin's warm breath, his soft lips caress that sensitive skin covering her eyes and she trembled. His lips trailed up and over her brows then gently down to her lashes again. He remained gentle and non-threatening but so very dangerous. She didn't want to stop him.

Cassandra didn't open her eyes and Dustin's assault on her senses didn't stop as his lips brushed softly down her cheek. With gentle fingers he untied the bow beneath her chin and lifted her bonnet off her head and pushed it aside.

His hands dug into the thickness of her hair and pulled the pins free. He draped her hair around her shoulders like a blanket.

"You need your hair down," he whispered as his lips nuzzled the lobe of her ear. "It will help keep you warm if we spread it around your shoulders like this. It's soft, thick, warm as a blanket."

Cassandra was past warm and getting hotter with each kiss, with each touch, with each sentence he spoke. There was something building inside her that made her want to please him as much as he was pleasing her.

Dustin's breath floated across her cheeks as the wind whistled harshly through the canvas. A corner lifted, bringing in a blast of cold air, but Cassandra hardly felt it. She was too attuned to Dustin.

"How are you feeling now?"

"Much warmer. Safe," she said, and reached up and started unbuttoning her velvet traveling jacket. "How about you? Toes cold with your boots off?"

"No. I'd say it's getting downright hot in here."

"It sounds good, doesn't it? The cold wind blowing outside. The wagon gently rocking."

"And you here safe in my arms. This is where you belong, Cassandra. With me is where you've always belonged."

Yes, she admitted to herself, even though she wasn't ready to admit that to Dustin. She had always loved him and now she felt as if she was beginning to trust him again.

He swiftly leaned forward and captured her lips again. His movements were no longer soft and shy. They were confident, commanding. She responded by instinct and parted her lips. His tongue probed her mouth. His hand slipped down and cupped her buttocks. He pressed her flush against his hardness.

The kiss deepened. A breathless fluttering filled her stomach. His mouth and tongue ravaged hers in a slow savoring kiss meant to seduce and be victorious. She felt excitement grow inside him. He was strong and demanding yet he tempered each touch with exquisite tenderness.

She knew his kisses well and the memory of his lips on hers mixed with the difference between then and now. The eagerness of the past was still there, only now she felt an intense desire to take it slow and savor every touch, every breath.

Dustin rolled her over and rose on top of her. She accepted his weight. It filled her with a sweet torturous longing to be completely his once again. Now here they were alone in the world with no one to object, no one to interrupt. It was time to find out if what had drawn them together years ago burned as hotly, as wildly as it had in their youth.

"We're moving into some dangerous territory here,

Cassandra," he said, with his breath hot and ragged on her cheek. "This is where you're supposed to stop me, isn't it?"

Cassandra considered his question for a fleeting moment and it pleased her immensely that he was leaving the decision up to her, but the urge, the desire to be with Dustin was too strong for her to deny. The truth was that this decision had been made a long time ago.

"I remember you told me that first day you were here that it wouldn't hurt me to bend a little."

"No, but I don't want to break you."

Her body softened and relaxed against him. She felt the bulge in his trousers nestled close to her womanhood. Her decision was made.

She sighed and snuggled closer. "You won't."

"You know what it will mean if we continue with this, don't you?"

"Yes," she whispered, and nuzzled the warmth of his neck with her nose and lips. There were no promises for tomorrow or forever this time. It was just the two of them wanting to be together again. She'd tried to deny this truth but she no longer wanted to.

With a new expectancy filling her, she kissed her way up his neck, letting her tongue come out and lave the scratchy skin over his chin and cheek. Tasting him released a sense of freedom she'd never felt before, leaving her with a confident feeling about what was to happen.

"Oh, yes, Cassandra," he said earnestly. "Don't be afraid to kiss me. To touch me."

"And you me. I promise I won't break, Dustin," she answered. "I want you holding me, loving me and making me yours." She slid her hands down to that warm part of him and caressed his abdomen, then let her hands search lower.

"Damn, it's hot in here. We have to get out of some of these clothes," he said huskily.

His lips continued to devour hers with mind-numbing

sensations as he helped her out of her traveling jacket. His fingers deftly worked the buttons at the back of her blouse, then he stripped the clothing from her arms and gently laid her down on the floor of the wagon. He reached into her camisole and lifted her breasts free of the lacy cups that had confined them. He caressed the tips with an open hand.

"I wish it was brighter in here so I could see more of you," he murmured hoarsely as he tenderly caressed her neck and shoulders and skimmed along the rising crest of her breasts.

Her nipples stiffened beneath the ever increasing pressure of his palm. The rotation of his hand sent curls of heat shooting through her abdomen, quivering her muscles beneath his burning touch.

"I might be embarrassed to have you look at me right now," she said, suddenly feeling shy at how wantonly she responded to his touch.

"Never. You are a beautiful woman. I've seen your breasts in the moonlight. They are the perfect size for loving."

Waves of pleasure radiated through her. It was sheer madness that the storm outside mirrored her feelings for Dustin. It was beautiful yet dangerous. It was cold yet comforting. It was fierce yet soft.

"I want to feel your skin on mine. I want to give you my heat and to feel yours. I'm not going to let our time together be cloaked with clothing."

Dustin rose up and shrugged out of his jacket and vest, then flung off his kerchief. Cassandra helped him unfasten the nickel-coated buttons on his shirt, then he tore the sleeves from his arms.

"Don't be frightened of anything I do. I'm not going to hurt you. I'm only going to love you, Cassandra."

"I'm not," she answered truthfully.

"I'm going to completely undress you but don't worry. I won't let you get cold."

166

He worked skillfully within the confines of the small area and quickly had her boots, riding skirt, and camisole off and thrown to the side. He fumbled with the buttons on his trousers but managed to get them and his longjohns pushed down his legs and off his feet.

He bent down over her again and closed his mouth over first one rosy tip of her breasts and then the other, not taking time to favor one over the other as he hungrily tasted her body. Cassandra was caught up in the joy of reviving the intimacy they had experienced that night in the garden. That had been so long ago. She was hungry for Dustin.

She stroked his back and spine, then slid her fingers up to tangle in his hair. Her hand traced the line of his shoulder and down his muscled arm. He trembled and she felt strength and power in his body.

Cassandra gasped and moaned and smiled as one sensation after another shot through her. He molded his hands over the fullness of her breasts as his lips gently sucked her nipples. With one fluid motion his hand slid down her rib cage over her abdomen to her most womanly part. She sucked in her breath at his caress. She quickly relaxed when the slow movement of his fingertips over her created a raging fire inside her. She tried to but she couldn't stop her body from rotating with his motion.

He rose onto her again and covered her. With his body on top of hers Cassandra's hands were free to comb the solid, muscled wall of his hips and buttocks. His body was firm, his skin smooth.

All her senses burst to life when he pressed his hard shaft against the softness between her legs and slowly, deliberately, continuously pressed into her, joining his body to hers. A fire burned inside her. It was frightening, exhilarating.

The jerky movements of his body and his rough breath showed his desperation to make her his as he pushed himself within her. Dustin kissed her lips, her eyes, her ears, and her neck. He whispered her name over and over again.

Her pulse beat so loudly in her temples she couldn't hear the wind anymore. She felt full, excited, complete.

She held herself rigid while he gently rocked against her, giving her time to get used to the fullness, the tightness of their joined bodies. Sensation after sensation quaked through her and even though the pressure built it also gave her a desperate feeling that she had to push harder, deeper, stronger, longer.

His thrusts became fast and sure. She arched to meet him. Grasping, clasping, clinging to him, she accepted his weight as her own. His body bore down on hers as fiercely as the storm that raged outside. The wind whipped the canvas against the wagon and Dustin whipped his chest against her breasts. She rose up to cup his body with her arms as an explosion of sensation burst through her so brightly she squeezed her eyes shut and fell against the plank floor with a loud thud.

A moment later, Dustin's hard jerky motions stopped. His head shot upward, his body stiffened, then he shuddered, falling breathlessly upon her.

He buried his face into the crook of her neck and breathed heavily, hotly on her damp skin.

Cassandra closed her arms around his back and held him to her, afraid he would disappear if she let go. She felt a deep rich sense of fulfillment. How could she give him up after what they had just shared? But how could she not? There were no commitments between them. Just man and woman enjoying each other.

"God, I can't believe how good that felt. Did I hurt you?"

"No." She shook her head and reluctantly removed her arms from around him. "I'm fine, but I think I scratched your chest."

"Don't worry about it if you did. Everything I felt was wonderful."

"For me, too."

He rose up and looked at her. "You mean that?"

"Of course I do."

"Loving you again was everything I knew it would be, Cassandra. You are a very passionate woman."

"I felt like I was going to burst out of my skin."

Dustin chuckled. "It does kind of feel that way, doesn't it? Are you cold?"

"No."

Dustin placed his fingertips against her cheek. "I think we need to talk seriously about the future."

"No," she said earnestly as that old fear of losing him gripped her, threatening to spoil what was happening between them. She understood there were no promises. Just tonight. "I don't want to talk about anything serious. The storm is still raging."

"All right, lady, tell me what you want me to do first."

"Start with a kiss."

He bent his head and gave her a soft brief kiss.

"No," she said. "Like this." She pressed her lips to his and gave him a hard, demanding, passionate kiss full of tongue swiping deep into his mouth.

"Oh, God yes, that's a kiss," he managed to murmur.

"No more talk."

"You always were bossy."

Cassandra smiled. "Telling people what to do is what I do best."

Chapter

·13·

A hand smashed against Dustin's face. His eyes flew open. A flat palm smacked his cheek. He bolted up and knocked his head against the canvas. Cassandra thrashed beside him.

"No," she muttered in her sleep. "It's dark. It's too dark. I can't breathe."

"Cassandra." He called her name and tried to catch her flailing arms. She whacked him beside the head again before he could catch her hand.

"I can't breathe!"

"Cassandra, wake up," he said louder, and gently shook her shoulders. "Open your eyes."

"It's dark. I can't see!" She struggled to get away from him.

"Cassandra, it's Dustin. Wake up. You're here with me. You're safe."

She jerked, stopped, and gasped a heavy breath that sounded loud in the silence around him.

"Are you all right?" he asked.

She calmed but she didn't answer him. All he heard was her heavy breathing. He realized then it was quiet outside. He didn't hear the wind. The storm was over. Shafts of moonlight found entrance into their hideout and faintly lit the wagon.

He had to find out what bothered her sleep. Dustin touched Cassandra's cheek with his fingertips. "You were dreaming."

"Dream? No, I couldn't breathe." She pushed her hair away from her face. "It's a recurring nightmare, not a dream."

"Like the one you had the other night?"

She nodded.

He rose and propped on one elbow beside her. "Tell me about it."

She hesitated. Her bright gaze moved away from his face. "It's always the same."

The air was cold. She'd flung the cover off them. Dustin reached down and pulled the coat up to cover her bare shoulders and snuggled her down on his arm again. Her body trembled but he didn't know if it was from the nightmare or the cold.

"Go on. I want to know and it might help you to talk about it."

"No. There's nothing to tell. It's not as if I'm afraid of someone or something."

He touched her cheek. "I'd never accuse you of being afraid of anything. You accept challenges and handle your life better than most men I know."

His words were a glowing compliment. The nightmares always made her feel weak and fragile. "It's always dark. It's as if something is pressing against my face and chest and I can't catch my breath. I've had the same dream for as long as I can remember."

Compassion filled him. He heard the frustration in her voice and saw the confusion in her features, but he couldn't let the subject drop. He had to know. She *needed* to know what plagued her and caused her to cry out in the dead of night.

He pondered. "Did you ever fall in water as a child

171

and almost drown? That would account for the feeling of darkness and not being able to breathe."

"No, I'm sure I would remember that, or someone would have told me about it."

"When did you start having the dreams?" He kept his voice soft and soothing. His fingers gently caressed her cheek and down her neck to the hollow of her throat.

"I know I've been having them since I came to live here in Wyoming with my grandfather."

"What did Thomas have to say about them? You told him, didn't you?"

"I mentioned it to him once and he told me I would get over them. I never talked about it again. I didn't want him to think I was a weak, weepy little girl, so I never told him they didn't go away."

He laid a gentle hand on her waist to reassure her. "He didn't try to explain what might have caused them?"

"He said I was adjusting to having lost my parents, the trauma of the trip out to Wyoming, my stepfather and—" She stopped.

"And what?"

She shook her head. "Too many things, too many deaths. It's not something I want to remember. It's not something I want to talk about."

"That might be the problem, Cassandra. When I knew you in Kansas City I never took the time to talk to you about your life. I was such a selfish bastard. We never discussed what happened to your family and what brought you to Wyoming, did we?"

"No. There was no reason to. It's not a happy subject. I wish I could forget what I do know."

Dustin realized just how little he knew, but how much he wanted to know about this woman who had captured his heart for the second time. He wondered how Thomas could have so easily dismissed a child's bad dreams. Had her grandfather just expected her to shake off all the fears she'd lived with since her mother's death?

"That won't make what happened disappear, will it?"

172

"No, but I wouldn't ever have to remember those things again."

"Maybe if you remembered it all we'd find out why you have the nightmares and how to stop them."

"There's so much, too much I don't recall from when I was a little girl."

She shivered again and Dustin took hold of her trembling hand. "Take your time and think. When is the first time you remember waking up because you couldn't breathe?"

At first he thought she was going to remain unresponsive to his probing questions, but as his eyes adjusted to the darkness and he could see her more clearly he saw that she struggled to remember.

"I—I think I was still in Kansas City. Yes. I remember standing in the middle of the bed. It was dark. Quiet except for my whimpering."

"Were you alone?"

"No. Juliana was standing in front of me holding a brass candlestick. Papa Ward lay on the floor by my bed bleeding."

"Juliana was your governess, right?"

Her face softened more and she smiled. "Yes."

A husky, faraway quality edged her voice. He didn't want her to have to relive any of this, but he knew the bad dreams wouldn't go away until she knew what caused them. He had to pressure her to talk.

"What had happened, Cassandra? Why was your stepfather bleeding? Did your governess hit him with the candlestick?"

"Yes. Juliana said Papa Ward had tried to hurt me and she had stopped him. I remember she took me in her arms and we left the house that night. I never went back to Kansas City until the summer I met you."

"Ward murdered your mother and blamed another man. I know he tried to kill you, too, when you were in Wyoming at your grandfather's, but Ward was shot, right?"

She tensed in his arms. He hated making her describe this tragic experience but a theory was forming in his mind. He had an idea where the blame should be placed.

Her breathing was labored but she managed a husky, "Yes."

Dustin rubbed his hand up and down her arm, soothing her with his touch. He was eager to offer her more than comfort but that wasn't what she needed right now. She needed to talk about her past.

"Did Juliana ever tell you what Ward was doing when he tried to hurt you?"

"Not that I remember now, but I must have asked. She must have told me. How many times do I have to tell you I don't want to remember?"

"He killed your mother in bed, didn't he?"

She pushed out of his arms and tried to rise. "Dustin, stop, I don't want to talk about this anymore. I wish I hadn't told you any of it."

"Don't get up." He held her down. "I'm sorry. I said that rather callously. I didn't mean to. I know it's upsetting for you to talk about this, but I want to help. I need to understand."

"Why would I want to remember something horrible? These dreams, or whatever they are, are just a stupid feeling that overcomes me sometimes. I live with it. It's not a problem, all right?"

Her softly spoken command was filled with an earnestness he couldn't deny. He would stop with the questions. For now. But he was determined they would revisit this subject again and again until the dreams were gone.

"Yeah, you're right. It's not a problem," he lied. "Come back into my arms. I'm cold without you."

He reached over and kissed her gently as if they had all the time in the world. Dustin wanted her to know he loved her. He desired her. She responded to his tenderness and settled down beside him again.

With love filling his heart he snuggled her close in his arms and kissed her more passionately, leisurely stroking the length of her silky back and hip. Heat rose up in him.

Finally, he raised his head and cupped her chin with his palm. "You know, I don't want anyone or anything making you lose your breath but me," he said against her lips.

"Right now, neither do—"

Dustin cut off her words with a deep passionate kiss that silenced her and heated his blood. He ran his hand down her outer thigh, then over to the downy thatch of soft curly hair between her legs.

"I hope you didn't think the night was over," he murmured against her lips.

"No," she whispered into his mouth. "I thought it was just beginning."

The air was clean and frosty as Dustin peeled back the canvas top and ventured a look outside. Fading moonlight shimmered on the white snow. A blanket of white stretched as far as he could see, covering the land, the trees, and the buttes. The fierce storm that had blown in so quickly had left nothing out of place. The landscape around the wagon was picture perfect. This land Cassandra called home was beautiful, beckoning.

A peacefulness settled over Dustin. He knew he didn't want to be a lawyer in Kansas City anymore. He wanted to marry Cassandra and live out here in the land that was called the Wild West.

Dustin threw his clothes on the driver's seat, then carefully climbed from beneath the makeshift covering so he wouldn't disturb Cassandra's sleep.

The temperature had risen to a bearable degree, but cold air nipped at his naked buttocks and the snow froze his bare feet as he hurried to step into his longjohns and trousers. He shivered as he donned his shirt and leather vest. He knocked snow from the driver's seat and sat down to put on his socks.

He smiled with contentment. Cassandra was like no

other woman he had ever touched. She was bossy but he liked that about her. She was determined and forthright. He liked those qualities, too.

Before they'd made love he'd asked her if she knew what their night together would mean and she said she'd understood. A feeling of victory washed over him. At last Cassandra was his, and this time he didn't intend to ever let her go.

Dustin knelt down on the floor by the seat. He brushed the light flaky snow away from the area and felt below the driver's seat. He smiled as his hand hit what he was looking for. There, safely tucked in the corner, was the package he'd stowed away before they left town. He couldn't believe the wind hadn't caught it and blown it away.

He crawled back into the wagon and down under his greatcoat with Cassandra. He watched how the faint moonlight sparkled off her hair and gave her white skin a golden glow. Her face was that of an angel in perfect peace.

He kissed her. Her eyes fluttered and opened. Dustin smiled at her. "I hate to disturb you, but the moonlight on the snow is so beautiful. I know it will be gone in a few minutes and I don't want you to miss seeing it."

She rubbed her eyes and sat up. She searched for her blouse. "Here, just put your jacket on for now. You can get dressed later."

He helped her slip her arms into her traveling jacket and fasten several of the buttons. He wasn't so sure he wouldn't make love to her before the sun rose high above the horizon. Already he wanted her again.

Dustin tucked the edges of his overcoat around her waist. "Keep this tight. I don't want your backside to get cold," he said.

"I'm afraid you are the one who's going to get sick without your coat on."

"My jacket is thick wool. Besides, the temperature is rising fast. The sky is clearing. I have a feeling all this snow will melt quickly when the sun comes up today."

She looked around as she brushed her long hair from around her face and rubbed sleep from her eyes. "It is beautiful. I've seen it like this many times, but I guess it's not easy for you to see the land in such repose where you live."

"Kansas City has its own beauty, but no, not like this. There are too many people, too many lights, too much activity around the town. I have to admit, Cassandra, that I'm drawn to this land of yours."

Her eyes searched his face and he didn't want to be found lacking the strength to stand beside her.

"Even with the hard work and dangers?"

He nodded. "Fear and danger can be around any corner. The city is full of it, but I admit I was worried when you pulled your gun on me the day I arrived."

A pensive smile eased across her lips. "I wanted to hurt you."

"I know. You were so angry and so confident I was intimidated."

She snapped her head around and looked at him. "You're lying. No one could intimidate you."

There was a heartiness to his throaty chuckle. "Yeah. You're right. Here, I have something for you."

"What is it?"

"You'll see. Open it. It's for you."

"I don't understand." She took the package.

"You will."

Cassandra untied the brown cord and opened the paper to reveal a beautiful black shawl with a six-inch fringe hanging from the edge. Excitement danced in her face as she gently handled the garment. An exquisite bottle of perfume lay nestled in the folds. She picked it up and took it to her nose. She breathed deeply.

She looked at him and smiled. "This smells wonderful and the bottle is so beautiful." She held it up to see it better. The oils in the amber colored perfume shimmered like iridescent bubbles in the moonlight. "I'm—I don't know what to say. Thank you."

"I'm glad you approve."

"Of course I do." She touched the knitted garment with care. "Dustin, this is so lovely, so expensive." She held it up where she could get a good look at it, then crushed it to her chest. "Oh, you shouldn't have bought these things for me."

He liked the way her eyes shined with surprise, with happiness. If she only knew how happy she'd made him last night, she'd know the way she felt about the shawl didn't compare to how glad she'd made him.

"Why not? I'll put the perfume in my pocket to keep it safe. Go ahead and put the shawl on." He helped her put it around her shoulders.

"It's so warm."

"That's what I was hoping. I remembered the one you wore to the bunkhouse that night didn't really keep you warm. This one should."

"You shouldn't have, but thank you."

"I have another package here that I was going to give to Olive, but under the circumstances I don't think she'll mind if we open it."

She shook her head. "Oh, no. If you bought it for her—" Cassandra stopped when he opened the paper and she saw the neat stack of tea cakes the size of a wide-mouth-jar lid. "I don't believe this."

"Hungry?"

"Yes."

"I bought a dozen from the man at the general store. Olive won't have to know if we eat half of them." He lifted an eyebrow. "Will she?"

"No. She'll never know you bought twelve."

"I thought you'd approve."

He gave her the first sweet cake and she bit into it. "Mmm. I'm so hungry I won't waste a crumb."

Dustin was hungry too, but he also wanted to get things settled between him and Cassandra before the sun came up and they had to start walking toward the ranch.

178

CASSANDRA

As far as Dustin was concerned he was ready to marry Cassandra before he went back to Kansas City.

He managed to eat one bite before he said, "I think it's time we talked, Cassandra. I don't want the past standing between us any longer. For me it doesn't. I want to make sure it doesn't for you either."

Cassandra looked up at him and wiped a crumb away from the corner of her mouth with the tip of her fingers. "As far as I'm concerned nothing has changed between us. Not the past and not the future."

Chapter

· 14 ·

"**W**hat are you saying, nothing's changed?" He tried to keep the desperation he suddenly felt out of his voice. "Everything has. We just spent the night together loving each other and I took that as a commitment to our future together."

"There was no kind of commitment discussed between us," she said with a defensive crispness to her voice.

Dustin coughed and cleared his throat. Dawn had edged its way up the dark sky and transformed twilight into daybreak. He had no trouble seeing Cassandra's clear, bright eyes. Her skin was golden, satiny. Her hair tangled attractively around her face and shoulders. She was dead serious about what she said and that scared the hell out of him.

He laid the sweet biscuit aside, having lost all taste for food. He couldn't remember ever being so satisfied after having been with a woman. She had to have experienced what he had.

He knew how to hold his temper in check and remain

unemotional, but this time, Cassandra's statement caught him completely off guard.

"The hell there wasn't," he answered, fear causing anger to get the best of him. "Last night when I asked you if you knew what it meant for us to make love you said you did. What happened?"

"Nothing. It meant there were no promises between us. I understood and accepted it. That's the way I wanted it."

Dustin tensed. She was saying all the wrong things. Any other woman who'd just spent the night with a man would be begging him to marry her. But not Cassandra. She had her own way of handling everything. He could live with her for fifty years and he was certain she would continue to find ways to surprise the devil out of him.

"It was a damn lot more than that, Cassandra," he said in an exasperated voice. "It was also a commitment for you to marry me."

She lowered her lashes over her eyes and looked down at the sweet bread in her hand. "No. Not for me it wasn't."

Her words wounded him. But Dustin wouldn't give up. He was determined not to let Cassandra know she'd just turned his world upside down. He loved and wanted to marry her. All he had to do was find a way back into her heart now that he was back in her life.

He hoped to remain calm on the outside but his stomach had started quaking. It was difficult to act cavalier when he was talking about his feelings for Cassandra. "So what are you saying? What happened between us meant nothing to you?"

"No, of course not," she argued in a soft voice that only added to his frustration.

"Good, because I'd really find that difficult to believe considering how you responded to me."

She broke off a piece of the tea cake and popped it in her mouth. After she swallowed, she looked back up at him and said, "I'm not going to lie to you, Dustin. Being in your arms, sharing this intimate time with you is something I've wanted to happen." She squeezed her eyes shut for only a moment, then opened them and continued. "At seventeen I wasn't prepared to have you make love to me then leave me. This time I know what's coming and I accept it."

The cold light of day chilled him. He saw his kerchief lying beside Cassandra. He grabbed it and pulled it around his neck, tying it so that it rode above his shirt like a cravat.

Cassandra knew how to make him feel like the bastard he was. "You think I'm going to leave you."

"Being with you again was everything I remembered. I'm not sorry we did it, but I don't expect it to happen again."

He hadn't disappointed her. Thank God for that, but he wanted more from her than a one-night poke. She deserved his name. His voice softened. "Was it enough?" he asked her.

She pierced him with a questioning expression. He thought he saw her stiffen. His insides jumped again. A raw thread of tension sprang between them.

"Enough? What do you mean?"

"Making love to me once. Was once enough for you and now you don't want me again? Because, I'm telling you, Cassandra, last night wasn't nearly enough for me. I still want you." He tried to keep his voice from rising. He tried to stay emotionless but his control failed him and for once he didn't care.

"I want the Triple R," she said curtly and turned away from his gaze and started wrapping the tea cakes. "It's all I have left and I won't lose it."

He resented her last remark. "How can you say it's all you have left when I'm telling you I want to marry you? Now, before I go back to Kansas City."

"We've already been over this."

She tried to act unconcerned as she folded the brown paper but she wasn't. He saw her hands tremble when she brushed the cake crumbs from her fingers.

Dustin was having a hard time with her behavior. He never in his wildest dreams expected her to be the one acting carefree about this. "Let's go over it again because I thought last night settled a lot of things."

"No. I'm not going to marry you, Dustin."

He shoved one foot into a boot. Her voice was so soft he worried that she might have believed what she said. Dustin drew in his breath as he put on his other boot. Anger at her, at himself, shot through him.

Cassandra started searching the wagon for her clothing, pulling each piece to her as she found it.

That was Cassandra. No gray, just black or white. No maybe, just yes or no. No middle, just left or right.

With his boots on Dustin relaxed his frantic movements and looked at Cassandra. His heavy-lidded gaze wandered over her face. She was beautiful, with her round chestnut-colored eyes, pert nose, and little rosebud mouth. Her cheeks were chapped but whether it was from the wind or his stubble of beard he didn't know. Her long hair hung around her shoulders so that it almost covered the new shawl he'd given her.

The tables had turned. Now Dustin was the one who felt jilted.

"I'm going to change your mind," he said more confidently than he felt.

She stopped her search for a moment and met his unwavering eyes. "My answer is firm."

He tensed as a thought struck him. "You're not thinking about marrying Webster, are you?"

"You know I've thought about it." She dropped her clothing in her lap.

Her answer didn't reassure him. "You can't marry him now. Not with the way you responded to me."

She folded her hands in her lap and sighed. "I haven't

had time to think that far ahead, Dustin. It's barely daybreak. So many things have happened the past few days I haven't given anything much thought."

"I made mistakes, Cassandra. I should have handled some things differently. I should have come for you sooner, but now that I've found you, now that I've loved you again, I'm not going to lose you."

"You have no choice. I've made my decision."

"I can't believe you don't think what we just shared is worth marrying for."

She started to speak, then stopped. He took that as a good sign that he was getting through to her.

"It's more than this desire we have to come together as a man and woman, Dustin. Your life is in Kansas City as surely as Landon's life is in Cheyenne."

Her words brought him up short. That was the hell of it. His life wasn't in Kansas. He knew that, but he wasn't sure Cassandra was ready to hear that he belonged in her life—wherever that might be.

"Marry me, Cassandra."

"No." She took off her shawl and started unbuttoning her traveling jacket. "Marriage isn't in the cards for me, Dustin. Everyone I have ever loved has left me. The Triple R is all I want and all I need."

"You're wrong and I'm going to prove it to you. You need me."

"No, you are wrong. You see, Dustin, I know that I'm strong enough to live without you. I made it through before when you left and I will this time, too," she said passionately.

"You don't have to. Marry me."

"I can't marry a man I don't trust, Dustin."

He reeled from the cruel sting of her words but managed to keep a straight face. How could he argue with her? So far he hadn't done anything to earn her trust again.

"I'm no longer foolish enough to believe everything is going to turn out like a fairy tale."

"You're usually right about things, Cassandra. That's one of the things I admire about you, but it's also one of the most annoying. Every now and then, though, you're wrong. This is one of those times. Whether or not you're ready to admit it again, you need me. You want me. You love me. I'm going back to Kansas City and get your money released and take care of some business, then I'm coming back for you."

"There's no need to come back."

She hesitated before she spoke. That was a good sign. Maybe his persistence was getting through. His confidence soared. His attitude changed to one of teasing. "I wouldn't stay away if you begged me."

"You bastard," she answered, matching his lighter tone. "I wouldn't beg you for water if my dress was on fire."

"Oh, yes you would. When I come back, I'm going to come courting. I'm in your life to stay, Cassandra, but I guess time is the only thing that will prove that to you."

When she didn't say anything else he asked, "Do you want me to help you dress?"

"No, I'd rather have a few minutes to myself if you don't mind."

"All right. I'll take a walk and give you some privacy." He waited a moment for her to look at him, and when she didn't, he jumped down from the wagon and trudged through the newly fallen snow.

God, he loved that woman. He wanted to always make her happy as he had last night, but he couldn't even get her to agree that she'd like him to return to Wyoming and court her.

He couldn't force her to forgive him for jilting her, but he couldn't let her go, either, Dustin thought as he walked. If he wanted her to soften and trust him again he had to be gentle and easy with her. She'd been through a lot in her lifetime. He'd hurt her more than he would have thought possible. Now he had to go slow and show by his presence that he was in her life to stay.

As soon as they made it back to the ranch, Dustin wanted to get his things together. He was eager to catch the train back to Kansas City and have Cassandra's money sent to her. Once she knew the Triple R was safe maybe she'd be willing to give him a chance.

Dustin planned to turn all his cases over to another attorney. There wasn't a one that he felt he needed to see to completion himself. One thing he was sure of was that his life was no longer in Kansas City.

He also intended to find out everything he could about Cassandra's past. He'd search the court records and old newspapers to find out all he could about her parents' deaths, her stepfather, and her flight to Wyoming. He'd also question his father. Since the firm was left in control of Cassandra's money, Gordon should know some details.

He also decided to try to contact Cassandra's former governess. Juliana probably knew more about Cassandra's past than anyone. Yes, that would be a good place to start.

The sun lifted above the horizon, spraying the white snow with a brilliance that hurt his eyes but immediately warmed him as he continued to walk and think. He was beginning to believe there was more in Cassandra's past than she knew or wanted to know. But Dustin wanted to know.

As soon as he had his practice settled, he was coming back to Wyoming to win Cassandra's hand for the second time. He was going to make it right between them. She might not know it yet, but she'd figure it out when he came back to Wyoming and started courting her like a gentleman.

A few minutes later Dustin strode back to the wagon. Cassandra was folding the blanket they had slept on. He knew she would pull herself together once he'd left her alone. She was too strong not to.

She'd dressed and made herself more than presentable. With her hair pinned at her nape in a chignon and her bonnet properly secured on her head once again, no one would ever know she had spent a passionate night in the wagon with him. That's the way he wanted it. It pleased him that she wore the shawl he'd given her.

There was an early-morning chill to the air but the skies had cleared and the sun had come out. It wouldn't be long before the heat melted the four or five inches of snow that had collected on the ground during the storm.

"Do you have any idea how far we are from the ranch?" he asked, more to start the conversation than with any real concern about the length of their journey.

He watched her gaze take in the landscape around them, and he wanted to pull her into his arms so desperately his muscles ached. Last night was only the beginning of rebuilding their trust, their love for each other. They'd been apart for five years. It was going to take time to heal, but he was willing to bide his time and wait for Cassandra to admit she loved him.

"It's at least half an hour's ride. It's hard to say how long it will take us walking."

"Are you sure you feel up to the trek? You didn't get much sleep."

Her eyes met his, then feathered down his face. Dustin's stomach contracted with longing. This wasn't how he wanted the morning to begin.

"I'm fine. The sooner we get home, the quicker we can get back for the supplies before poachers or Indians raid the wagon."

Dustin reached into the wagon, picked up his hat, then settled it on his head. "I'm ready."

"There's something I want to say before we start."

"All right."

She took a deep breath and looked him in the eyes. "I know we talked about a lot of things since we've been stuck out here. I want to make sure you know that the only thing that is important to me is that I get the money I need to save and rebuild the Triple R."

A resigned chuckle with a slightly hard edge floated up

from his chest. "There's no misunderstanding between us on that account. That has been clear to me since the first day I arrived."

She lifted her chin. "Good."

"However—" He waited for her to look into his eyes again before he said, "There are things I want to know the answer to and I intend to find them when I'm in Kansas City."

"What kind of things?" she asked warily, searching his face again.

"I'll tell you when I get back."

She scoffed, letting him know she didn't believe he'd be coming back.

"All right. Then let's wa—" She stopped and pointed behind him. "Riders."

Dustin turned and looked behind him. "One rider, several horses."

"Yes. Look. I think it's Jojo. He's bringing our horses. The mare must have made it back to the barn." A smile spread across Cassandra's face. She started waving to him. He signaled her the same way.

"I guess that long trek home we were expecting won't happen now," Dustin said.

"You almost sound disappointed," she said, turning to him.

Dustin smiled. She'd recovered from their earlier conversation. He liked that. "I can't say I minded having you to myself."

A frown crossed her brow. "Dustin, I don't want you to say anything to—"

"Cassandra, you don't have to worry. I don't kiss and tell."

"You all right, Miss Cass?" Jojo asked as he stopped his horse in front of them.

"Yes. We're fine and so glad to see you," Cassandra said. She walked over to her horse and patted her nose and neck.

"I'm sure glad to find you two safe," Jojo said. He

threw his leg over the saddle and jumped down. "I was more'n a mite worried when the mare arrived at the barn first thing this morning pulling the harness. When you didn't make it back yesterday afternoon I assumed you stayed in town to wait out the storm."

"It wasn't storming when we left town," Dustin told him. "Just flurries."

"Is everything fine at the house?"

"Nothing going on there. How's Red Sky?"

"The doctor says he's not out of danger yet but it's looking more likely that he'll make it."

"Glad to hear it. I'll hitch my horse to the wagon and bring these supplies on in."

"We had some trouble with the wheel," Dustin said. "It might need some work before it'll roll."

"I'll take care of it if you two want to ride on to the ranch."

"I'll take you up on that, Jojo," Cassandra said. "I want to get home."

Dustin wanted to talk to Jojo so he turned to Cassandra and said, "You go ahead. I'll stay here and help Jojo with the wagon." He smiled at her. "If you don't ride too fast, I'll catch up with you in a few minutes."

"I plan on riding like the wind," she said and took her reins from Jojo. "I need to clear my head."

"Not with this much snow on the ground," Dustin remarked. "Promise me you'll ride sensibly or I'm going with you now."

She gave him a fake smile. "My words were figurative."

"In that case, I'll help you mount."

"Help Jojo. I'm doing fine on my own."

When Cassandra rode away Dustin joined Jojo at the wheel. He knelt in front of the hub. "We didn't have so much as a wobble when we rode into town."

"That's a long ride for nothing to show up. Could be the snow had the bolts freezing up. I'll take care of it."

Dustin nodded. "I'm going to be leaving by late

afternoon. I need to catch the first train back east in the morning."

"Been nice knowing you," Jojo said and stuck out his hand. "I won't forget what you did for us."

Dustin shook his hand, knowing Jojo was referring to Rodney. "Red Sky's not going to be back for a while. I'd like to hire a couple of more men to stay around the Triple R just to keep watch. I know Cassandra's worried about rustlers. Do you think you can find some out-of-work cowboys for me?"

"Sure I can." Jojo's mustache twitched. "But what is Miss Cass going to say about that? I work for her, not you."

Jojo was loyal. Dustin liked that. "She and I have already reached an agreement that I'm going to advance her the money to pay the back wages she owes. I'll give her enough money to hire three more men. See what you can do about getting some of them to come back today. I want to make sure nothing happens to Cassandra while I'm gone."

"Mr. Bennett is a fine, fine man. Never had anyone give me tea cakes before. Never have," Olive said to Cassandra for the third or fourth time. "He would sure be a nice man to have around here all the time."

"Then I suggest you marry him. That should keep him around," Cassandra said, finishing the last bite of her pancakes and sugar syrup. She didn't want to think about Dustin or talk about him but Olive hadn't stopped since he'd walked in and handed her those little cakes.

"Me! Good gracious. You know I'm old enough to be his grandmother. I was thinking about you getting a husband, not me."

Cassandra picked up her coffee and sipped. It was hot and strong, just the way she liked it. "I don't need one, and I don't need gifts."

"Well, that's a mighty fine shawl and sweet smelling

perfume he gave you. What kind of woman wouldn't like nice presents?"

"Me. I shouldn't have accepted them." But how could she not? His giving the gifts to her had touched her all the way to the core of her being. Her grandfather had never forgotten her birthday and there were always small gifts on Christmas Day, but no matter what she said to Olive, Dustin's gift of the shawl and perfume would always be very special.

"Hush that kind of talk now. There's nothing wrong with a fine gentleman like Mr. Bennett buying you that nice warm shawl."

Cassandra drained her cup and set it on the table. "I'm going to the barn to find the seeds we stored last winter."

"You thinking about putting in a garden when snow's on the ground?"

"It'll be gone tomorrow." And for reasons she didn't want to explore too deeply she felt like planting flowers.

Cassandra walked out on the back porch and closed the door behind her. She stopped and looked out onto the white landscape. The house had a magnificent view of timbered hills and the mountains in the distance. Often in the spring and summer she would see pronghorn or mule deer feeding and drinking at the creek. Occasionally a fox or timber wolf would get brave enough to hang around the ranch.

Snow outlined the barren tree limbs, sprinkled the bushes, and covered the ground. She smiled when she thought of Dustin awakening her just so she could see how beautiful the moonlight played on snow. She had always loved the winter, with its frigid air and skies that were so gray and low they hung like a warm blanket over the earth. She loved the way the land looked clean and innocent after a winter storm. And now, every time it snowed she would think of Dustin.

She leaned against the porch post. She closed her eyes to the beauty around her and Dustin's face came to mind. No, she didn't want to think about him. Ever. But as she thought that a soft smile tweaked her lips.

How could she not think of Dustin and the storm? When they had lain together she had felt they belonged together. How could she have told him she didn't need him? Because she didn't want to trust him and open herself for that intense hurt again. If she never loved again she wouldn't lose again.

She had doubts that Dustin meant it when he said he would return. She expected him to get back to his life in Kansas City and forget all about her. But what if he did come back? A tiny bit of her heart thrilled to the idea of Dustin riding up to the front porch and sweeping her off her feet.

"You wouldn't be doing anything fanciful like day-dreaming, would you?"

Her eyes popped open. She cringed at Dustin's voice as he walked around to face her. He would have to catch her daydreaming—and about him.

"I was trying to remember where I put some seed," she fibbed without guilt.

He gave her a knowing smile. "We didn't get much sleep, did we?"

Cassandra's heart lurched as she realized that Dustin was wearing the same clothes that he had worn when he arrived at the Triple R. He didn't have to say a word. She knew he was leaving. Again. She didn't know why it felt like a knife in her stomach. She knew he was going back to Kansas City, she wanted him to, so why did it feel as if he were ripping her heart from her chest?

"—because of everything that happened," he said.

She had no idea what he'd said. She moistened her dry lips. She realized her hands were shaking. She had to get control of herself.

After clearing her throat, she said, "I guess you ended up staying a few days longer than you planned."

"I'm not in a hurry to leave, but I know you need your

money, and I have some things to take care of in Kansas City."

He was so handsome in his starched white shirt, string tie, and black jacket. His blue eyes seemed to sparkle against the crispness of his shirt. "Yes, I guess you have clients and business waiting for you."

Dustin nodded. "I've left an envelope with Olive for you. There's enough money in it to pay all your ranch hands their back wages just like we talked about—and to pay the new ones I hired until I get back."

"Fine—" She shook her head as his words soaked through her addled mind. "No, wait. What did you say about hiring extra men?"

"Jojo said he knew which cowboys were out of work. He's gone after them now. He'll be back by dark with three more men."

Startled, she stared at him a moment. This news should have outraged her.

He's taking over your life.

Someone needs to.

No, you can take care of yourself.

It's nice to have him to lean on.

He'll think you're weak.

"I can't believe you hired men for this ranch without talking to me first. Just because I spent the night with you doesn't mean you can take charge of my life."

Dustin remained calm. "I'm not taking charge. I'm helping. There's a difference. With Red Sky gone you and Jojo need help."

"I can take care of myself," she spouted in a curt tone.

A pang of doubt that he'd return hit her and she knew it showed in her face.

Dustin looked deeply into her eyes. "I'm coming back, Cassandra. I want to make sure you're here waiting for me when I do."

Inside she felt a trickle of warmth that Dustin cared enough to worry about her, but she refused to let herself get sucked into his promises. She'd been hurt too many times by people who said they wouldn't leave her.

"I left instructions that the men are to start rebuilding the bunkhouse in their spare time."

"Dustin, I object to—"

"Overruled." He smiled.

"I don't have the money yet for the lumber or the—"

"You will have. Don't worry, you will have."

He was so damn appealing with his smile and handsome good looks. If he didn't leave soon she was going to do something crazy like throw her arms around him and kiss him.

"Just go, Dustin," she whispered earnestly.

Dustin settled his hat down on his head. "I'll be back."

Chapter

· 15 ·

The starched collar and tight cravat choked Dustin as he walked down the handsomely panelled hallway that led to his father's office. His boots made no sound on the carpeted floor. The two-story building of the law firm of Bennett, Lucas, and Farrell was located in the busy section of Kansas City known as Banker's Row.

Dustin was glad to be back only because he knew this was his farewell to the city, to the firm, and to his father. The next time he left he would be free of any responsibilities to the law firm.

Once he'd made the decision, he felt good about it and knew he was doing the right thing.

The train ride to Kansas had seemed to take forever. It was ridiculous, he knew, but at times Dustin felt he would have made better time by horse. At least he wouldn't have been stopping in every little whistle-stop on the plains.

Dim corridors and small rooms had the usual smells of cigar and pipe tobacco, burned wood, and lemon oil. Occasionally he'd pass by an open doorway and catch the scent of a spicy cologne or woodsy musk.

His father's office door was open. Dustin stopped just outside. Gordon sat behind his expensive, dark mahogany desk with the newspaper in front of his face, completely concealing everything but his hands. A cup of coffee sat nearby and a cigar burned in the jade ashtray a client had brought him from the Orient. Nothing had changed inside this building, but everything had changed inside Dustin.

Dustin raised his hand and rapped on the door with his knuckles.

"Come in," Gordon said, but didn't bother to lower the paper.

He knocked again. The paper fell down in a rustle of sound. The chair legs scraped on the wood floor.

"Dustin, you're back." The tall, broad-shouldered man rose with a big smile on his face. "When did you get home? Last night, or are you just in?"

"Late yesterday," Dustin said, entering the cold, formal room. Gordon walked from around his desk. They shook hands. There had never been more affection than that between the two of them.

"Sit down and fill me in. Do you want coffee?"

Gordon sat on the edge of his desk and crossed his feet at the ankles. He was in excellent health and fine form for a man approaching the age of fifty.

"No. I'm fine."

"You've been gone much longer than I expected. Tell me, did you spend all this time on that ranch with Cass Rakefield or did you take some unexpected detours along the way?"

"No unscheduled stops." Dustin took a seat in the leather wingback.

"Interesting." Gordon folded his arms across his chest and managed to look relaxed. "I want to hear all about that ranch and about our dear Cass. How is she?"

She's beautiful, wonderful, loving, incredible. She's worried about the ranch, sad about losing her grandfather, doubtful I'll return.

But Dustin couldn't say any of those things to his father. "She's all right."

"All right? What does that mean? That tells me absolutely nothing. What shape is the ranch in?"

"If you're asking me if she needs the advance she's asked for the answer is yes. Everything we read in the papers was true. That whole cattle industry has been devastated by the harsh winter and late spring."

"But twenty-five thousand dollars sounds excessive, surely? That's a lot of money for a twenty-two-year-old woman to be in charge of."

"She's more than capable of managing the funds. Her grandfather taught her well."

"Sounds like she can manage you, too. It certainly didn't take her long to get you on her side, did it?"

Dustin hated it when his father was critical. "She's worth millions and she's never touched a penny of it to buy so much as a new hat. I'd say she's entitled to as much of it as she wants."

"I see." His father snapped to his feet and walked around his desk and took his chair. "She is most certainly entitled to what she needs, but that's as far as I'll go to agreeing to that."

Dustin knew he wasn't going to be reasonable when it came to Cassandra. It didn't matter if she needed it. If she wanted it that was enough for him.

"I assume Cass is well and that she hasn't suffered from the illness that took her grandfather, but you haven't told me what kept you so long at her ranch."

He had no doubt that his father was interested in how it went between him and Cassandra. Gordon had always wanted them to marry, but not because it would make Dustin happy. It had always been for the money and prestige of handling the Rakefield fortune.

"One of the things that kept me so long was that I had to help Cassandra with an incident involving poachers."

"Cassandra? Good heavens, I didn't think anyone called her by that name."

Only me. "She's grown into her name. It suits her now."

"Mmm," Gordon continued, pressing a finger to his chin in a thoughtful manner. "Poachers? Nothing too serious, I hope. I've heard they can be a damn nuisance on open rangeland."

He didn't want to have to tell his father about shooting Rodney. That wasn't the kind of thing a man talked about to anyone. It had to be done. The sheriff had accepted what happened with few questions. It was over. No reason to go into details his father really didn't want to hear.

"Nothing that can't be cleared up in time."

"Good. And how's she doing without her grandfather? I remember she was extremely fond of him."

She's courageous.

"His death was hard on her," Dustin admitted, "but she has everything under control."

"Did you find her figures about cattle, land, and equipment to be correct?"

"Absolutely. I'm going to write up a full report. I'll have it on your desk in a day or two."

"Good. It can't be easy for a young woman to manage a ranch that size."

"She's capable," Dustin defended. "I see no reason why the firm shouldn't wire her the money she's asking for immediately."

"Well, of course we'll go by the rules governing the trust, Dustin." He picked up the paper and started folding it. "And how did it go between the two of you? Any problems there?"

She was angry at first but she softened. "No. She was surprised to see me, but she soon realized I only wanted to help her."

"I thought as much. I've wanted you to go see her for a long time. Well, since you won't answer any of my diplomatic questions, I'll be blunt. You were gone longer than I expected you to be. You said you didn't make any other stops. Is your romance with her on the mend? Are wedding plans in the future?"

Not yet, but there will be. Dustin wasn't ready to tell his father that. Not here in his office and not until Dustin was ready to leave Kansas City for good.

"I don't have anything to say about my personal relationship with Cassandra."

"Then why did you come into my office? You do like to try my patience, Dustin. I'm telling you now if you don't marry Cass someone else will. You're running out of time."

The muscles in Dustin's neck were taut with frustration and ached to relax. He knew Gordon would get around to marriage. He always did.

"I don't want to get into this with you."

"How well I know." He smacked his paper down on his desk and asked, "Will you come for dinner tonight?"

Dustin rose. He knew when he was being dismissed and for once it didn't bother him. He was happy to leave. "I don't think so. I'll be working late on my report, and I have a lot of other things to do concerning work."

"Yes, I'm sure you need to catch up. Later in the week then, perhaps?"

"Definitely. There are some things I want to discuss with you at length."

"And what would those be about?"

"Cassandra's parents, her stepfather, in general I want to talk about her past."

Gordon's eyes narrowed only slightly. Dustin could have sworn this surprised Gordon.

"I don't know what I can tell you that you don't already know."

"Maybe nothing," Dustin said.

"Why didn't you question her?"

"I did, but she was so young she remembers very little about her parents."

"I can't imagine why you'd be interested in her past. It's her future that you should be concerned about. And the future of this firm, I might add. We can't afford to lose the Rakefield estate."

"Oh, I assure you I'm concerned about Cassandra's future. I have to get busy on that report."

Dustin left his father's office and walked down the hallway and around the corner to his own office, which overlooked the back street. He looked around the panelled room with the dark green draperies and masculine furniture.

No, he didn't want to be here. He didn't want to work in these clothes, in this office, in this city anymore. He wanted to check fences, brand cattle, and ride horses on the range. He wanted to wear banded collar shirts and leather vests, not cravats and fancy waistcoats. He wanted to pursue poachers and help Cassandra rebuild the Triple R. Most of all he wanted to make love to her again. He wanted sweet kisses in the moonlight and he wanted to marry her.

A faraway feeling swept over Dustin. He remembered back in time to being in the garden with Cassandra. She'd said that she wanted their first time together to be under the moon and stars. Now he understood why. An intense longing filled him.

Dustin had to find a way to make Cassandra see that he was all she needed. He had to prove to her that he'd changed and that she could count on him for anything she needed.

An uneasy feeling crawled over Dustin. His only worry was Webster. Now that the banker knew what Cassandra was worth Dustin suspected he wasn't going to go away peacefully. The man worried Dustin.

Dustin wasn't going to feel comfortable until he finished what he had to do in Kansas City and made his way back to Wyoming and Cassandra.

* * *

Cassandra stood on the front porch staring down the lane that led up to the house. She knew she had to stop coming outside and watching as if she expected Dustin to come riding up the road. He'd only been gone a week. Hardly enough time to even get to Kansas City and back again.

Yet, she found herself coming outside to look down the road. She wished he'd never told her he was coming back. Too many times she'd found herself wanting that to be true. She didn't like spending her time thinking about him. She hated the thought of turning into a lovesick woman pining after a man.

But she missed Dustin.

Contrary to what she'd told Dustin, she believed he would see to it that she got the money she'd asked for. Although she had good reason not to, she trusted him to do that for her.

She couldn't believe how lonely the house seemed without Dustin around. She couldn't believe how he'd filled the house, how much she'd enjoyed having him with her. She missed their banter, his chuckle, his smile. His carefree outlook on life. There was something to be said for how easily he took things, how he seldom let things rile him, and how he never lost his temper with her.

Yes, she missed him and she hated that she did. If only she could put him out of her mind. She squeezed her eyes shut for a moment and when she opened them her breath caught in her chest. A rider was coming up the lane. Her heart started thudding crazily. Her hand held a death grip on the porch post as she strained to identify the person on the horse.

Slowly she exhaled and relaxed her shoulders. A stab of disappointment sliced through her. It was Landon.

"Damn you, Dustin Bennett, for making me care about you, for making me care whether or not you come back," she whispered passionately.

It didn't surprise her that the rider was Landon. He'd

been coming every Saturday for three months now. She should have remembered. She wasn't looking forward to seeing him. She expected that he'd want to stay for dinner since he was coming so late in the day. If Olive remembered that it was Saturday she hadn't mentioned it to Cassandra.

A big smile split Landon's face as he dismounted and threw his reins over the hitching rail. "I can't tell you how good it makes me feel to see you on the porch waiting for me. How are you, my sweet?"

Cassandra pushed her disappointment aside and smiled at Landon. "I'm all right, and you?"

"Couldn't be better if it was a hot day in January," he said, walking up the steps to join her on the porch. He took off his hat and stood in front of her. "I stopped by to check on your ranch hand before I left and I have some good news for you."

Expectation filled her. "Is he ready to come home?"

"By the first of the week."

"That's wonderful. I've been so hopeful."

Landon moistened his lips. "It was a long ride out here and—ah—"

"Oh, I'm sorry. Of course it was. Please come inside. I'll have Olive prepare you a cup of that tea you like."

While Landon settled himself in the parlor, Cassandra talked to Olive about the tea and dinner. A meal was the least she could do for him since he had made the trip out to the Triple R.

"Now," she said, taking a seat opposite Landon on the brocade covered settee. "Tell me what else the doctor had to say."

"Not much. You should be prepared to come get him in two or three days, but don't expect him to be ready to work for several more weeks."

She nodded. "Thank you for checking on him for me."

He beamed at her praise, but his smile quickly ebbed as he said, "I do want to keep you happy, Cass. Nothing is more important to me than you."

His words made her uncomfortable. "Landon, I wish you wouldn't say things like that."

"That's right. You don't need pressure from me. I'm sure you got enough of it from your house guest. I guess you heard about the words I had with him?"

She frowned. "You mean Dustin?"

"Yes. I hear he's finally left town, and good riddance, I say."

Perplexed, Cassandra shifted on the sofa. "He left a week ago. What are you talking about, having words with him?"

"It was the day of the snow storm. He was in town on your wagon, although I didn't see you."

"That was the day I saw Red Sky and we told the sheriff what happened to Rodney."

"Well, while you were busy I ran into Bennett at the general store and he went out of his way to make me jealous of him. Didn't he tell you?"

"Well, he told me he saw you but not what was said," she answered, having a difficult time believing Dustin was really worried about Landon, even though she hadn't actually admitted to Dustin that she wasn't going to marry the banker.

"I'm not surprised he never mentioned it to you. I'm sure he wouldn't want to be seen in a bad light in your eyes. No need to go into the details of his rude behavior. It seems my little talk with him worked. He's gone, you're alone once again, and I'm glad."

Cassandra decided not to tell Landon that she was certain Dustin's leaving had nothing to do with him. Landon wouldn't believe her anyway. "Tell me what happened between you two. Did you have a fight?"

He took a deep breath and sniffed. "Not quite, but Bennett managed to ruin my brand new suit. I let him know I wasn't happy he was buying those personal items for you. I knew he couldn't win your hand with fancy perfume. I set him straight about us, and he now knows that you and I will be married one day."

Cassandra drew back. "Landon, how could you say that? I've not agreed to marry you."

"Only because I haven't insisted you give me a final decision. I understand that a woman needs time to make up her mind and I intend to give you that time."

"Landon, I'm not going to let you go on thinking I might marry you. I'm not."

"Are you planning on marrying anyone else?"

"No."

"Then there's no reason to give me an answer until I ask for it. Now with that settled, I have other news for you."

She stiffened. An uneasy feeling settled over her. She didn't like Landon's attitude. Something about him was different. "What news?"

"Well, I know that you are not just a rancher who has some money available to her. You are a wealthy heiress." His words sounded like a glowing compliment. He reached over and placed his hand on top of hers. "Why didn't you confide in me sooner about this?"

Cassandra pulled her hand away. "I don't consider it anybody's business but mine."

Landon ignored her as if she hadn't rebuffed him. "It's no wonder you wouldn't agree to sell the ranch. You could easily pay a foreman to manage it for you. You could buy a brand new carriage with velvet cushions and ride back and forth to check on it if you wanted to. My word! You could buy the whole town of Cheyenne."

"The money has never been important to me. It doesn't matter how much there is."

"It's been my experience, Cass, that the only time money doesn't matter is when people have more of it than they know what to do with. Didn't you know that if you'd told me about the money you have at your disposal there would have been no question about the bank where I work lending you the money for your mortgage? But you don't have to worry about any of that now. I had the money so I paid it for you this morning."

Cassandra jumped up. "Landon! You paid off my mortgage? You had no right to do that."

"Why? You had been asking for loans all over town. I thought you'd be happy. Cass, you are an heiress. We're going to be married. It was the natural thing for me to do."

His innocent act only made her madder. "No, it was the wrong thing to do and I want you to go get your money back."

Cassandra felt as if she were beginning to lose control over her own life. She rubbed the back of her neck. It didn't do any good to get angry.

"Cass, I was only trying to help."

"Well, you didn't. You made a mess. Now fix it and get your money back. I wish everyone would stop trying to help me."

"Excuse me, Miss Cass."

Cassandra pivoted toward the doorway. "Yes, Olive," Cassandra said, welcoming the housekeeper's interruption.

"I have Mr. Webster's tea."

"Thank you. Set it down on the table and I'll let you pour it for him."

Olive placed the tray on a small table, then walked over to Cassandra. "Jojo just got back from town. He brought good news. We can bring Red Sky home next week."

"Yes, that is good news. Landon just hold me."

"Jojo brought this telegram, too. It was the only mail you had."

Cassandra's pulse increased rapidly. Why did every little thing remind her of Dustin? She silently chided herself for thinking it might be from Dustin. "Thank you, Olive." She turned to Landon and said, "I'm sorry I don't feel up to dinner tonight, Landon."

"Are you sure? I can—"

"I'm sure, but enjoy your tea before you go."

"Of course, I understand," he said tightly. "I'll check with you in a few days."

The paper seemed to burn in Cassandra's hand. She couldn't get to her office fast enough. She shut the door behind her and quickly ripped open the envelope. She took a steadying breath, then looked down at the writing.

> My dear Cass:
> Dustin's recommendations received and reviewed. The firm has deposited the total sum of three thousand dollars into your bank in Cheyenne. With all good wishes,
>
> Gordon.

Cassandra gasped as the paper fluttered soundlessly to the floor. Dustin had duped her again.

Chapter

· *16* ·

Cassandra waited her turn to disembark from the passenger locomotive. It was the first time she'd ridden a train but it wasn't an unpleasant experience. In fact, she found that the train was much easier on the body than a horse or wagon. She'd been able to sleep without too much difficulty on the long journey, and she had chatted several times with an older lady who was traveling farther east. Cassandra wouldn't have minded the train ride at all if she'd been coming to Kansas City for a different reason.

On the trip, she'd tried not to think of Dustin and what he'd done. She tried not to think about the night they had spent together during the storm, but that was impossible. She would always remember his touch, his taste, and all that they had shared. What bothered her the most was that she'd believed him when he told her he'd see that she received her money. She trusted him to do what was right. Why hadn't she been able to see through his charm? He hadn't kept his word five years ago. What had made her foolish enough to believe he had changed?

Cassandra lifted the hem of her heavy cotton skirt and

stepped off the train onto the wide plank platform, having no idea where she was except that she was in the city of her birth. She'd lived here for six years, and she had visited here for three months five years ago, yet there was no familiar feel to the place as she looked around.

The reason she had never wanted to come back to Kansas City was because she had never wanted to see Dustin again. He had circumvented that by showing up at her ranch. Now she had no fear of this town.

Mid-afternoon sunshine fell across her face. A tepid breeze stirred the air and fluttered loose strands of her hair across her eyes. Already she could tell that the temperature was much higher than in Wyoming. Spring had definitely come to Kansas. She stuffed wayward curls of hair under her dark brown bonnet and moved away from the train steps.

Her satchel was heavy, even though she traveled light, packing only one other change of clothes and her night rail in a large buckled case she'd kept with her on the train. All along the journey she had watched women board and disembark with as many as three and four trunks. But Cassandra didn't plan to be in town any longer than it took her to get the money she needed.

She looked around and saw a number of people milling about the depot. Some laughed and talked while others received joyous hugs and kisses of greeting. A pang of loneliness struck her and she wondered whether, if she'd telegraphed Dustin's father of her arrival, he would have come and met her. But it was too late to think of that now. She'd been so angry with Dustin she hadn't thought clearly for days.

The first thing she needed to do was find a hotel and get settled. Once she'd done that she could make her way over to the law offices. It was getting late in the day but she didn't want to wait until morning to see Dustin's father. She didn't need another night to sleep on what she had to do.

"Excuse me there, Mum?" a lad of about thirteen said

to Cassandra. He reached up and yanked his gray felt hat off his head and smiled at her. "Ay're ye waiting for someone ta pick ye up or will ye be needing a ride ta'day?"

Cassandra looked at the lanky, well-groomed young man with the Irish accent. "Well, I'm not waiting for anyone, but I'm not sure I need a ride. I don't have any trunks. I expected to walk."

"What would ye want ta be doing that for? That baggage you 'ave there in your 'and looks ta 'eavy for ye ta carry ta me, Mum. Where will ye be a'eading? I 'ave my wagon over there." He pointed behind him. "And my fare is the cheapest in town. I'll be glad ta take ye wherever it is ye want ta go."

Cassandra warmed to his friendly smile and pleasing accent immediately. His clothes were old but clean and his dark auburn hair looked presentable.

"All right, maybe you can help me. I need to go to the hotel."

"Which one will ye be a'wanting?" He jabbed his hat back on his head and took her satchel from her hand. He started heading toward his wagon.

"Ah—well, maybe you could suggest one that doesn't cost a lot of money."

"'Ow about the Silver Spoon Boarding 'ouse? Ye get two meals a day with the room. And the mum who runs it is a friendly sort. It's not in the center of town, which makes it more affordable ta your pocket."

Cassandra was feeling better already. "That's sounds like the kind of place I'm looking for. Tell me, do you know where the law offices of Bennett, Lucas, and Farrell are located?"

"Not right off the top of my 'ead, but if ye got the address, not to worry, I can find it."

"Good. I'd like you to take me to the boarding house and then to the lawyers."

He stopped and turned toward her. "I'll 'ave to charge you extra for that, Mum," he said.

209

"I understand," she answered and allowed him to help her onto the wagon. "What's your name?"

"Patrick. Named after my saintly uncle who was always giving some poor soul a 'elping 'and."

Cassandra laughed and it felt good to release some of the tension she'd been feeling since she'd received that damning telegram. "All right, Patrick, let's go."

Cassandra had no idea Kansas City was such a big place. Her knowledge of the area had been limited when she'd been here before. She thought Cheyenne had become a big place but its size was nothing compared to this area. Patrick had taken left and right turns down short streets with three- and four-story buildings. They passed fancy carriages pulled by expensive horseflesh and old wagons pulled by nags. She saw properly dressed men and women strolling along the boardwalks and ragamuffins darting across the road in front of them. This city was a busy place.

Patrick found the law offices without any problem and stopped in front of a two-story brown building. She asked him to wait for her while she made her call.

Her stomach fluttered and she held tightly to the reticule hanging from her wrist as she climbed the steps. She noticed that the names of the lawyers were written on the glass door as she entered the building.

A short, husky young man with wire-rimmed glasses perched on the bridge of his nose rose from his desk and greeted her. "May I help you?" he asked in an overly proper-sounding voice that did nothing to make her feel welcome.

Cassandra took a deep breath, trying to calm the jittery feeling making her stomach twist. "Yes, I'm here to see Mr. Bennett."

He laced his fingers together and rested them on his round girth. "Which Mr. Bennett? There are two who work here. Senior and Junior."

"Yes, how could I have forgotten? Senior," she answered quickly, knowing she didn't want to see Dustin at all. "Mr. Gordon Bennett."

He stepped back to his desk and looked down at a book in front of him, flipping one page back and forth a couple of times. He looked up at her over the top of his spectacles and asked, "Do you have an appointment with Mr. Bennett, Miss—"

"No—no. But I'm sure if you tell him Cassandra Rakefield is here, he'll see me," she said with more confidence than she was feeling.

The young man's mouth formed an O for a moment. "Of course, Miss Rakefield. I recognize your name as one of our clients. Have a seat, please. I'll go tell Mr. Bennett that you are here."

Cassandra watched the young man walk away. She didn't want to sit. She'd had enough of that on the train. What she needed was to move around and work off some of the tension building inside her. She took several deep breaths and tried to prepare herself for her meeting with Dustin's father. She remembered him as a polite, well-spoken man who seemed eager to have her a part of the family. Now she knew it was only because of her money.

She was nervous just being in the offices. She didn't want to see Dustin again. She didn't want to hear his excuses.

"Cass, my dear sweet girl. What an unexpected surprise. How are you?"

Pivoting on one foot, Cassandra turned and faced Gordon Bennett. He looked just the way she remembered him, an older, fuller, more sophisticated version of his handsome son.

Gordon took her hand in his and looked her up and down. "My word," he murmured softly, then smiled at her. "You are more beautiful than you were five years ago. That son of mine should have married you when he had the chance."

Cassandra ignored his compliments and his reference to Dustin. She knew his true feelings now. He had never been interested in her or her happiness. Always it was her money. The only thing she wanted to do was get to the business at hand and be done with this man forever.

"Mr. Bennett, I'm glad you could see me on short notice. I wasn't sure you would be available."

"What nonsense. Even if I were visiting with the governor, I'd make time for you. But, if Dustin had told me you were coming to town, I wouldn't have been so surprised."

Cassandra pulled her gloved hand free of his. "He didn't know. Besides, I didn't come to see him. I came here to see you."

His eyebrows flew up in a questioning expression. "Oh, well, I hope nothing is wrong and this visit is no more than a social call. Come into my office and let's talk." He lightly touched her arm. "Would you like refreshment? Tea or water perhaps?"

"No, thank you. I'm fine," she said, following him down the wide, dimly lit hallway. They passed several open doors and Cassandra cringed each time, fearing Dustin might pop out of one of them.

"Dustin isn't in just now," Gordon said as if he could read her mind. "He left more than an hour ago to run an errand. As late in the day as it is, I doubt if he'll be back to the offices today. No matter, we'll see him later tonight. He's coming for dinner."

She heard his reference to both of them seeing Dustin tonight. She didn't want to tell Gordon that his son was the last person she wanted to see.

Cassandra walked into Gordon's office. It was heavy with the smell of pipe and cigar smoke. Hot coals glowed in the fireplace, giving the room a warm cozy feel.

"Sit down and tell me what brought you all this way. Not that I'm unhappy to see you, but naturally I'm a bit confused if Dustin doesn't know you're here. I've not been able to get much information from Dustin about you since his return from your ranch. I hope nothing is seriously wrong."

CASSANDRA

A stab of pain quickened Cassandra's heartbeat as she seated herself in the wingback chair. Just as she suspected. Dustin had lied to her about what he planned to do for her. She had been a fool to trust him to tell his father everything about the ranch.

"Well, I'd like to get right to the point, if I may."

"By all means, dear." He rested his hip on the edge of his desk. The silver that lightly peppered his hair gave him a distinguished look. She could imagine Dustin looking as sophisticated twenty years from now.

"I came here to plead my own case since Dustin did such a poor job of doing it for me," she said, unable to keep her feelings in check.

Gordon's eyebrows shot up again. "Dustin do a bad job? I don't know what you mean."

Cassandra lifted her shoulders. It was clear Gordon Bennett didn't want her saying anything unflattering about his son. "I asked for twenty-five thousand dollars. I only received three." She didn't mind the bitterness that showed in her voice. She'd rather he hear that than the hurt she was feeling over Dustin's betrayal again. "Yes, I consider that a very poor showing of a man's work."

"Well, even though Dustin's work needs no defending I feel I must. To his credit he did recommend we give you the full amount."

It was her turn to be shocked. "He did?"

"Oh yes. He was quite adamant about it." Gordon folded his arms across his chest in a relaxed manner. "But, frankly, Cass dear, we couldn't see where you needed that much money to be responsible for, so we gave you enough to cover your yearly mortgage."

Cassandra clasped her hands in her lap for a moment and tried to think. Dustin had tried to help her. But why didn't he telegraph her and tell her what to expect from the firm?

"I need that money," she announced emphatically.

"Yes, we went over that. Dustin explained everything in a detailed report."

If Dustin told them the predicament she was in, what had happened? She was trying hard not to get angry but she was losing the battle. She lifted her shoulders defiantly. "Then what is the problem?"

"There isn't one as far as I can see."

She was beginning to feel he was being deliberately obtuse and that angered her all the more. "I need the rest of the money I asked for. The problem is that I didn't get it and that's why I'm sitting here right now."

"We gave you what we considered a fair amount for your needs. After your—stepfather—was no longer in charge of your trust, the executive committee decided no large sums of money would be paid out of it."

Dustin hadn't told her the will stated that. "Why?"

"Well, let's just say that he wasn't judicious in his spending habits. We, of course, have no way of knowing what your mother's intentions were, but my guess is she wouldn't want your fortune wasted."

"Waste my fortune? I'm not a simpleton," she remarked, her irritation increasing. "This is the first time it's been used in over fifteen years. I'd hardly consider that wasting it." She didn't try to control the anger in her voice.

Gordon shrugged his shoulders and spread his hands out palms up. "I didn't make the rules, Cass. I only ensure they are kept."

"Just tell me what I have to do to get more money."

"You are always free to apply for extra funds. The committee will weigh each request separately."

"Fine. Consider that I've requested another twenty thousand and write the damn check."

"It doesn't work that way. We have to be careful what we allow you to spend it on. We'll be happy to approve a thousand here and there, but we simply don't feel you are capable of managing a large sum like twenty thousand."

Cassandra leaned forward in her chair. "If I can manage a spread the size of the Triple R, I'm capable of managing a few thousand dollars!"

"Your request is noted. I'll speak to the committee."

It bothered her that she was furious and he remained quiet, softspoken, and unruffled. It must have taken him years to perfect that demeanor. Angry demands would not work with this man. She had to find a different angle and that was going to take some time to figure out.

"I think I understand where you are coming from now and I know what I have to do."

"Good." He smiled. "I'm sure your mother would be pleased with us. We have invested your money wisely and made you a very wealthy woman."

"Yes," she answered tightly, "but what good does it do me if I'm not allowed to spend any of it on things that are important to me."

"That's what you have us for, dear. To take care of it for you." He stood up straight. "Now, where are your bags? I expect you to stay with me."

Cassandra rose. "No thank you. I've already booked a room."

"That's nonsense. I want you to stay with me. Tell me where your things are and I'll send my driver after them. As I said, Dustin is coming to dinner tonight and I know he'll want to see you."

"I'm staying at a boarding house."

"I won't hear of it."

"My mind's made up." She turned to go.

"Then I insist on knowing where you're staying."

"If you must, it's the Silver Spoon."

"Hmmm. Never heard of it. Must be new. I can't keep up with everyone who has rooms to rent in the city anymore. There was a time when I knew every merchant in town. Not anymore."

Cassandra felt stiff and out of sorts as she walked to the doorway. She didn't want to be in the same room with this man one minute longer.

"Now, that's one thing I won't take no for," Gordon was saying as he followed her out.

"I'm sorry, what was that you said?"

"The cattlemen's club is having a special spring dance Saturday night. I want you to be my guest."

"I might not be in town and even if I am, I didn't bring clothes for a dance."

"That's one of the nice things about a big city. You can buy your clothes already made and just have the finishing work done. I insist. You can't come all this way and leave before sampling a few things the city has to offer. I'll have Dustin talk to you about it and about getting you out of that boarding house and in my home where you belong."

Cassandra rushed her goodbye and walked out of his office. Right now Dustin was the last person she wanted to see, even though she had to admit she was feeling a little better about him. Maybe he had really tried to help her. Maybe he could help her even more—if she could bring herself to make him an offer of marriage.

She turned and headed out of the office where Patrick was waiting to drive her back to the boarding house.

It wasn't time for dinner and it wasn't dark, so Cassandra decided to take a walk and think. She was sore from so much sitting. The day was warmer than any they'd had back home. She enjoyed being out in the tepid air.

With her reticule hanging from her wrist, she took off at a leisurely pace down the boardwalk. Occasionally she would meet someone and nod her head as a greeting. As she walked, her mind kept going back to one thought. If she were married, her husband would have control over the money, not Gordon Bennett and the law firm. And that always brought her back to the thought of whom she should marry. Dustin or Landon?

Both men had good and bad points. But after much thought she came to the conclusion that her first impulse was right. She couldn't deny the fire of desire that burned inside her for Dustin.

She wasn't sure she could trust either of them to give her the money she needed for the ranch without some written agreement. Mr. Bennett had said that Dustin asked that they approve her advance, but she didn't know how hard he had argued her case. He knew how badly she needed the money. She was sure of that.

Cassandra stepped down and realized she'd run out of boardwalk. She looked up and noticed it was dusk and she'd strayed into a different area of town. She'd been so deep in thought that she hadn't noticed that she'd walked so far. There were no buildings in front of her. She was supposed to know better.

She had no idea where she was, but she didn't remember making any turns. If she walked straight back the way she had come she would no doubt end up at the boarding house.

She turned and stepped back onto the boardwalk. Her gaze darted around the area. Garbage and trash littered the streets and the buildings looked run down and empty. Doors hung half off their hinges and window panes were broken or missing altogether. How could she have not noticed she was straying into the wrong side of town?

She picked up her pace, walking much faster than when she'd started. In the distance she saw two men huddled together on one corner. Their talking was loud and their laughter raucous. Smoke drifted up from between them. Her hand slid over to her hip. "Damn," she muttered. If she had been in Wyoming she'd have her pistol with her.

Cassandra felt uneasy, but tried to talk herself out of being frightened. She could handle herself. Her grandfather had taught her how to throw a few punches in case she ever got into a fight, but he'd always warned her that the best thing to do was avoid one. She knew what to do. Walk fast, look straight ahead, and don't take offense if the men made ribald comments as she passed. The main thing she shouldn't do was show fear.

Her hands made fists as she brought her arms up to rest at her waist. She was furious with herself for getting in this position. As she drew nearer, from the corner of her eye she saw one of the men throw down a cigarette and they started across the street toward her.

Night seemed to have fallen all at once. It was dark. She felt that familiar pressing on her chest, the lack of air to breathe. Chills popped out on her body. No, she wouldn't allow that fear to overcome her. She had to remain in control and get herself out of this.

She thought about running but knew that would do no good. They were ahead of her, and there was no help behind her. Suddenly the two men rushed up, flanking her. They each grabbed one of her arms, lifted her feet off the boardwalk, and started carrying her backward.

"What are you doing? Put me down. Stop!" Cassandra struggled to free her arms. She kicked but only managed to tangle her legs in her petticoats and skirt.

"Settle down, honey. We ain't gonna hurt you," one of the men said.

The other man laughed. "Yeah. We're gonna love you. Lovin' don't hurt none."

Terrified, Cassandra looked behind her and saw they were forcing her down an alley that looked like a labyrinth of darkness. Knowing she was no match for two strong men she screamed as loud as she could.

She was slammed against the wall so hard it took her breath and rattled her senses. Fear held her rigid as she tried to regain her breath.

"Shut your damn mouth," one man said, as his big hand slapped over her lips. His meaty fingers dug harshly into her cheeks.

The men held her off the ground and against the wall. She kicked and bucked trying to free herself.

"Don't worry," the other man said. "I'm gonna fill that mouth so full she can't scream."

Cassandra was frantic. Screaming wasn't going to help. Her grandfather's words rushed to her mind. If a man gets you down kick like a hornet-stung mule right between the legs.

She brought up her knee and sank it hard into the man's crotch.

He groaned and bent double. His hold on her weakened and she jerked her arm free and landed a closed fist up against the other man's cheek.

He grunted. A hand smacked her across the face, knocking her head against the wall and sending sparkles of light flying in front of her eyes.

"Damn, bitch!"

Suddenly she was lifted and thrown to the ground. She tried to scream but it sounded more like a weak moan. Her arms were pulled up and over her head. One of the men fell on top of her. His foul breath fanned her face. She bucked against his weight.

The man laughed. "I got something big and hard waiting for you, sweet lips. Keep her quiet until I get my pecker out and have me a go at her. I'll hold her for you when I get through."

Hands pulled and groped at her skirts, pushing them up her legs. Cassandra struggled to clear her head and break loose so she could fight.

Fear and determination spurred Cassandra to action. She refused to be bested by these two dirty men. Now that her legs were free of the heavy petticoats and skirt she could kick harder and that's what she intended to do.

A hand closed around her mouth again and she bit down hard. The man yelped like a whipped dog. A fist landed in Cassandra's rib cage, but she ignored the pain. With all the strength she could muster she brought her foot up and kicked the man soundly in the crotch. He howled and fell moaning against the wall.

One to go, she thought.

Dustin's heart thudded wildly. Cassandra was in danger. Madness gripped him. He heard another scream. She was close. With a shaky hand he pulled his derringer from his jacket pocket and palmed it, ready to shoot. His feet pounding the boardwalk, he ran frantically.

He flew past an alley before he knew he was upon it. Skidding to a stop, he wheeled around and rushed back to the opening. It was so dark he could hardly see down the narrow passageway. He stopped and listened, but all he could hear was his own heart slamming against his chest. He took a deep breath, forcing his heart rate to slow down so he could hear any sound.

The stench of garbage filled his nose and the taste of fear coated his mouth. He started to turn away when he heard a muffled groaning. His chest tightened. He took a couple more quiet steps down the narrow passageway, then held his breath and listened again. Rage overtook him when he heard something like a prolonged moan. He inched closer and caught the sounds of struggling and labored breathing.

His first thought was to rush forward shooting at

whoever touched Cassandra, but fear for her safety held him in check. He knew the sane thing to do was to go slowly and find out what he was up against. His derringer was a double shot pistol but there could be more than one or two men.

Prickles of awareness coated his skin. Sweat trickled down his neck as his eyes adjusted to the darkness. In the distance he saw the outline of something white on the ground and knew it had to be Cassandra. He crept forward with his pistol pointed to kill. The dark shape of two men came into view.

Suddenly one of them flew back against the wall, holding his groin and groaning. Dustin smiled.

"The other one's mine," he muttered and rushed forward.

Dustin cracked the handle of his gun against the temple of the man crawling on top of Cassandra. He grunted and slumped to the side with a moan and a dull thud.

Cassandra was already scrambling to rise from the ground. Dustin reached down and grabbed her hand and helped her up.

"Dustin, thank God you found me," she whispered huskily.

He longed to hold and comfort her but knew they were in danger. Not wanting to wait around to see if either of the men was out cold he said, "We'll talk later. Let's get out of here now."

Dustin took off running, pulling Cassandra behind him. He knew she was tired and weak from fighting, but he wanted to get her safely away from her attackers.

They cleared the alley with no sound of either of the men chasing them, but Dustin didn't slow down. He kept running, holding on to Cassandra with one hand and clasping his derringer in the other. He didn't let them stop until they passed under the third street lamp and could see people walking along the boardwalks.

Catching his breath, Dustin looked behind them.

There wasn't any sign of the men following them. He put his pistol away, then they continued to walk fast. Close to the boarding house where Cassandra was staying Dustin saw a bench in front of a general store so he ushered her over to it so they could sit down.

Finally feeling they were safe, he turned his attention to her to see how badly she was hurt. Cassandra held her left side with both hands. Her chest heaved as she gasped for air. Her blouse was torn at the shoulder and her hair had been torn from underneath her bonnet. With the backs of his fingers he brushed her tangled locks away from her face and lifted her chin so he could look at her.

She lifted her lashes and her dark gaze met his. Her eyes were luminous with unshed tears. "Thank you for your help," she whispered. "I don't know what I would have done if you hadn't—"

"Shh. You know you were doing a good job of taking care of yourself."

Her tone and expression were filled with gratitude Dustin didn't feel he deserved. He had managed to rescue her but not before she'd been hurt. Dustin's stomach wrenched as he looked at her face. Her upper lip was swollen and the skin was broken in the corner of her mouth. A red welt showed underneath one eye. The damn bastards had struck her more than once.

He caressed her cheek with the tips of his fingers as his gaze searched out every detail of her face. "Did they—"

"No," she answered quickly, not allowing him to ask his intended question. "I was hit a couple of times. That's all."

He noticed that her swollen upper lip barely moved when she spoke and he wanted to slam his fists into the faces of those men. He reached into his pocket and pulled out his handkerchief. Softly he touched the cut on the side of her mouth. She winced but didn't pull away from him.

His chest swelled with pride that she'd put up a good fight, but he wanted to admonish her for not being cautious. Dustin desperately wanted to hold her and show her how much he loved her.

He couldn't keep the emotion out of his voice when he said, "I was so damn scared when I heard you scream."

She exhaled a ragged breath. "So was I," she admitted. "How did you find me?"

Dustin heard footsteps and looked up. His hand automatically went to his pocket. A man and woman walked by chatting quietly with each other. After they passed, he relaxed again.

"Gordon told me you had shown up at our office this afternoon. Thank God he had the foresight to ask where you were staying. The owner of the boarding house told me the direction she'd seen you walking."

He trembled when he thought that he could have been too late to save her from those men. He couldn't think about the possibility that the men could have easily raped her, then killed her before he arrived.

"I think I'm safer in the high country facing grizzly bears than I am on the streets of this city," she said, touching a trembling finger to the corner of her injured mouth.

"You just wandered onto the wrong street."

"The late afternoon was warm and beautiful, I was stiff from the train ride, and I had so much to think about that I lost track of time and where I was going."

"What are you doing getting a room in this section of town? What are you doing in Kansas City? Why didn't you let me know you were coming to—" Dustin stopped. "No, don't answer any of those questions right now. You're coming home with me, then we can talk."

"Dustin, I've already paid for my lodging and—"

"To hell with that. My father let you get away with that argument but I'm not going to." He rose and took hold of her hand. "You're coming with me—over my shoulder or walking beside me. It's your decision."

* * *

The hot wash in the claw-footed tub had felt so good Cassandra stayed in until the water was winter cold. Even though she was sore in several places where she'd been struck, she'd scrubbed with sweet-smelling soap until she no longer felt those men's hands groping and clutching at her body. She then dunked her head under the water and washed until she felt thoroughly clean.

She'd felt welcome inside Dustin's house the moment she entered. It wasn't large, but in it she'd felt safe and much too comfortable to admit to anyone. It had made her feel good when he'd said, "You're coming home with me."

After one look at the very modern bathing room Dustin had built into his house, with its inside, flushable commode and the fancy tub installed with running water connected to it, she knew she wanted to look into having one of the newfangled things put in at the Triple R.

When her fingers started wrinkling and her wet hair lay cold against her skin, Cassandra stepped out of the tub and quickly dried herself. She took her clothing out of her satchel and saw Miss Watkins lying on the bottom. She smiled and left the doll where it was. She didn't know why she'd brought it, but she wouldn't have felt right leaving it. This town was once Miss Watkins's home, too.

Cassandra dressed in the only other suit of clothing she'd brought with her. She'd have to wash and mend the clothes she'd taken off before she could wear them again.

The bedroom Dustin had given her was small but beautiful, with gold embossed wallpaper decorating the walls. Gaslights mounted on the walls gave a soft, romantic light to the room. Dustin had made a fire in the fireplace that made her room warm and toasty.

The draperies that hung from the two windows flanking the bed were made out of a rich-looking eggplant-colored velvet. Thrown over the bed was a matching velvet coverlet that had been piled high with pillows in colors of butternut, bisque, and summer wheat.

After she had finished dressing she sat down at the

dresser to dry and pin up her hair. On top of the dresser lay an ivory-handled woman's comb and brush set and a pretty perfume bottle decorated with dried flowers and a ribbon fashioned into a bow. She was reminded of the beautiful perfume bottle Dustin had given her, and she smiled.

As she slowly looked around the room she couldn't help noticing how this room had been prepared for a woman. Dustin didn't know she was coming to town so it had to have been made ready for someone else. Only a man with a mistress would have such a room.

A pang of jealousy stabbed through Cassandra's heart. She squeezed her eyes shut and shook her head. She had to remind herself that what Dustin did and who he did it for was of no concern to her.

Cassandra had lain with him that night in Wyoming because she knew she would always love him, not because she was looking for any kind of commitment. When Dustin had first shown up at her door, she thought fate was being cruel. But now she was glad he'd come back into her life for a short time and given her such wonderful memories.

Dustin was a handsome, healthy, eligible young man. There was no way he would have spent the last five years without being with a woman.

A knock on the door startled her. Her eyes popped open and she looked around and said, "Come in."

Slowly the door opened and Dustin walked in carrying a tray. She rose from the cushioned bench.

"What are you doing dressed?" Dustin asked. "I expected to find you in your nightclothes in bed resting."

"And I expected to come downstairs when I finished my hair. I'm not a weakling that faints at the first sign of trouble."

"No, you're not," he agreed. "But you need to rest, and I need to take care of you." He set the tray on the dresser in front of her. "I don't know my way around a kitchen too well. My housekeeper didn't prepare anything tonight so I put together what I could find. Sit back down."

She looked at the tray and couldn't help smiling. On a plate lay two pieces of bread, a square of cheese, a small dish of apple butter, and a cup of milk. She looked up at him and smiled. "Thank you for going to so much trouble."

"It wasn't." His gaze flitted softly down her face.

"I know you're expected at your father's for dinner. I don't want to keep you any longer."

"That's not a problem. I cancelled that when I learned you were in town."

"You shouldn't have."

"I wanted to. The redness under your eye is going away and the swelling in your lip is going down. Your injuries could have been so much worse."

She nodded. "The pain's almost gone away, too."

"Good. Sit down and eat."

Cassandra did as she was told and started spreading the spicy apple butter onto the bread. Dustin pulled the slipper chair over to the dresser and sat down opposite her.

She offered him a piece of the bread. Dustin shook his head. "It's all for you. I had some while I was preparing your tray."

"This room is very nice."

"I'm glad you like it."

"I do." She glanced up at him. "Very feminine. How clever of a bachelor to prepare a room in his house that would be so pleasing to a woman."

"Well, a man never knows when he might have to rescue a damsel in distress and have to put her up for a night or two."

She picked up the knife and cut a small piece of cheese and popped it into her mouth. It was sharp, dry, and delicious.

"Have you had to do that before?"

"What? Rescue a damsel or put up a woman for the night?"

She hesitated. He seemed to be enjoying this conversation a little too much. What was she doing, pestering him for information? She didn't care if he had twenty mistresses. "Rescue a woman."

"Not to the extent I did tonight."

They were quiet for a moment and she ate another piece of cheese.

"I'm disappointed. I thought you were going to ask me how many women had stayed in this room."

"That's of no interest to me."

"Liar."

Damn him for being so smart.

Dustin settled back against the chair and asked, "Why didn't you send me a telegram and tell me you were coming to town?"

Thankful he had let the subject drop she said, "I was angry with you."

"That's nothing new."

"I didn't want to see you."

"That makes me feel real good," he remarked in a sarcastic tone, then hurried on to say. "What made you take a room in one of the worst sections of town?"

"How was I supposed to know it was a bad part of town? I had to stay in a place I could afford." She ate a piece of the bread.

"Afford?" Dustin leaned forward. "Dammit, Cassandra. Hasn't it sunk in yet that you are a millionaire? You could buy that whole section of town and have money left over."

Cassandra put the bread down and wiped at the corner of her injured mouth with her fingertips. "That's what you keep telling me, but what good does that do me if I can't get any of it when I need it?"

His eyebrows drew together in a frown. "What do you mean? Haven't you received your advance yet?"

"Oh, yes," she said unhappily. "I received all measly three thousand dollars."

"What about the rest of it?"

"There is no rest of it. Gordon made it clear that's all I'm getting. And I'll have to give every dime of that to Landon because he had already paid my mortgage payment for me."

"What?"

"Yes. When Landon found out about my inheritance he made arrangements with the bank to pay off my entire mortgage. Now I'm indebted to his bank for the balance of the loan."

"That dandy little prig. I bet he was willing to climb up the sky and pluck the moon for you, too, wasn't he?"

"None of that matters, Dustin. The fact remains that even though the mortgage payment has been made, I have no money for cattle or anything else. Which means you didn't do what you promised, which doesn't surprise me."

She picked up her cup of milk and drank thirstily, not wanting to see Dustin's face after her last remark. He was sure to take offense.

He waited a long time before he replied. "Which was why you didn't want to see me," he murmured, and sat back in the chair again. "I recommended the committee give you—no, I *told* the committee to give you all of it, I swear. I went into Gordon's office this afternoon to ask him if he'd sent you the money but I forgot about it when he told me you were here."

Cassandra picked up her napkin and dabbed the milk from her mouth. She desperately wanted what he said to be true. She wanted to believe he was in there fighting for her. "Well, they didn't."

Dustin ran his fingers through his hair and it fell neatly back in place. "It's unconscionable that Gordon would let them do that after the conversations we've had. I explained everything to him. I wrote up my report and told them to wire it all. I just assumed they took my advice. Dammit, that was what he was supposedly sending me out there to do."

Dustin shook his head in disbelief. "Gordon knows I'm through playing games. He knows I don't give a damn about the firm or your money, but he can't let go of my life."

Something about what Dustin said and how he said it struck a chord in Cassandra and she believed he had tried his best for her.

"His objective hasn't changed since the first time he mentioned your name to me. He wants you to marry me because of the money."

"Yes."

"I tried and I couldn't do it. I damned myself and put you through hell, but Gordon won't give up."

Suddenly, Cassandra was desperate to outsmart Gordon and wrest control of her inheritance from the firm. Dustin's father was no better than her stepfather had been. Gordon had tried to manipulate Dustin to keep control of her trust.

"I knew that money was tainted," she whispered. "It seems all my life that someone has wanted it."

Dustin's features softened. "The money isn't tainted, Cassandra. The people are. The power money brings does strange things to people."

Cassandra felt as if a weight had been lifted from her shoulders. She knew what she had to do. "Your father might not be violent but he's as unworthy as Ward Cabot. I've decided you were right when you said the only way to get control of my inheritance was to marry. All I have to do is decide whether the man will be you or Landon."

Dustin stiffened perceptibly but he kept his tone light when he said, "You like to drive me crazy, don't you?"

Perplexed by his reaction, Cassandra continued to stare blankly into his eyes. "What do you mean?"

"Teasing me with talk of marrying Webster."

"Dustin, I'm not teasing."

Chapter

· 18 ·

He cursed softly. "You're not going to marry that plaid-suited dandy."

His confidence surprised her but his insight didn't. She smothered the impulse to protest and simply said, "You don't know that."

His eyes didn't waver from hers. "Yes, I do. If you were going to marry Webster you would have said yes the first time he asked you."

It rankled that he knew her so well. She should have taken offense at his presumptuousness. How could she when he spoke the truth? But she wasn't about to admit that. "What makes you so sure?"

"Because that's the sort of thing love makes you do. When I asked you to marry me you said yes immediately. It didn't take you months to decide your answer."

She rolled her shoulders uncomfortably. "I don't remember that I agreed right away," she fibbed and immediately felt bad for doing so. But how could she let him know that she remembered all the little details about the summer she spent with him?

A smile touched his eyes, making them shimmer like

moonlight on water. "I do. It was a hot night late in June. We were in the parlor of the house your grandfather had rented for the summer. You threw your arms around me and said, 'Yes, yes, yes!'"

He was so engaging in his portrayal of her, she had to smile, accepting his accurate account of how she'd behaved that evening. "You're playing with me, Dustin, and I'm serious about this."

He studied her face for a moment, then said, "You don't love Webster. You never have and you never will."

"You can't know that." She challenged his confident assertion again.

The glow in his eyes intensified. "Sure I can. You love me. You always have and you always will."

Cassandra sat back and considered his proclamation. Dustin was right. She didn't love Landon. She never would. And yes, she would love to be able to once again shout that she would marry Dustin. But something inside her wouldn't let her put aside the past hurts. She'd given Dustin her love and trust once before and he'd deserted her.

Old feelings of losing those she'd loved forced her to remain quiet even though she knew Dustin desperately wanted her to agree with him.

Edgy, she rose from the dresser stool and strode away from him. "Dustin, I need some time to think right now. I don't know what I'm going to do. I'm tired of fighting but I know I can't give up now."

Dustin followed her to the other side of the room and stood in front of her. "You aren't alone anymore, Cassandra. I'm going to help you. Since I returned to Kansas City I've been on a fact-finding mission for you. I'm learning all I can about your past. I've read old newspaper articles about your parents' deaths and—"

"Dustin, no, I don't want to hear."

She tried to turn away from him but he caught her upper arms and forced her to look at him and listen.

"Cassandra, you need to know the facts about all these things that have happened to you and your family."

"Why? It's over. Reading about what happened to my parents won't bring them back or change the past," she defended her lack of curiosity.

"No, but it might help you understand it."

"There are certain things you just learn to live with. You cope. That's all."

"You need to know the good things about your parents too. From what I've read your mother was as beautiful and demanding as you are, and as independent."

Cassandra softened. "Really? Grandpapa Rakefield never talked about my mother or father. I always assumed it was because it hurt him too much to remember his son."

"That could be, I guess. I've found out a lot of things about them I think you should know. I've kept everything I've found. I'll give them to you later and you can decide if and when you want to read them."

Her heart swelled with love for him. It was hard to believe he'd taken the time to do that for her. "That was kind of you."

"I wanted to do it. I've tried to contact your old governess and—"

"Juliana?"

"Yes. According to the newspapers she caused quite a stir in this town for weeks when she kidnapped you."

Cassandra pulled out of his grasp and he let her go. "Juliana's not old and she didn't kidnap me. She saved me from a murderer."

"From what I've read she was a very courageous woman." He paused. "You've never questioned her about what happened that night she kid—took you away from Kansas City?"

"No," Cassandra confessed. "It's the lawyer in you wanting to know these details, Dustin."

He exhaled heavily. "Maybe, but I think it's just that

I'm concerned about you, and I think you should know more about your parents and how they lived."

She swallowed down the lump in her throat. "If I don't know it can't hurt."

"You believe that?"

"Yes. It's worked for more than fifteen years. It's easier to deal with what I don't know."

"I can't force you to want to know about your past. I have the information I've collected on them so far. Just let me know when you're ready for it."

His gentle persistence made her relent and say, "Maybe someday I would like to read about them."

Dustin nodded. "Before I left the ranch I promised you I would get your money for you and I will. We'll go to my father tomorrow and talk to him."

"What makes you think we can do together what we haven't been able to do separately?"

"Because I believe in us. I believe that together we can do anything we want to do."

His words warmed her, gave her encouragement. "But Dustin, you don't understand. I've decided I want the whole damn trust, not just twenty-five thousand."

A grin lit his face again. "That sounds like the Cass I remember. You are the most fiercely independent woman I've ever met."

"I've always had to be." Cassandra walked over to the window and pushed the drapery aside. She saw a void of darkness. It would be so easy to rely on Dustin. He was so strong, so confident, yet so easy. For him there were no problems.

She whipped around and locked her gaze on his. "What would you do if I asked you to marry me?"

The grin faded into an inquisitive smile. His bright eyes held steadily on hers. "I'd say, yes, yes, yes."

Cassandra was making herself nervous but she couldn't stop her questioning. All she could think was that marriage would get control of her inheritance away from the firm. "What would you say if I asked you to sign papers giving me complete control over my trust?"

"I'd say yes." His voice was softer, more cautious this time.

"What would you say if I told you that's what I wanted to do?"

He paused for so long she started to tremble with expectancy.

"I'd say what do I get out of the marriage?"

She moistened her lips and thought for a moment. She couldn't believe she was saying these things to him. She wasn't even taking the time to think things through.

Cassandra cleared her throat and put the burden of answer back on him. "What did you expect to get from the marriage when you first suggested it the day you arrived at the Triple R?"

His gaze remained firmly on her face. "A wife in my home, in my bed, in my life."

"But—your life is here in Kansas City and the reason I'd want the money is so I can keep the ranch."

"No. If we married, my life would be with you."

She gulped loudly, unable to control what was happening between them. She rubbed an open palm against her forehead. She had to stop herself. She wasn't supposed to trust him, was she?

"I can't believe I'm doing this. I can't believe I'm actually considering the possibility of marrying you. I've pretended to hate you for so long."

A breathy sigh whistled past Dustin's lips. "Cassandra, let me make this easy for you." He stopped and shook his head. "I know I'm going to regret what I'm about to say, but sometimes we have to make decisions that we spend the rest of our lives trying to change. I have a feeling this could be one of them. I'm not going to marry you, Cassandra."

She gasped. She couldn't move. Only Dustin had the power to render her incapable of thought.

He took a long step toward her. "Not right now anyway. Don't get me wrong. I want to. Hell, I do! But I want to marry you for the right reasons, not the wrong ones."

"What do you mean?" Her voice was shaky. She took a step away from him.

"I need to know you trust me completely."

Cassandra's mind raced. Trust him? No. Yes. Maybe? No. She wasn't ready for that, and she wouldn't be pressured into admitting anything until she knew for certain she could put her trust in him. Her silence gave Dustin his answer.

"I want to marry you because you've admitted you love me, you can't live without me, and you'll spend the rest of your days happy with me. But more important than that is that I want to marry you because I've earned your trust and your love. I'm deserving of you, Cassandra, and proving that to you is more important to me than just having you use my name to get what you want. I don't want to marry you so you can get your money. I need an emotional commitment from you. I need to know you believe I can make you happy."

He stood so tall, so erect, so at ease with his decision, Cassandra felt chilled. He was asking for her faith in him, in his love, in his ability to take care of her. She was hurt. He'd hurt her again by telling her he wouldn't marry her. She needed him. When was she going to learn that he couldn't be trusted? She must have been insane to allow him so close to her again that she was thinking of marrying him.

"No. No, I can't commit to any of those things," she said with all the earnestness she was feeling inside.

"Can't or won't?"

"Your choice. They mean the same."

"Don't close me off here, Cassandra. I'm taking a big risk here. I'm taking the chance that you won't go back to Wyoming and marry Webster or some other man just to get your inheritance. I'm hoping you'll give me the chance to do this my way first." His eyes never left her face.

She sensed his sincerity. For all the confidence he'd shown earlier, she could see he was worried she might marry Landon. She knew she wouldn't marry him. Not even to get her money, but she wasn't ready to tell Dustin that.

"What do you have in mind?"

He let out a deep breath of relief. "I believe Gordon denied your advance in hopes you would do exactly what you did—travel to Kansas City. I'm sure he still wants us to get married and this is his way of getting us together again."

It made sense. "I think you might be right about that, but it doesn't change the fact that I want to take control of my inheritance away from the firm."

"Right, and we don't want him to know. Tomorrow morning we'll go see him and ask for a copy of your mother's will. I've never actually seen it. I'm assuming you haven't either."

"No."

"I'd like to look over it." He looked pensive for a moment. "There may be a clause, a word, a sentence, or something in there that's been conveniently overlooked all these years."

"I've never questioned that before."

"You've never needed to." He moved closer to her and let the backs of his fingers lightly caress the red skin under her eye. "Does it hurt?"

"Only when it's touched."

"Oh. Sorry."

He jerked his hand down so fast Cassandra smiled. There was so much about him she liked. There were so many good reasons to love him. At times like this she wondered why she couldn't commit to him. Why didn't she just go with her gut feelings as she had that night they spent in the wagon and abandon all her doubts?

"I know you're tired. I'm going to let you get some sleep, but remember I'll be right next door if you need me tonight."

She nodded.

He lowered his head and pressed a soft, brief kiss upon her lips. "I know I hurt you badly in the past, but I'm not going to give up until I've proven to you that I'm not the bastard I was when I left you. I love you, Cassandra, and I want to marry you. Don't forget that."

Somewhere deep inside she felt desperate to acknowledge her changing feelings for him, but a deep-rooted distrust held her in its clutches and she allowed him to walk out of the room without a comment.

"Dustin, Cass, come in," Gordon Bennett said with a wide smile on his face. "Sit down and make yourselves comfortable. Obviously Dustin found you last night."

"Yes."

"Good. I wish he'd brought you back to my house for dinner. No matter. We'll do it another time. I hope you plan to be here for a long time."

"I'm not sure right now."

Dustin couldn't help noticing the satisfied smile on his father's face as he and Cassandra exchanged pleasantries. Dustin was more convinced than ever that the wily old fox had orchestrated Cassandra's journey to Kansas City. He refused to give up. He was still trying to manipulate them.

"I don't think I had time to tell you yesterday, Dustin, but I took the liberty of inviting Cass to the cattlemen's dance for you."

"But I told you, I didn't come prepared to attend a function like that," Cassandra spoke up quickly.

"Nonsense," Gordon remarked. "I told you it would be easy to buy a dress in this town."

While they talked about the dance, Dustin's thoughts drifted away from the conversation. He'd had a hell of a night forcing himself not to steal into Cassandra's room and crawl into her bed. He hungered for the taste of her again, but he was determined to take it slow and court her. She had to admit she loved and trusted him.

He'd meant it when he told her he was taking a risk in not accepting her proposal of marriage. A big risk. He knew better than anyone how stubborn she could be once she set her mind to something. And she wanted control of her money.

His hope was that he could find a way—a loophole— and get her money and redeem himself in her eyes. Then, she wouldn't be the one proposing to him. He'd be the one asking for her hand—again. He didn't like to admit it even to himself but he was scared that might not happen. Cassandra was strong willed, and at times Cassandra was unpredictable.

"Isn't that right, Dustin? Tell her."

Glancing up at his father he blinked several times to clear his thoughts. "What was that?"

"The dance."

"Oh, yes. I hadn't planned to go until Cassandra came to town." He turned to her. "But I'd very much like to take you. We don't have to stay long."

"I'll agree to think about it."

"Well, with that settled there is another thing I want to discuss. Dustin, I think Cassandra should stay with me. I don't like the idea of her staying in a boarding house even though I'm sure she is perfectly safe there."

Dustin suppressed his smile as he continued to look at Cassandra.

"That's already taken care of. She's moving into my house. This morning I made arrangements with my housekeeper to stay and act as chaperone."

"Splendid."

"One of the reasons we're here is that Cassandra and I were talking last night about her mother's will and how her trust was set up. Neither of us has ever seen the paper work. We'd like to look over the document."

Gordon cleared his throat. "Well, I'd be happy for you

to see it if we had it. Years ago it was destroyed in a fire, along with some other papers. It was back when we used oil lamps. One was accidentally overturned on a desk. As I recall, several important documents were lost." He looked directly at Cassandra. "But I assure you the trust was set up properly per your mother's instructions."

Dustin didn't miss the concerned glance Cassandra threw his way. He had watched and listened to his father carefully. Gordon's voice grew stronger as he talked, but to Dustin it sounded as if his father was making up the story as he went along. Dustin had no recollection there had ever been a fire at Bennett, Lucas, and Farrell.

"Is there no documentation left that substantiates what my mother's will stated?" Cassandra asked. "Have I only your word that my mother didn't want me to have control of her estate until I reached twenty-five?"

He placed a finger on his chin. "I'm thinking there's not. Your stepfather was living at that time. Have you looked through his papers for a copy?"

"Ah—no. I have no idea where his papers might be."

"I'll do some asking around and see what I can find out for you," he said in a placating, fatherly tone. "Cass, dear, this is not the sort of thing you need concern yourself with. Tell her, Dustin. We'll take care of her."

"Actually you made a point that brings up a good question," Dustin said. "Cassandra was living in the family mansion when she was kidnapped—"

"Dustin," Cassandra interrupted.

"I'm sorry," he said, giving Cassandra a sheepish grin. "When she was taken from her home. Her stepfather was killed in Wyoming. What happened to the house?"

Gordon shifted in his chair. "It was sold."

"Who sold it?"

Gordon cleared his throat again as a wrinkle of aggravation formed between his brows. "The firm of course."

His father was edgy and Dustin wanted to know why. He never thought he'd have to use his interrogation skills on his father. "So then someone here would know what happened to Cabot's personal papers and things."

"I would assume so, yes," Gordon said, rising from his chair.

"But you didn't personally see them and you don't know what happened to them."

"That's right."

His father was good. Short answers to probing questions. "Can you give me the name of the person who handled the sale and personal effects?"

"Not right off. It's been a few years. As I said, let me look into a few things and see what I can find out for Cass."

"I'd like that," Cassandra said in a conciliatory tone.

"I'm thinking this came about because we only approved a portion of the money you wanted." He pointed a finger at her and said, "I intend to take up your request for another advance the next time the executive committee meets.

"Now you two run along and start looking for a gown for the dance. I'm sure Dustin can help you find the shops in town. Dustin, we'll talk later."

"Yes," he told his father and ushered Cassandra out into the corridor.

After they had walked a safe distance from his father's door Dustin said, "There was something about what my father said and how he said it that bothered me."

"I don't think he was happy we questioned him."

"He wasn't. I have an idea."

"What?"

Dustin stopped just outside the reception area. "We're going to break into his safe."

"What?"

"Gordon has a safe in his office behind that picture with the waterfall."

"Do you think my mother's will might be in there?"

"Could be. It wouldn't hurt to look. I've never heard anything about a fire in the offices."

"Can we really break into his safe? Isn't that dangerous, not to mention criminal?"

"More or less, but we're not going to take anything. We're just going to see what's in there. Besides, I doubt if my father would file charges against his son and his most important client."

"How do you break into a safe? Don't you need dynamite or something like that?"

He grinned. "Or the combination."

Her eyes flashed. "Do you have that?"

"Boys do like to plunder their fathers' offices. My father is a meticulous man. He wouldn't trust his memory, so he wrote it down. There's no saying he's kept it in the same place all these years, but it's worth a shot."

"Good. When will we do it?"

Dustin gave her a cunning grin. "I'm delighted at how quickly I could turn you into a criminal."

Cassandra started to smile, but suddenly she looked as if she'd seen a ghost. He touched her arm. "Cassandra, what's wrong?"

Her face changed again as her lips broke into the brightest smile he'd ever seen. She shrugged off his hold and started running. Dustin saw a tall, rugged-looking cowboy with a six-shooter strapped to his hip stretch out his arms and catch Cassandra in his embrace.

He hugged her, pressing her firmly to his chest. They kissed soundly, though briefly, on the lips.

Dustin's gut twisted.

Chapter

· *19* ·

Cassandra left the man's arms as quickly as she went into them and flew into the arms of a pretty woman who had hurried up beside them. They hugged. They laughed, then hugged again. Joy was evident in their faces.

Suddenly Dustin knew who these people were, but he couldn't figure out what in the hell they were doing at the law firm. He relaxed and walked closer.

Cassandra turned and looked for him. "Dustin," she called, motioning with her hands. "Come meet Rill and Juliana Banks, the two dearest friends I've ever had. Rill, Juliana, this is Dustin Bennett."

The cowboy quickly gave Dustin the once over and stuck out his hand. Dustin was obliged to shake it, but he wasn't prepared to like any man who would grab Cassandra in such an intimate way and put his lips on hers.

Rill's expression was friendly, his handshake firm. He looked every inch the working cowboy, from his collarless shirt and leather vest to the worn Stetson he held in his hand and the gun belt that rode low on his hips.

Dustin's starched collar and wide cravat seemed to tighten around his neck.

"This is Juliana," Cassandra said, her smile beaming.

Somehow Dustin knew the ex-governess hadn't taken her eyes off him since he had walked up. He didn't mind her looking him over. He intended to look them over, too. He wanted to know more about the people who'd once been so much a part of Cassandra's life.

Juliana didn't offer her hand as she said, "I've heard a lot about you, Mr. Bennett."

Her smile, if that, indeed, was what the slight movement of her lips was, gave him his first hint she was wary of him. Dustin was sure the smile wasn't genuine. It didn't reach her big blue eyes. And why should it? He was sure that, close as she and Cassandra had been over the years, Juliana had to know everything about his and Cassandra's past.

"And I've heard a lot about you, Mrs. Banks," he answered, prepared to meet her on whatever ground she chose.

Now that he was closer to her he could see that Juliana was more than pretty. She was beautiful in a soft classic way. All her features seemed to fit together perfectly from her small nose to her shapely lips and big expressive eyes. Her matching dress, bonnet, and traveling jacket made her look very much a properly dressed lady.

"I have to admit, Mrs. Banks, I was looking forward to meeting the woman who turned Kansas City upside down by—leaving town with the wealthiest little girl in the state."

A flash of appreciation showed in her eyes before she answered, "The feeling is mutual, Mr. Bennett. I have been looking forward to meeting the man who was once engaged to Cass."

"I won't have the two of you continuing with this mister and missus formality talk." Cassandra glared from one to the other. "It's Juliana and Dustin, isn't that right, Rill?"

"Always has been. I don't see any reason to change now."

Cassandra smiled at him and said, "Now, tell me, what are you two doing here in Kansas City? How's your father, and where are Cassie, Vickie, and William?"

"Whoa! One question at a time. We left the children back in Texas with my brother. We brought my father up here earlier in the week to see a specialist and we have hope he'll be better. My parents are at the hotel. If we'd had any idea you were here we would have already come to see Dustin."

"But why are you here at Dustin's office?" Cassandra asked.

"We received a telegram from Mr.—" Juliana paused. "From Dustin."

"I told you I was trying to find your old—" Dustin stopped and cleared his throat. "Your governess."

"Yes, but I didn't know you asked them to come to Kansas City."

"I didn't."

"He didn't."

"Oh, no, he didn't."

Dustin, Rill, and Juliana all spoke at one time.

"His telegram only stated that he was seeking information about your past and that he could be reached at this address," Juliana stated.

"The message was sent to my ranch," Rill said, taking up the story. "My foreman forwarded it to my father's ranch in Texas. My mother was planning a trip to bring my father up here to see the doctor, so we decided to come with them and see Dustin."

"We wanted to know if anything was going on that we should be concerned about. We had no idea you were here."

"But we're glad you are," Rill said.

"Yes," Juliana agreed. "Of course we recognized Dustin's name as the man you were once engaged to." She paused again and looked at Dustin. "Quite frankly,

Cass, we've been a bit worried about why he'd want to know anything about you. So we wanted to see Mr. Ben—Dustin—and talk to him before we leave."

Cassandra smiled affectionately at Juliana. "Will you always worry about me?"

"Always. I'm glad you're here too. Now we can find out from both of you what's going on."

Dustin had been right. Watching Juliana now with Cassandra, he was certain that she hadn't really smiled at him. She wasn't prepared to accept him. Yet.

Cassandra turned to Rill. "I hope everything will turn out all right with your father."

"I think it will. We weren't expecting you to be here, so we've already planned to take the train back to Texas late this afternoon."

Cassandra's smile faded. "Of course, I understand. I'm so glad to see you if only for a few hours."

"In that case," Dustin said, glancing around the office. "I suggest that we all go to my house for lunch. It's only a short distance away by carriage. While my housekeeper prepares a meal we can talk. We'll have more privacy there than anywhere else."

Juliana looked at Rill.

"I'm agreeable to that."

"What do you say, Cassandra?"

She looked over at Dustin and gave him a sweet, appreciative smile. His heart soared.

"Dustin's right. Let's go."

Rill and Cassandra headed out the door immediately but Juliana hung back and Dustin waited for her. "Cassandra," Juliana said to Dustin. "My goodness. No one has called her that since she was seven years old. She's preferred Cass since Cropper started calling her that when we made the trip to Wyoming."

"I used to call her Cass, too, but she's grown up and it no longer fits her. She's Cassandra now," he said and made a sweeping motion with his hand for her to precede him out the door. She was gracious enough not to question him, but he couldn't help smiling as he felt that just for a moment he'd earned a tiny bit of respect from Juliana for noting that Cassandra had changed.

Rill and Juliana's carriage followed the one Cassandra and Dustin rode in. Cassandra couldn't help noticing that Dustin was unusually quiet. It wasn't a long drive but in the close confines of the small rockaway buggy, time seemed to stretch.

"Dustin," she said, when she couldn't take the silence any longer. "I want to thank you for bringing Juliana and Rill to Kansas City. I'm so happy to see them, if only for a short time."

"You know I can't take any credit for their coming here. I never expected them to come to Kansas City. I hoped they would contact me by letter."

"I think your telegram disturbed them. Juliana has always been protective of me."

"Undoubtedly, though Juliana was very careful not to let her ruffled feathers show."

"What do you mean?" she quizzed him. "Juliana never gets flustered. That's one of the things that's so easy to like about her. I'm certain she was just as surprised to see me as I was to see you the day you showed up at the Triple R. She knows we parted on less than favorable terms."

"I don't guess she has any reason to like me."

"She didn't like what our broken engagement did to me. For a long time Juliana tried to fill in as a mother, but when she started having her own children it became too much for her to travel between the two ranches. Cassie is my namesake, but we're nothing alike. She's as sweet and soft-spoken as her mother."

"How boring."

"Dustin."

"But I can see why you love them."

If his tone hadn't been so somber she would have

thought jealousy prompted his remark. Something was definitely wrong. "I do love them. After they brought me to Wyoming, they could have left me and never come back. Rill's ranch is more than a day's ride from the Triple R. But they never forgot about me."

Dustin turned away from her without saying anything.

"If you are happy for me that they are here, why are you so quiet?"

He jerked back around to stare at her. Her stomach tumbled when she saw his grim expression.

"I was just thinking about how much I hate seeing another man's lips on yours and what I should do about it."

"What do you mean?" she asked.

The dim lighting inside the carriage seemed to add texture to his strong features. She wanted to reach out and touch his clean-shaven cheek.

Slowly his features softened. "Rill. He kissed you on the mouth."

He was so serious it stunned her and for some inexplicable reason it pleased her. Amusement filled her and she said, "You're jealous of Rill?"

Dustin nodded. "I don't want anyone's lips on yours but mine."

"Rill's old enough to be my father, Dustin."

"Doesn't matter. I don't like it."

"Then why don't you do what you did after Landon kissed me?"

His eyes searched her face. "You haven't let that dandy kiss you since that night I was there, have you?"

Her heart thudded at the thought of being so honest to a man who could hurt her so deeply. "No," she whispered.

He slid one arm around her waist and the other up over her shoulders and pulled her close. He lowered his lips to hers and said, "I've always thought you were the smartest woman I've ever known. Now I'm sure of it."

Instinctively, her hands landed open palm on his shoulders. She stretched up to meet him as her breasts molded against his solid muscles.

His lips brushed against hers and lingered, moving warmly and tenderly. His fingers caressed the soft skin at the hollow under her chin, then sketched a trail over her jaw and up to her cheek. The feathery skim of her skin heated her passion and she responded ardently to his masterful touch.

A wave of wanting swept through her. His breath, his lips, his tongue mingled with hers and captured her thoughts.

She wanted to disrobe and feel his skin upon hers as she had that night they spent in the wagon. It had been a dream come true for both of them, she was sure of that, and she couldn't help wondering if Dustin was remembering that time right now, too.

When he finally let her go she felt dreamy with desire.

"How was that?"

"Wonderful. Why did you stop?"

"Because the carriage stopped, and I don't think you want Juliana catching you looking at me with eyes heavy with passion."

"Oh!" She jerked up and straightened her dress. "We could have been caught kissing."

"I wouldn't let that happen." Dustin opened the carriage door but turned back to Cassandra and said, "Just so you'll know. I never forgot about you, either."

He hopped down and reached back inside for Cassandra. She placed her hand in his. She felt his strength, his warmth, his honesty, and suddenly knew she was beginning to believe him.

As soon as Cassandra and Juliana had closed the door to the bedroom Juliana turned to her and said, "I'm not entirely happy with the fact that you are staying in Dustin's home, Cass."

The minute Cassandra had suggested that she and

Juliana come up to her room to freshen up it was clear that Juliana didn't approve.

Cassandra had to force herself not to smile. She liked the fact that Juliana cared so much about her that it mattered how she behaved and if she did the proper thing.

"I'm staying here, but you don't have to worry. Dustin has been a gentleman."

"But for how long? You two do have a past," Juliana said, removing her bonnet.

"I believe we're both constantly aware of that. Why don't you sit in the slipper chair and I'll take the dressing stool."

"This is a lovely room. Was it decorated for Dustin's mother?" Juliana asked.

"No," she said, as an odd feeling of protectiveness washed over her. For some reason she hated admitting to Juliana that Dustin was less than perfect. "Dustin's mother died when he was young."

"I see." Cassandra knew that Juliana had come to the same obvious conclusion that she'd come to last night. This beautiful room in Dustin's home had been prepared for Dustin's lady friends. That bothered Cassandra too, but dare she admit, even to herself, that she was jealous of any woman who kissed Dustin?

"He's very handsome," Juliana said as she sat down and started unbuttoning her traveling jacket.

Cassandra plopped down on the stool. "Yes, but that's not what draws me to him, Juliana. Grandpapa Rakefield arranged for so many handsome men to visit me at the Triple R that I lost count."

"I know," Juliana said with a sigh in her voice. Her features softened for the first time since she arrived. "It's the way he looks at you, smiles at you. The way he makes you feel inside when he walks into a room, when his hand brushes yours."

"You must feel the same way whenever Rill looks at you."

Juliana laughed lightly. "Even after all these years of marriage, I tingle inside whenever he smiles at me."

"That's the way I felt when I met Dustin and that's what I felt when he walked into the barn a few weeks ago. All the feelings were there inside me and I hated every one of them for being alive."

"You don't want to love him, but you do?"

Cassandra lowered her lashes and nodded. "I've tried so hard not to love him, but I—I can't stop, I can't destroy these feelings inside me, but it's as if I can't accept them either."

"Some hurts never mend. Do you want that?"

"No, of course not."

"What about Dustin. Is there any indication he's in love with you? Have the two of you talked about this?"

Cassandra pondered for a moment. "We've talked. He admitted he didn't know if he truly loved me when I was seventeen or if he just desired me. But now he says he's sure he loves me, but—"

"The infamous But. It's the past that bothers you, isn't it? You thought he loved you, but he left you and you don't know that you can trust him."

Cassandra nodded. "That's exactly right. I want to, but something inside me won't allow me to open myself up to him and trust him completely again."

"But you're trying to overcome that? Is that why you are here in Kansas City?"

"Our relationship isn't the reason I'm here. Sometimes I think maybe we can renew what we once had, but I have those doubts. I can't give him everything that's inside me as I did before. I'm not willing to take a chance and be hurt like that again."

"Why don't you start at the beginning and tell me how you ended up in Kansas City in Dustin's home?"

"Oh." Cassandra faked a short laugh to lighten the mood. "You don't have three days here. Hardly three hours. There's not time to tell you everything."

"I'm sure there's a short version of the story."

"I'll try. I did as you suggested before you left for Texas and wrote to the law firm about needing an advance, to Gordon Bennett, Dustin's father. Instead of money, he sent Dustin."

"Did you have any idea that he'd send his son?"

"Of course not. We hadn't had any communication in nearly five years. Dustin said he was there to inspect the ranch and report back to the committee at the law firm so I could get the money."

"So what did he do? Spend a day or two there and then leave?"

"Well, he ended up being there longer than that because of too many things that I don't have time to go into right now. Anyway, before he left, he promised to make sure I received the twenty-five thousand I'd asked for. But, when the check arrived, I only received three thousand and a terse note saying that was all I was going to get. So I packed a bag and came here to persuade the firm I needed the money."

"And have you done that?"

"No. I discovered that Dustin's father and his committee don't think I'm capable of managing a few thousand dollars." She threw up her hand in frustration. "I couldn't believe it. Mr. Bennett was so damn condescending I wanted to scream, 'Look at me!' I'm twenty-two, I'm educated, and more than able to take care of myself, run the ranch, and manage my own damn money if I want to." She inhaled deeply. "I'm sorry. I didn't mean to get carried away, but I've had it up to my hat with those tight-fisted fuddy-duddies who control my inheritance."

"So where do you go from here, Cass?"

"Dustin and I are working on a plan. We've asked to see my mother's will but we were told it was burned in a fire a long time ago."

"Yes, I believe that to be true. I remember your grandfather telling me that years ago when we first arrived in Wyoming."

Cassandra's hopes of finding a copy plummeted, but she tried not to let it show. "Dustin is hoping we will be able to find some kind of document that will support what the firm is doing in hopes there's a clause that will allow me to get control of the trust fund before I turn twenty-five."

"So marrying is out of the question."

"I asked him and he turned me down."

Juliana inhaled sharply. "You don't mean that."

"Yes. But he was right to do it. I asked for the wrong reasons and he declined for the right reasons."

"I'm worried about you, Cass. What can we do to help? That's why we're here."

Cassandra smiled and touched Juliana's hand. "Just being able to see you and talk to you has helped more than you'll ever know."

"Why does Dustin want to know about your past?"

"He's hoping to find a way to get the money out from under the firm's control. I'm sure he was hoping you knew something about the will."

"I wish I did. If your grandfather never saw it, I don't think there is one."

"Well, I won't give up hope that a copy of it will show up somewhere. Do you have any idea what happened to Papa Ward's personal papers after the house here in Kansas City was sold?"

She shook her head. "No. I never came back, and I know your grandfather didn't care what happened to anything that belonged to Mr. Cabot. As far as I know he only communicated with the law firm one time. I remember him telling me he wrote to the firm and told them to sell the house and any other property and put it in the trust until you decided you wanted to do something with it."

Cassandra sighed. "Yes. That's all I'm aware of, too. I'm sorry you made this trip for nothing."

"For nothing? What do you mean? I told you we were

coming anyway. How could this visit be wasted? I've seen you, haven't I?" Juliana squeezed Cassandra's hand. "I only wish I could help you settle your feelings, your doubts, about Dustin."

"Yes, I could use some words of wisdom."

Juliana took another deep breath. "Maybe I do have some departing words for you. My Auntie Vic always taught me that other people came first and that my dreams and happiness should be second to my employer's. She told me that I was to deny any romantic feelings I might have and live only to serve my employer."

"Did you believe her?"

"For a long time. Rill helped me to see that she was wrong. What had made her life complete wasn't what I needed. You know, Rill left me one time, too."

Cassandra snapped her head up. "No. I don't believe you."

"Oh, Rill's leaving wasn't as dramatic as Dustin's. Rill left me at the Triple R to take care of you and went to his own ranch."

"What did you do?"

Juliana smiled. "I went after him. You can give up on a lot of things in this world, Cass. Your ranch, your inheritance, but the one thing you don't want to ever give up is love. You'll never be happy if you do."

Cassandra closed her eyes for a moment. "But it hurts so when you lose those you love."

"That won't change, but sometimes we get lucky and love lasts forever."

"There is no forever, Juliana."

"You're much too young to be that cynical. Think about what I've said. I still have the greatest respect for my Aunt Victoria, but I thank God every day that I didn't listen to her when it came to love. I listened to my heart and it was right. Listen to your heart, Cass."

A knock sounded on the door. "That must be the

housekeeper with our refreshments." Cassandra started to rise. Juliana stayed her with her hand. "Will you think about what I just said?"

Cassandra smiled affectionately at her. "I've been thinking about it since Dustin came back into my life. I just haven't heard my heart's decision yet."

"I'm glad you declined Cassandra's offer of a walk in the garden, Juliana," Dustin said. "I wanted to talk to you alone before we have to take you to the depot."

"I sensed that. It's why I declined and Rill accepted her invitation."

"Would you like to sit here in the parlor or out on the garden patio?"

"In here is fine. I'm sure we'll have more privacy. But I believe Cass has already informed me of what you want to talk about. I'm afraid I can't add anything to what your father told you. Fifteen years ago I was told by Thomas Rakefield the will had been accidentally burned."

"I see. So Cassandra talked with you about the will."

"Yes, you did say you wanted to talk about her past. That is what you had in mind, isn't it?"

He nodded. "I'm glad to hear you knew about that, but when I wrote to you I had a different line of questioning in mind for you."

He had her attention. She looked serious. Good. It was a small thing but he liked the idea that he could shake her ever-so-proper veneer.

"What's wrong?"

"A recurring problem that I think is serious, although Cassandra makes light of it most of the time."

"Tell me."

Her assertiveness reminded him of Cassandra. "Cassandra says you were aware that as a child she had nightmares."

"Yes, as a child—" She stopped, a startled expression sweeping across her face. "Surely she doesn't still have them? Does she wake in the middle of the night unable to breathe?"

"The nightmares continue to plague her. I've questioned her at length, and she says she has no clue why she has them."

"Oh dear. I had no idea. I remember I did speak to Mr. Rakefield about them and he assured me they had stopped. No, no. What he said was that Cassandra no longer mentioned the nightmares."

"They didn't stop. She just stopped talking about them."

A look of agony crossed Juliana's face. "The poor child. I had no idea."

"I had hopes of finding out from you what might have caused them. I want her to be free from them."

"So do I. We didn't tell her when she was so young because we were afraid it would traumatize her even more if she knew how her stepfather had tried to murder her."

"Tell me what happened."

"I awakened in the middle of the night to sounds I didn't recognize. I rose and peeked through the doorway separating our two rooms. Ward Cabot held a pillow over Cassandra's face. Her legs kicked, her small hands clutched his arms and strained to remove the pillow, but her strength was no match for his."

"Damn son of a bitch," Dustin muttered. "I'm glad the bastard is dead. I'm not going to apologize."

"No need to. I agree with you."

"What did you do?"

"I was frantic. I grabbed the first thing I saw, a brass candlestick, and struck him on the head. Cass and I fled the house almost immediately. That night we hid in a covered wagon in the stockyard." Her voice and expression softened. "It just so happened it was Rill and Cropper's wagon. They were on their way to the Wyoming Territory. A lot of terrible things happened because of us. Cropper was shot by Ward's men. We didn't think he was going to make it. Cassandra left her doll with him to keep him company while he recovered. It was the most unselfish act I've ever seen from a child or adult. After her mother died Cass never went anywhere without Miss Watkins, but she left the doll with Cropper. I was so proud of her."

Dustin thought of Rodney and Cassandra. She could easily have sent him away, but no, she had to try to save him first. "I've seen that unselfish side of her."

"I guess you know the rest of the story."

He nodded. "Most of it anyway. Cassandra doesn't want to talk about that part of her past. I don't think she wants to know what happened."

"Probably because so much of it was so very bad for someone so young. She had so much to cope with because of her stepfather."

You learn to deal with it and you go on. Dustin remembered the words Cassandra had spoken to Rodney that late afternoon at the Triple R.

She looked in his eyes. "Ward Cabot wanted that money for a long time. He killed her father and her mother and he almost killed Cass. You couldn't say anything too bad to describe that man."

"No wonder she thinks the money is tainted."

"I just wish I'd known Cass continued to have the dreams. Maybe I could have helped her. I hope telling her will stop them."

"That's what I'm counting on. I think I hear Cassandra and Rill coming back inside. Before they get here I want to thank you for saving her life. It was a brave thing you did, taking her from her stepfather like that. It couldn't have been an easy thing to do."

Gratitude burst on her face like sunrise. "Thank you for saying that. At the time, no, it wasn't easy. I worried that I had done the right thing. Now, when I look back on that time, I know we made it to her grandfather's because of Rill and Cropper."

"Then thank them for me, too."

She smiled. A genuine smile. No wonder she'd captivated Rill's heart.

"Dustin, do you think you would have made a different decision about jilting her if you'd known all that you know now about what Cass had gone through in her life, how much she lost?"

Like Cassandra, Dustin had been a different person back then. He'd been too selfish and too immature to appreciate Cassandra's pain even if he'd known. He looked into Juliana's eyes. She deserved the truth.

"Probably not."

Chapter

·20·

The whistle blew, the engine chugged, the wheels screeched and whined as the train pulled out of town. Dustin noticed that Cassandra's eyes moistened as she waved goodbye to Juliana and Rill one last time. After having spent an afternoon with her friends, Dustin knew why Cassandra had such great admiration for them.

Juliana had proven herself to be Cassandra's protector and Rill had gained Dustin's respect by not prying into the details of his relationship with Cassandra. He appreciated that Rill sensed enough about him to know that Cassandra's welfare and happiness were uppermost in Dustin's mind and heart. Not that Dustin would have told him anything even if Rill had started acting like a long-lost father.

The train disappeared around a corner but Cassandra continued to watch the dark curling smoke fade into the air. Dustin remained quiet. He knew she was taking time to compose herself before she faced him. Cassandra didn't like him to see tears in her eyes. He didn't like them to be there.

Late-afternoon sun had turned the blue sky to shades

of gold, copper, and brown. A light breeze stirred the warm air and feathered his hair. Several people milled around the platform and depot. It made Dustin smile to think that children and adults came to the depot just to watch the trains pull in and out of the station.

Finally, Cassandra turned toward him dry eyed and said, "You'll never know how much it meant to me to see them today. It was like receiving a gift."

Dustin felt guilty about taking credit for that. "Cassandra, I didn't know they'd have a reason to come to town when I telegraphed them, and I certainly didn't expect you to be here."

"All that doesn't change the fact that I wouldn't have seen them if you hadn't solicited them."

"I know you hate to see them go."

"They are the closest people I have to family now. It was good for me to talk to Juliana. It's been months since I've seen her. The winter was so harsh neither of us could travel to visit. Then Grandpapa Rakefield got sick and I had to take care of him, and she had to leave for Texas because of Rill's father. I've missed her."

"Well, I can't say I mind you being indebted to me. I won't hesitate to call in the favor."

"Cass! Is that you?"

Dustin jerked around at the sound of her name. He swore under his breath. Landon Webster scurried toward them. The jacket of his brown plaid suit flared out behind him. He held his bowler hat on his head to keep the wind from blowing it away in his mad dash to get to them.

"It *is* you, Cass," he said, out of breath as he skidded to a stop beside them. "For a moment I thought I was seeing things. I never dreamt I'd be lucky enough to find you here at the depot. I thought I'd have to check every hotel and boarding house in town."

"Luck indeed," Dustin muttered.

"Landon, what are you doing here?"

"I came to file a complaint with the railroad about the delays along the route from Cheyenne to here."

"You came all the way to Kansas City to file a complaint?" she asked.

Webster chuckled. "Oh, no. I thought you meant what was I doing here at the depot. I arrived earlier today. After I settled into my hotel, I came back here to file my—"

He stopped when he glanced over at Dustin and saw his glare.

"Evening, Bennett. Glad to be home?"

"Couldn't be happier, now that Cassandra is visiting," Dustin remarked dryly.

"Landon, what in heaven's name are you doing here in Kansas City?" Cassandra asked.

"Following you," Dustin replied for him.

"That sounded like an accusation."

"It was intended to."

Webster gave him a dirty look. Dustin guessed the banker didn't know it would take a hell of a lot more to intimidate him than that weasel face. Dustin was beginning to get more than a little suspicious about Webster.

"Landon, why are you following me?"

"Guess," Dustin said. He held up his hand and rubbed his fingers and thumb together, suggesting money was Webster's motivation.

"I resent that," he barked.

"Dustin, let him answer for himself."

Webster took off his hat and smoothed down his hair. "In a way I guess I am following you, but certainly not for what *he* is indicating. Why are you at the depot? Are you returning to Wyoming already?"

"No, I was here to see some good friends—never mind what I'm doing here," Cassandra said in an exasperated voice. "Why did you say you're following me?"

"That's what I'd like to know," Dustin said. "But he keeps changing the subject."

Webster didn't bother to look at Dustin again. "I'll explain all that, but first I wanted to tell you I went to Dr.

Smithers to look in on the Indian who works for you, but he's already gone back to the Triple R."

Damn! Landon Webster wasn't what Dustin or Cassandra needed right now. Just last night Dustin had refused to marry her. He hadn't been that worried about the banker stepping in when he was back in Cheyenne, but now he was here, winning smiles and favors from Cassandra by checking on her wounded ranch hand.

Dustin's gut wrenched. He was suddenly hit with the fear that Cassandra might ask the banker to marry her. There was no way Dustin could afford to let the two of them be alone together. If she asked the prig to marry her he'd march her right over to the justice of the peace before she had time to finish her sentence.

Cassandra's smile glowed with happiness. "Thank you for doing that for me, Landon. I was hoping nothing would happen to delay his going home."

"I was glad to do it for you."

Dustin remembered his talk with the doctor. He probably couldn't wait to get the Indian out of his way. "That is good news, but surely Webster didn't follow you to Kansas City just to report on your ranch hand?"

"No, but I would have." Webster smirked at Dustin. "I know how concerned she's been about his recovery."

"Tell me, Landon, how did you know I left town?"

"Mr. Baker from the depot was in making his weekly deposits. Of course everyone in town knows that we're en—almost engaged. He just happened to remember you buying a ticket and asked me if you were going to Kansas City to buy your wedding gown."

Dustin's blood boiled. He didn't like the thought that anyone in Cheyenne thought Cassandra was going to marry that sap banker. She wasn't.

"Naturally I made arrangements as soon as I could to come and assist you."

"You think I'm here to buy a wedding gown?" Cassandra exclaimed, her gaze darting from Webster to Dustin.

"Oh, no, Cass, not me. Mr. Baker thought that. I, of course, knew you must be here because of your inheritance problems."

"I take it you didn't set Mr. Baker straight on his wrong assumption," Dustin said.

Webster glanced at Dustin, then quickly gave his attention back to Cassandra. "I thought you might need me to help you. I know you think you're capable of dealing with the business and financial terms of an account as large as yours. I thought perhaps I could assist you in some way, considering I've been in banking for quite some time now, and I'll be in charge of your affairs once we're married."

"She's not marrying you," Dustin said, but inside he smiled. Maybe he didn't have to worry about Cassandra offering to marry Webster after all. If he kept up this kind of talk he was going to drown his own hopes of making a wealthy marriage all by himself.

"That's very thoughtful of you, Landon," Cassandra said. "I'll call on you if I need help."

Dustin gulped. "Wait a minute, Cassandra. You can't be serious about this. Don't you see what he's trying to do?"

A smile appeared on Webster's face. "I'm trying to help her. And why not? Taking care of money is my business."

Smug-ass dandy, Dustin thought.

Cassandra turned to Dustin. "I said *if* I needed help. Your firm has had complete control of these accounts for over fifteen years. It probably wouldn't hurt to have someone I trust have a look at them."

"Someone you trust?" Dustin said, not believing she was going to let that dandy anywhere near her money.

"Let me spell it out for you, Bennett. She doesn't trust you or your firm."

Dustin took a step toward Webster.

"Dustin, Landon. Please don't argue, or I won't let either one of you help me."

"What about what we talked about last night?" Dustin asked, reminding her of their plan to break into his father's safe.

"I think we should go ahead with that."

"What are you talking about?" Webster asked.

"None of your business," Dustin told him as a twitch of frustration started in his cheek.

"Cass, where are you staying? I'd like you to join me for dinner tonight so we can discuss this further without any more unpleasant interruptions."

"She already has plans."

"I do?"

"Yes. Remember we need to discuss the details about how we're going to execute our plan."

"Now see here, Bennett. I asked her first."

"The three of us will go to dinner together," Cassandra announced.

"No," the two men said in unison.

"Then none of us will. I'll dine alone while you two stay here and snort and charge like two bulls."

Cassandra turned to walk away, but Dustin caught her arm and stopped her. "You made your point. All right, the three of us."

"Good." She returned his smile. "Landon, tell us where you are staying and Dustin and I will meet you. Dustin has his own carriage and it will be easier if we come and join you."

He sniffed. "Very well, my dear. As Dustin said, whatever you want, I'm happy to agree with."

"A whole evening with Webster is more than my stomach can take," Dustin said as he opened the door to his house.

"I noticed you were quiet during dinner," Cassandra said, stepping into the lighted foyer.

"I figured if I left him to talk enough about himself and your inheritance you'd see what a fortune hunter he is." He glanced over at her. "Did you?"

"What?" she asked innocently as he helped her take off the shawl he'd given her. It pleased him that she had brought it with her and that she'd worn it.

He loved it when she teased him and pretended not to know what he was talking about. He hung his hat and jacket on the coat tree by the door. "I'm going to have a glass of brandy. Care to join me?"

"Yes, I'd like that. Pour yourself a double. Your temperament has been less than cordial tonight and you need to loosen up."

"Have I ever been cordial around Webster?"

"No. I guess not. He told me about his incident with you in town."

"It doesn't surprise me he went crying to you about that. I wonder if he told the whole truth."

"Probably. His story wasn't favorable to you. It seems you ruined a brand new suit."

"Good. That makes me feel better."

Dustin quirked his brows as they walked from the foyer of his home into the parlor, and he asked, "Were you serious about wanting a brandy?"

"You seem surprised. I've been enjoying a glass of brandy in the evenings with my grandfather since I was sixteen."

"He let you drink that young? And something as strong as brandy?"

"That's right. By the time I was ten years old my grandfather didn't baby me about anything. With his only son gone, he knew I'd have to take over the ranch one day. He started grooming me for it shortly after I arrived. He didn't want me to be soft. He insisted I know how to take charge, issue orders, and take command of a situation so the men who work the ranch would respect me. He also wanted me to know how to hold my liquor, as he always said."

"So that's why you're always so tough around everyone. That's why you work as hard or harder than any of your men. Thomas did a good job."

She made herself comfortable on the small, wide-striped settee. "Yes, but he loved me. I always knew that, although he never told me until shortly before he died."

"I guess it was enough that he showed it and you felt it when he was hard on you."

She nodded. "I'm told I was a spoiled little girl from the day I was born, so he probably didn't have to push me too hard to take the lead. It's always seemed natural for me to do it."

Dustin believed that. Taking the top off the decanter, he asked, "When you agreed to marry me five years ago, was that the only time you ever considered leaving the ranch?"

"Yes."

His back was to her so he couldn't see her expression but her hesitant tone made him know that she hadn't wanted to answer his question. As many things as they had shared recently, there were other things she didn't want to admit to him.

He liked the fact that she had the courage to handle everything herself. He liked the fact that she was here with him in his home. Since he'd been back in town his nights had been long and restless. He was eager to finish this business with her inheritance and his clients and take her back to Wyoming where they belonged.

"Thomas was going to let you marry me even though he'd been grooming you to take over the ranch?"

"I told him it was what I wanted. He wanted me to get married and have children. He was just hoping I'd finally accept one of the ranchers or cowboys he was always bringing home to meet me."

"Why were you willing to give up the ranch, Cassandra?" he asked, turning back to her.

"Dustin." She almost whispered his name. "You don't have to ask that. You know why. You know me better than Juliana."

That admission surprised him. Flattered him. Elated him.

"No one has ever been able to make me madder, sadder, or happier than you can."

Her eyes sparkled with honesty. Her lips were a tempting rosy shade of pink. At that moment he wanted to drop the glass he was holding and take her in his arms and kiss her more than he could remember ever wanting anything.

"Should I take that as the beginning of a change in our relationship to something more along the lines of commitment?" He walked over and extended the glass to her.

She took the brandy. "It was a compliment."

"Then I'm flattered," he said and hoped his voice didn't register his disappointment.

"We're getting far too serious. I wonder where your housekeeper is. I thought she was supposed to chaperone me."

Dustin did as she suggested and poured himself a double. He kept thinking the natural conclusion to this evening should be for him to take Cassandra upstairs to his bed and make love to her, and she was talking about chaperones.

"She's doing exactly as she was told. If she hears you scream she's to come running with broom in hand. Otherwise, she's not to be seen or heard."

Cassandra laughed lightly. "I don't think that's the role of a chaperone."

"Really? That's what I was always told." He sat down beside her.

Cassandra gave him a disbelieving expression. "Who told you that?"

"Every man I've ever asked."

She laughed again. "You're incorrigible at times, Dustin."

"And you are the most beautiful, the most tempting woman I've ever met."

Dustin watched her take a sip of her drink. The brandy coated her lips. The muscles in his groin tightened. He liked the way she responded to him. Every time he'd put his arm around her shoulder, touched her hand, brushed her lips with his, she had responded to him. He was eager to have her underneath him again, ravishing her body all through the night.

But he wanted so much more from her than gratification. He could get that from any woman. He wanted Cassandra's love. Would she ever be willing to give him that unconditionally as she once had, or had he really messed up last night when he didn't accept her offer of marriage?

He wanted to ask her if he'd made the second biggest mistake of his life when he refused to marry her last night, but he wasn't prepared for her answer.

He had thought he could be patient. He thought he could wait until she was willing to accept the kind of commitment he wanted from her. He wanted her love, her passion, and her trust. But last night he didn't know Webster was going to show up in town and fill her head with all the wonderful things he could do for her.

Her gaze searched his face for a moment. "You said we need to discuss the details of our plan."

Dustin sipped his brandy. She obviously wasn't ready to talk about their relationship.

"Yes," he said, giving in to her wishes. "I had a lot of time to think about it while Webster was talking tonight. Without knowing it, Gordon gave us the perfect solution. He invited you to the cattlemen's dance tomorrow night. I think that's the perfect time to do it."

"Why?"

"There will be little chance of any of the lawyers staying late at the office or dropping by. Most everyone will be at the party. We'll go early so it will seem as if we've been there a long time, but we'll leave while the night is young. We'll make sure we spend time with Gordon and maybe have a dance or two before we leave. There will be so many people there Gordon won't miss us until long after we're gone."

"It sounds like the perfect time to do it, but there is a small problem."

"What?"

"I didn't come prepared for a dance. I will have to get a dress and I don't know if I have enough money to buy fancy ready-made clothes."

Dustin chuckled. "You are indeed the poorest rich young lady I know. Don't worry about money. I will see you have more than enough tomorrow to buy dresses, shoes, petticoats, or bows for your hair."

"Even ready-made dresses have to be fitted properly and there may not be enough time to make the alterations."

"We'll make it worth the seamstress's time to make sure you have a dress."

"Thank you. I'll pay you back when—"

He put his finger to her lips to silence her. "I don't have as much money as you do, but I can certainly afford to buy whatever you need."

She nodded, and when Dustin took his finger away from her lips he had a consuming desire to stick it in his mouth and suck her taste from his skin. He took another sip of his brandy instead.

Cassandra cleared her throat and said, "What about the combination to the safe?"

He reluctantly returned to the subject. "It's written on the underside of the bottom drawer on the left side of his desk."

"Has your father changed desks?"

"Not that I'm aware of, but it's been a long time. The ink could have faded beyond recognition."

"What will we do if we can't read the combination?"

"Blow it open."

"Dustin, are you serious?"

"Not at this point. It's just an option. There's something else I decided tonight while Webster talked. I want to do this on my own. That way if there's trouble you won't be implicated in any way. I'll have the driver bring you here, then return for me."

Cassandra was shaking her head before he finished his sentence.

"I'm with you all the way on this. It's my inheritance we're talking about here. I'm not going to let you do this alone, no matter what the risk."

Admiration for her soared within him. He loved her. He wanted to marry her. Why in the hell had he rejected her plea last night? Because he wanted her to marry him because she loved and trusted him. But looking at her now, he wondered why that seemed so damn important last night. Right now he wanted her no matter the terms. His body was making him painfully aware of that, and instead of helping him fight his desire for her, the brandy was increasing it.

"I'm glad you trust me to help you with this."

She reached over and touched his cheek with the tips of her fingers. Her soft touch sizzled against his skin and made him tremble. He had a feeling she knew exactly what she did to him.

Her gaze held fast on his. "Can I, Dustin? Can I trust you?"

He knew she wasn't just talking about her inheritance. "I know you have doubted me for a long time. I understand I have to earn your trust. I'm going to." He paused and trembled again. Did he dare say the rest? "Right now I can show you how much I love you, then you won't ever have to wonder about that again."

He saw in her eyes that she was contemplating his offer. Should he push her? Should he stay quiet and let her make the next move? She'd touched him, but what did that mean?

"Making love and pretending that nothing stands between us won't alter anything. My position hasn't changed since we talked last night. I'm not ready to make any kind of emotional commitment to you."

His throat suddenly felt dry. He sat back and took a

big sip of the brandy, letting it burn his throat and stomach. "Are you still considering marrying Webster?"

"Dustin, the only thing I know right now is that I intend to get my inheritance away from your father. And I'm going to take the steps to do that one day at a time, starting with the dance tomorrow night."

"Then I'll take whatever I can get." He set his brandy down and slid his arms around her, entrapping her with his strength. He bent his head and claimed her lips with his. They were soft, moist, and ever so good and pleasing but he had too much passion burning inside him to linger over the gentle kiss. His tongue thrust deeply into her mouth and he savored the taste of her.

He was desperate to claim her for his own, to sate his pent-up desire, but this time he wanted their loving to be just for Cassandra.

It had been hell trying to keep his hands off her the past two days. He grabbed a sofa pillow and put it behind her head, then gently laid her back against the corner.

His hand moved to her throat and caressed the soft skin there. He would have never thought he was capable of loving as much as he loved Cassandra.

With eager fingers he unfastened the buttons on her blouse and pushed it open. He slid the straps of her corset cover off her shoulders and pulled down on the garment until her breasts were free for him to touch. He moved his lips down her neck, across her shoulder to her breast. He opened his mouth and tasted a rosy nipple. It hardened beneath his flickering tongue.

"How does it feel, Cassandra?"

She made a soft moan and whispered, "Wonderful."

He loved to please her.

Fondling and kissing her breasts hardened his shaft until it was painful. It was madness to go slow and give her this time to simply indulge in the way he could make her feel when he wanted to plow deeply within her warmth and find his own pleasure, his own release. A fiery heat of love for her drove him to deny his own passion and continue pleasing Cassandra.

He wanted to tell her that he'd missed her like crazy and that she belonged with him forever, but he didn't want to do anything that might keep her from enjoying what he was doing right now. He could tell her those things later. And he would.

He slid his hand under her skirt and gently pulled down her drawers.

"What are you doing?" she asked softly as her hands played in his hair.

"Loving you. Relax and enjoy what's going to happen to you, Cassandra. You don't have to do a thing. I'm going to make love to you."

His hand slid down to the moist cove between her legs as his lips continued to pleasure her with kisses. He savored the way she gently moved beneath his hand.

With a delicate touch, his finger played with that most sensitive spot of her womanhood, stroking and pressing. He could feel the pleasure growing inside her. Her breath became shallow.

Cassandra's hips began to move beneath his touch, faster, harder until she arched her back and gasped before slowly easing back against the pillow.

Panting, she asked, "How did you do that?"

He arranged her underclothes and lowered her skirt. "With my finger."

"I know that, but I mean, well—you know—I thought you had to be inside me."

He chuckled attractively. "I have so many things to show you about making love."

Her eyes sparkled with wonder. She smiled and threw her arms around his neck. "Then let's get started."

"Not here." He removed her arms and closed her blouse. "I've made love to you on the floor of an arbor, the flatbed of a wagon, and now a sofa. This time we're going to the bed." He rose and reached down for her hand.

Cassandra laid her hand in his.

Chapter

·*21*·

The high-necked, banded collar blouse with the leg-of-mutton sleeves fit her body like a glove. The sheer beige lace had been stitched over a silk tunic liner. The matching taffeta skirt fell in an upside-down V shape and the seamstress had expertly fitted a wide band of matching velvet around her waist.

Cassandra had felt positively wicked buying the expensive clothing but she'd had little choice. All the dress shops she visited had already sold out their evening clothes because of the dance.

With the help of a few pins Cassandra fashioned her hair in a loose bun at the back of her head, then pinched her cheeks a couple of times before walking down the stairs. When she walked into the parlor and saw Dustin standing by the window waiting for her she felt the tiny curls of thrill deep in her abdomen that she used to experience when she dressed for him.

Her mind drifted back to last night and how he'd unselfishly denied himself pleasure until he'd made her weak with contentment. That had been a delightful, wondrous surprise. Later when he'd taken her to his room and laid her on the crisp white sheets she gloried in the way he made her body come alive over and over again.

Heaven couldn't be any finer than what she'd experienced last night. Clouds couldn't make her feel any lighter and no man could have made her feel more special, more loved than Dustin had when he'd joined his body with hers. With every touch, every kiss, every soft breath he'd told her that he loved her, but when again he'd asked for verbal confirmation from her that she felt the same for him, the words stayed in her throat.

Although she didn't say a word or make a sound he must have sensed she was standing in the doorway. Dustin turned and saw her. His eyes lit with pleasure, with admiration, with hunger, and she desperately wanted to respond to those things and tell him all was forgiven and forgotten. But something inside her held her tight and wouldn't let her go, wouldn't free her to tell Dustin what she was feeling for him.

"Cassandra, you are always beautiful, but tonight even more so. That dress looks as if it was made for you."

"Thank you. You are as handsome today in your dinner jacket as you were five years ago."

"I feel older, more mature, wiser."

She smiled at him and said, "I see you as finer, more powerful, seductive."

He smiled appreciatively. "I like your choice of words better than mine." He walked over to the rosewood Sheraton sideboard. "I have a bottle of champagne. I thought we'd have a glass before we go."

"I've never had champagne before. I hear it's very good."

"I think you'll like it. It's the perfect way to start an evening such as this."

"All right." She took the glass of bubbling liquid from him and put it to her nose. It didn't smell fruity or flowery like most wines and it didn't have the strong fermented scent of most ports and brandies.

"To a successful evening."

She tipped her glass to his, then sipped the light yellow liquid. It was slightly sweet and tingled on her tongue. She smiled. "Mmm. I love it."

"I thought you would. Sit down and enjoy your drink."

Cassandra walked over to the settee. "I thought Landon might contact me this afternoon, but I never heard from him."

"I never told him where you were staying."

"Dustin," she admonished but his possessiveness thrilled her.

"I'm surprised he didn't go to your offices and ask your father."

She saw Dustin hide a smile. "I was sure he'd think of that so I told him only a few of the lawyers work on Saturday and Gordon wasn't among them." He took a seat beside her. "I could get used to this," he said.

"Champagne?"

"No. You and me in my home."

"Dustin, let's don't get into that tonight."

"All right. There's another reason for the champagne tonight."

"What's that?" she said.

Dustin made himself comfortable beside her. "It has to do with the real reason I contacted Juliana."

A feeling of unease swept over her. "I thought it was to see if she knew anything about the will."

"She told me the two of you discussed that, and I'm glad you did, but what I wanted to talk to her about was the dreams, the nightmares, or whatever they are that disturb your sleep."

"I can't believe you told her about that. How could you?" She started to rise from the settee, but Dustin caught her hand and stayed her.

"I want to help you. Don't get upset. Cassandra, you shouldn't be bothered by these—dreams that awaken you in the night."

"That's beside the point. It wasn't your place to say anything to her about my life. I—I didn't want her to know."

"I think the problem is that you don't want to know. It's as if you're afraid to know about your parents, your childhood. Cassandra, Juliana and I think we know why you have the nightmares."

"I—you do?"

"That's the only reason I contacted her. Now, do you want to know what she had to say or should we put the champagne away and go on to the dance?"

Cassandra took a deep breath, suddenly finding it harder to breathe. "I'm not sure I want to know."

"Why?"

"Dustin, I've never heard anything good about my childhood before I came to Wyoming," she answered, resisting him. "It's all bad. Why would I want to know any more?"

He took the glass from her trembling hand and set it down. "Because it might help you to get over the dreams. You'd like that, wouldn't you?"

"Yes. Yes, I would like them to stop."

"The night Juliana struck Ward with a candlestick and fled the house with you, your stepfather was holding a pillow over your face. He was trying to smother you."

He was trying to smother you. Dustin's words echoed in Cassandra's mind and she squeezed her eyes shut. She saw an indistinct, shadowy figure of a man looming over her. Something soft came down over her face. She couldn't breathe. She tried to push it off, but the pressure held her to the bed. She kicked. She shoved at the pillow but she couldn't move it.

Cassandra's chest tightened. She felt pressure against her face. She couldn't breathe. "No." Her eyes popped open.

"Yes," Dustin soothed her. "That's why in your dreams it's always dark and you can't see anything. Your face was covered with a pillow. That's why you feel as if you can't breathe."

Cassandra's hand flew to the base of her throat. Her breath became choppy as those familiar feelings washed over her again. She shook. "I think I remember now. I think I saw Papa Ward standing over me, but why didn't Juliana ever explain all this to me?"

Dustin gently pulled her against his chest. His embrace was warm, comforting, safe. Cassandra snuggled deeper into his arms and nestled her cheek against the soft, expensive wool of his dinner jacket.

"At the time, she was afraid it would frighten you more than you already were. When she realized you didn't remember what Ward was doing to you that night she didn't tell you because she didn't want you to remember what happened. She wanted you to be free from those memories. What she didn't know was that you remembered the symptoms but not the cause, and you haven't been free from it all these years."

"When she said he was trying to hurt me I always thought he was going to hit me with the candlestick and she'd somehow managed to take it away from him."

"No."

"Why didn't I remember that?"

"I think you blocked it from your memory. Nobody wants to think someone has tried to kill them, especially a child."

"I haven't wanted to remember any of that part of my childhood. Do you think knowing that Ward tried to smother me will stop the dreams?"

He drew away from her and with the tips of his fingers lifted her chin so she could look into his eyes. "I hope so." He kissed the tip of her nose. "Now, the next time you wake up feeling as if you can't breathe you know what has caused it and you don't have be frightened. Ward Cabot can't hurt you. You can put those horrible memories out of your mind now. Nothing like that is ever going to happen again."

Cassandra took a deep breath. Looking at Dustin, listening to him, made her believe him. She drew away from the safe harbor of his embrace. "I hope you're right. Thank you for finding that out for me. I know Ward strangled my mother, then blamed it on one of the servants. I guess he didn't want another murder on his hands so he was going to try to make it look as if I had died in my sleep."

"I think you're probably right. He must have been a madman."

"Yes, he was," Cassandra said. The last time she had seen Ward came back to her as clearly as if it had been only yesterday. "I remember we were in the old ranch house. I was standing on the stairs. Juliana was trying to shield me with her body, but I saw Papa Ward, Grandpapa Rakefield, Rill, and some men I didn't know. I remember Papa Ward shot one of the men, then Juliana pulled her gun out of her purse. I kept hearing gunfire."

Dustin lowered his head and gently kissed her lips. "Don't think about that. You can put that behind you now. I want you to read the things I've read about your parents. There are good things to replace the bad."

"I will."

"Now, remember what I once told you?"

His lips were moist, tempting. "You've told me many things."

"But this was very important that you remember. I don't want anything taking your breath away but me, Cassandra."

He bent his head and captured her lips again. He pulled her close and pressed her breasts against the hardness of his chest. The horrors of the past faded from her mind and she melted against Dustin.

His kiss was gentle, persuasive, enticing her to remember only him. She so much wanted to believe that Dustin would be in her life forever. Was Juliana right about not giving up love? Cassandra was beginning to believe she wanted to find out.

"When are you going to admit that I'm the only man who can put stars in your eyes?" he whispered against her lips.

"I'll admit to that right now," she answered in kind.

He kissed her again, a longer, deeper kiss that burned into her heart and soul. His tongue moved into her mouth and met hers. She felt his possessive hunger. She would have loved to forget about the dance and what they had to do and stay in Dustin's arms.

Tapping her reserve of will power, she slowly pulled away from Dustin.

"When are you going to admit that you love me and you can't live without me?" Dustin asked.

She was oh, so tempted, but until she knew she had complete trust that Dustin would be in her life forever as she had once before, she had to hold back.

"We have a lot to accomplish tonight. I think we should be going."

Chandeliers glistened, music played, and couples danced in the ballroom of the hotel as Dustin walked in with Cassandra on his arm. Women in brightly colored gowns mixed with men in their dark suits and white shirts. The windows had been raised to let in fresh air but scents of musk, perfume, and smoke hung like a thick cloud in the room.

Men laughed, women chatted, and young ladies giggled as Dustin glanced around the crowded dance floor, searching for his father. What he saw was Cassandra receiving more than her share of looks, smiles, and interest from eligible men and curious stares and unfriendly glares from the young women. Not only was Cassandra beautiful, she was new and bound to cause a stir.

"You are getting more attention than a fish in a crystal bowl," Dustin said.

"Then maybe you should take me out on the dance floor so we can melt into the crowd."

He smiled down at her. "I didn't know you were so eager to be in my arms again."

"I'm eager not to be set upon by strange partners wanting to dance with me."

"In that case, let's find my father and make sure he knows we're here. Let's go this way. I think I might have seen him."

Finding Gordon proved to be an arduous task. Friends and acquaintances alike stopped Dustin wanting to be introduced to Cassandra. Many eyebrows shot up as his friends recognized Cassandra as the young woman he was once engaged to. Dustin could imagine the gossip swirling around the room.

"Cass, my dear. How lovely you are," Gordon said when at last they found him. He took her hands and kissed her on each cheek. "I'm so happy you decided to join Dustin. And I see that someone saved the most beautiful dress in town for you. You are absolutely stunning tonight, my dear."

"Thank you, Mr. Bennett."

Gordon turned to Dustin and shook his hand. "I hope you know you are the luckiest man here tonight, but from the looks I see Cass getting you might have some competition."

"I'm aware of that," Dustin said, not wanting to share Cassandra with anyone. "We were stopped ten times trying to get to you. Cassandra has caused quite a stir."

"As it should be. This is a sort of reunion for the two of you, isn't it?"

Dustin wanted to think of it that way but Cassandra was elusive. He knew she loved him and needed him but she had to come to that realization.

His father bent over and whispered, "Don't let her go this time. Something tells me you won't get another chance."

Dustin tensed, blinked. His eyes narrowed. No, he wasn't seeing things. That was Landon Webster heading toward them with a big friendly smile on his face.

Damn! Somehow the banker had managed to wrangle himself an invitation to the dance. Dustin had to think quickly. He didn't want Gordon talking to Webster.

Dustin touched Cassandra's arm and whispered, "We might have trouble. Look straight ahead."

He saw her surprise when she saw Webster. "I don't believe this."

"Me either. He's become a regular pain in the ass," Dustin murmured so only she could hear.

"I'll take care of him," Cassandra said.

"No, I will," Dustin said. "For good this time."

"Dustin, don't cause trouble."

"Cass, I've never seen you looking so beautiful," Webster said, taking her hand and kissing the back of her palm. "I have to admit I had hopes of seeing you tonight."

If Webster's eyes had been his mouth he would have devoured Cassandra in seconds.

"Landon, I—we had no idea we'd see you here."

"Obviously not. You never mentioned a word to me that you were coming. I tried to find out where you were staying, but—"

"Webster, I'm surprised to see you here," Dustin said, cutting him off.

"I just bet you are." He smirked, then turned to Gordon. "And I've no doubt who this fine gentleman is. You have to be Dustin's father."

Gordon reluctantly stuck out his hand. "All right, if I have to be, I will. And who might you be?"

"Landon Webster, from Cheyenne."

"I see. And whose guest are you this evening?" Gordon asked tightly.

"Mr. John Tutwiler, from the Cattlemen's Bank."

"Oh, yes. I've done business with the man," Gordon said.

"Landon," Cassandra said, snaking her hand around his arm. "I don't believe you've asked me to dance. You did intend to, didn't you?"

"Ah—er—yes, of course." He beamed with arrogance when he looked at Dustin and said, "Would you gentlemen excuse us?"

Dustin knew exactly what Cassandra was doing. He was glad she had stepped in, but he didn't like the thought of Webster's hands being anywhere on Cassandra's body.

"Is there something going on here I don't know about, Dustin?" Gordon asked as soon as Cassandra and Webster walked away.

"What do you mean?"

"Sounds like he's interested in Cass and you just let him walk away with her."

Dustin didn't take his gaze off Cassandra and Webster as he replied, "He was courting Cassandra when I went to Wyoming. He followed her here."

"He's probably a fortune hunter," Gordon said matter of factly.

"You'd certainly know one."

"That was an unnecessary remark."

Webster led Cassandra to the far side of the dance floor and Dustin turned to his father. "I don't think so. Cassandra knows the whole story."

Gordon remained stiff. "I don't know what you're talking about."

"I told her what I'd written in the letter you never gave to her. She knows everything, from the time you wrote to her grandfather and asked him to bring her to Kansas."

"There was no need to let her see that scribble. It was filled with half-truths from a love-bitten young man who suddenly had an attack of nobleness."

His father amazed him. "Is that what you considered it?"

"You should know better. A good lawyer would never let his client make a full confession. I don't have to tell you that."

Dustin chuckled ruefully. "And to think I almost ended up like you."

"Am I so bad to want you to have the things I never had as a young man?"

"Yes. You wanted them at Cassandra's expense. She was seventeen and blissfully in love. I manipulated her into thinking I loved her all because I wanted to make you proud of me and secure my place in the firm."

"And you sacrificed that for the sake of your conscience."

Dustin nodded, realizing he wasn't going to get his father to admit to any wrongdoing. "I'm sure you thought so at the time, but you've done all right. The firm has continued to control the Rakefied fortune and I've managed to secure some wealthy clients without having the heir to the fortune as my wife."

"It could have been so much easier for you if you'd married her when you had the chance." Gordon pursed his lips as his gaze drifted to the dance floor. "Once word gets around town who she is she'll have more suitors than she can handle. I suggest you go break in on Cass's dance. If you don't marry her someone else will. And you're already five years late."

Gordon turned and walked off, leaving Dustin to wonder why he even bothered to try to make his father see that what they had done to Cassandra was wrong.

Cassandra was twirled around the dance floor by Landon yet again. After the champagne and kisses from Dustin, Cassandra was looking forward to dancing with him but instead she'd found herself stuck to Landon in order to keep him away from Gordon.

"I need to rest, Landon," she said after the third dance in a row. "Can we get some fresh air?"

"Of course. You should have said something. I thought you were having a wonderful time."

"I was." They walked out onto the patio. The air cooled her skin and she thought about Dustin. She remembered how he'd smelled, how he'd tasted when he'd held her and kissed her earlier that evening. She wanted to be dancing with Dustin, not Landon.

She turned to face Landon and he pulled her into his arms and kissed her soundly, quickly on the lips, then let her go.

He smiled at her. "I've wanted to do that all evening, my love," Landon said. "I've missed holding you in my arms and kissing you. I promise I'll make it up to you when we return to Wyoming."

Cassandra was too stunned to respond.

"When we're married you'll have to learn not to be shy with me. If you're tired, say so. I can't read your mind, you know."

"I'm not going to marry you, Landon. How many times do I have to say it?"

He blinked rapidly. "What—what do you mean? I haven't asked you for a final answer to my proposal. I'm willing to wait."

Cassandra was tired of Landon's innocent act. "Forever? That's how long it will be."

"It doesn't matter if you don't love me, Cass."

"Landon, it's more than that."

"It's Bennett, isn't it?" Controlled anger flared in his nostrils as he spoke. "He's probably trying to make you believe I want to marry you for your money. That's not true. Remember, I asked you before I knew you were an heiress."

"I know that and so does Dustin. I was less than truthful about Dustin when he first came to the Triple R. He was and has always been more than a family friend. He's the man I was engaged to five years ago."

"I know. I found out some time ago, but that doesn't matter to me. You were under no obligation to tell me anything about your past. And you said yourself, that was years ago."

"I'm not talking about the past now. I'm talking about the future. I'm not going to marry you."

"Do you plan to marry Bennett?" His voice was tight, brittle. A twitch started in his eyes.

"That's none of your business, but there is no chance for you and me, Landon. Ever," she said, suddenly feeling uncomfortable with his behavior. "If you're going to insist otherwise we can't be friends."

He drew a short, sharp breath. "So it is Bennett. I see now he's the one I need to be talking to. Not you."

A curl of suspicion crawled up Cassandra's back. "Stay away from Dustin, Landon. My business with him has nothing to do with you. Now, I'm going back inside." She turned and walked away.

"Are you sure Landon left the party?" Dustin asked Cassandra again as the horse and carriage clipped along the dark city streets at a brisk pace.

"Yes. I looked everywhere for him. I left him rather abruptly and later remembered I was supposed to be keeping him away from your father."

Cassandra's tone bothered him. "Webster didn't try anything, did he?"

"Of course not."

Dustin wasn't sure he believed her but he wouldn't press the matter right now. "I couldn't believe it when I saw him tonight. If I'd taken time to think about it I would have known he knew someone in town, but I try not to think about Webster. Why did you let him hold you so close when you danced?"

"Close?" Cassandra turned toward Dustin and their arms brushed, sending a thrill across her breasts. It was too dark to see his face clearly, but his voice let her know how disturbed he was. "Dustin, there was at least twelve inches between us at all times."

"It didn't look like it from where I was standing."

She smiled to herself. "Jealous?"

"Hell, yes."

Cassandra laughed. She should tell Dustin she wasn't going to marry Landon and put him out of his misery, but the carriage slowed and she was reminded of what they had to do. She'd tell him later.

As soon as they stopped Dustin jumped out and reached back inside to help Cassandra. "It's not too late for you to let me take care of this alone," he said. "You don't have to be involved in this part of it."

Cassandra looked up into his eyes. She wanted to be involved in everything he did. "I won't let you keep me out of this. I want to be a part of it."

Dustin nodded and took hold of her hand. He told his driver to wait for them, then he and Cassandra went inside the dark office building of Bennett, Lucas, and Farrell. Dustin lit a lamp in the reception area and in several offices on their way to his father's office. The night was warm but Cassandra felt chilly. She didn't care for the deception but Gordon Bennett had left them no choice.

"Why are you lighting so many lamps?" she questioned, thinking the darker the better.

"If anyone should happen by, I wouldn't want the single light to show that we were in Gordon's office. Beside, it's best if we don't look like we're hiding anything."

"It's after midnight. Do you think someone might come by, as late as it is?"

"Lawyers stop by their offices for a variety of reasons at odd times of the night, Cassandra. We'll deal with it if it happens."

The only sound she heard as they made their way down the dimly lit corridor was the hissing of gas jetting through the pipes nestled inside the plaster walls.

When they stepped inside Gordon's office a feeling of remorse gripped Cassandra. She wasn't any good at deceit. She didn't like what they were doing. She stopped and took a deep breath. She was convinced there was no other way to best Gordon Bennett and the committee that controlled her inheritance, and she desperately wanted to beat them.

Before he tried the bottom drawer, Dustin checked all the other drawers. "Nothing's changed. He still keeps his Scotch and pistol in the top drawer."

"What would he want with a gun?"

"The same thing you would. Protection."

"How many coyotes, wolves, and renegade Indians do you think he gets in here?"

Dustin smiled. "We may not wear them on our hips but most of the men in Kansas City have weapons. It wasn't too long ago that there were gunfighters roaming this town."

Dustin picked up the pistol and checked the cylinder.

"Is it loaded?" she asked.

"It would be useless any other way."

"And I thought this town was civilized. Come on, let's get busy."

The bottom drawer wasn't locked so Dustin quickly pulled it out and set it on the floor. Cassandra knelt beside him and they carefully lifted the papers and folders out of the drawer, then turned it over.

Dustin whispered, "The numbers are faded but I think we can make them out."

"Yes, all but one. Is that an eight or a zero?"

"An eight," he said.

"No, I think it's a zero."

He looked up at her and smiled. "If eight doesn't work we'll try the zero."

Cassandra's stomach jumped as Dustin removed the waterfall painting and carefully laid it against the wall.

"Call the numbers out to me," he said.

"Twenty-nine to the right. Forty-three to the left." It was so quiet in the room Cassandra heard the clicking of the spinning wheel as Dustin turned the dial. "Thirty to the right."

Dustin threw a glance at her over his shoulder. "Thirty-eight," he said and turned the wheel again. He grabbed hold of the handle and jerked up. Nothing happened. Dustin wiped his hands down the sides of his trousers, then started over. "All right, we'll try a zero."

Cassandra held her breath as Dustin pulled up on the handle for the second time. The door swung open. She gasped.

There were stacks of papers almost two feet high on one side of the safe and stacks of one-hundred-dollar bills on the other side. "Dustin, look at all that money." She turned to him, astonished. "What does he do with it?"

"He probably sits at his desk and counts it."

"How could anyone be that obsessed with money?"

"I'm sure it goes back to his never having any when he was young." Dustin grabbed a stack of the folders. "Take a handful and let's get started."

"What are we going to do? We don't have time to go through all those papers," she said, suddenly feeling overwhelmed.

Dustin turned to her. "Of course we do. We have until daylight or until we get caught. Whichever comes first."

Dustin and Cassandra sat cross-legged on the floor going through the files one by one. Dustin had been in one position so long he was getting a cramp in his leg, when a document caught his attention.

"This is unbelievable," he said. He rose and held the piece of paper up to the oil lamp that sat on the edge of the desk as his eyes scanned down the page.

"What?" she asked from where she sat on the floor. "Did you find the will?"

"No, I found something better."

"What?"

"Twenty-five years ago, my father was in business with Ward Cabot."

"My stepfather? No! That can't be true. Your father and—and the man who murdered my parents knew each other?"

Dustin nodded. "According to this they knew each other very well."

"What is it? What does it say?" She jumped up and looked over his shoulder.

Dustin shook his head. "This is a document that dissolves a partnership they had in a business. By the date, it looks as if Gordon and Ward had an unauthorized banking business going for about three years. Apparently they loaned money for a high rate of interest. From what I can tell, Gordon put up the money and Ward actually ran the business. The company was dissolved shortly after Ward married your mother. Guess Ward didn't feel he needed to strong-arm anyone after he married your mother."

"Everyone knows he married my mother for her money and then he killed her. How is that paper going to help us?"

"It means that ethically my father should have declined to represent your mother in the matter of the will and trust since he had previous business dealings with Ward Cabot. Take my word for it that this is not the kind of story Gordon wants anyone in town to know. Clients would leave the firm in droves if they knew he'd continued to administer your trust knowing that he was once in business with the man who murdered your parents and tried to kill you."

Dustin laid that paper aside, and started stacking the other folders back into the safe.

"What are you doing? We haven't found the will."

"We don't need it. We have something better." Dustin stared at Cassandra. "Gordon has two choices. He can free your trust or destroy his reputation."

"Too bad you'll never get the chance to find out which choice he would make," Webster said, walking into the room with a pistol held in his hand.

Dustin tensed. His hand automatically flew up to where he kept his derringer.

"Don't try it, Bennett."

"Take it easy, Webster," Dustin said, hooking his

thumbs under his lapels and spreading his coat wide. "I don't wear a firearm on formal occasions."

"Landon, what are you doing with that gun?" Cassandra demanded.

"Pointing it at you, my dear."

"How dare you? Put it down." She took a step toward him.

Dustin tried to stop her. "Stay where you are, Cassandra. He means business."

"Do as he says, Cass. I will shoot you."

"I'm not afraid of guns and I'm not afraid of you."

"I suspected you knew about Cassandra's inheritance right from the start, but you put on a good act," Dustin said, already planning how he could reach the revolver in his father's desk.

"Yes, I was proud of myself, and it was working until your father sent you to Wyoming."

Defying Dustin's order, Cassandra moved from behind the desk and said, "What the hell are you two talking about?"

"He was courting you for your money," Dustin explained. "Now stay where you are," he said in a voice that he prayed she wouldn't question. He didn't want Cassandra to get between him and Webster.

"That's the problem with being an heiress, Cass," Webster said. "Nobody loves you but everyone loves your money."

"You bastard," she whispered.

"Oh, it gets worse."

"Stay calm, stay quiet, and stay put, Cassandra," Dustin warned, but never took his gaze off Webster. "Just tell us what you want."

"Let me explain some things before I pull the trigger." He kept the pistol pointed at Cassandra but looked at Dustin. "I've been dying to tell you this. Your father is the one who sent me to court Cass."

"That doesn't surprise me," Dustin said, but it did. He

hadn't known how low his father would stoop. It angered him that Gordon would put Cassandra in danger. Forcing himself to keep a straight face, he said, "He had me do the same thing five years ago."

Webster frowned. "Yes, but you didn't have the balls to go through with it and I do. Only he double-crossed me, first by not telling me she was worth millions and second by sending you to make up with her."

"What do you want, Webster?"

"I want the money your father promised me. When you showed up I had to pretend I didn't even know who you were. Tonight I had to pretend I didn't know your father. I knew I'd never persuade her to marry me with you around so I tried to force her to sell the ranch. I could have been happy with the amount those Englishmen were willing to pay for it. I tried to get the president of the bank to sign the deed over to me when I paid off the mortgage but the son of a bitch wouldn't do it. I had to follow her here and keep pretending to be a love-bitten fool."

"And now you won't get anything," Cassandra said in a voice filled with contempt.

"That's where you're wrong." He turned his cold gaze to Cassandra. "After our little talk tonight, I decided if Bennett was out of the way, you'd come back to me. So I hid and waited for him to leave the dance. Of course, Cass, I assumed he'd drop you by your hotel and I'd follow him and shoot him in front of his house when he got out of his carriage." A wild gleam shone in his eyes. "But I see you two had others plans. I'm glad I followed you inside now that I see all that money in the safe waiting for me. And I consider it a bonus that I get to kill you, too."

"You're not a murderer, Webster," Dustin said. "Take the money and go."

Cassandra smirked at Webster. "You don't have the guts to kill anybody, Landon," she remarked hotly.

"And if you tried, I wouldn't send the law after you, I'd go after you myself."

Webster chuckled. "You don't think Mr. Bennett went to church looking for a man like me, do you? I might have acted like a weak-kneed fool but I'm not. I've conned a few old women out of their money and I had to do away with a man once. Didn't bother me at all to pull the trigger."

Dustin inched closer to the drawer that held the gun, while Landon talked to Cassandra. It seemed as if she was deliberately trying to rile him.

"Let me handle this, Cassandra," Dustin said in an irritated tone.

"It's my money he was after."

"Well now he's after my father's money so stay out of this."

"I don't have time to listen to you two squabble."

Dustin glanced at Webster and knew he was going to fire.

"Get down!" he yelled to Cassandra as he dove for the drawer.

A shot rang out.

The drawer slid open.

Two more shots sounded.

Cassandra screamed.

A stinging pain tore through Dustin's upper arm. His hand closed around the handle. He lifted the gun and fired, hitting Webster in the chest. Webster's eyes rolled back in his head. The pistol dropped from his hand with a clatter as he slammed to the floor.

Cassandra ran over to Dustin. "Dustin, you're shot! I saw the bullet hit you."

He looked at his arm. It stung like hell. Blood stained his white shirt. "I don't think it hit the bone. How about you? Are you hurt?"

"No, no, I'm fine."

"Thank God."

"If he'd been a better shot we'd both be dead now."

She wrapped her arms around Dustin's chest and hugged him tight for a moment, then said, "Let me take off your cravat and tie it around your arm until we can get you to a doctor. We need to stop the bleeding."

"The police patrol this street. I'm sure someone will be bursting through the door any minute now. I'll have to stay until someone gets here."

He walked over to Webster and turned him over. He was dead.

Cassandra came up beside him and asked, "Now do you believe me?"

"About what?"

"The money's tainted."

Dustin knew why Cassandra thought that. Her stepfather, Dustin's father, Landon, and even Dustin had once been after that money.

"I told you, it's people who are bad. Not the money. Remember that."

Chapter

·22·

"Dustin, Cass, what happened?" Gordon said, rushing into his office early the next morning. "The police said there'd been a break-in at my office. I wasn't told you'd been hurt."

"I told them not to tell you."

"What happened to your arm?" He glanced around the room. "What are the two of you doing here? My God, Dustin, what happened?"

"Sit down, Gordon, we have a lot to discuss."

Cassandra walked over to stand beside Dustin, who leaned on the edge of his father's desk. The police had arrived and Landon was carried away. She and Dustin were questioned about Landon's death and released. They went straight to the hospital and had a doctor take care of Dustin's arm.

She felt good, right, justified about what they were about to do. Gordon Bennett's reign over her inheritance was about to come to an end. She was sorry about Landon, but just as she couldn't dwell on what had happened to Rodney, she couldn't blame herself for

293

Landon's fate either. They'd both made their own choices.

Dustin said he was fine about what they had to do, but Cassandra knew it couldn't be easy for him. Gordon was his father even if he didn't call him by that name. She couldn't help wondering if what they were about to do would destroy their relationship forever. She took a deep breath. That was a chance they had to take.

Gordon's serious demeanor didn't change after he took his seat. "Somebody better start talking."

"I can make this part short. Landon Webster, the man you hired to marry Cassandra, has been killed."

"Killed?" Gordon rose, visibly shaken.

"Since he couldn't get the money you promised him by marrying Cassandra, he decided to try to kill me and get me out of the way."

"I—I can't believe this!"

"It's true. What angers me most is that you endangered Cassandra's life. She could have been killed. I don't know if I can ever forgive you for that."

"No, I wouldn't do that to her! I've always cared about her."

"No, you cared about her money. When Webster found her with me last night he decided he'd kill both of us and rob your safe."

"This—this is incredible. It's an outrage. I—I don't know what to say. I was only trying to keep—"

"The money at the firm," Dustin finished for him.

"Cass needed to get married. You wouldn't marry her. I—I thought Landon was a man I could control. I thought he'd be happy as long as I gave him a few dollars to put in his pockets each month. I had no idea he was such—such a bad person." Gordon shook his head in disbelief and sat back down.

Cassandra walked over and laid the file they'd taken from Gordon's safe in his lap.

He opened it. His body jerked. He snapped around to look at the painting of the waterfall, hanging neatly in its place on the wall. He glared at Dustin. "How did you get this?"

"We took it from your safe last night," Cassandra admitted. "That's what we were doing here when Landon arrived."

Gordon paled. "How did you know it was there? How did you get the combination? I've never given it to anyone."

"Boys like to snoop when they're young," Dustin said.

Gordon's gaze darted nervously from Dustin to Cassandra. "I'm ashamed of you, Dustin." He shook a trembling finger at his son. "You've been pawing through my private papers like a common thief."

"You are the one who should be ashamed of yourself, Mr. Bennett," Cassandra said, stepping forward and defending Dustin. "We were looking for a copy of my mother's will when we found that."

"I told you the will was accidentally burned. That's the truth. Why didn't you believe me?"

"We never would have found this if we had," Dustin replied. "Why didn't you excuse yourself from handling Cassandra's trust? You knew that it could be considered a conflict of interest."

Gordon's agitated state continued as he picked up the papers and smacked them against his leg. "There was no need. I was no longer in business with Ward Cabot."

"But you had been just three years before. And when he was killed, you must have known that someone might think it unethical for you to be managing the estate of the woman your former partner killed."

"No one who knew me would think that!" His voice shook. "I had nothing to do with that woman's murder, no more than I had anything to do with Landon's death tonight."

The mention of Landon let Cassandra know that Gordon Bennett would never admit to any wrongdoing. "When my stepfather was spending my inheritance with the carefree hand of a drunken cowboy, didn't you think something might be wrong?"

"They—tried and convicted a man for—for her death." Gordon stopped. His bottom lip trembled in outrage. "I had no idea Ward killed your parents until the whole story was released in the papers years later. True, we had a business together for a short time. I gave him money to lend and he always paid me back with interest. That's all I knew about him for a long time. He handled everything else. I never confided in anyone about my arrangement with Ward."

"How did it come about that this firm was chosen to administer the trust after my stepfather was killed?"

Gordon took a deep breath. "Your mother set it up that way. I was Ward's attorney. My firm was already well respected in town when they married. There was nothing wrong with what we did."

"That's a matter of opinion," she said.

His voice softened as he turned his eyes on Cassandra. "I've always taken good care of your inheritance. Not a penny was wasted or invested recklessly. I've earned every dime I've been paid from your trust. When I learned what Ward had done, I felt bad about it. I wanted to do right by you and make your inheritance grow. I'm satisfied I've done my best."

"How do we know you weren't in with Ward from the start?" Cassandra asked.

"How dare you?" Gordon shook.

"It's a legitimate question," Dustin said, moving closer to his father. "How do we know that you didn't know Ward planned to kill his wife and his stepdaughter for that money?"

"You can't seriously believe I'd be involved in something like that."

Cassandra wondered if they'd gone too far. She felt sorry for the man who now looked much older than his fifty years. She didn't believe Gordon had anything to do with Ward's crimes, but she had to suggest it. Gordon had left them no choice.

"It doesn't matter much what we believe, Gordon," Dustin admitted. "What will your other clients think? Especially those who don't know you as I do."

"Well—I—I don't see any reason why they have to know about this. My God, Dustin, my business with Ward happened more than twenty-five years ago."

"I want control of my trust," Cassandra said before she had second thoughts. "Or I'll go from here to the newspapers and tell them about your business dealings with my stepfather."

Gordon jumped up again. "I can't do that. The will stated the firm was to manage the money until you're twenty-five if anything happened to Ward."

"I'm prepared to take you to court over this," Cassandra said. She glanced over at Dustin. He nodded for her to go ahead with their plan. "We can handle it quietly here and now so only a few people in the firm know or I will take you to court and everyone in Kansas City will know about your relationship with a murderer."

"There was no conflict of interest." Gordon's voice shook again.

"Some clients might look at the moral and social implications of your involvement, Gordon. I suggest you do what Cassandra wants and give her control."

Gordon looked over at Dustin for a long time. Finally, he dropped his hands in his lap. "All right. I'll turn over the trust to her if you insist, but not out of any fear of this leaking to the town and the firm losing business. I'm doing it for you."

"For me?" It was Dustin's turn to stare at his father. Gordon's words stunned Dustin. His father had never indicated he cared what Dustin thought about him. "I'm not falling for that line. You're not interested in anyone but yourself."

"Of course I'm doing it for you. You are my only son. I

have to save the firm's reputation for you, Dustin. I'll draw up the papers to release control right away."

"Cassandra," Dustin said, "would you wait for me in my office?"

"Of course," she said and left the room.

Dustin had to hand it to his father. He never changed.

"The will was destroyed," Dustin said. "Why didn't you burn this document, too?" Dustin asked. "No one would have ever known."

Gordon lifted his chin. "There was no need. I didn't do anything wrong."

Dustin knew his father would never give in on that point. "You might not have done anything wrong, but I have," Dustin said, feeling more relaxed now that he knew Cassandra was going to get what she wanted, what she deserved.

"It's too late for apologies now, Dustin. The damage you caused breaking into my safe can't be repaired."

Dustin chuckled. How like his father to think that, and just when he was beginning to feel sorry for him. "I'm not talking about that. You were right, I should have married Cassandra when I had the chance. I've been meeting with clients since my return from Wyoming and telling them that I'm leaving the firm."

"You can't mean that. Dustin, how much more bad news can I take? I've built this firm for you."

"I don't want it. I'm going to Wyoming and do my best to win Cassandra's trust and her love. What kind of role you have in my life from now on will be up to you."

The evening grew late. Cassandra paced in the parlor of Dustin's home waiting for him to return. When the clock struck ten she told the housekeeper to put dinner away and go to bed.

Cassandra hadn't seen Dustin since she left his father's office. He told her he would join her later but he never showed up. He sent word that he had pressing business to take care of and would see her at home. She desperately wanted to talk to Dustin.

Her mind was going wild. She was beginning to believe that he hated her for what they had done to his father. Because of her, Dustin had been forced to kill Rodney and Landon. What would she do if he never wanted to see her again?

She was taut with worry when she finally heard him coming in the front door. Cassandra took a calming breath and walked into the foyer to meet him. His hair was tousled. He looked tired and as if he needed a hug from someone who loved him.

"How's your arm?" she asked softly.

"It's going to be fine," he said. "I didn't know if you'd be up."

"Of course. I've been worried about you."

"I'm sorry. I guess I forgot to tell you that I'd be late tonight."

"Did you have dinner?"

"Yes, I hope you weren't waiting for me?"

"No," she lied. "Can I get you a brandy?"

His eyes searched her face as if he wasn't quite sure what she was up to. "All right," he said and followed her into the dimly lit parlor. "How did your afternoon go? Did you sign all the papers?"

"Everything's taken care of." She walked over to the sofa table and took the stopper out of the leaded cut crystal decanter. She poured the amber liquid into a glass.

Cassandra handed Dustin the brandy glass but made no move to pour one for herself.

"You're not having one?"

She shook her head. "I need a clear head for what I have to say tonight."

"That sounds ominous. Maybe you should have made this a double shot for me."

Cassandra remained tense. "I know it wasn't easy for

you dealing with your father the way we had to today. Especially after—Landon."

"It was necessary."

"Thank you for helping me," she said with all the gratitude she was feeling.

He shrugged. "I'm not sure my father is totally guilt free but I'm not sure what he did was wrong either. I guess I'll sort it all out in time."

"I've been thinking along the same line." She moistened her lips nervously. "Gordon was right about one thing."

"What's that?"

"I have no idea how to manage the kind of money I have. All I ever wanted was enough to rebuild the Triple R."

"Don't worry, I'm sure you'll learn how to handle it in time. You're the smartest woman I know."

"Thank you," she said, but she didn't know when she'd felt so inadequate.

"Then you have what you wanted, Cassandra." Dustin threw back the brandy as if it were a shot of cheap whiskey.

She clasped her hands together in front of her. She wished she wasn't so nervous about telling him that she loved him and wanted to spend the rest of her life with him. "I thought I did."

His eyes locked with hers.

A quiver of longing shuddered through her. She quickly placed a finger on his lips so he wouldn't speak. "I realized this afternoon that I had enough money to do anything in the world I wanted to do, and you know what I decided?"

Cassandra felt his lips tremble beneath her fingertip. He stepped away from her. "We've been at this too long for you to tease me like this, Cassandra."

"I want to marry you."

"Why? You have your money now. You don't need me."

She thrilled to his bravery. "I want you."

"Your life is in Wyoming. Mine is here in Kansas City."

He was making her work for the answer she wanted but she didn't mind. She knew he wanted to be sure she was ready to give up the ranch that had been so important to her and put her complete trust in him, rely only on him for her security and happiness.

Cassandra's throat felt tight. "You asked me not long ago if you were the only one I was ever willing to give up the ranch for and I said yes. That's still true. When you left the ranch I missed you. I found myself wanting you to come back to me."

"Why?"

"Because I love you, Dustin. I've put the past behind me. I want to start over with you as your wife."

"And what about the trust?"

"I talked with your father late this afternoon. I'm going to leave the money with the firm, for now anyway. Except for what I need, of course."

"I don't believe this."

"It's true."

His eyes sparkled with surprise. "But you wanted to take it away from Gordon and the firm."

"I wanted to take the control away from them and *we* did. I can draw from it anytime."

"If you're happy with that, then so am I."

"I appreciate all you've done to help me with the ranch, Rodney, Landon, your father." She stopped and moistened her lips. "You were there for me every time I needed you. Thank you."

"I wasn't doing it for gratitude." His voice lowered. "I wanted much more than that."

"How about my love?"

"That's a good start."

Cassandra smiled. "My life is with you, Dustin, wherever you are. I'm putting my complete trust in you."

Dustin gently gathered her in his arms and pressed his

face in her neck. "Cassandra," he whispered. "I've been going through hell thinking you'd walk away from me when you got your inheritance. I wouldn't have blamed you if you had. I knew you loved me and wanted me but I didn't know if you could forgive me."

"I had to wait until I was sure I could come to you free of everything connected to our past."

"And are you?"

Cassandra smiled. "Yes. Completely. Forgiven. Forgotten. I finally figured out what Juliana was trying to tell me. I can give up the money and the ranch but I can't live without you."

A possessive glint shone in his eyes. "You don't have to give up the Triple R for me, love. As soon as I returned to Kansas City I started making plans to leave the firm. That's what I've been doing yesterday and today. When I told you I was restless and not sure I wanted to do law work anymore, I meant it. I also meant it when I told you I was coming back to Wyoming for you. So how about it, Cassandra, am I welcome at the Triple R?"

She gave him a teasing smile. "It's a lot of hard work. You'll have to get better at handling horses, and you'll have to wear your gun on your hip, not under your jacket."

He smiled. "I'm up to the task."

"It gets downright frigid in Wyoming during the winter months and most of spring."

"I'll have you to keep me warm. Marry me, Cassandra."

"Yes, yes, yes!" Cassandra laughed as she hugged Dustin tighter. She had never felt so free yet so committed. "I loved you, Dustin, even when I swore I hated you."

Dustin looked down into her eyes. "You are like no other woman in the world, Cassandra Rakefield, and I love you."

"You can call me Cass. It was childish and selfish of me to tell you that you couldn't call me that."

He took hold of her hand and pressed it to his lips and kissed her fingers. "No. Cass no longer fits you. You are Cassandra."

He pressed her body to his, his lips to hers. Cassandra felt joy in embracing this wonderful man whom fate had brought back to her. He kissed her hard as her hands traced the contours of his back and shoulders. She opened her mouth and fondled his tongue with hers.

Reluctantly Cassandra moved away from the kiss. Dustin groaned his disapproval.

"Take me upstairs," she murmured.

Dustin smiled at her. "That sounds like an order. Are you planning on being the boss when we get married?"

"Cropper told me bossing people is what I do best."

"Not anymore." Dustin swooped down and hooked one arm under her knees and the other around her shoulders and lifted her into his arms.

"Dustin, what are you doing?"

"I'm going to show you something that you do better than bossing."

She reached over and gave him a happy, carefree kiss. "I love you, Dustin."

"I love you," he answered, and reached down and claimed her lips for his own.

· *Epilogue* ·

Five months later

Cassandra walked out the back door and stood on the porch. A contented smile spread across her lips. She leaned a shoulder against a post, propped her hands on her slightly rounded stomach, and watched her husband chop firewood.

Ranch life suited Dustin. He was up every day at first light strapping his gun to his hip, eager to ride the range, check the fences, or settle a dispute between the hands. He didn't seem to mind the backbreaking work that challenged him from dawn to dusk.

Sometimes fate had a way of making bad things turn out well. If she and Dustin had married years ago they would probably be living in Kansas City and she probably wouldn't have the respect for him that she had today.

Her love for him swelled inside her.

She watched him as she walked down the steps and over to where he worked. His hands gripped the ax handle. His shirtsleeves were rolled up past his elbows showing muscles bulging with the power it took to split the logs.

"You look like you could use a break," she said as two pieces of wood fell to the ground.

Dustin laid down the ax and smiled at Cassandra. "All right, I'll sit on the steps with you for a few minutes."

"I made fresh coffee. I'll get some for you."

"In a little while," he said. He helped her sit down, then settled himself beside her. "It's hard on you, isn't it?"

"What? Being pregnant? Of course not. I don't even get sick in the mornings anymore. You know that."

"I'm talking about the ranch. You want to be out on your horse, checking those new cows we made into steers last week and bossing the hands around."

Cassandra looked at the wide expanse of blue sky, flowing green hillsides, and snow-crested buttes. "Yes, I miss it, but Dustin, I couldn't be happier that I'm going to have your baby. I want to have the son my father never had. I want him to have this ranch someday."

"In that case, if the first baby is a girl I promise you we'll keep trying until we have a son." He reached over and kissed her softly on the lips. "We can name him after your father and your grandfather if you want to."

"You'd do that for me?"

"Of course I will. You gave me a second chance. You've given me so much I can't imagine I'd deny you anything you wanted."

"The only thing I've done is love you."

He reached down and kissed the side of her mouth. "I'm a very lucky man. I love it here on the ranch, Cassandra. It's hard work but I can't wait to get started in the mornings."

Cassandra laughed lightly. "I had a feeling you felt that way. I'm glad you wanted to live here and learn to be a rancher."

"Me too. You're a good teacher, but a tough one just like your grandfather."

"That's a nice compliment." She paused, then said,

"There's something else I want to tell you before you get back to work."

"What's that?"

"I've decided to give a large portion of my inheritance to that hospital in St. Louis that Juliana and Rill told us about when they were here last week."

He picked up her hand and kissed the back of her palm. "I think that's the best decision you could have made. You never wanted that *tainted* money anyway." He winked at her.

"I know you like to tease me about that. And I want you to know that I'm not being foolish. I've decided to keep enough so that we'll be able to see the ranch through bad winters, unless, of course, you'd like to take your father's offer and go back to being a lawyer."

"Hell no. I have no plans to go back to Kansas City and I made it clear to my father that if wants to see us he will have to come here."

"Do you think he will?"

"I have a feeling he just might, once the little one is born."

Cassandra laughed and curled her arms around his neck. "I hope so, but I don't know how he'll feel about me giving most of the money away."

He pulled her gently to him. "I'm not worried about Gordon and I don't want you to. I'm a better rancher and a much happier man thanks to you."

"And I'm the happiest woman in the world. I love you, Dustin."

"I love you, Cassandra."

Author's Note

A drought in the spring and summer of 1886 left ranges parched in Southwestern Montana and parts of Wyoming. Cattle were weak and vulnerable to the blizzards that ravaged the area from November through February of 1887. Hundreds of thousands of animals froze or starved to death. History records that sixty to ninety percent of most herds perished and many ranches were put out of business because of the devastating effects of the harsh winter.

For the sake of my story I used this event as the historical basis for *Cassandra* even though the book was several years later.

I hope you've enjoyed my books set in the West. *Ransom* and *Juliana* are still available from Pocket Books if you missed reading them. Check with your local bookstore for a copy.

I love to hear from readers and I respond personally to every letter. Please write to me at 2433 Thomas Drive, Suite 181, Panama City Beach, FL 32408.

POCKET STAR BOOKS
PROUDLY PRESENTS

HELLION

GLORIA DALE SKINNER

Coming soon
from Pocket Star Books

The following is a preview of
Hellion. . . .